Legends of Daer: Champions of Tylwyth

R.S. Howell

Maximus Publishing—Langley, KY
ISBN: 979-8-218-02106-1
Library of Congress Control Number: 2022911659
Title: Legends of Daer: Champions of Tylwyth
Author: R.S. Howell
Digital distribution | 2022
Paperback | 2022

Dedication

I have so many people that deserve to be dedicated to this work. There have been so many people who kept me going when I felt like giving up. My wife, Brittany Howell, who stood by my side through the happy times, the hard times and the darkest of times, but with her help we managed to get the work complete. My best friend Bernie Blankenship who guided me when I felt lost, provided me words of wisdom when I couldn't find any and helped keep me strong. My children, who I wanted to create the work for in the first place. My mother, Beth Moore for providing me with the time needed to write and finally my grandmother. Ruby Newsome has kept me humbled through the whole process. She was there in the beginning; she was there during the writing and creating. She has always been someone I could turn to and for that I am thankful.

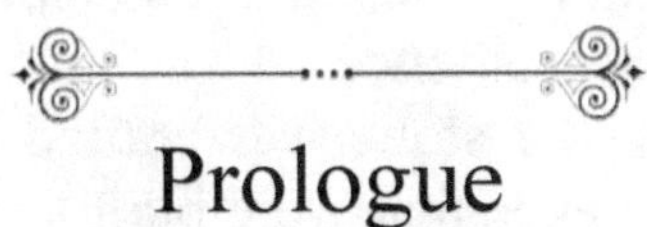

Prologue

Lyer Island was a free and fertile land that found prosperity, despite being ruled without a king. Instead, it was governed by a council populated by the head of the region's various clans. This small council would meet at a grand hall constructed within *Sparrow's Lake* to speak on important matters happening on the island. Twice a year they came together to discuss the great harvest. It is held a week before the embrace of Spring so they could speak on what crops were in need of planting. Then, a fortnight before the Kiss of Winter, they come to terms on what could be split between each clan and what could be traded to the other kingdoms. *Hyland* relied upon the crops to help see them through the long winters, but farms weren't the only thing the island was home to and ambassadors sailing on their decorative galleys in the hopes of trade weren't the only visitors. Scholars traveled to the island to visit the great *Library of Zephyr* and some came to take their vows at the *Vepters Academy*.

The only place a boat could safely anchor was at *Seagulls Harbor*. It was a large port town where a dock was constructed that could house twelve galleys. The town offered lodging if you could handle the horrendous smell of fish and the constant squawking of the seagulls that gave the town its name. Fish shops were everywhere the eye could see, but every so often you could spot a tavern offering warm food and drink to help ease a knotted stomach from the harsh travels across the *Unforgiving Sea*. Many entered those establishments in the hopes of finding someone that could help them traverse the many leagues it would take to get to the grand hall.

Sparrow's Lake was home to over half the clans of the island and it was where the majority of crops were grown all year round. To the north of the village was a lake of water so pure you could see the bottom. At its center was where the grand hall had been built. It was a modest building of a single story, but it took up the majority of the island. Within was a long wooden table where the twenty men could sit comfortably and eight hearths burned to provide heat during the colder nights. The wives would cook a meal for their husbands, the youngest child would serve, and the eldest child was expected to observe the meetings in silence.

A beautiful bridge of stone was crafted to allow passage from the grand hall to the cottages that were built to accommodate the families, and at the center was an elegant four-story building. It was erected as a means of storage for the crops that had been harvested. Along the small stream coming from the lake was a mill that was built by Doukan McGee, the miller, and for a small fee he would grind your grain into flour. All the clans of the village were busy tending to the harvest, the smell of baking bread hung heavy in the air, and soon it would be time for supper for all those living in *Sparrow's Lake*.

Kirkland stood from the ground, stretching his back. He had been hard at work since before the sun ever kissed the sky, but he saw that he was only halfway through the massive field of wheat he was assigned to harvest by his father. He exhaled a sigh of disappointment. The muscles in his arms, legs, and back burned. His shirt was soaked with sweat. He ran the length of his forearm across his brow. His heart dropped as he looked up to see his father approaching through the unharvested wheat.

Torgath Strongfellow was often mistaken as a giant by those who would visit the island. He stood three feet taller than the average man and his body was bulging with muscles he built over the years tending to the fields. His sun kissed skin was covered in sweat that glistened, his auburn hair bounced as he walked, and a toothy grin could be seen through his thick beard of the same color. A scythe rested upon his round, right shoulder as he waved to his son. "You have made great progress, my boy," he called out as he reached the young man. "You should fetch some water and rest your back. I'll finish this up for you," he said, softly placing a calloused hand on the shoulder of his child.

Kirkland lowered his head in defeat. "I'm sorry I failed you."

Torgath scoffed as he placed a thick finger underneath the chin of his son and lifted his gaze back up. "You have done no such thing, my child. I am truly proud to call you my son," he assured him with a toothy grin. "Now, fetch some water and rest," he said, ushering his child behind him as he went to work on the field.

Kirkland watched as his father swung the scythe with ease and was astonished to see just how much a single swipe managed to cut down. He looked at his small arms that were throbbing and gave them a squeeze. *Will I ever be as strong as you?*, he thought, releasing a soft sigh before making his way toward the village. He glanced to his right to see Vincent McRobert and his five sons plucking corn from the stalk. Peering to his left was Old Man Gregory Deary digging in the dirt with his three sons and two daughters for the potatoes. Everyone worked tirelessly to see that the village prospered, everyone, but him.

Kirkland's eyes were swollen with tears and they stung at him, but he refused to let them escape. He quickly approached the door to his cottage and he gently pushed it open to step inside. "You're home early," his mother's gentle voice filled the room.

Kirkland stepped slowly through the cottage to the kitchen and slumped down in a chair at a small wooden table. "Father sent his disgrace home," he said, letting the tears finally break free and run the length of his cheeks.

Magdalene Strongfellow had a slender body that she kept hidden under layers of clothes. Her yellow hair was twisted around and pinned at the back to keep it off her shoulders and out of the dough she had been kneading for supper. She often carried a gentle smile that warmed the hearts of others, but when one of her children was hurting, she became fierce. The fire that burned in her eyes when she was angry made even her husband cower. She looked up from the counter and at her crying son. "What exactly did your father say?" Her once soothing voice became cold as she asked her question.

"He said for me to fetch some water and rest my back," he admitted, lifting his head to reveal the tears that were still flowing.

Magdalene released a heavy-hearted sigh and rushed over to wrap her arms around her son. "My sweet boy," she said, her voice returning to normal. "Your father didn't mean anything by sending you to get some rest. Your father knows just how hard the great harvest can be on a boy of seventeen and he was just looking out for you," she whispered as she ran her fingers through his thick auburn hair.

Kirkland ran his arm across his eyes to wipe away the tears. "I just feel like such a failure," he admitted with fresh tears forming in his eyes.

"Well," Magdalene said, dabbing the eyes of her son with the fabric of her dress. "You shouldn't. We are all proud of the fine young man you have grown into," she said with a smile. "You will do great things in the years to come Kirkland, and I can't wait to witness each one."

Talking to his mother always made him feel better. "I won't let you down," he said with a sniffle. "I believe I will get some water," he exclaimed, pushing himself up from the table.

Kirkland made his way over to a barrel and pulled the lid. The clear liquid rippled to the sudden movement, but as it calmed, he gazed upon his reflection. He looked at his thick auburn hair that was slicked to one side thanks to his mother, his light green eyes focusing on the little freckles that lined the bridge of his nose, and the small scar just above his right eye that he got while roughhousing with his younger sister. He carefully dipped a clay vessel down into the liquid causing the reflection to ripple away and drank deep from the tepid water.

He could hear his mother going back to the kitchen. "Supper will be ready soon. Can you go get your sister for me?" She requested, from a soft smile.

Kirkland gave her a nod as he finished the last of his drink, and placed the clay vessel back down. "I'll see if I can find her," he said, stepping out of the cottage.

Kirkland knew where he could find his sister before he even agreed to the task, but he wasn't thrilled about the location. At the Eastern side of Sparrow's Lake was a woodland area full of tall, thick trees that covered the ground with an eerie shadow. He came to a stop just outside of the small forest. "Isabella! Can you hear me!?!" He screamed, leaning against one of the trees, but all he could hear from her was a giggle.

Kirkland released a heavy sigh. He knew by her response that she was going to force him to come find her within the forest and that filled him with dread. He looked out into the darkness to see thick roots that sprouted forth from the ground, long vines swirled around many of the trees, and some even dangled from the branches. A cold breeze blew within the shade that made his heart leap with fear. It was a nightmarish place that scared him and his sister knew that. "Mom sent me to get you for supper," he said in frustration through clenched teeth, but all he got was another giggle from her. "Please don't make me come after you," he pleaded.

"Let's play a quick game, Kirky. See if you can find me," she replied before going completely silent.

Kirkland stomped his foot in frustration. "I'm in no mood to play, Isabella!" He screamed, but received no response.

Isabella Strongfellow was two years younger than her brother, but she was almost as tall as him. She refused to wear the dress her mother purchased from the seamstress and instead covered her slender body in the clothes her brother grew out of. She had auburn hair that she kept cut short. Her dark green eyes saw everyday as a new adventure. She would spend hours climbing the trees, swinging from the vines, and roughhousing with boys. Her body was covered in bruises, but nothing could ever hold her back. Kirkland remembered a time she had fallen from a tree breaking her arm and the vepter had to make a splint to make sure it healed properly, but the very next day she was out chasing Edward McRobert around. She was stubborn and he knew that she wouldn't budge from her hiding spot until he came to find her.

I should just leave her out here, Kirkland thought, looking back at the village, but he knew that he would get into trouble if he returned home without his sister and he slowly turned his gaze into the gloom ahead of him. "Fine!" He screamed, slamming his fist against the tree he had been leaning on. "I'll come find you, but you better not scare me," he said before stepping into his nightmare.

The shadows surrounded him as he inched his way deeper into the forest, cautiously crossing over the thick roots that sprouted from the ground. He thought back to a time he was playing within the forest and his trousers got snagged. He remembered the hysterical laugh of his sister as he screamed thinking something had grabbed him. He shook the fear of that memory from his head. He moved slowly through the vines that dangled from the trees, making sure to examine them thoroughly. It wasn't that long ago when his sister forced him into the forest in search of her and she slid down one of the long vines tapping him on the shoulder. He trembled with anger as he remembered his sister laughing at his terror-filled scream.

Kirkland leaned against a tree to catch his fleeting breath. He ran a hand along his forehead to remove the sweat that was pouring down his brow and turned his gaze upward. He had lost track of time while searching for his sister. He knew that night hadn't befallen the land, but he wanted to see just how much longer it would be before the sun would set. The canopy of trees blocked all sight of the sky. He released a heavy sigh as he pushed himself up off the tree and stretched his back. His feet ached from all the walking, but he sauntered onward. He wasn't going to let his guard down this time. His sister might have forced him to play her game, but he refused to give her the satisfaction of scaring him again.

The forest was starting to darken as he stopped to catch his breath. It had been some time since he last heard anything from his sister, and he started to wonder if she had returned home without him. "Isabella!" He screamed in frustration, but no answer came to him.

If she left me, he thought, but those thoughts were disrupted by something taking hold of his shoulder. He let out a terror filled scream, and turned around abruptly to look upon his assailant. The sudden movement caused him to stumble back. Tripping over a rock he dropped to the ground slamming his head against a root that was sprouting up. He could see his sister with a wide grin, and he could hear her screaming his name, but all of it soon faded.

Kirkland slowly opened his eyes to see the thick root his head hit. He took notice that the tip of it was pointed up, and if he would have fallen a few inches to the right it would have impaled him. He fought against the tears that wanted to fall. He refused to let his sister see just how hurt he was, and he pushed himself up to a sitting position, but his sister was no longer standing before him. In her place was a tall tree that loomed over him. The branches outstretched like boney hands reaching for him. He scrambled to his feet in a panic. What little light that filtered through the leaves of the trees had vanished, and he found himself cast into an endless void. Sweat covered his brow as he turned in half circles looking at every tree that seemed to draw closer in the darkness.

"Isabella?" He called out to his sister in a soft whisper, but as the name emerged from his lips the ground rumbled beneath his feet. He was swallowed up by it, but before he could process what was happening, he was standing in a field of harvested wheat.

Kirkland was confused as he looked around him for answers, but he stopped searching when his gaze fell upon his family standing at the front door of their home. His father stood with a scythe resting upon his massive shoulder, his sister was on one side with her hands on her hips, and his mother was waving her hand for him to come to them. He was frozen at the center of the field. He desired to be with them, but found that his body wouldn't move. Tears fell from his eyes, and the call of a raven pulled his attention away from his family. Looking into the sky, he could see the bird, but it was unlike any he had ever seen. It covered the whole sky with its body, its golden amber eyes cut into his very essence, and terror gripped him as its beak parted.

The monstrous raven unleashed a sound that caused the world to quake in fear and it swooped down. It transformed into a slender framed man as its feet touched the ground. The wings folded back into a black feathered cape, his body was covered in black leather that clung to his body, and upon his head was a helm crafted to resemble a raven. The beak came to a point with no signs of being able to part, but the golden ember eyes stayed fixated on Kirkland as he slowly lifted his arms. Fire rained down, screams of the dying echoed out, and a thunderous charge could be heard from within the two portals that appeared behind the raven turned man.

Kirkland was frozen with fear as he watched monstrosities he could have never imagined emerge and stood behind the man. He tried to rationalize what he was seeing by comparing the hulking beast to that of his father, but they stood three hands taller, they had biddy eyes of crimson, and they looked more muscular. Their hair varied based upon the creature wearing it, but regardless of the color or length adorning their scalp a thick patch covered their chest, back, and shoulders. Two tusks bulged up from their lower teeth, but the points came to a stop just at the bottom of their eyes. They had different types of jewels hanging from them, and some even had tusks broken, but they weren't the only monsters to come forth.

Kirkland watched as pale slender men stepped out to form their ranks alongside man. They were different from the first batch that came through. They had long white hair that hung just past their shoulders, purple eyes, small of frame, and their smooth faces looked more like marble than flesh. They wore long black robes, their arms folded at the chest with their hands hidden inside the sleeves, and as they took their place in the long line they began to harmonize in a chant.

Kirkland forced his head to turn to look in the direction his family had been standing, but all he could see was the fire that was still falling from the sky. Tears flooded his cheeks as he tried to comprehend what he was seeing, but looking back to the raven turned man he could see that the portals had closed. His massive army of creatures stood at his back, and with a point of his finger they charged across the bloodied battlefield toward Kirkland. He wanted to flee from them, but his body wouldn't respond to his commands as he stood powerless while the creatures came for him.

They were almost on him with their weapons of war. He could see the anger that burned in their biddy eyes, saliva dripping from their opened mouths, but as they were about to collide his body relented its frozen posture causing him to jerk awake. He sat straight up with his arms covering his face in defense. He could hear a soft sobbing at his side, and the sound of something burning ahead of him. He was afraid to lower his arms, afraid that he would be greeted by the nightmarish creatures that were charging for him, but he forced his eyes to slowly open so that he could gain sight of what was happening around him.

Isabella was sitting beside him with wide eyes locked on something ahead of them. An orange glow flashed across her face, and he lowered his arms to see that the tree he was leaning against was now on fire. "Isabella, what did you do?" He asked slowly, moving his gaze from the tree to his sister.

Isabella shook her head as she lifted a trembling finger to point at him. "That wasn't me, Kirky. You set that tree on fire," she said with fresh tears streaming from her eyes.

Kirkland rubbed the back of his head. "What are you talking about?" He asked, standing up from the ground and dusting himself off.

Isabella stood up, but didn't bother with knocking the dirt from herself. "I was hiding inside that tree," she said, pointing to the tree that was on fire. "When you leaned against it, I grabbed your shoulder to let you know you had found me, but you tripped, and bumped your head," she said, kicking the small root that was protruding from the ground. "I tried to wake you, but you wouldn't respond to me. I thought you," she said, running her arm across her face to wipe away the tears. "You were so still, it looked like you were barely breathing, but then you sat up, and two balls of fire shot out of your hands at the tree," she confessed, taking hold of his hands, and looking at his palms.

Kirkland released a sigh as he pulled his hands free. "How could I use magic?" He asked moving his gaze from the burning tree to the palm of his hands.

"I am curious about that myself, young man," the tremulous voice of an old woman echoed out.

Kirkland leaped up from the ground in surprise, but the pressure that had been steadily building behind his eyes made him disoriented, and caused him to retch. The world was spinning as he lifted his head up to see that the old woman had come into view, but was just standing there watching him. She leaned heavily on a thick stick due to her crooked back, her body was covered in a tattered cloak that was coated in mud around the bottom, her unkempt toes peeked out from underneath it, and a wisp of white hair sprouted from behind the hood that she used to conceal her face from him. She pointed a long bony finger at him. "What might your name be, child, and who are your ancestors?" She asked wheezing.

Kirkland rubbed the nape of his neck in the hopes of relieving the pain he was in. "I am Kirkland Strongfellow, son of Torgath Strongfellow, son of Lockland Strongfellow, and who might you be?" He asked.

"Strongfellow," she repeated. "One of the original families to settle Sparrow's Lake. proud people, but I don't recall any of them capable of harnessing such magic," she said leaning heavily upon her walking stick.

Isabella shifted a single step closer toward her brother, but never removed her eyes from the old crone. "Who are you?" She asked, placing a hand upon the hilt of an unsheathed dirk.

"My given name is Agatha," she said, lifting a shaking hand to pull back her hood. "But those of Sparrow's Lake call me the witch of the woods," she said, flashing a feeble smile that showed her only tooth.

Kirkland was familiar with all the tales involving the witch of the woods, but none of them gave any indication that she was a bad person or one he should fear. The Moordoon family were amongst the first settlers of Sparrow's Lake, and they possessed a sight that would give them a glimpse of things to come. They would gather herbs that grew within the forest for their concoctions, and potions that the villagers would seek out to aid them with their ailments. Her assistance didn't cost any coins, as she didn't have any need for that, but she did require trade. When the McDoyles were having trouble conceiving a child they traded four fat pigs, and within nine moon cycles they had four healthy sons. When a curse had stolen the sight of Darleen McMurphy, she took a mirror made of silver, and the young woman was able to see again. The most recent miracle she had performed was with Nat Lyons newborn. The baby wouldn't stop crying, and the vepter of the village had tried all their remedies, but nothing soothed the child. They paid the witch a dozen fresh eggs, two chickens, and an old milk cow. At the end of the night their baby no longer wailed uncontrollably.

Kirkland knew that under normal circumstances they wouldn't have anything to fear of the witch, but the only thing she holds dear is the forest, and her wrath was not something any wanted to befall them. He gave a shake of his head. "We are sorry for what happened to the tree. It was not our intention to burn it," he said, moving his eyes from her.

Agatha chuckled. "The tree can be forgiven, but only if you are willing to pay the price for it," she said with a smile.

Kirkland looked around confusedly in search of what she might be after, but he hadn't brought anything from the house with him, and the only thing his sister had was an old worn dirk that she wore at her side. He held out his hands as he shook his head. "I am afraid I don't have anything to give," he confessed half-heartedly.

Agatha gave a laugh that chilled his blood. "You have knowledge young man. Tell me how you managed to conjure such power to burn that tree, and I shall forgive you for doing it," she said, pointing a bony finger at him.

Kirkland looked back at the tree, the fire had engulfed it, but the flames appeared to be contained to stop it from spreading. He released a sigh before turning to face the old woman. "I'm afraid I don't know how I did that," he revealed in shame.

Agatha scoffed with a shake of her head. "I have spent my entire life dedicated to learning all the magic I can. I have felt other witches come into the forest, I have encountered dabbling wizards in the craft, uneducated novices trying to find their way in life, and even the old foolish wizard prime, Patherias, but in all of them I have never felt such power as I did when you set that tree ablaze, and you want me to believe you did it by accident?" She asked, laughing.

"It's the truth," Isabella interjected the answer to Kirkland's surprise.

Agatha licked her dry, wrinkled lips. "If you aren't going to give me the payment I require," she said, stabbing her staff into the dirt. "Then I will just have to take it out of your flesh," she remarked as vines burst from the ground, and took hold of the children.

It happened so fast that Kirkland had no time to react as the vegetation came to life wrapping around his wrist, ankles, and even one around his throat. He watched as the same happened to his sister.

She struggled against the vines, trying to take hold of her weapon, but she was soon overpowered, and left restrained. The old crone chuckled as she hobbled closer to the two. "Such a pity that your sister has to suffer the same lashing as you," she said as two vines crept up behind them.

Kirkland struggled against his restraints. He didn't know what to do, his sister was the one that always had a plan, the brave, and tough tomboy out rough housing with other boys from the village, but in this moment she was powerless. He watched as tears streaked down her cheeks from her eyes, and he could feel his heart break. "Stop," he demanded as the vines prepared for their first strike. "Promise that no harm will come to Isabella, and I'll tell you how I set the tree on fire," he lied.

Agatha chuckled as she stepped closer to Kirkland and took in a deep breath. "There is an ancient magic coming from you, child, but you have no idea how to use it," she said from a soft smile. "If you did, I would already be dead," she remarked while walking over to sit upon a large rock. "Magic isn't something that is used by accident. It requires years of training, and even then, the use of it isn't guaranteed," she said in a wheeze.

Kirkland shook his head. "Until today I thought magic was just a part of the fables mother told my sister and me before bed. I never even considered it to be real," he confessed as he watched his sister fight against her restraints.

Agatha released a sigh. "You have so much potential, child, but I fear time is something you are lacking," she said, turning her head to gaze out into the forest. "Perhaps there is a way for you to grasp a better understanding of your power, but it will come at a price."

"What would you have for this help?" Kirkland asked, pulling his eyes from his sister and locking them on the witch.

Agatha gave him a chuckled cough. "I'm afraid the price isn't of my own making, child. I will have to use a forbidden magic that isn't used in this world, but it is the only way to know for sure where you draw this power from," she said while shifting on the rock in search of comfort.

Kirkland huffed his disappointment. "What will you have to do?"

Agatha licked her lips. "The spell I use will tap into your bloodline, and it will place you in a deep sleep. It will feel like a dream as you walk in your ancestors' shoes, reliving their past lives, enduring their hardships, and rejoicing in their victories. From that we will know where your power comes," she said leaning heavily upon her staff.

Kirkland lowered his head to look upon the ground. "Do it," he demanded, closing his eyes, and taking in a deep breath.

"Stop!" Isabella screamed. "Why are you agreeing to this? You are supposed to be the smart one, and yet you are about to do something so incredibly stupid. You don't even know what this spell will do to you. It could kill you, Kirky," she choked out as tears began to swell in her eyes.

Kirkland knew that it wouldn't be without risk, but he had a thirst for knowledge that could never be satiated, and his sister often told him that his curiosity would be the death of him. He lifted his head to meet the red, puffy eyes of his sister, and he could feel her heart breaking at the thought of losing him, but he forced her a half smile. "You need not worry about me, sweet sister. You know my curiosity," he said before looking back at the witch. "Are you going to do this or not?"

"Stop it!" Isabella screamed as Agatha shifted off the rock, and started her incantation. "Why does it have to be Kirkland? Can I take his place since I am his sister?" She asked through clenched teeth.

Agatha flashed a feeble smile as she stepped closer to Isabella, and inhaled deeply. "What are you thinking Isabella? It's too dangerous for you," Kirkland protested while fighting against his restraints.

Isabella gave him a frustrated look of anger. "Why do you think it would be too dangerous for me? I'm stronger than you, faster than, and more courageous," she proclaimed.

Agatha chuckled before stepping away from the feisty girl. "I'm afraid I can't use you, my dear. You don't seem to have any trace of the power your brother has," she exclaimed looking back to Kirkland. "Are you ready?"

Isabella sobbed uncontrollably. "Please, don't do it," she begged.

"I have to," Kirkland half-heartedly admitted, looking away from his weeping sister. "Do it before I change my mind," he demanded, relaxing his head as best he could.

Agatha closed her eyes while speaking in a language that Kirkland didn't understand. She lowered her head, and lifted the tip of her staff to point in his direction. A nauseating feeling of dread came over him as he continued to listen to her incantation. He started to struggle against his restraints, fear had taken hold of him, and he no longer wished to go through with the spell. "Wait, I've changed my mind," he cried out, but the witch flashed a half smirk as she opened her crimson eyes, and pushed the tip of her staff against his chest causing a light to erupt from it.

Kirkland's blood boiled, filling him with excruciating pain. He wanted the witch to stop her spell, but when he opened his mouth to make the request all that would come from him was his agonizing scream. His head was spinning making him nauseous, and the world around him went dark. He was alone within the void, but a bright light sparkled before him. Reaching out a hand he took an unsteady step toward it, and in a magnificent flash he found himself standing on an overlook within the Emerald Forest with King Gorre Theodred.

Kirkland was looking through the eyes of his ancestor, and he was studying twelve enormous ships that had beached upon their shores and the twenty others that were still on the water waiting for their chance to breach. He watched as men marched from the vessels dressed in bronze armor carrying long spears, and round shields that covered them from thigh to neck.

Kirkland knew the equipment they carried, but he got the overwhelming feeling of fear as his ancestor had no idea what he was looking at. These outsiders were trespassing on his king's land, and they moved like warriors, and he was filled with dread as he watched them form a border with their shields. Others moved swiftly from the vessels to erect a makeshift camp of white tents along the beach, and the ships that were emptied had been torn apart so they could use the lumber to craft a wall just behind the line of shield carriers. The speed that these men worked was remarkable, but another ship washed ashore, and a thick wooden plank was dropped down so the massive beast could be ushered off the vessel.

Kirkland knew that the beast was known as an elephant, and they were well used in the lands of Slanderia, but he had never seen one so close before. The massive beast shook its head making its ears flop against its head, it lifted its trunk showing the ivory tusk that came out of its mouth, and it unleashed a deafening sound that shook his ancestor. They watched as a stable was crafted from the lumber taken from the ship, fifteen elephants were corralled together with an enormous trough built along the sides of it where the beast could take water, and be fed, but they weren't the only creatures to emerge from the ships.

From a different vessel stomped another beast that Kirkland recognized. The rhynos were shorter in stature than that of the elephants, but still enormous when standing next to a normal person. They had long horns that protruded from their nose, their small ears twitched when bugs landed on them, and the men tending to them did so with extreme caution. He watched as twenty of them were corralled into a separate stable than the elephants, but they also had a trough to which they could be watered and fed.

A hand grasped his shoulder causing him to turn and look at the king. Gorre Theodred was ruler of the Emerald Forest with long silver hair that hung just past his shoulders, he wore his crown that was crafted from the wood of Virundal, the tree of life, and it was elegantly dressed with gems upon it. His light purple eyes twinkled as he stepped up beside the ancestor of Kirkland. He was tall, and slender. "What do you think they want?" He asked, looking at the outsiders that were covering his shore.

Kirkland's mind was opened to what transpired as if he had lived it, but he knew that he was just going through the motions of his ancestor, Ralolen, who was a seasoned warrior. He fought against the evils of Hyland in service of his king, endured hardships, and was bestowed the nickname Silver Archer due to his skill with his longbow, but the strangers that plagued the beach worried him. He released a heavy sigh. "I know not of their true intent, but I believe we should report this to the wizard prime, and see what he has to say," he said.

Kirkland's body twitched as the dream shifted. He was now standing within a frozen forest high atop a snowy mountain. In place of leaves the trees were covered with icicles, and on their branches hung icy blue fruit. Reaching up he plucked one from the cold branch, the touch of it chilling his hand, and he took a bite. He felt his teeth chill as his mouth was filled with a refreshing minty flavor, but a surprisingly warm liquid washed down his throat. The Minova was always the sweetest fruit, but also the hardest to ever come by. He looked out at the quaint cottage and he savored his meal. The home of the wizard prime, he had almost given up hope on finding it, but there it was before him. Plumes of white smoke poured from the chimney, and they could see the dim light through the stained-glass windows. They approached the cottage unhindered by the snow beneath their feet. A sharp gust of cold wind washed over them. Their leaf capes flapped at their back, and flakes of snow danced elegantly around them as they arrived at the front of the small cottage.

Ralolen took a position at the right of the aged door that barred their entrance, and King Gorre made ready to knock upon its surface, but as he drew up his hand the door creaked open. The warmth from within caused their faces to flush, and they could see the smile of a child. The boy looked to be no more than twelve years, but his eyes told a different tale as he looked at them from one blue, and one green. "King Gorre, Master Ralolen, I have been expecting you," he said, stepping to the side so they could enter.

Ralolen stepped through the door, and he could feel the magic that was being used on the cottage. The outside appearance was just an illusion making it look as if it only had a few rooms, but once he stepped through the entrance the spell was broken, and he could see that the home of the wizard prime was enormous. They made their way down a small hallway, passing a number of doors on both sides of them, and they entered through a large double door at the end. A massive table of oak sat at its center with a map of Hyland etched on its surface. Small wooden pegs covered it to show the different kingdoms, the territory they controlled, and even the giants were represented on it.

The young wizard released a sigh as he stepped around the table, and moved some of the pegs. "I suppose you have come to talk about the strangers who have set up camp along Ashire," he said, placing the markers further south.

King Gorre bowed his head. "We sought you out, Aster, in the hopes of finding out where these outsiders came from, and what they want," he admitted as he watched the wizard move another twenty pegs north of the shore.

Aster lifted his gaze from the table. "Even my knowledge has its limits, King Gorre, but it would seem they came across the great sea, and if I had to muster a guess at this time," he said, studying the map. "I would say they came to invade," his voice made Kirkland's skin grow cold, and another sharp pain caused the dream to shift once more.

Kirkland felt the anxiousness of Ralolen as he continued to look through the eyes of the ancestor. Across an open field stood a sturdy wooden fort that had been built using trees that were cut down from the Emerald Forest, but the makeshift structure wasn't what bothered

Ralolen. It was the enormous force of bronze soldiers that gathered in front of it, and their beast was what had his ancestor nervous. He gazed upon a formidable wall built from the bronze shields the outsiders carried, and behind it stood sixty thousand men. The elephants steadied themselves with the help of a rider, a massive structure built upon their backs that carried several hundred bowmen, and the rhynos could be heard, but not seen. It was a force that filled even the veteran warrior with fear.

Ralolen looked back at his small force of twenty thousand, the combination of his king's army and that of King Virion Regynald. The others were coming, but it would be a fortnight before they would arrive. He released a sigh looking once more at the formation of the outsiders. He still didn't know their true intentions, but the wizard prime believed them there to invade our lands. They started cutting down trees from our beloved forest to build their crude structures, and that was when we tried speaking to them, but our words proved different than theirs. In a panic those that were chopping down our trees attacked with their tools, and we were forced to defend ourselves against them.

Aster feared that the death of those outsiders would be the spark that would ignite a war between us. He quickly wrote a letter to the commander of these barbarians while we tossed the dead bodies across the back of several horses, and selected an envoy to deliver the items to the fort of the outsiders. The wizard prime told us that the letter gave a detailed explanation of what transpired within the forest, and that it requested that the one who leads speak to our king about their intentions. We did not know if they would accept what Aster had told them of their deaths, but we wanted to be ready should they seek war against us.

Kirkland felt the horse grow uneasy as a man thick of chiseled muscle pushed his way through the shield wall, and out into the open field. He wore a cloak of crimson that dragged the ground behind him. A sheathed short sword dangled at his hip, strapped to his left arm was a round shield that covered him from thigh to neck, and in his other hand was a long spear. Plates of bronze ran the length of his legs from his knee to the top of his foot. The gauntlets that covered his forearms stretched from his elbow to the bend of the wrist. The bronze helm that adorns his head made him look fierce. Covering his cheeks down to the chin with a thick piece covering his nose down to the tip.

In a puff of smoke, the boy wizard appeared in the field. His dark blue robes lightly touched the tall grass, his dirty blond hair flowed with the breeze, his twisted staff poked into the dirt, and the amethyst that was embedded at the top glowed a brilliant purple. "I am Aster Debias, the wizard prime. I am not permitted to join one side or the other for fear of tipping the balance of nature, but I can be of use to both sides. I will be a bridge for the conversations that transpire here today," he said from his boyish smile.

The stranger held up a hand, and gave a shake of his head. "Your services will not be required this day, wizard prime," the stranger said in the tongue of Ralolen's people. "I am known as Guthric Maximus, a warlord of this army, and as you can plainly hear I have already been taught the language of this land," he boasted from a dark, and chilling voice.

Kirkland could feel the shock of his ancestor, but could see it through the eyes of Ralolen upon the face of the wizard prime. Aster leaned against his staff, and gazed heavily upon the outsider. "So it would seem. Would you be against telling us who enlightened you in this speech?" He asked, his boyish smile never failing.

"Let's get through one thing at a time," Guthric replied from a half smile that could hardly be seen. "I have come to speak to an elvish king about the twelve men he slaughtered, and of our intentions. Could you bring him out?"

Aster turned to look back at the elves who had amassed to greet the outsiders. King Gorre Theodred sat upon a palfrey of dark gray that was stomping a hoof against the ground. He was garbed in a pale green tunic, a cape of leaves pinned at his neck, and his weaved crown of birch rested elegantly on his brow. His longbow was fixed about his chest, a quiver of arrows rested on his back, and with a flick of his wrist the horse slowly trotted him out into the field to meet with the outsider. "I am King Gorre Theodred, and this is King Virion Regynald," he said, introducing the other elf who rode up alongside him.

King Virion Regynald was on the back of a palfrey of black and white. He was garbed in an icy blue tunic, he wore no cape, but he did have a longbow of his own strapped about him with a quiver of arrows. His long platinum hair was pulled back and held in place by a crown weaved from the pine trees that grew within his region. His dark violet eyes sharply peered at the stranger as they came to a halt at the side of Aster, but the two kings didn't go alone.

Kirkland watched through the eyes of his ancestor as they rode up to take their place just behind their king. At Ralolen's side was the sworn protector of King Virion Regynald. Yllaven Simimar wore an icy blue tunic to match that of his lordship, but it was stretched tightly across his massive chest. He stood two hands taller than Ralolen, his platinum hair rested down to the small of his back, and in place of a longbow he wore a crude hammer that he had taken from Tieban Gorgtov Frognasher. A giant who threatened to kill King Virion Regynald so that he could claim SnowBird Mountain, and Yllaven challenged him to a *kunnia*.

The battle would take place atop the mountain where four spectators from each side would make sure that honor was kept. The battle started as the sun kissed the sky, but no victor would be crowned until it had gone full circle. Both combatants were beyond a point of exhaustion, but Yllaven managed to dodge a blow from Tieban's hammer, pulling the weapon free of the giant's grasp; he brought it down on his head and took the life of the chieftain. With the death of the would-be chieftain the others fled screaming *bane of giants* in their harsh tongue, but none from that tribe would ever challenge King Virion or his champion ever again.

Guthric gave a quick nod of his head. "Two of you are here. Which one of you was the one responsible for the death of my men?"

King Gorre broke his gaze from the outsider. "The fault falls on me, I'm afraid," he admitted, looking back in the direction of the stranger. "My men asked them to stop cutting down the trees, and they attacked us. We do not kill unjustly," he said looking over at Aster.

Guthric gave a quick nod of his head. "I told everyone that they should take the opportunity given, and learn the language of this land, but it would appear that not everyone heeded my advice," he said, releasing a heavy sigh. "They were dispatched to gather more wood before I arrived at the fort, or else I would have made sure someone had gone who could have spoken to you," he admitted, pulling the tie of his helm, and lifting it from his head.

His shoulder length black hair was coated in sweat, his piercing blue eyes scanned the field, and he took in a deep breath of the fresh air that swirled around him. A soldier stepped forward from behind the wall of shields. The bronze armor that covered his body fully glistened in the sunlight, his shield matched that of the others, and he held high a long spear as he stepped up to stand beside Guthric. He handed his helm to the soldier before running a hand through his thick, but trimmed beard. "That feels better," he said, taking hold of his spear once more, and looking at the elvish kings. "We had thought the death of those men meant you were hostile, and we were prepared to defend ourselves to the last man," he admitted from his half smile.

King Virion wasn't known for his patience as he shifted on the back of his horse. "Why have you come to Hyland!?!" He asked harshly.

Guthric took a moment, his eyes scanning every inch of the battlefield. "We came to these fertile lands in search of a new home," he answered calmly.

King Virion gritted his teeth in anger. "Do you intend to steal our land!?!," he screamed in frustration.

"We did not come with the intention of stealing your land, but you have to understand that we cannot return to Slanderia," Guthric said, the grip on his spear tightening. "Now, we have come to establish settlements in these lands, and we hoped that war could be avoided," he said looking back at his enormous force. "But if we can't come to some agreement then we are prepared to fight for," he said in a booming voice of confidence.

King Gorre tossed up his hand to prevent King Virion from speaking. "If there is a way to prevent blood from being shed then we will consider it, but before we put any thought into anything you have said we will have the answer to our question. Who has been teaching you our customs?" He asked lowering his hand to grip the mane of his horse.

Guthric inhaled deeply. "I don't see any harm in you knowing the identity of my teacher," he said, turning his head slightly to gaze upon his army. "You should come on out."

A man stepped out from behind the shield wall wearing an elegant robe of lavender that was trimmed in silver, he had a chest plate of bronze that also covered his shoulders, a quiver of arrows was on his back, and he carried a beautifully crafted recurve bow with the sunlight reflecting off the many gems that decorated it. The cape he wore was lavender, but hung only to the small of his back, his helm resembled that of Guthric's, but with some small differences. He walked with a smooth stride as he moved from the shield wall to stand at the warlord's side, and he gave him a simple bow. He carried no shield, but the hilt of a short sword could be seen dangling at his hip.

Guthric placed a hand upon the shoulder of the war-commander that stood two hand lengths shorter. "This is the one who told me all about your customs, your land, and how to speak to you. I found him on a small raft muttering to himself, he was half-crazed from starvation, and dehydration. It wasn't easy nourishing him back to health, due to the barrier created by our different languages, but eventually I learned how to speak to him. Allow me to introduce War-Commander Druindar," he said as the man removed his helm.

Kirkland felt his ancestors' heart drop at the reveal of who brought the Slanderians to the shores of Hyland, but it was King Virion who spoke first. "How dare you bring these outsiders to our land. You were banished for performing blood rituals!" He screamed, freighting his horse.

Druindar flashed a smirk that made his light purple eyes twinkle, his white hair was cut short to his head, and he dropped his helm on the ground to free his hand. "You should have killed me when you had the chance," he mocked, pulling free an arrow from his quiver. "I have returned home and now I ask you. Will we have talks of peace or will it be war?" He asked, nocking an arrow in his bow.

"What do you have in mind for terms of peace?" King Gorre asked in haste.

Guthric gave a nod to his massive army, and from it came another soldier. He wore armor, but carried only a rolled-up parchment. "I have written what is known as a *Coranata*. In the lands of Slanderia it signifies peace between rival armies, and I have taken the liberty of writing it in both our languages. Give it a read," he said ushering for the soldier to carry it over to the elvish kings.

Ralolen was lost in thought as he remembered what the open field they stood in once looked like. The tall ancient trees that stretched to the sky, offering shelter and shade from the sun. He felt a stinging in his heart to see them rendered to nothing, but a stump. He watched as the bronze covered man saluted the warlord, and marched toward them carrying the parchment tightly in his hand, but the silver archer was more focused on the traitor. "A ghaoth chluasach," he softly whispered his spell, and a gentle breeze whirled through the Slanderian army.

"This is folly," the wind carried over to Ralolen as the traitor continued to speak. "They will never agree to the coranata. They will just stall until the other kings can join with them against us. We should attack."

"I will not kill needlessly, war-commander," Guthric said, but the spell was starting to fade. "I seek peace," was the last thing the wind carried, but he could plainly see it wasn't all the warlord had to say.

King Virion snatched the parchment from the bronze covered man eagerly. "Give me that!" He demanded harshly.

Ralolen edged his horse closer in anticipation of the soldier reacting to the severe gesture of the hot-tempered king, but to his surprise the man just saluted them, and then made his way back across the field. The red wax seal had an image of a howling wolf, but King Virion paid it little mind as he broke it in half, and unraveled the scroll so that he could read the words etched on it. "They can't be serious," he said through clenched teeth, handing the coronata over and looking back to his champion.

King Gorre released a heavy sigh as he unrolled the parchment, and Ralolen watched as his majesty read over the document that was supposed to be about peace. "Twenty-four," he muttered letting the parchment roll back together as he looked to the other king.

"They are barbarians," King Virion said from a snarl. "They want us to just give them our lands and our children. I would rather have war," he declared through clenched teeth.

Aster rushed over to the two kings. "Let's not be too rash in our thinking. Their numbers are many compared to yours and they have beasts of war that will fight with them. May I read the coronata they have drafted?" He asked with an outstretched hand.

Ralolen moved to stand at the side of his king as the rolled-up parchment was handed to the wizard prime. "What did it say, my king?" He asked, steadying his horse.

King Gorre lightly groaned while rubbing the back of his neck. "It states that it is a declaration for peace. They are afraid of tainting the land with bloodshed, and want to avoid the countless deaths that often come with war, but what they are asking is too much. If we agree to their terms they will take half of my kingdom, and that of King Virions," he said in a whisper.

Ralolen looked over to see that the other king was distracted with speaking to his own champion, and wasn't listening to their conversation. "That explains why King Virion said they just want us to give them our lands, and I'm just guessing from your words that they have requested twenty-four of our children to be given to them too," he said, releasing a sigh.

King Gorre gave a quick nod. "They want twelve of our male nobles, and twelve of our female nobles to marry nobles of theirs. Apparently, it is how they solidify an agreement between rival armies in the lands they came from," he said, shifting his position on the back of his horse. "If it comes to war, do you think we can win?" He asked, turning his gaze from the massive Slanderian force, and looked to his champion.

Ralolen was worried about going to war with the outsiders since he saw them landing along their shores. The thought of fighting against them with their vast numbers, polished equipment, and enormous beasts was not something he relished in. He released a heavy sigh. "It would not be an easy battle, my liege. We know very little of our enemy, and we have to consider that Druindar has told them everything about us. Going to war against them would be unwise," he said, lowering his head in defeat.

Aster rolled up the parchment, and stepped to stand before the two kings. "I can understand why you are willing to go to war, King Virion, but we have to find another way of resolving this conflict," he advised, stuffing the coranata into his robe. "They are just searching for a new home. I know they have requested too much land, and asking for twenty-four nobles is outrageous, but I believe these are things that can be negotiated."

"Can you set up a meeting where we could talk about these matters?" King Gorre asked quickly before Virion could speak. "If they are willing to alter their request to something more suitable, I don't see why peace can't be achieved."

King Virion was clenching his teeth in his anger. "Make the arrangements wizard," he snarled coldly.

Aster bowed to the kings. "I shall go to speak to the warlord," he said, and within a blink he was transported across the field to stand before Guthric.

Kirkland groaned in agony as a sharp pain in his chest caused the dream to shift. He was still on the field, but he was now looking through the eyes of the Slanderian warlord. "I'll speak to the kings about altering the terms of the coronata," Guthric said before handing his weapons over to the soldiers at his side.

"You can't be serious," Druindar scoffed. "We have presented them our terms, and to alter it now would be a sign of weakness. I say we just take it all."

Guthric flashed a look at the elf that made him cower. "I have seen the tragedies that come with spilling blood on a field. I will not destroy this land like others have done to Slanderia," he said harshly. "Demetris, Phelx, Cornelious, and Sven. Come forth," he demanded and the shield wall parted so that the men could emerge. "I want you four to watch Druindar, and if you think he is about to do something stupid, kill him," he commanded in a firm tone before looking back to the wizard with a smile. "Go get the elvish kings."

Kirkland felt the great strength of this ancestor. A raw power that made him feel indomitable, but he could also see the brilliance of his mind. Guthric knew that he had the upper hand against those born of Hyland. He held the numbers against them, he understood their magic, he had weapons to stand against it, and his army was well trained in the art of combat. If it came to war, he knew that he could win, but he was also mindful of the effects it would have on the land. *Roz, titan maiden of wisdom, and beauty. Guide me in these negotiations to keep peace between us,* he prayed to himself as they met at the center of the field.

Guthric gave them a respectful bow, but kept his eyes on them. "The wizard stated that our terms were unacceptable," he spoke, in a clear and calm voice.

"You want the majority of our kingdoms, and twenty-four of our people to wed yours," King Virion hissed as he encircled the Slanderian.

Guthric released a heavy sigh placing his hands on his hips, and nodding. "What would you find agreeable?"

"Your surrender and departure from our lands," King Virion said angrily.

Kirkland could feel the rage burning within his ancestor. Guthric took a deep breath trying to keep calm. "Going back to Slanderia isn't an option," he declared.

King Gorre held up his hand to prevent the other king from speaking. "You said that once before. Why can't you return to your home?" He asked in a calm voice.

Guthric inhaled deeply. "Slanderia is a vast place, but where I am from it is nothing more than a wasteland. A desert of scorching sand for as far as one can see, and the very few places that prove to have fertile ground have been taken by the emperor. Those of us who are able hunt the desert for food and water. Most of us make a living fishing the *Dreaded Sea*, but none of it goes to the starving people of the *Scorched Sand*. Anything that is caught, killed, gathered, or scavenged is taxed by the emperor. Those who had enough of his tyranny fought back against him, but they were quickly put down by his army," Kirkland could feel the rage being replaced with sadness as his ancestor told them of his home.

"I had given up hope of anything better than the harsh life I had, but then I found him. The elf you call traitor," Guthric paused to look back at the elf that was being detained by his men. "He was half-dead from starvation, and driven mad by thirst. I thought him a lost cause, but my sister managed to nurse him back to health. It took some time, but I managed to learn his language, and then he reignited my hopes for a better life. He told me stories of lush fields where crops could grow, and streams of fresh drinking water. I was ready to set sail, but he warned me of his people. The ones who banished him from his home."

Guthric paused to collect his thoughts as he put his gaze on King Gorre. "Fearing that I wouldn't be given permission to stay in a land of new hope I went to the emperor. I told him about the lands to the west, and how fertile they were. He provided me with the means to bring an army across the Dreaded Sea, but he took my sister as a prisoner. If I fail to make settlements here, he will kill her and I would rather raze this world to cinders instead of living without her. So, going back to Slanderia empty handed is not an option," he declared.

King Gorre glanced at the other king briefly before putting his eyes back on the man before him. "The twenty-four weddings, is that meant to force the emperor to keep his word on peace?" He asked, steadying his horse.

Guthric shook his head. "The emperor has no honor," he said looking back to his army, and then taking a small step closer toward them. "Regardless of what you choose to do he will come across the Dreaded Sea, kill your strongest warriors, enslave the rest, and take all of this for himself," he said, holding out his arms.

"He can try," King Virion snapped.

"He will succeed," Guthric returned defeatedly. "This force you see amassed behind me isn't even close to his full might."

Kirkland could see the fear setting into the eyes of King Gorre, but it was Ralolen that stepped forward to speak. "Then we need to negotiate a new coronata with you," he declared, bringing his horse to a halt at the side of his king.

King Gorre nodded. "Can you defeat him?"

Guthric gave a shrug. "I could certainly be of help. Though the majority of my force is constructed from his men, that doesn't make them loyal to him. I could easily convince them to join me," he said from a sly smile.

King Virion's face was flushed as the vein in his neck pulsed. "What do you want?"

Guthric rubbed the back of his neck. "You know what I want. I want to make this place my home, but I also want my sister to join me here in this new world. You don't want to give me a majority of your kingdom, that's fine, but give me enough to build homes for my people. I will need lumber for our houses, stables for our animals, and the dwarven folk who traveled with me are just beside themselves with anxiety to mine ore from that mountain," he said pointing to the snowy peaks that could be seen to the north. "They will build themselves a kingdom inside of it, but they are very resourceful. We will need their craftsmanship if we hope to stand against him," he said, taking a deep breath.

"What about the twenty-four marriages?" King Virion asked from a soured tone.

Guthric gave him a nod. "Would two marriages be too much? I will wed a female of your choosing, and one of your males can marry one of my most trusted schildmaids."

King Gorre rubbed his forehead just below the crown. "I have a son who has come of age that will marry this schildmaid of yours, but I'm afraid all my daughters are already pledged in union to others," he admitted looking to the others.

King Virion shook his head slightly in disagreement, but Ralolen placed a hand upon the shoulder of his king. "My sweet daughter, Kaylessa, has just recently come of age, and I was in the process of finding her a suitor," he said, looking the Slanderian up and down. "If it meant keeping Hyland safe, I would promise her hand to him."

Kirkland's stomach twisted as the dream flashed, and darkness took him. He was still within the memories of his ancestor Guthric, but his sight was gone. The sound of a baby wailing gave light to why as the

Slanderian lifted his head, and opened his eyes to gaze at the small babe that was bundled in fine silk. The mother fell back into the sweat covered sheets, she gave a panting smile, and squeezed the hand of Guthric. "See our son?" She asked with a tear running the length of her cheek.

Guthric flashed her a grin as he wiped the tear away with his thumb, and kissed her gently. "He is healthy, and beautiful," he said, touching his forehead to hers.

"What will you name him?" She asked, taking the bundled babe from the midwife that her husband insisted on them having.

Guthric uncovered the face of the baby to get a better look at him. "Thallan Maximus," he said with a lighthearted chuckle.

Kirkland was in awe at seeing the birth of a child, but it was also the first time he got a good look at Kaylessa. She had shoulder length platinum hair, her dark violet eyes were full of peace, and her skin looked more akin to porcelain. She was breathtakingly beautiful as she smiled at her new baby. "I like that name," she said, moving her gaze to her husband.

Guthric gave her a wink. "I'm glad you like it," he said, kissing her forehead. "He is the first of his kind. A child born of elvish, and human blood."

"He will do great things," Kaylessa said, nestling down into the bed. "I'm going to sleep. Will you watch over me?" She asked while fighting to keep her eyes open.

Guthric lifted the babe up from her arms. "We will not leave your side, my love," he replied, kissing her hand, and watching as she drifted off to slumber.

Kirkland felt an intense pressure in his head making him feel as if his eyes were going to pop out, and the memory shimmered in his blurred focus. "Foolish boy," an unfamiliar voice echoed through his mind. "You are meddling in powers you can't even comprehend."

Kirkland screamed in agony as the dream shifted, he was sitting beside a large lake, the image that looked back at him was not that of Ralolen or Guthric. This ancestor was a beautiful woman, her light purple eyes were filled with unfallen tears, and her silver hair hung just past her shoulders. She sniffed as she ran her sleeve across her eyes blocking Kirkland's sight. "Aleesia, you out here?" Guthric asked as he emerged from behind the trees, and into the clearing where the pond was.

Aleesia quickly ran the sleeve of her long shirt across her face. "I am," she said from a broken angelic voice.

Guthric sat down beside her, and put his arm around her. "What's wrong, honey?" He asked, squeezing her tight.

Aleesia's eyes betrayed her as more water flowed from them, and down her porcelain cheeks. "I'm afraid something bad is going to happen to you, daddy," she admitted, pulling her knees up against her chest, and resting her head upon them.

Guthric chuckled lightly. "Nothing bad is going to happen, sweetie. I'll have your grandad Ralolen, and brother Thallan with me the whole time," he said from a smile.

Kirkland could feel the fear that was overwhelming her. "Why does it have to be you, and them? Can't King Gorre find someone else?" She asked in between her sniffling.

Guthric kissed his daughter on top of her head. "I was the one that brought Druindar back to these lands, I was the one that allowed him to escape the encampment after we signed the coranata, and because of those actions I have to be the one to confront him," he said causing Aleesia to look at him, but the vision blurred.

Kirkland felt his blood freeze as the dream shifted. The cave was cold, and damp, but he knew that he was still looking through the eyes of Aleesia. He could feel the panic that made her heart race as she cautiously made her way down deeper. She was trailing someone that was just outside of his sight, he could see the faint light of their torches, and even hear them as they traveled ahead of her, but as they stepped through a small opening, they went silent. Her heart pounded in her chest as fear and panic gripped her tightly, and she quickened her pace to clear the opening. "Got you," a familiar voice called out, making her scream in fright.

Guthric quickly turned her to face him, and he placed a hand over her mouth. "Aleesia," he said shockingly. "I told you to help your auntie with your mother. Why are you following us through this cave?" he asked quietly, and slowly removed his hand so that she could answer.

Aleesia took a deep breath to calm herself. "I was worried about you, and so I came to help," she admitted with watery eyes.

"You shouldn't have come, granddaughter," Ralolen said, stepping from behind a stalagmite, and her brother came from the other side, shaking his head.

Aleesia shook her head. "But father said that there was nothing to worry about. I came to make sure of that," she said, drying her eyes.

Guthric released a heavy sigh. "Stay close to your brother, and do exactly what I say," he said looking to Thallan.

Her brother gave a nod and the four of them examined the large room they found themselves in. It was a large circular room with stalactites hanging overhead, stalagmites were everywhere, and at the center was a weathered makeshift shack. Guthric placed his hands on his hips as he gazed at the structure. "Do we take a chance and go in?" He asked looking over to Ralolen, and then to Thallan.

"I do not sense any magic lingering here," Ralolen said as he cautiously stepped closer. "But that does not mean he hasn't set something more barbaric for any who trespass."

Guthric rubbed his chin before looking at his children. "Thallan, watch your sister, and wait here. Make sure you don't take your eyes off her. You know how she is," he warned from a slight smile before stepping through the door.

Thallan placed a hand upon the shoulder of his sister. "Father will be fine, sweet sister. He is a tough old man," he said from a soft smile.

Aleesia knew that her father was one of the strongest warriors in all the land, but something just didn't feel right about the whole thing. Druindar had been in hiding ever since the coranata was signed. His thrust for vengeance drove him to make an attempt on King Virions life, but thanks to father it failed. He was placed in a cage, his magic was drained from him, and there he waited for judgment to be passed on him. Father was heavy of heart because the hopes of finding a new home blinded him to just how bloodthirsty Druindar really was, but after his magic was stripped from him by the wizard prime her father released him under the veil of night, and no one had ever heard from him since.

Aleesia sighed as her body quivered from the cold and dampness of the cave. "Are you freezing?" Thallan asked as he unpinned his cloak, and draped it over her shoulders.

Aleesia welcomed the warmth of the thick fur cloak her brother wore, but it still didn't put her mind at ease. "Something just doesn't feel right," she said looking up to her brother. "Druindar has been hiding in a place where even magic couldn't find him, and after thirty years he resurfaced to attack the small village of *Frosty Meadows*," she said looking back to the shack that was being lit by the torches of the two searching it.

"How do you know it was an attack on the village?" Thallan asked, crossing his arms about his chest, and glaring at his sister.

Aleesia shook her head. "I don't have any confirmation that it was an actual attack, but I do know of the letter King Virion sent to King Gorre about it being abandoned, and of the letter left for father instructing him to come to this cave," she said, turning her gaze up to her brother.

Thallan held a shocked expression as his sister recounted everything that his father had told him in confidence. "How do you know all this?"

Aleesia placed a hand on the arm of her brother. "I can walk into a room, and no one notices I am even there," she admitted looking back to the shack.

The two stood in silence as their father emerged from the small shack. He was carrying a tome in his hand, and their grandfather was walking while turning the pages of another. "Thallan, I want you to take your sister and return to King Gorre. Give him these, and tell him to make a call to arms to the other elvish kings," he said, handing the book over.

Ralolen slammed the book he was reading shut. "Go with haste, grandson. We will try to find more clues of what is going on, but need to be prepared for anything," he said, handing over the tome to Thallan.

Aleesia looked at the covers of the books, but nothing was inscribed on the outside to give her any inclination of what they were about. Thallan gave a salute, and placed a hand on the shoulder of his sister. "Let's go," he said, handing his torch to her to carry.

Aleesia didn't put up a fight as they made their way through the small door leaving the room that contained the shack, but she paused to look back. Her father walked behind the old wooden structure followed by her grandfather. The light of their torches fading leaving nothing, but darkness. "I'm not going back with you," she said in a huff, and taking a step back away from her brother.

Thallan's face flushed with annoyance as he turned to look at his sister. "Father said for me to take you back, and that is what I am going to do," he said, taking a step closer.

"I'm sorry, brother," she said quickly before turning on her heels and running across the enormous room that held the makeshift cabin.

Aleesia knew that her brother had no chance at catching her. She had always been swift of foot, and because of that she was given the nickname *Guandreal*, which meant Zephyr Swiftness. She worried that the fire at the end of the torch would go out, and she watched as it flickered in her haste, but the flame continued to fight against the odds. She could hear Thallan struggling behind her, and eventually his heavy wheezing started to fade. She ran around the corner of the shack, but stopped to look back. Her brother was doubled over in an attempt to regain his lost breath. "Iginata tumalas," she whispered through heavy breathing, making the fire burn brighter. "I have to make sure father is safe," she said, turning to take the only opening that was behind the shack.

Alessia cautiously descended further into the depths of the cave. She walked with the torch held high above her head making the light dance off the glistening walls, each step was meticulously placed to keep her from slipping over the wet stones that made up the path, but she kept her eyes forward into the unknown darkness ahead. Her mind raced with the stories she was always told of the monsters that dwelled within the dark, and she imagined those beasts hurting her father. Her heart pounded in her chest with fear, but she kept going. She clenched her teeth, drove the thoughts from her mind, and continued to make her way. Nothing was going to prevent her from making sure that her father remained safe.

The tunnel she traversed narrowed in places causing her to have to walk through sideways, but in other places it grew so wide that her torch couldn't push away the darkness of the full room. She walked until her feet ached, and the muscles in her legs throbbed. She kept looking for signs that she was gaining on her father, but she hadn't even seen the light of his torch since he walked around the back of the cabin. With a fluttering heart of panic, she quickened her pace along the path, and as she turned a sharp corner, she could see a small door being lit by torch light from the other side.

Aleesia slowed her pace as she walked toward the door, but the painful groans of those within the room filled her with dread. She pressed against the wall so that she could peek inside the room without drawing attention to herself, but a small gasp emerged from her as she looked upon the horrors of the room. Along the back wall were massive steel cages that held women, and children while the men were shackled to the stone cave with thick chains. They all were too weak to even hold their heads up, the children were unable to cry any longer, the women continued to hold them as tight as their frail bodies could, and then men lay defeated upon the ground, but she saw that the source of the groans were coming from them.

Aleesia choked back a cough as she covered her nose. The rancid smell that was flowing from the room was going to cause her to retch, but she didn't want to let anyone know that she was there, and so she fought against the urge. She watched as her father stepped a little closer to the dais that held the pedestal where Druindar stood. "What are you doing?" He asked, pulling his sword from the sheath.

Druindar looked up from the book he was reading from the pedestal with a smile. "I am doing what you were too weak to do. I am going to wash this world clean, and make it ready for him," he said, dipping his fingers into a chalice, and then running them across his cheek just under his eyes.

Guthric placed a hand on the hilt of his sword. "Who are you talking about?"

Druindar held out his arms. "*Bahaal*," he said before reading from the book.

"We have to stop him," Ralolen said, firing an arrow in the direction of the traitor.

The projectile was deflected by an unforeseen force, and Druindar laughed hysterically. "You are too late Silver Archer. Bahaal has already placed his blessing on me for gathering him an army. Now that you are here to witness it, I will open the portal to release him back into our world," he said, plunging his hand down into the chalice, lifting it out and flinging the blood across the room.

Druindar started chanting, but Aleesia was unfamiliar with the words he was speaking, and as a whirlwind formed within the room Guthric fought against the winds that threatened to knock him off his feet. "Who is Bahaal?"

Ralolen shook his head. "He was one of the first elves. He was corrupted by *Avgrunnen*, and was the first to use blood magic. Those abominations that threaten the kingdoms from the shadows were amongst his first creations. He was banished by the Wizard Prime to another plane, and has remained there for centuries," he screamed over the opening vortex that appeared at the side of the dais.

"And now I am free," a dark voice echoed out.

Aleesia watched in shock as an elf stepped from the maelstrom, but he didn't look like any of the other elves she was accustomed to. He had ashen skin, dark red eyes that pierced her soul, and his raven-colored hair flowed down to rest upon the polished skulls that were strapped to his shoulders. He wore robes of crimson that touched the ground lightly, a leather belt was tied around his waist holding a small dagger that dripped blood, and his toothy grin gave her chills. He took in a deep breath of the putrid air. "It has been too long since I have smelled the intoxicating smell of fear," he said, setting his gaze upon Guthric and Ralolen.

Bahaal held out a hand causing a blast of energy to force the two of them off their feet. "Now to finish what I started so long ago," he said looking at the ceiling.

Guthric groaned as he tried to stand from the ground, but found that his body wasn't responding to his command. "Why can't I move?" He asked in a strain.

"He was gifted the control of blood by Avgrunnen," Ralolen forced out in a groan.

"I have done what you asked master," Druindar said, kneeling at the feet of Bahaal. "Grant me what you promised. Grant me the power to finally get my revenge on those who have wronged me."

Bahaal placed his other hand upon the head of Druindar. "I shall give you power, but not for your petty vengeance. You will be the one to lead my army, but your desires shall be wiped from you. You will live to serve only," he said from an evil laugh as his eyes glowed red and crimson poured from them.

Druindar clutched to his chest as he screamed in agony, but his cries weren't alone as those being held prisoner joined him. Aleesia watched as their bodies began to change. The Slanderians that were held captive started to double in size, their bodies becoming thicker of muscle, tusks pushed forward out of their mouths, but each was unique in how it appeared. Some came out of the bottom, some from the top, a few had more than one, and some had up to four. Their skin remained the same color it was before the magic changed them, but their eyes turned black with a small red pupil.

The elves that were locked up alongside the hulking Slanderians suffered a similar fate, but their porcelain skin turned to ash, their hair faded to a pale white, but their tall, slender bodies remained the same.

Their eyes were deep pits of darkness, and, as they groaned in their agony, small tusks could be seen forming, but not visible with their mouths closed. Druindar stood from the feet of his master revealing that he suffered the same fate as his brethren, and he moved to stand at the side of the one who deceived him.

Bahaal turned his attention to the two he was holding down on the ground. "Now for my two generals that will lead my army," he said from a smile as Guthric and Ralolen started twisting in pain.

"NO!" Aleesia screamed as she ran through the door and stood in defiance between her elders. "You will not take them!" She yelled, filling the room with a brilliant light of pure energy. As it faded, she saw that she was standing alongside the big lake she would often visit when she felt uneasy.

"What happened?" Guthric asked in bewilderment as he quickly stood up from the ground and wrapped his arms around his daughter.

"Had to save you," Aleesia managed to whisper before letting sleep take her.

The world was spiraling out of control for Kirkland, and it made him feel nauseous. "Foolish boy! This must end!" The ancient voice echoed in his head.

With a brilliant flash of radiant light the dream shifted, and Kirkland was on a battlefield fighting against the creations that Bahaal made with the prisoners. He could feel that he was no longer looking through the eyes of Aleesia as this ancestor gracefully dodged an attack and made an opening. Kirkland watched as the youthful hands quickly plunged the sword he was holding into the neck of the enemy and moved onto the next as the lifeless corpse collapsed to the ground.

Kirkland took a deep breath as the dream played out for him. He knew that the hulking Slanderian creatures were known as orcs and those created from the elvish prisoners back in the cave were called druhir. He could feel the fatigue setting in with his ancestor as another enemy was cut down. The battlefield was littered with thousands of corpses, black ooze flowed from the creations of Bahaal, and they pooled together with the crimson streams of the others that had been cut down during the war.

"Eridin, be mindful of where you are," Guthric called out as he sliced the head off a druhir and deflected the attack of an orc.

Eridin danced beneath the thick axe head of an orc and plunged his sword into the chest of a druhir. "How much longer do we need to hold them?" He asked, flipping backwards to avoid the axe head once more and get closer to his grandfather.

Guthric was older with his gray hair and salt and pepper beard, but his body was still taut with muscles as he hit an orc with the shield he carried, knocking it to the ground. "We will hold them for as long as needed, grandson," he said, plunging his sword into the chest of the monster. "We have to give our injured the time they need to retreat across the bridge of *Tirthos*," he said, as a horn echoed across the bloody field and the army of Bahaal stopped attacking.

"What are they doing?" Eridin whispered to his grandfather as the survivors of their small band closed ranks and made themselves ready for another assault.

Guthric let his eyes scan the enemy ahead. "Bahaal is here," he declared through clenched teeth. "Be ready to run, grandson. We will lead the enemy to the path between Luminar and Gilger. The narrow gap will cause them to funnel down to a more manageable number at a time. It should provide us with the edge we need to hold them until Aster is ready," he said, never moving his eyes from the enemy.

"You have fought well," Bahaal said as his throne was carried from within the ranks by six orcs and sat down before his army. "But why fight me?" He asked from a sly smile.

"We fight to keep our freedom," Guthric responded, pointing the tip of his sword at him.

Bahaal laughed heartily as he stood from his throne and folded his arms behind his back. "You think you have freedom?" He asked, but didn't wait for them to answer. "Everything you have done has been orchestrated by Zephyr and his primordial favorite. Avgrunnen has shown me their big plan for this world and he granted me the power to disrupt their work. I offer you the same enlightenment. Just kneel at my feet," he said from a smile.

"None of us will ever bow to you or your master," Guthric growled. "You spout nothing but lies! Your deception might work on those weak of will, but your words have no effect on us," he declared, gripping his shield tighter.

"Such a pity," Bahaal remarked from a forced frown. "I had hoped to make you one of my generals," he said, giving a shrug. "Guess I'll just have to settle for a lifeless corpse once my soldiers kill you," he boasted, twisting his fingers over his head to give them a sign to attack.

xxxviii

"Retreat!" Guthric screamed as the army of Bahaal charged toward them.

Kirkland could feel the fear of Eridin as they ran from the bloody battlefield in the direction of the twin mountains to the west. From time to time, he would glance back to see how far away the enemy was, but with every look they appeared to be gaining on him. Panic settled into his chest, but as they were about to be overcome, they managed to rush into the narrow gap between the two mountains and the orcs were forced to funnel in after them. "Shield wall!" Guthric screamed his command and his men obeyed.

They turned on their heels holding up their shields letting the chasing orcs smash against them. The raw strength of their enemy was almost too much for them to hold, but each man that held up a shield managed to stay on their feet. Archers quickly opened fire from behind the shield wall, letting arrow after arrow fly into the horde, and long spears were used to stab at the orcs that pushed against the shields. The enemy roared in frustration as they were being held back, but Eridin knew that the strength of his grandfather's soldiers wouldn't last, and eventually the stronger orcs would bash their way through. The young man looked to the sky with eyes full of tears. "Please help," he prayed to the sky and the clouds turned dark.

Guthric smiled as lightning flashed in the darkening sky. "He is ready," he said, touching the shoulder of the nearest soldier. "On my command make an opening and retreat."

The soldier gave him a nervous shake of his head as he gritted his teeth and was slowly being pushed backwards in the dirt. "This is as far as we go, sir," he said. "We will continue to hold them while you escape. Just make sure Bahaal pays for what he has done," another soldier said as they took a step in unison to push back against the enemy. "It was an honor to fight at your side," another said. Then they all roared in a unified battle cry.

"It was a great honor to stand with each and every one of you," Guthric said with unfallen tears in his eyes. He turned to look at the five archers and five men carrying spears that were behind the shield wall. "Aster is ready and we need to get across this bridge before the attack," he commanded.

Eridin's heart was heavy with pain as they made their way out of the ravine and he stole one last look of the ten men standing firm against the orcs that continued to try to push them back. They managed to clear the natural bridge of Tirthos as a blast of lightning fell from the sky striking the top of both mountains and causing large boulders to fill in the gap. Eridin could hear the roar of a giant wave forming north of them. He looked to see that it was traveling toward the bridge. Once it crashed into the bridge, it was completely destroyed. He dropped to his knees to weep. His mind flashed with so many mixed emotions about what had just transpired. His body ached, his heart pained him, and his lungs burned. He quickly wiped away his tears as his grandfather sat down beside him.

Guthric placed a hand upon the shoulder of his grandson. "Don't be ashamed of the tears you are shedding, grandson. Those feelings are a part of what we are fighting for. It's what those men sacrificed their lives for. Our emotions are what assures us that we are living and we must stand to never let anyone take that away from us," he said from a half-hearted smile as tears streaked his cheeks. "Let's get to Sunset Falls and regroup with King Gorre," he said, standing up and pulling his grandson to his feet.

Kirkland felt the vines growing tighter around him as his body convulsed and the blood drained from his nose dripping from his chin. The dream quickly shifted, but he was still looking through the eyes of a fleeing Eridin. Fear took the very heart of his ancestor as he rushed across a small bridge to his grandfather and collided into him. "They are coming," he muttered hysterically, looking back to see the encroaching enemy.

Guthric flashed a half-smile to his grandson. "Your mother has already escaped with the majority of the kingdom. She is heading for Hywind Forest. Make sure that the town is evacuated and make your way to her," he said, moving his gaze to the enemy and tightening his grip on his long spear.

Eridin knew by the way his grandfather was dressed he didn't intend to flee the kingdom. He held his round bronze shield on his left arm, the long spear was gripped in his right hand, and the short sword hung from his hip. He shook his head and tugged to the crimson cape of his grandfather. "Escape with me," he begged.

Guthric gave a slow shake of his head. "I am too old to run, grandson. I will hold the enemy here while you escape. I will make them regret ever coming this far," he said, without breaking his eyes from the enemy.

Eridin pulled his longbow from his back and nocked an arrow, but the stern look of his grandfather made his knees tremble. "I said to retreat to Hywind Forest. Now go!" Guthric commanded firmly, but seeing the shock and fear in the eyes of his grandson made him realize just how harsh he was being and it broke his heart. "I'm sorry for my sudden burst of anger, grandson. I'm just afraid," he admitted softly. "I need you to escape from this place. I need you to watch over our family, Eridin. You will have to see that our legacy continues after this menace is brought to a stop. Now, please run," he pleaded, and with a sniffle the boy ran.

"Come and face death!" Guthric screamed.

Eridin stopped his retreat to look back at his grandfather and he marveled at how brave he looked. His silver hair dancing in the breeze, the strength he still had as he held the shield up awaiting the enemy, and his dominating presence as he stood in defiance of the massive army that was clamoring toward him. The narrow bridge meant that only two orcs could assault him at a time. The bridge covered an enormous chasm that would prevent anyone from being able to jump over it, the depth of it would kill those that fell from it, climbing down the smooth surface would have been next to impossible, and the climb back up would take too much time. The only way the army of Bahaal could assault Guthric was if they traveled north to another bridge and crossed over to their side, but the entire force had chased Eridin through the city. "It's like he knew," Eridin whispered as he pieced together his grandfather's plan.

Guthric was the one that asked him to scout the enemy, but when they saw him, he panicked and ran. He led them through the empty streets, and right to the narrow bridge that his grandfather was now protecting. A volley of arrows rained down, but the only purchase they could find was that of orc flesh and bronze. The monsters roared in pain as they tumbled off the bridge and two more stomped ahead to take their place, but they were quickly slain by the aged veteran soldier. "Is that the best you have to offer!?!" He roared, holding his arms out as two more lumbering orcs made their way toward him.

"That is enough!" Bahaal's voice called down from the sky as the other two orcs were killed and their bodies fell from the bridge. "You are truly remarkable. Your tactical brilliance amazes me. Your tenacity and ferocity would be a great addition to my army," he said as he descended down on the back of a winged beast.

Kirkland recalled the monstrosity from the many fables his mother would tell him. The origin of dragons were unknown to those around, but many stories were written depicting the creatures and where they came from. The black scales of the one that carried Bahaal, glistened from the sunlight that managed to peek through the clouds and it screeched as it landed on the ground. It stood on four legs, its massive wings folded back to rest upon its back, and its long neck glowed a fiery red before a flame burst from its maw into the sky. The monster struck fear into the heart of Eridin, but Guthric just chuckled and, while the beast wasn't paying attention, he hurled his long spear at it. The bronze tip plunged into the chest of the dragon causing it to wince in agony and a blood curdling screech emerged from it. "Your overgrown lizard doesn't scare me," Guthric declared, pulling free his short bronze sword and holding his shield up in defiance of the army ahead of him.

"Kill him!" Bahaal demanded, and the orcs started their assault.

Guthric blocked their attacks, but each blow from their weapons were starting to take a toll on his bronze shield. The dragon managed to pull free the spear and tossed it to the side. Bahaal laughed maniacally. "Kill him SynDrake!" He commanded.

"I am not one of your creations to be controlled," SynDrake said in a domineering voice. "You are a deceiver and I have seen the truth of the matter. I will aid you no longer," he said, pulling Bahaal from his back and tossing him to the side like he did with the spear.

"You will submit to my will," Bahaal said, standing up from the ground and using the blood from the ground to restrain the dragon.

SynDrake roared as the blood wrapped around him. "You think your pathetic magic can hold me? I was ancient before your race even opened its eyes. I am a creation of pure magic and as long as magic flourishes, I will remain all powerful," he declared, extending his wings and breaking the spell that sought to contain him. "I was the first gift Zephyr gave to his primordials. I was bestowed the almighty's blessings long before you were even a concept in the mind of Deware. I am ancient and my power is beyond your grasp. I can see into the heart of this warrior and it is pure, unlike yours. I will aid you no further, he proclaimed before disappearing into the sky. Guthric chuckled as he killed two more orcs. "Looks like your big threat abandoned you," he remarked as two more enemies slammed their axes against his bronze shield.

"I've had enough of your defiance!" Bahaal screamed as he conjured several blood spears and hurled them at Guthric.

The old soldier blocked two that came directly at him, but Bahaal was able to control them and he caused four to maneuver around Guthric, stabbing him in the back. The blood spears pierced through his body before turning back to liquid. "That all you got?" He asked, spitting his own blood out at the two orcs that came for him.

He pulled up his shield to deflect their attacks and he stabbed the one on the right into the chest, but the attack from Bahaal slowed him. The arrows of the druhirs managed to get to him before he could lift his shield. The orc on the left cried out as he fell from the bridge with a dozen of the arrows piercing his back, but the rest found purchase in the chest of Guthric forcing him to drop to his knees. "You finally kneel," Bahaal sneered as he made his way to the bridge and started across it.

Guthric's breathing was sporadic as he let his shield drop from his arm, and he gave a shrug as Bahaal came to a stop at him. "I'll never kneel," he said as he lunged with his short sword, plunging it deep into the chest of his enemy and driving him over the side.

Eridin whimpered as he watched his grandfather disappear over the edge with their enemy, but he didn't have time to investigate as the army of Bahaal took notice of him and charged toward him. "We need to get out of here," Aster said, taking hold of the boy's shoulder. Using his magic, he teleported them out of the fallen kingdom.

Kirkland felt the dream shift as the teleportation engulfed his ancestor. He was now standing on the roof of a tall tower as two dragons flew high overhead fighting against enormous bat-like creatures while giants helped the elves and humans stand against those that assaulted the tower from the ground. He was still looking through the eyes of Eridin, but the boy was now a man. He was firing arrows at the *grumblins* that were fighting the dragons in the sky, but he wasn't the only one on top of the tower defending it. Ralolen was dancing around attacking the flying creatures. He looked as if he hadn't aged any over the many years that Kirkland knew had passed. At his side was Kaylessa. The children of Guthric were also holding off the rooftop assault. Aleesia, Thallan, and the four others stood side by side firing their arrows. "Watch out mother!" Eridin screamed as he fired an arrow into the chest of the creature.

Aleesia quickly turned to see the monster crash at her feet, dead. "Whatever you are trying to do, Aster, you better hurry. I'm not sure how much longer we can hold these creatures off," she declared, releasing an arrow and nocking another with haste.

"When I banish you this time, Bahaal," Aster spoke softly, "Stay gone," he finished, lowering his head.

Eridin looked at the wizard prime who was at the center of the tower wearing a polished steel breastplate, a sword dangled at his hip, a steel helm adorned his head, and gauntlets that covered from wrist to elbow on both arms. He was beneath a magnificent stone archway decorated with different colored gems that matched the jewels on his armor and he was chanting something that Eridin couldn't make out. He could feel the power that was building within the young man that stood before him. Aster slowly lifted his head showing that his eyes had gone white and slapped his hands together, causing a wave of energy to burst forth.

A vortex slowly formed overhead and it started pulling the people on the island into it. "If this continues it will destroy your mind and leave you as nothing but a husk. The spell must be broken, but I still fear what the consequences of that will do to you. For me, just using what power I have already will require a fortnight of rest to recover, but it is a price I am willing to pay to try and save your life," he said as the dream froze and shimmered.

"I will send one of my most trusted friends to check on you and do what he can to aid you in whatever price will be paid for this."

"Who are you?" Kirkland interrupted to ask.

"I am Patherias. I am the one who took up the mantle of wizard prime when Aster disappeared, but even we have limits to our magic," he finished as Kirkland felt a tug to his mind that caused his body to seize and he collapsed to the ground.

He could feel someone shaking him violently. "Kirky, are you alive?" Isabella called out in a whimper.

"Patherias," was all that Kirkland could muster before letting sleep take him.

Chapter 1
Price of Magic

Isabella gritted her teeth as tears ran from her eyes and she clutched the linen sheet that was covering her brother. It has been three nights since the events with the witch of the woods and Kirkland showed no signs of waking from his slumber. She closed her eyes, but all she could see in the darkness was that of her brother struggling against the vines that restrained him, the agonizing screams, and how lifeless he fell to the ground when the witch disappeared. Her heart stung within her chest. She felt responsible for what happened to him. Had she not forced him to play in the forest, he wouldn't have drawn the attention of the witch. "Kirky," she sniffled out. "If you wake up, I promise I'll never make you play with me anymore," she offered, but the boy continued to lay motionless. She laid her head down beside him. "Please wake up," she whispered, before closing her eyes and letting sleep take her.

"Isabella," the soft voice of her mother whispered. "Honey, you should get to bed. I'll sit with him and come get you should he wake up," she offered from a half-smile.

Isabella gazed into the eyes of her mother and she could see the sadness that dwelled there. "I don't want to leave him," she said, taking hold of the cold hand of her brother.

"Isabella," Torgath said in his deep voice as he stepped into the room. "Do as your mother said and get to bed," he demanded, holding the door to the bedroom open so she could step through.

Isabella stood from the chair, the tingle in her legs caused her to lean on the bed, and her mother rubbed them to help the feeling return. "Promise me that you will come get me the moment he opens his eyes, no matter when it is," she begged, pushing herself upright and ambling toward the door.

Magdalene offered a quick nod as a tear streaked down her cheek. "I promise, sweetie," she uttered, before turning her attention to Kirkland.

Isabella stepped out through the door, and Torgath closed it behind her. She inhaled deeply, but turned her gaze to the ceiling of their home. *Please, please give my brother back,* she prayed, causing her heart to sting.

What are we going to do, Torgath?" The voice of Magdalene could be heard outside the closed door and Isabella pressed her ear against it.

Isabella didn't know what to expect from her father. Despite his muscular physique, he was always well-mannered, soft spoken, and the voice of reason. She knew that he was upset by what happened to his only son, but she didn't know what he could do about it. "I intend to travel to the Library of Zephyr," Torgath said, breaking her thoughts as his heavy footfalls moved from the door bringing him closer to the bed. "I am going to find the wizard prime and he will help our son," he said, causing a chill to run down her spine.

Isabella pushed away from the door, and quietly made her way to her room across the home. She pushed open the door, her head was spinning, she didn't know what to do, but knew that her father would need help. She grabbed a small satchel from under her bed of straw and stuffed it full of things she thought she would need. She grabbed extra clothing, a linen sheet from the top of her bed, and eased her door open to see that no one was in the kitchen. She tiptoed through the home to wrap up a fresh loaf of bread that was delivered that day, some salted beef, and filled two waterskins until the lid was hard to twist back on. She moved all her gathered items to the main hall of the house. She knew that her father wouldn't be too keen on the idea of her going, but she wasn't going to let him leave without her. She sat beside her satchel on the hard wooden floor and hugged it tight while looking intently at the door to her brother's room. "I'll save you Kirky," she whispered through a yawn and without warning darkness took her.

Isabella awoke to the sound of birds chirping outside her window, and she sat up quickly as the realization set in that she was laying in her bed. She gazed out the window to see the midday sun and she rushed from the bed. Her satchel was sitting in the corner of the room. The only thing it contained were the clothes she had packed. She threw open her bedroom door and ran across to the small room where she knew her mother would be.

Isabella burst through the door of her brother's bedroom, her startled mother leaped up from the chair, and stood ready to defend her child, but calmed when she saw that it was only her daughter. "Bella, you scared the life out of me," she admitted, placing her hand on her chest and sitting back down.

"Where is father?" Isabella asked without hesitation.

Magdalene shook her head. "He has gone to the Library of Zephyr to find what he can about the wizard prime, his sanctuary, and what might have befallen our son," she said, placing a hand on Kirkland's and gently moving his hair out of his face.

Isabella clenched her fist. "When did he leave?" She asked, her body twitching from the anger she was suppressing.

Magdalene sniffled. "He left at first dawn. Right after he carried you to bed," she admitted softly as she turned to face her daughter. "Bella," she paused for a moment to catch the tears that broke free of her eyes with a linen cloth. "Promise me that you won't go after him. My heart can't handle having both my children hurt," she said, covering her face with her hands.

Isabella felt her anger turn to compassion as she watched her mother cry and she slowly walked over to put her arms around her. "I promise everything will be fine, mother. Just keep your focus on Kirky," she said, kissing the forehead of her mother and making her way out of the room, closing the door behind her.

"What do I do?" Isabella asked in a whisper, leaning back against the door and looking down at her feet. She lifted her gaze to look around their small house. The door to her bedroom was still open, but if she wanted to catch her father then she wouldn't have time to repack everything she had. She gave herself a once over checking her clothes and rubbed the back of her neck. "I'm going," she declared softly, making her way across the small living quarters to the main door, stopping only to slip on Kirkland's boots. "I'm sorry, momma," she whispered, pushing open the front door and stepping out.

Isabella stepped over the hand-woven baskets that the villagers were leaving at their door. The smell of fresh baked bread made her stomach rumble, but she shook her head. *Not enough time to eat,* she thought, pulling the blankets back to see the contents of the baskets. She quickly removed all but two jars of jam and then started taking portions from each other basket to put into the one she intended to take. She covered them all back over with the blankets, lifted hers, and made her way toward the stables. If she was going to have any chance of catching her father, she would need a fast horse to carry her.

The stable was at the edge of the village going toward Seagulls Harbor. It was a huge two-story structure that expanded the length of four homes, the horses could be heard from outside the building, and a small house was built alongside it for those that worked the stable. Though three clans dealt with the upkeep of the building only one dealt with the lending of horses. Anlon McGlothen was a man not keen on having his time wasted, but Isabella was hoping that he would be away from the stables. If he was gone, the task of horse handling would fall to his eldest son Irick and she was always able to convince him into doing what she wanted.

She could see the stable just ahead of her, but it was more active than normal. Four men emerged from within carrying large tomes and trinkets. She could tell by the chains that wrapped around their arms that they were vepters from the academy. *They must be here to see Kirky,* she thought to herself as one of them approached her.

He was taller than the others, but was much older than them. His hair looked as if it retreated from the top of his head and found refuge on his face. His bushy eyebrows were the same color as his facial hair and his stone-gray eyes were reddening from his travels. He cleared his throat and stood as straight as his back would allow him. "Young lady," he said in a raspy voice. "Could you tell me where the young boy is that refuses to wake?" He asked as the others crowded around him.

His robes were of ivory meaning that he had passed all the trials to become a vepter, he wore a signet ring of a crow on his right hand, and those who traveled with him were wearing deep black robes letting her know that they were still training. One had started the links of his gauntlet on his left arm, but the others had yet to start. They all waited patiently for her to answer them and she flashed them a charming smile. "He isn't far," she said, pointing in the direction of her house. "Just keep going that way and you will see a house with baskets at their front door. That will be where you can find him."

"Very good," he exclaimed, looking at his entourage. "Come quickly," he commanded and they all walked in the direction she pointed.

Isabella watched them scuttle off for a moment before she continued toward the stables. She stepped to the opening where the horses were and she could see the carriage that brought the vepters to Sparrow's Lake. It wasn't anything special, but it looked sturdy. It was pulled by four well-bred horses that were being led to a stall and she could see the person she would need to speak to. Irick was a young boy of barely sixteen in age. He had the same eyes of his father, but lacked the wisdom that Anlon picked up over the years. He smiled at the sight of Isabella and rushed to greet her after securing the horse within the stall.

"Isabella," he said gleefully. "What brings you to the stables?"

Isabella flashed him a charming smile and placed her hands behind her back. "I came to see you, silly boy," she said playfully.

Irick chuckled at her lightly. "Sure, you did," he mocked, placing his hands on his hips. "You can tell me the truth," he declared from a smile.

Isabella gave a shrug. "I need a horse, Irick. I have to catch my father before he gets too far ahead of me," she said, looking away from him shyly.

Irick shook his head. "I can't give you a horse. You are just a girl."

"You don't think a girl can travel alone?" She interrupted to ask in anger.

"That's not what I meant," Irick defended, putting his hands up, ready to defend should she attack him. "You are barely fifteen and it's not safe out there for you. Wild animals hunting for their next quick meal, bandits looking for their next steal, and unsavory people who would do despicable things to you. I will not be a part of you getting hurt," he admitted, stepping away from her and going back to the horse he was tending to.

Isabella could feel the familiar sting of unfallen tears. "Please, Irick. I need to help Kirky," she begged.

Isabella," Irick started, but paused to look her over. "Do you even know where your father is going?"

"He is going to the library to research the wizard prime," Isabella softly whispered.

Irick gave her a quick nod. "Do you know where the library is?" He asked, brushing out the horse he was working with.

"North of here," she said proudly. "I need a horse, but if you can't help me then I'll just have to walk there," she admitted, looking away from him.

Irick released a grunt as he hung his head down and squeezed the bridge of his nose. "Wait for me by the large oak tree we like to play in. I'll see what I can do," he said in a defeated tone.

"Thank you," Isabella whispered before making her way out of the stable.

She wasted no time in making her way to where the large oak tree sat. It was one of many, but what made this one stand out was the hole they had burrowed out at its base. They would often spend time playing inside the tree. Irick would often want to play as if they were husband and wife, but she would always turn that down. She didn't like the idea of belonging to anyone. Her father would often say that she was like her mother in that way and how hard he had to fight to win her affection. She slowly climbed inside the tree and pulled back the blanket over her basket so that she could enjoy a small portion of bread and jam.

Isabella was trying to chew, but found it hard as she thought of her brother. The stories he would read to her before bed and how he was always there to comfort her when she was sick. He was always so cautious, never wanted to be adventurous. He liked his books and learning what others had accomplished through the words written on pages, but she was a person that craved adventure. She rested her head against the smooth surface of the hollowed-out tree and she could see that it was starting to get dark. "Guess Irick isn't coming," she exclaimed, disheartened. "I should have known better than to wait on him," she remarked, fixing her basket before emerging from the tree, and taking a quick glance back into the village.

"Leaving without me?" Irick's familiar voice called out.

Isabella looked in the direction of the stable to see the young man riding toward her. He was leading a small brown palfrey, but he looked different. His dark brown hair bounced with each step the horse took and a sheathed sword flopped up and down at his side. He smiled, making his big brown eyes twinkle as he pulled his horse to a stop at her. "Ready to go?" he asked, sliding from the saddle and standing before her.

He had changed his clothes from the ones he was wearing earlier, the sword belt he wore wasn't his, but it was altered to fit him, and he was giving her a grin that made her legs feel weak. "Isa, are you sure you want to do this? No one will ever know that you had planned to leave for the library and we can still go play in the forest before it gets too dark," he offered while checking the saddle to the palfrey he was leading.

Isabella hated when he called her Isa, but she didn't have time to squabble over a nickname. She didn't know how far her father was, she didn't know how long it was going to take to get to the library, and it was already getting dark. "I have to save my brother," she said, looking at the ground.

Irick tucked a single finger under her chin and lifted her gaze to meet his. "Then we should be going," he said from a soft smile.

Isabella shook her head. "You can't go with me. Your father will kill you," she said, taking his hand and letting him help her onto the saddle.

"He won't kill me," Irick said, getting back on his own horse. "He will beat me until I wish I was dead and then put me to work in the stables," he admitted with a nervous chuckle. "But I am not letting you go alone. I am going to stand at your side, protect you from all that I can, and see you safely to your father. Then hope he doesn't kill me for helping you," he said, steadying his horse.

"I don't think I packed enough rations for the both of us," Isabella said, looking down at the small basket she carried.

Irick gave her a quick nod. "I know," he said, pulling some salted beef from one of the saddle bags. "I packed enough food to last us a couple nights, and some changes of clothes for us. They are my clothes, but we can make them so they can fit you," he said with a shrug. "Now....you ready to go? The journey to the library takes some time and we are losing daylight," he said, shifting in the saddle.

Isabella released a heavy sigh. She wasn't going to admit it to Irick, but she was slightly relieved he was coming with her. She left her house in such a hurry she had completely forgotten to grab a weapon to take and she didn't really know how to use a sword. The closest thing to training she ever had was when playing swords in the forest with sticks, but she was good enough to never be struck by those she played with. "Try not to be a burden, Irick," she said, putting her heels to her horse and leading it away from the tree just outside the village.

"The library is this way," Irick said with a chuckle, putting his heels to his own horse and getting them going in the right direction.

Isabella turned her horse to follow behind him. "I knew that. I was just waiting for you to lead the way," she said, closing the gap between them and riding at his side.

"Sure, you did," he mocked, but the two of them watched as they sauntered along the side of their village, watching the houses pass by them one at a time, and the fading light covering them in shadow. "Your home is just right through there. Are you sure about this?" He asked, pointing in the direction that would take her home.

"You asked me that already," Isabella said as they started around the enormous lake at the edge of the village.

Irick gave a shrug. "I'm just wanting you to make sure this is something you want to do. We will be away from the village for a few days. We will travel a great deal and might even see monsters out there. You think you are prepared for all that?" He asked with a sly grin.

Isabella knew that Irick had traveled all over Lyer Island with his father. They would often escort travelers to the library or those seeking to take their vows to the vepter academy, but nothing he said was going to change her mind. She was set to help her brother and she would face anything that dared try to stop her. "I am ready to face anything if it saves Kirky," she declared, gripping the reins of his horse tighter.

Irick gave her a nod. "Then that will be the last time I ask you," he admitted with another shrug. "Be mindful of wolves in the forest," he said, pointing ahead of them. "They are cunning creatures that hunt in packs."

The sky was darkening as the sun had almost completely vanished over the horizon, a sliver of moon could be seen high overhead, and a blanket of white stars speckled the endless void, but all that was blocked from sight as they crossed the threshold of the forest. The thick leaves of the tall trees shrouded the ground in endless darkness. Irick pulled free a long stick that had bandages wrapped around one end of it, he gently poured a liquid from a waterskin, and using a tinderbox he made a torch to give them light. He handed it over to Isabella before doing the same to make another for him. "It's not much, but it will give us some sight to where we are going," he declared, holding his high.

Isabella could feel fear gripping at her heart as they traversed the dark forest. She was accustomed to being home before the sun completely vanished from the sky, but now she was out traveling to a strange place and she didn't know what could be lurking out in the woods. The shadows looked alive, but when she would move her torch all she could see was a towering tree ahead of her. A guttural howl from deep within the forest caused her to yelp in fright and Irick bellowed with laughter. "Scared?" He asked without stopping.

Isabella was terrified, but she didn't want him to know. She cleared her throat, adjusted herself in the saddle, and drove the fear she was feeling down deep inside of her. "It only surprised me," she admitted proudly.

Irick chuckled lightly. "Sure, it did," he mocked, rubbing his eyes with the hand that held the reins and yawning. "I wish I would have known you intended to run away from home yesterday. I would have gotten more sleep," he said from a smile.

"I didn't run away from home," Isabella scolded with a snarl. "I am going to the library to help father find a way of waking Kirky back up," she said, glancing to her sides for any sign of life in the dark.

Irick gave a quick nod. "What do you intend to do to help?"

Isabella took a breath as the question echoed in her mind. She wasn't sure how she would help, but she knew that she couldn't just wait at home and do nothing. "Father wasn't there when the witch cast her spell on Kirky and he wasn't present to see what it had done to him. The anguish he felt," she paused to quickly wipe a tear from her cheek. "I tried to explain it, but words can't describe what I witnessed. I'm hoping that the keepers of knowledge will be able to see it through magic or something."

Irick's eyebrows raised. "Makes sense to me," he exclaimed, moving his torch to the side to make sure nothing was prowling to his left.

Isabella dwelled on the events of her brother and the witch. She wanted to protect him from what was happening, but each time she struggled against the vines they just grew tighter. She thought of the anguished screams her brother would let out, the amused chuckles of the old hag, and the bewilderment she had when he spoke in an unfamiliar language. The despair welled in the heart of Isabella as she tried to push those memories from her mind, but she found that it was all she could focus on. She yawned heavily. "Are we almost out of the forest?" She asked, but was greeted with no answer.

Isabella lifted her gaze to see that she was alone. Irick had simply vanished and she felt fear grip her. "Irick?" She called out in a panic, but found no solace.

Where did he go? She asked as she started looking around frantically.

A low guttural growl came to her from within the forest, quickly followed by several others causing the palfrey to leap around in fright. Isabella fought to stay on the horse's back, but found it impossible and she tumbled from the saddle. She landed on the ground knocking the air from her body. The snapping of a twig caused her to rise up quickly, noticing a dozen glowing yellow eyes within the forest, but what really drew her attention was the enormous wolf that slowly prowled forward. It was twice the size of her horse, its maw was agape with drool pouring from its lower jaw, and its ears twitched as it glared at her with icy cold eyes.

Fear gripped at her heart, tears filled her eyes, but she clenched her hands into fists to keep them from trembling and she gritted her teeth. She didn't know what the beast intended, but she wasn't going to just let it take her without a fight.

The creature whimpered as it lowered its head. "You have tremendous courage, child," a soft voice echoed in her head. "That is something I value above all else. I will grant you my power and be your guide on things to come."

The wolf slowly turned to show her its back, but moved its gaze to look upon her once more. "You will face many trials throughout your life, but you will never have to face them alone," the voice finished as the wolf walked back into the forest and vanished.

Isabella slowly opened her eyes to see an early morning sky and that she was being cradled by Irick. "What are you doing?" She screamed loudly as she raised up and looked around.

Irick twisted his finger in his ear. "I can see you are awake," he declared, shaking his head. "You fell asleep last night and I barely caught you falling from your saddle. So, you are welcome for that," he said, bringing his horse to a halt.

Isabella scratched at the back of her head, the dream still fresh on her mind, and the wolf that spoke to her. "Did we encounter any wolves in the forest?" She asked, half-heartedly as she got on her own horse and they got moving again.

Irick shook his head. "We heard some off in the distance howling around, but never saw any. Why?" He asked from a slight grin.

"No reason," Isabella remarked quickly. "How much further to the library?"

Irick took in a deep breath, his eyes reddening from the ride and lack of sleep. "We should be able to see it if we continue to ride straight, but I am hoping to encounter your father soon. I would like to rest my eyes," he said, unleashing a massive yawn.

Isabella shook her head at him and she glanced around at her surroundings. She could see the peaks of mountains far off in the distance, but the clouds looked to be covering their tops. The edge of the forest they had emerged from was barely visible, but the trees still loomed high, and the tall grass they were riding through swayed gently in the fresh breeze that swirled around them. She was amazed at what glamorous sights lay beyond the village and the small forest she played in. She took a deep breath as her mind fluttered back to the dream she had the night prior, the wolves encircling her, and the large one that spoke to her without moving its lips.

She wondered if what it had said had anything to do with Kirkland or if there was some secret meaning that she just wasn't understanding, but as she was lost in her thoughts, the sound of combat snapped her back to reality and she immediately locked her eyes on Irick just ahead of her. She followed the actions of her young escort as they both put heels to the sides of their horses and traveled at a full gallop in the direction of the noise.

She held tight to the reins of the horse, trying to keep from falling from the saddle as the palfrey ran across the open field. Her heart was racing as the commotion grew louder. She worried that the fighting had something to do with her father and she didn't know if he had taken a weapon with him. She watched as Irick clumsily pulled free his sword, ready to defend himself from anything, and it didn't take long for them to see what was happening.

She could barely see those involved, but she noticed that fifteen men riding horses had encircled one man who was standing over another that lay motionless and outside the circle sat an elegantly dressed man on a black stallion. He wore robes of midnight traced in gold, a thick beard covered his face, his hair was long, resting on his chest, and he held aloft a sword she had never seen before. It was thin at the hilt, but widened as it got to the tip. It was two hand lengths by the time it got to its end. She moved her gaze from that man to see if she could get a better look at who they had encircled. Even from her distance away, she could see that mountain of flesh and she had no doubts who it was. Her father was in danger, but Irick released a groan that caused her to look at him. "I hate bandits," he exclaimed with an eyeroll. "For Isabella!" he screamed, putting his heels to the side of his horse.

She watched as her young escort charged toward the overwhelming odds, their concentration breaking to look at him, and her father using the distraction to his advantage. The massive scythe he often used to harvest the crops emerged over his head. He swung, stabbing one of the men in the chest and her father moved with a quickness to plunge the blade into the back of another. The sharpness of his weapon cut through the breathable robes with ease, sliced into the flesh, and the length of the blade caused it to completely puncture through the chest of the man stabbed in the back. Both attacked cried out as they fell from their horses and the beast thrashed around trying to get away.

The men on horseback looked back to her father, but by then Irick was on them. She watched as the young man stabbed one of the bandits in the back as he rode past and came to a halt at her father. The man that was stabbed still had the short sword stuck in his back as he fell from the saddle. She could see Irick looking at his empty hand and she could see that he was talking to her father, but she couldn't hear what they were saying.

The bandits pulled away from their prey, regrouped around their leader, and she noticed that the man dressed in elegant robes was now looking at her. Panic filled her breast as he pointed his blade toward her and four men charged toward her. Her whole body trembled as they came closer, knowing she didn't have a weapon. She had only play-fought with the boys of the village. She had no idea what to do. "NO!" Screamed Torgath, but he was being contained by the remaining bandits that weren't coming for her.

Irick had reclaimed his sword and headed for her, but the bandits were closer to her. She was overcome with fear as they drew dangerously close with weapons drawn. She didn't know what to do, she wished Kirkland was with her, he always knew what to do. Then, the image of the enormous wolf engulfed her mind. She remembered the black fur that covered its body, its fiery eyes, the rows of sharp teeth it licked, and just how powerful the beast looked. If she could be as menacing as the wolf, she wouldn't just be sitting on top of her horse with tears streaking from her eyes, watching the bandits get closer.

Her attackers held their swords high above their heads, ready to attack once they were close enough. She could hear the growl of the wolf as she threw out her hands in reaction to the blades coming down on her. A growl emerged from her as a whirlwind swirled around the bandits, lifting both man and beast from the ground. She watched as they fought against the wind that twirled them around effortlessly, their cries muffled by the ferocity of the whirlwind that carried them higher, and as quickly as it came it disappeared letting those it held prisoner fall.

Bones cracked and broke as the bodies smashed against the ground. Isabella was in awe of what just transpired. She could feel herself slipping from the back of the horse, but she lacked the energy to catch herself. She fell hard on the ground, causing the horse she was riding to gallop off in fright. *What just happened?* She asked herself, but her thoughts were disrupted by the booming voice of her father.

"Why is she here?!" He screamed in a voice that she was unfamiliar with.

"She came looking for you," Irick replied sheepishly.

Isabella tried to move her head to see how close they were, but she lacked the energy to even move a finger. All she could do was watch the clouds through hazy eyes. They moved so gently across a pure blue sky, so elegant it made her forget that she was almost struck down by bandits, but her serene sight was broken as her body was snatched up from the ground. Her face was pressed against the sweaty chest of her father. "Bella, honey, are you alright? Can you speak to me?" He asked in a panic while rocking her.

"Tired," she squeaked out before succumbing to sleep.

Isabella slowly opened her eyes to see a fire burning brightly beside her and she could see her father slowly turning a skewered piece of meat over the flame. The smell of the cooking food was intoxicating and it made her stomach grumble. "Father?" She managed to squeak from a dry throat.

Torgath rushed toward her and gently cradled her in his massive arms. "I am here, daughter," he said, his eyes sparkling with unfallen tears. "You frightened me, Bella. You weren't supposed to follow me," he scorned her softly, but poured some water into her mouth slowly.

The liquid was welcomed by her dry mouth and she could feel it as it drained down her raw throat. "I couldn't let you go alone. I was there when the witch did her spell and I thought I could be of help," she said softly before taking another drink.

"Take it easy on the water, Isa," Irick cautioned as he knelt down beside her. "You have been asleep for two days and I don't want you to choke."

"Two days!" Isabella screamed as loud as her throat would allow. "What happened?" She asked over the grumbling of her stomach.

"Fetch her some food, Irick," Torgath commanded, and the boy obeyed without question. "We don't know what happened, daughter. The bandits were about to strike you and a cyclone of dust lifted them high into the sky before dropping them. It was something I had never seen before," he admitted while helping her sit up on her own.

"You must be starving," Irick said, handing her a large chunk of the meat.

Isabella put a hand up to her forehead; she was sweating, her head was spinning, and her stomach was rumbling. "Thank you," she replied as she took the meat from him.

The warm grease drained down her throat as she chewed quickly. She chomped into another bite just as she swallowed the first. "Slow down, Bella. I don't want you to choke," her father japed with a smile. "No one is going to steal your food," he said, taking a bite from a massive chunk of his own.

"Tell me child, have you always been able to do magic or did it just happen after your encounter with Lucian?" An unfamiliar voice asked from within the tree line.

Torgath bounced to his feet, tossing his unfinished meat to the ground and putting his fist up in defense. "Who said that!?!" He screamed in the direction of the voice.

Irick quickly took position at his side with his sword drawn, but before he could say anything the voice returned. "I mean you no harm," the man said as he stepped out of the tree line and into the light of the campfire.

The man was only a hand shorter than her father, but his body was thin. He walked with the aid of a long wooden staff, a green gem glowed lightly from it, and he wore a wolf pelt that had been fashioned into a cloak. The brown robes showed only slightly as he walked and his stringy long salt and peppered hair bounced as he made his way closer. She could see that he had a thick beard to match that of his hair, but what she noticed more than anything was that his right eye was covered by a leather strap. "I am known as Uthric the wanderer. I came from the sanctuary to check on a small boy that Patherias said might be in danger and to my amazement, I felt a great power coming from this direction," he said, burying his left hand into his beard.

"You came from the sanctuary?" Torgath asked through clenched teeth.

Uthric gave him a nod. "Patherias cautioned that the boy could be unwell due to the power it took to break the spell. He sent me in his stead to offer what assistance I could," he said, bowing to them slightly.

"Why are you here and not helping him?" Torgath asked.

Uthric buried his hand in his thick beard. "I have already been to see him, but I am afraid there is nothing that can be done to help the boy awaken. The vepters are doing their part to keep his body nourished and make him comfortable while he slumbers," he said, leaning against his staff.

Isabella stood from the ground. Her legs were shaky from the two days without being of use, but she focused on keeping them under her. "What is wrong with my brother?" She asked while trying to take a step, but her legs weren't ready and she found herself collapsing.

"I got you," Irick said, quickly dropping the sword and catching her.

Uthric looked up at the black sky that was freckled with stars. "Do any of you know anything about magic?" He asked, looking back, but seeing that they were clueless on the matter and he released a heavy sigh. "This will be a long tale and not one I would like to make standing. Could we gather by the fire while I explain things?" He asked, holding out a single hand. "I will sit across the flame from you three, if that will ease your worry about my intentions," he offered from a smile that was mostly covered by his beard.

Isabella felt a comfort looking at the humble man that stood before her. "You aren't going to use blood magic, are you?" She asked as the memories of what happened to Kirkland played out in her mind.

Uthric shook his head. "I am not going to cast anything on any of you. I am just going to regale you with tales and explanations," he said, inhaling deeply.

Torgath grunted, but he lifted Isabella up off the ground. "If you are going to tell us stories then it might be best if we all sit for them," he said, carrying her over and sitting her down on furs around the campfire. "You sit there where I can keep my eye on you," he said, pointing to a spot across the flame and Irick took a seat beside her.

Uthric groaned as he nestled down on folded legs, his staff resting on his shoulder and head. He gazed into the fire, his one eye twinkled as it danced, he looked to be mesmerized by the flame, and the gem at the head of his staff glowed just a little brighter. "Everything in this world is touched by magic through the life granted to them by Zephyr and his primordials, but some of us are a little more blessed than others. Now, no one knows truly why this person is bestowed this power and that person isn't. That knowledge has been lost to time, but what we do know is that not everyone who can use magic is the same," he said before blowing on the fire and causing an image to appear.

Isabella watched as the fire revealed an old man. He was thin, the blue robes he wore looked to be too heavy for him, his long white beard came to a stop at the top of his stomach, on top of his head was thinning white hair that was cut short, and his long-twisted staff held a bright red ruby on it. Beside him was a woman garbed in dark blue robes, she carried a thick tome against her chest, and her chestnut-colored hair was wild and free. "Wizards, like myself, require something to help us focus our magic. Gems are what we use and though many place them at the head of their staff, like me," he said leaning his wooden stick over to show his gem that was still pulsating. "Others will have them embedded into other trinkets like books, bracelets, necklaces or something else that they will be holding while using their magic. All wizards are encouraged to keep a tome of the things they have encountered, spells they have used, and when their lives are coming to an end that book is passed down to someone who can succeed them. Most wizards are noble and good, but there are some that harness evil within their heart," he paused, allowing the image in the fire to change.

The flame turned black as the old man and young woman were replaced with two others. The man was dressed in black robes, his long black hair covered half his face as he dropped something into a cauldron of bubbling liquid and started chanting. The woman was dressed in robes of the same color, but her hair was a dark brown. She danced around the cauldron while chanting in unison with him and both of them sliced their hands letting their blood mix with the liquid. "Witches and warlocks use rituals to cast their spells. They mostly deal with curses, but not all of them are evil. Some use their knowledge of herbs to concoct potions to help those in need," he said before whispering an incantation to the fire.

The flame turned a robust green as the two figures were changed once more. The man's hair turned light brown and was cut short. He was dressed in garments of light green with leaves adorning it. He was speaking to a flower that had yet to bloom, but as he spoke it shook to life and opened its petals to reveal its beauty. He handed it to a woman with long light brown hair, her green robes matched his, and she smelled the sweet smell it contained. "Druids are one with nature. Their power comes from a spirit animal, and that is why I asked if she could use magic before the encounter with Lucian," he said as the fire turned back to normal and he put his one good eye on her.

Isabella nervously shook her head, but it was her father that spoke. "Are you trying to say that my children are wizards?" He asked, wrapping his massive arm around her.

Uthric gave a shrug. "I'm not sure if they would be classified as wizards, but they do have the ability to cast spells. Tell me what happened with your brother in the woods and don't spare any detail," he said, conjuring a rock to appear behind him so he could sit back against it.

Isabella inhaled deeply before she retold the tale once more to the old wizard. She told him how Kirkland conjured a fireball, how the witch of the woods came, and the blood magic she used on him. Tears rolled down her cheeks as she described the agony that her brother appeared to be in as he struggled against the vines and how it all just ended. Their bindings released them, letting them fall to the ground, the witch was gone, but her brother was left unresponsive before her.

Uthric raised up off the stone. "Fascinating," he remarked, burying his hand in his thick beard and nodding. "Was that the first time the boy had ever used magic?" He asked, focusing his only eye on Torgath.

Her father grumbled lightly as he grinded his teeth. "I was unaware that any of my children possessed the ability to use magic," he admitted shamefully.

Uthric waved his hand slightly. "A person not touched by magic could never know one that has. We are only able to sense them because of the scarcity of the power left in our world. Magic is used by turning the energy of the wielder into the spell they are calling on. Our bodies can only sustain so much before it becomes burned out and that is why those of us touched by magic can always sense others who might be using their power uncontrollably. That way we can seek them out, teach them the ways of using the power and the consequences of using too much too fast," he said, looking down at his hands and forcing a smile to them.

"Is my son going to be alright?" Torgath asked, clenching his fist in anger at what the answer might be.

Uthric released a heavy sigh. "Your son will wake up, but it is hard to tell when. When we use magic, it requires that we use our own energy to do so. Depending on the spell will depend on how long it will take for that energy to replenish. Patherias will slumber for at least a fortnight to regain the energy he spent breaking the spell that the witch used on your boy, but your son conjured a fireball, without a focus, and then went through the blood magic spell of the witch right after. There is a reason that blood magic is forbidden to be used. When he wakes it is unknown exactly how well he will be. She forced him to relive his ancestors' lives and the mind is not equipped to withstand that," he said, gazing back at the fire and taking in a deep breath.

Isabella released a heavy sigh. "The old witch said that I didn't have a trace of magic within me and that's why she had to use her spell on Kirky," she confessed, looking first at her father and then to the old man.

Uthric gave a slow nod as he stretched out his legs. "Interesting. Then that means your power came to you after the visit with Lucian," he admitted, standing up and walking over to the cooking meat.

"Why?" Isabella asked, but didn't wait for anyone to answer. "Why would the wolf spirit bestow this gift on me?" She questioned, looking down at her hands.

Uthric gave a shrug as he sliced a sliver of meat off and started chewing. "I'm not going to pretend to know the mind of a spirit animal, but he chose you as a disciple and with that came a taste of his power. You are a druid, girl," he said from a toothy grin that was slightly hidden behind his mustache. "Knowing that I will be able to train you more efficiently," he admitted, slicing a bigger piece of meat and walking back to his seat.

Isabella's stomach churned with nerves. "When the spell broke the witch just disappeared. What happened to her?"

Uthric grunted as he finished the meat. "Using blood magic is unpredictable, and it requires sufficient energy. Plus, she would've had to use even more of her energy to prevent Patherias from breaking her spell at the very start. If she didn't drain herself completely then her body would have teleported to her *slumbering circle*, but with the times she deflected Patherias when he was trying to break the spell, I would say she died and her body turned to ash," he admitted, laying back against the rock.

"Slumbering circle?" Isabella asked, scratching the back of her head.

Uthric gave her a quick nod. "Anyone that uses magic has one. It's a sacred place that is created by the person so that their bodies can rest and regain spent energy without worry. When a person touched by magic uses up too much energy then they fall into a deep sleep, while they slumber their bodies are vulnerable unless they have protectors," he said, ushering to Irick and her father. "Establishing a slumbering circle takes time, but it is one of the first things done after someone finds that they can wield magic. I will guide you on how it is done and then I will teach you how to use the magic that was bestowed on you," he said from a smile.

Torgath grumbled lightly. "Why are you willing to help?"

Uthric inhaled deeply. "I am from the sanctuary. Finding inept magic users and training them to be better is what we do," he said, resting his head back on the rock. "When your son wakes, I'll give him a proper examination and then train him as well. Magic isn't something that should be used on a whim. It needs to be cherished, it needs to be preserved or else we will lose it from this world and that won't be good for anyone," he admitted, lifting his head to put his one good eye on all three of them.

"Can magic really be lost?" Isabella asked, looking up to her father.

Uthric grumbled as he sat up. "I assure you it can," he said quickly before clearing his throat. "There once was a time when magic flourished and those blessed by it could call on it freely," he said, pulling the cork from a waterskin at his hip. "In the beginning, Zephyr created time and space. An endless void of darkness, but with a snap of his fingers he brought forth the world. He worked tirelessly shaping it to his liking. He made the mountains, the valleys, rivers, streams, and lush forests. He stood back to admire his work, but found it lacking," he paused to drink deep from his waterskin.

"The world was cold and dark," he continued, pushing the cork down into the waterskin. "With the wave of his hand he conjured a ball of fire, but he couldn't leave it too close to the world he just created or it would have burned everything. He hung it up in the sky, far enough that it wouldn't catch anything on fire, but close enough to provide warmth and light. He looked out at what he had created, but found it empty. He lifted a mighty hand full of dirt from the ground, cupped a hand of water in the other and brought them together. He fashioned the first primordials from this clay, brothers *Deware* and *Avgrunnen*. He bestowed a small fraction of his power to them so that they could continue to fill his world with beauty while he rested and Deware wasted little time in setting out to work," he paused to stand from the ground and made his way over to the cooking meat.

"Deware created the elements of the world. He used a small portion of fire from the sun to create *Aldmari*, he took a handful of dirt to give life to *Grund*, using water he birthed *Vatn*, and with the very breath he was given he created *Vindr* and he used these four elements to give us the seasons we enjoy," he said cutting him another slice of meat off. "Avgrunnen watched as his brother worked tirelessly and to not be outdone, he tried to conjure an element of his own. Using the shadows, he created *Ginnung*, but he was without form. Seeing that his creation lacked the beauty that his brother's carried, filled him with jealousy," he stated, tossing the chunk into his mouth and cutting off another large slice before walking back to his seat.

"Deware created the elven race and bestowed on them a small fraction of his power. They could call on his elements at will, but it would take an immense amount of time to imbue them with this power and so he conjured an enormous tree where they could slumber peacefully," he ripped a large bite off his chunk of meat and chewed it quickly. "He watched over his creations, but he grew impatient. The dwarves came next, he wanted to make them a strong race, one that could mine the ore Grund created in the mountains, but due to their stocky build they ended up only being half the height of the elves. Though they could not call upon the elements at will he did grant them the ability to work with stone and the minerals that were mined. With that, they created remarkable things that still stand to this day, the library of Zephyr being one of them," he said, looking in the direction of the library.

"He looked at the dwarven race he created out of stone and felt he could improve on them. Using the same method Zephyr used in creating him, he birthed the human race. They were as tall as the elves and almost as stout as the dwarves, but they would also be unable to call upon the elements at will. They were ambitious, courageous, they sought adventure, they used the resources around them to build, and using those same resources, they found a way of using magic," he said from a smile as he finished the last of his meat.

"What was Avgrunnen doing while Deware was creating all this?" Irick asked, sitting forward in awe of the story being told.

Uthric gave him a slight nod. "Avgrunnen was creating, but he was unable to create anything that would rival his brother. In his jealousy, he created the *primevals* to tempt the different races, but Deware was able to catch him. He found that he was unable to destroy the primevals and so he created hope to help his creations overcome them. Avgrunnen was angered by what his brother created and so he created fatigue to hinder the creations, making them weak with sleep, but Deware then created another sphere that would hang in the sky to separate day from night and it would be cooler so that his creations could rest to regain the strength stolen from them. In an attempt to plague the dreams of the races, Avgrunnen created *Nightmyre* to keep them from getting a peaceful sleep and Deware created *Droyma* to bless them with good dreams instead. Upset that his brother had a counter for everything, he sought to corrupt the elven race while they continued to slumber. He bestowed upon them the knowledge of blood magic, but Deware was able to give them the warning of how that magic corrupts the user," he paused to drink deep from his waterskin and pushed the cork back down into it.

"Though most of the elves took the warning there was one who desired the power promised by Avgrunnen," Uthric continued rubbing his good eye. "Bahaal used the magic that was bestowed to him to take over. He wanted to be ruler of the world and with his power he succeeded. Deware couldn't just destroy him as it would go against the desire of Zephyr and so he created the wizard prime to do what he couldn't," he said through a yawn while stretching.

"How do you know all this?" Isabella interrupted.

Uthric released a gentle sigh. "All this is within the *Paavi*."

"What is a Paavi?" Isabella asked, looking up to her father.

Uthric released a displeased groan. "The Paavi is a collection of sacred texts about the creator, but the Paavi isn't the only tome we have at the sanctuary. We have stories of the *Slanderian Conquest, The War of Blood*, and *The Great Banishing*."

"Great Banishing?" Isabella interrupted with a whisper.

Uthric shook his head. "That was when Aster banished the blood god and his endless horde to another plane. The spell he used took so much energy that the only thing that survived was the artifacts he used, but no one can find them to verify that knowledge. Some also believe that is the reason magic has been slowly fading from this world," he said, turning his head away.

Isabella moved to speak, but strong winds began swirling above their heads causing Uthric to jump to his feet in a panic. "Are you doing this!?!" He screamed as he looked around.

Isabella shook her head nervously as a bolt of lightning cut the sky and a vortex appeared before them. "What is that?" Torgath screamed at Uthric over the sound of the swirling wind as he wrapped his massive arms around the two children.

Uthric held out a hand, his lips were moving, but Isabella couldn't make out what he was saying over the wind and the gem at the end of his staff was glowing bright. "I can't stop it," he admitted as the vortex lifted him from the ground and pulled him through it.

Isabella watched in horror as the wizard disappeared into the spiraling abyss. Her father, despite all his strength, was powerless to move them away from the vortex that threatened to pull them in and with every attempt her father made, she felt them getting a little closer to sharing the same fate as the wizard. She could see the tears mixing with the sweat as her father continued to fight against the whirlwind, but he was growing weak. She reached up, placing a hand on his cheek. "Isabella," Torgath managed to groan as the vortex pulled them through.

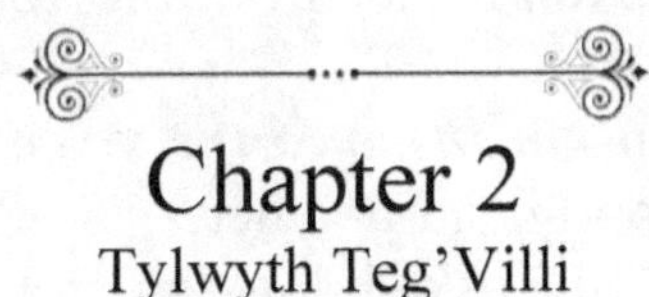

Chapter 2
Tylwyth Teg'Villi

Isabella found herself weightless as she swirled around in the darkness of the vortex that pulled her and those with her inside. She remembered the tight grip of her father as he struggled against being dragged into the whirlwind that just appeared over them, but in spite of his strength, the cold dark vortex was not going to be denied its victims. She drifted peacefully through the void, but her serenity was torn asunder by the loud echoing crack of thunder. She placed her hands over her ears, her heart raced, and her head pounded.

"I can see you girl," a voice called out from the swirling darkness, but it wasn't a voice she recognized. It was cold and made her body shiver. "Free me and I shall grant you even greater power than the wolf. I can even save your brother," the voice promised, but there was just something about it she didn't trust.

Images of her family flashed through her mind. She worried for her father who was lost within the same void as she was, her brother that was slumbering in an endless sleep and her mother that was beside herself with grief. She wanted to help them, but she didn't trust the cold voice. "Free me from this prison, child," the voice returned, breaking her concentration on her family.

"I can't," Isabella cried out in defeat.

The void shook as the voice roared with anger. "Useless mortal! Begone from my sight!" He screamed, causing a light to appear and she felt herself being pulled through it.

Isabella felt the soft grass under her, she could hear the wild animals playing in the distance, a cool breeze blew across her brow, and the smell of fresh air was intoxicating. She slowly opened her eyes to see a pristine blue sky through the breaks in the leaves of the trees that surrounded her. She raised up and squeezed the back of her neck. Her head pounded, but she needed to find out where she was.

She knew that she was no longer on Lyer Island. The grassy field they had established their camp for the night was now a lush forest and everyone she was with were gone. *I can even save your brother,* the words that were spoken to her from the void echoed in her head and she shivered.

You were right to not listen to the voice, a different, calmer voice echoed in her head and it startled her.

"Who said that?" She asked, looking around, but the heavy footfalls of someone approaching drew her attention.

"Are you alright, Bella?" Torgath asked as he emerged from within the forest and hurried over to his daughter. "Have you seen Irick?" He asked while examining the girl for any injuries she might've sustained.

Isabella shook her head. "What happened?" She asked.

"I might have an explanation," Uthric offered as he emerged from the opposite direction of where her father came from. "We have arrived in one of the different planes that was created by the Wizard Prime Aster during the Great Banishing," he said, pulling a piece of bark off a tree and tossing it into his mouth. "I believe we are in Tylwyth Teg'Villi," he announced just before spitting the chewed-up bark on the ground.

Torgath released a heavy sigh, but flashed a soft grin to his daughter. "Nothing seems broken," he remarked before putting his gaze on the wandering wizard and his demeanor changed to anger. "How do I get my daughter home?" He asked in a terrifying tone.

Uthric tossed up his hands in defense and shook his head. "I'm not rightly sure," he replied, but wasted no time in continuing as Torgath stood from the ground. "In all the years I have traveled the world I have never heard of someone opening a portal to the other planes. The magic it would require to tear through the veil would surely kill any that tried it within the *Peili'Marfach Kone,*" he said, burying his hand inside his thick beard.

Torgath grunted his frustration. "I don't understand any of that," he admitted through clenched teeth. "What I want to know is how do I get back home to my wife and son? Can you do it?" He asked, taking another small step closer to the wizard.

Uthric held the tip of his staff out in the direction of the large man getting closer to him. "I'm not sure."

"If you tell me that you are unsure of one more thing, it will be your last," Torgath interrupted harshly while pointing at the wizard.

Uthric was slightly startled by the aggression of the massive man. "I am truly sorry, but the only knowledge we have of this plane is that it existed and beyond that we have nothing. I'm just as lost as you in this world," he declared as the gem started to glow at the end of his staff.

"Fighting amongst ourselves is going to get us nowhere," Isabella said, standing from the ground and stretching. "We need to find Irick and then look for someone native to this plane," she said, stepping up beside her father.

Torgath looked at his daughter, a slight smile crept across his face as he marveled at her and he gave her a nod. "When did you become the mature one?" he asked, but didn't wait for an answer as he looked at the wizard. "She is right. We need to find the boy that was pulled through the vortex with us and then look for a way home," he declared.

The gem at the end of Uthric's staff stopped glowing and he used it to lean on instead. "Do we have anything that belongs to the boy? I can use it to scry for him," he said with a smile.

Isabella looked down at the shirt she was wearing. "I have something, but do I have to give you the whole thing?" She asked, bashfully looking at her father and then to the wizard.

Uthric shook his head. "Just a sliver of it will do," he said, pulling free a small dagger and cutting a small piece from the sleeve. "It will take a little time for me to perform the ritual, but once I am done, I will know where the boy is," he said while using the end of his staff to draw images in the ground and he sat between them.

Isabella laid her head against the arm of her father. "I hope Irick is alright," she declared, closing her eyes and releasing a yawn.

"I'm sure he is fine," Torgath remarked confidently.

Isabella wished she could be as optimistic as her father, but she just couldn't seem to shake the feeling of dread that has been plaguing her since she emerged from the vortex. The voice that spoke to her from the darkness was overwhelming, it was so cold and filled her with terror. *Useless mortal! Begone from my sight!* The chilling last words she heard before she was expelled from the vortex echoed in her head and caused her to shiver.

Torgath wrapped the arm she was leaning against around her and squeezed. "Are you cold?" He asked, rubbing her arm to warm her.

Isabella released a heavy sigh as she laid her head against the muscular side of her father. She always found solace being in his arms, as if nothing could ever harm her, but not even this safe haven could put her at ease. She inhaled deeply, a gentle breeze blew across her brow and with it came a scent. She couldn't understand what it meant, but she felt compelled to follow it. She sniffed the air as she stepped past Uthric and disturbed his concentration. "Blast it all girl."

"This way," she interrupted him before he could scold her any further.

Isabella pushed deeper into the forest being mindful of the small twigs that could alert any to her presence. She sniffed the air; the aroma was stronger now and it was sweeter causing her to salivate. She realized that the scent she was following was that of cooking food, she didn't know how much time had passed since her last meal, but judging by the rumbling of her stomach it was too long. She wasted no time in continuing her pursuit. She continued to make her way toward the sweet aroma, leaping over protruding roots and forgetting all about her companion that was still missing. Her mind was focused on filling her empty stomach.

The smell of cooking meat became stronger, but that wasn't the only aroma that filled the air. The stink of sweat and blood was now mixed with that of the sweet scent of the slowly roasting meat. She halted her pursuit, hiding behind a massive tree, but close enough she could see the small encampment down below. She looked back to see that she had put a great distance between her and those that followed her, but as they came into view, she lifted a single finger up to her lips to warn them to be quiet as they approached.

The two of them halted their advance and looked in the direction she had pointed to see the small camp. They proceeded slowly toward her, making sure to keep the noise of their footfalls down and though it took more time they managed to reach her without giving away their position to those within the camp. Looking at the camp she could see that which was drawing her toward it, the cooking meat over a small fire, but the creature that was turning the spit was one she had never seen before. It was twice the size of her father, it was rounder of shoulder, thicker of muscle and it was covered in scars. It had bronze colored skin, long black hair that was braided down its back, two large tusks that protruded from the bottom lip with the tip coming to just under the eyes and it had thick metal pierced through it.

Isabella broke her gaze from the creature to look at the wizard. "What is that?" She asked, moving her gaze to her bewildered father.

"I have a theory based on the scripters I've read from the sanctuary, but I'm unsure just how accurate they are," Uthric confessed while scratching at his chin. "In some of the last writings of Wizard Prime Aster, he mentions creatures created by the blood god that match the description of that thing. He called them orcs and stated that they were bloodthirsty creatures of immense strength. I believe we should stay clear of that camp for now," he advised and Torgath gave a nod in agreement with him.

Isabella released a heavy sigh, she desired the cooking meat, but she knew that the wizard spoke true and she needed to find her friend before these creatures did. She moved to stand from the ground, but movement within the camp caught her attention. "What's going on?" She whispered as another orc emerged from within the enormous tent at the center of the camp and it was carrying a prisoner that had been bound with rope.

The orc that was carrying the prisoner appeared just slightly larger than the one turning the spit and the first one stood at attention as the other approached. It slammed the body it was hauling down on the ground at the fire. Pushing the other orc to the side, it lifted the helpless creature up and screamed in its face.

Isabella gasped at the sight of the prisoner. Even through the swollen black eyes and all the lacerations that covered his face, she could tell that it was Irick they had tied up. Blood poured down his face, his lips were busted, his hair was a mess, and the orc lifted a burning log from the fire. It said something in a guttural voice, but she didn't understand the language. It held the flame close to the face of Irick and she felt a rage take hold of her. A low growl emerged from her throat. She didn't know how many were truly in the camp, but she couldn't just stand by and let them hurt her friend. She unleashed a frightening howl as she charged toward the orc that was about to scorch her friend with the burning log.

The orcs looked toward her, but before they could react, she was already on the chest of the one that was about to burn Irick. She buried her fingernails deep into its flesh and without hesitation she sank her teeth into its neck, making it drop the log near Irick's face. With a jerk of her head, she tore the throat of the orc out and its black blood oozed from the open wound. It covered her mouth and poured down the chest of them both. The orc was able to dislodge her from its chest and toss her to the ground, but as it turned to look at the other orc, it dropped to a knee. Its mouth moved as if it tried to speak, but no words would emerge as it collapsed to the ground and succumbed to death.

Three others emerged from other tents around the large one at the center. The one that was turning the spit pointed at her and yelled in the same guttural voice as the one she had killed. They grabbed what weapons they could before charging toward her.

Isabella felt a power surge through her body. She slowly lifted her hands causing the ground to rumble beneath the feet of the orcs. They slowed their advance in bewilderment. Pulling her hands apart she caused a great chasm to open up beneath her attackers. Two of them managed to leap to the side of it, just missing the inevitable fall, but the other two weren't so lucky. As the ground opened up, they fell inside and Isabella slammed her hands together causing the chasm to close on them.

She looked at the two that remained with a smirk and they attempted to retreat from her in fear, but she wasn't about to let any who might have hurt her friend escape. She held out her hands and wiggled her fingers. Vines within the forest appeared to be mimicking her movement. She moved her hands toward the orcs that were almost out of the camp and the vegetation of the forest quickly wrapped around them. She could hear their bones snapping, their agonizing screams of pain, and all at once everything fell silent.

"Isabella, stop this!" Torgath screamed as he took hold of her shoulders.

The rage that had clouded her judgement was lifted. She didn't feel remorse for those she had killed, but she couldn't believe how quickly she succumbed to the anger. It wasn't like her to throw caution to the side and put herself in danger. She knew that she could be childish, but that was only when she was playing in the forest with Kirky. She slowly turned to look into the worried eyes of her father. "I'm sorry," she said softly, turning her gaze to the ground in shame.

Torgath pulled his daughter in against his chest to squeeze her tight, but before anything could be said the old wizard finally reached the camp. He sat on a large rock, his wheezing echoed out as he looked at the devastation caused by Isabella, and then he looked to her. "How do you feel, child?" He asked from wide eyes.

Isabella gave a shrug while still being embraced by her father. "I feel great," she admitted. Despite all the carnage she unleashed on the camp, she didn't feel drained of energy or even tired in the slightest.

Uthric scratched his chin. "Fascinating," he remarked as he walked over to examine the vines and the orcs that were tangled lifelessly inside.

"Irick," Isabella said, pushing away from her father and quickly making her way over to her badly beaten friend.

Irick was still lying beside the fire, the burning log was just a smoldering ember beside his head, but she kicked it to the side as she knelt down beside him. She gently placed a hand on his shoulder, but he recoiled at her touch and a small whimper emerged from him. "I'm here, Irick," Isabella said softly in an attempt to calm him.

Irick's body twitched and he made the sounds of crying, but his eyes were too swollen to let tears push through. "Is that really you, Isa?" He asked in a weak and feeble voice.

"I'm so sorry this happened to you, Irick," Isabella said as she carefully examined the wounds on her friend. "What happened to you after we were taken by the rift?"

Irick groaned in pain as he tried to sit up, but found that he was lacking the strength. "I remember the world going dark. I was alone and scared. I remember feeling your father holding us tightly, but in this void, there was nothing. I don't know how long I was there, but I felt a breeze blow across my brow and when I opened my eyes, I could see a pristine blue sky through the leaves of the trees. I was just lying there trying to figure out what happened when those creatures found me. They grabbed me. I tried to fight against them, but they were so strong and once they had me tied up, they started screaming at me. When they would fall silent, I would try to speak to them, but then they would beat me," he admitted shamefully.

Isabella released a heavy sigh. "I'm sorry this happened to you, Irick, but I'll never let this happen to you again," she promised from a soft smile, the black blood still smeared across her mouth and drying on her linen shirt.

Irick moved to speak, but he was interrupted by a loud scream from within the enormous tent at the center of the camp. "Isa," he whimpered in fear as he tried to move, but found that he still couldn't budge.

"Calm yourself, Irick," Isabella said calmly while looking toward the tent. "Do you know how many were in this camp?" She asked, looking back to her badly beaten friend.

Irick coughed harshly. "I'm sorry. I don't know," he admitted as the sound of iron begin rattled echoed out.

Isabella stood from the ground. "Don't worry, Irick. I will not let anything else happen to you," she promised, looking to the others. "Uthric, see what you can do for Irick's wounds while father and I check on what is making that noise," she commanded and the old man scratched at his chin.

"I'm not sure what I can do," Uthric confessed while digging through his satchel. "I am still unclear on how magic works in this plane. The power you just used would have sent even the wizard prime to his slumbering circle for at least a night to rest and yet you have no signs of weariness," he remarked, pulling free a canister. "I do have this healing balm that we make at the sanctuary. On our plane it helps numb pain and speeds up the recovery of simple wounds. It can't bring the dead back to life or save someone from a mortal wound, but it will make them more comfortable until they breathe their last," he said while examining the wounds on the face of Irick. "It shouldn't take more than a week for these wounds to heal," he advised from a smile and went about administering the sweet fragrant salve.

Watching Irick grit his teeth through the pain of the old man's touch caused Isabella to bite her lower lip. Her heart ached seeing her friend in such pain, but another roar from within the camp caused her to turn her attention in its direction and the rattling of iron piqued her curiosity. She looked intently at the massive tent where the noise was coming from. She didn't know what to expect on the inside of it, but she figured whatever was yelling from within was a prisoner or else it would have charged out of the tent during her attack. She looked back at her friend once more before moving her gaze to her father and the two of them crept upon the tanned leather flap that made up the door of the tent.

Pulling back at a corner just enough to where they could see inside, Isabella noticed the tent was erected around a thick tree and around it sat more orcs that had been clapped in iron. They were positioned with their backs against the tree, their arms extended over their heads, and some looked to be sleeping. The one that was fighting against his restraints had shoulder length black hair and his body was thick of muscle, but covered in scars. He snarled showing two small tusks protruding from his bottom lip and he was screaming something that

Isabella didn't understand. She glanced at her father, but she knew he didn't understand the language the orc was speaking.

"What can we do?" She asked in a whisper to her father.

Torgath inhaled deeply and shook his head. "We should speak to the wizard and see if he knows something we can do. I see eight bedrolls within the tent and you only took care of five. That means three are still somewhere," he said, releasing the corner he was holding up and ushered his daughter back toward the old man.

"This is going to hurt," Uthric told Irick just before he snapped the arm of the boy causing it to crack.

Irick released a muffled cry before passing out and Isabella released a low growl unintentionally causing Uthric to look back at her. "It had to be done," he assured her calmly. "Had I not set the arm back then it would have healed improperly and he would have lost the use of it," he explained while placing a splint on the arm. "I have done all I can for the wounds you can see, but there is nothing I can do for the stress the orcs put on his mind. He is a strong young man and hopefully he can overcome the fear they have beat into him," he stated, looking back at the two of them and releasing a heavy sigh. "What did you two find?" He asked, placing the lid back on his container.

Torgath cleared his throat. "We discovered that there are possibly three unaccounted for orcs," he declared, looking around for any signs of them. "There are also six others bound to a large tree within the tent, but only one is tugging at his chains. He is saying something, but we don't understand his language and we are hoping you might be able to."

Uthric pulled free a linen square from his satchel and cleaned the salve from his hand. "Let's go see this orc."

"Can Irick walk? I don't want to leave him out here in his condition if there are three more orcs out there," Torgath declared, making his way over to the boy.

Uthric gave him a shake of his head. "The injuries the young man suffered were severe. They weren't life threatening, but they will prevent him from being active."

"Then I will just have to carry him," Torgath announced, lifting the boy from the ground and tossing him over his left shoulder with ease.

Irick groaned over the sudden movement and Isabella shook her head. "Try to be a little gentler, father," she scorned, but didn't wait for a response as they made their way toward the tent.

Stepping inside they saw the orc that was rattling his irons look at them and his eyes widened. He roared at them in his language causing the others to slowly lift their heads. They all roared in their language while thrashing their chains against the tree and Isabella could see that the loud commotion they were making, made her father uneasy.

"Can you understand them?! Can you tell them to keep quiet?!" Torgath asked in haste as he gently laid Irick down on the ground and quickly made his way back to the entrance.

Uthric shook his head violently. "I'm afraid I don't know their language!" He yelled in exasperation over them.

Torgath gritted his teeth. "There has to be something you can do. Don't you know any spells that can help with this?!" He asked, peering out of the tent.

"I have heard of ancient spells that the druids were able to do, but I have never done the spell and it is too risky for me to try it now," Uthric declared harshly.

Torgath pointed to the wizard with anger in his eyes. "We have to be able to speak to them," he declared, stomping over to the old man. "Do the spell and tell them to calm down before it is too late," he demanded, pushing his finger into the chest of the wizard.

Uthric shook his head. "There is just too much that could go wrong with a spell like this. It could steal the mind of one of us or even both of us. That is a risk I cannot take. Not even the druids did it without caution," he proclaimed as he held tight to his staff.

Isabella closed her eyes. *Great Wolf Lucian, I ask that you guide me in what needs to be done,* she prayed. An image of her placing her hand on the forehead of the orc, cut through the darkness. She slowly opened her eyes, looked at her father who was still arguing with the old wizard, and she quietly made her way over to the chained-up orc. The closer she got to the prisoner the more details she could make out, though he was a hand shorter than the ones she killed outside the tent, he was still bigger than her father and he snarled at her as she placed her hand on his forehead.

A radiant light burst from the touch and in an instant her mind was filled with the memories of the orc. She could see that he was the youngest of six, the training he had endured, the friends he made, and that he was from a clan that sought peace with the other races that filled the realm. She understood that there were a multitude of clans, but not all of them were like his. Some were bloodthirsty and felt that the race of orcs was superior to the others. She could see that the orcs were warriors. Taught from birth that death on the battlefield was more noble than retreating, but that there is a difference in giving up on a battle and performing a tactful retreat to regroup. Her heart broke as she watched the *Black Sword Clan* attack his clan, burning their homes, slaughtering their people, and carting off those that weren't killed in the battle.

"Isabella!" Torgath screamed.

Isabella felt the calloused hands of her father gripping tight to her shoulders and he was shaking her violently. Her head was pounding, the memories of the orc were blending with her own, but she was sorting everything out. She held up her hand to stop her father from screaming at her again. "I'm fine," she reassured them.

Torgath was grinding his teeth. "What did you do?"

Isabella released a heavy breath. "I did what I had to do so that we could speak to the orcs," she admitted, rubbing the back of her neck.

Torgath's face flushed with anger, but he took a deep breath in to calm himself as he looked into the eyes of his daughter. "I need you to stop doing things recklessly, Bell. My heart can't take much more of it," he declared as his eyes became misty.

Uthric cleared his throat as he stepped closer to them. "Was that the spell the druids used to learn the languages of others?" He asked, examining her for any repercussions to using magic.

Isabella furrowed her brow causing wrinkles to appear on her forehead and shook her head lightly. "I'm not sure of the spell. I prayed to Lucian and asked him to guide me. He provided me with a vision of touching the forehead of the orc," she admitted, looking around her father and at the orc.

The orc looked dead, but she could see that he was still breathing. Uthric scratched at his chin. "Fascinating!" He declared, glancing at the orc and then back to Isabella. "Did the spell teach you their language?" He asked with an inquisitive smile.

Isabella rubbed her forehead. "The spell didn't just teach me their language, but it revealed everything to me. I know about the different clans of orcs; some are peaceful and some are ruthless. The one I touched is known as *G'Nash*, he belongs to the *Black Root Clan* or what is left of it," she paused to collect her thoughts. "There is this religious sect that is growing in power known as the *Eye of Avgrunnen*."

"Eye of Avgrunnen?!" Uthric interrupted her with wide eyes. "Are you talking about the primordial?"

Isabella gave a shrug. She felt nauseous and dizzy, but she squeezed the bridge of her nose. "I'm not sure of those details. Its leader is a druhir named *Doden* and no one knows where he came from, but his power can't be denied," she said, fighting to stay upright.

Uthric was lost in thought as he buried his hand in his beard. "Hmm, I need to know more about this….," he paused as he searched for the right word, "cult," he said, lowering his arm to his side and leaning heavily on his staff.

"I agree," Isabella said, turning her attention to the orcs that were still chained up. "They were heading for the city of *Y'Melenor*. It's a home to elves."

Uthric's one eye twinkled with excitement. "Elves," he repeated the word happily. "I've heard rumors of their magic. They are one with the elements and supposedly capable of calling upon them at will. I'm sure I could use their knowledge to find us a way home," he said with excitement.

Isabella gave him a nod. "If they are as powerful as you say then they might have a way of helping Kirky too," she said, looking at the orcs that were in chains. "We can also research this Eye of Avgrunnen, but first we should set the other orcs free."

Uthric scratched at the side of his head. "Are you certain that they won't attack us once they are free?"

"I know that you are scared, but we are not here to hurt you. If you will give us time then we will earn your trust. We are going to free you from those chains and all we ask in return is that you don't attack us," Isabella called out to those that were still conscious.

The one closest to her snarled and grumbled. "What did you do to G'Nash?"

Isabella shook her head. "I did what I had to so that I could communicate with you. He is still alive, I can hear him breathing," she assured them. "Now, can I have your word that you will not attack us once we have freed you from your shackles?" She asked, now knowing that there is nothing the orcs value more than their word.

The orc was larger than G'Nash, the top of his head held no hair, but he had a thick black beard that was braided in two spots. The tusk on the right was long, thick, and pierced with golden rings, but the one on the left was broken. His body was covered in healed scars. She could see that he was grinding his teeth and as he released a defeated breath, he closed his eyes. "You have our word," he said lightly.

"They have given their word they won't attack once they are freed," Isabella relayed the message to the others. "Now to set them free," she said while trying to stand up, but found that she lacked the strength to do so.

Uthric gave a slight shake of his head. "You have done enough, child. It is time I stop living in fear and use my magic," he said, leaning on his staff and using his magic he caused the shackles to break open.

The arms of G'Nash dropped heavily to his side and he slumped to the ground. Isabella watched as the orc she was speaking to moved so that he could examine him. "How is he?" She asked, rubbing her forehead.

"He is resting," the orc replied, placing his head against that of G'Nash and whispering a prayer to their ancestors. "Who are you?"

"I'm Isabella Strongfellow," she said, placing her hand against her chest and then pointing to her father. "He is Torgath Strongfellow, my father, this is Uthric the Wandering Wizard, and lying over there is Irick McGlothen. We were violently pulled from our world and now we are lost in yours," she declared, looking at everyone she had introduced.

The orc groaned a sigh. "I am Gh'Rys."

"I know," Isabella interrupted him. "You are the shaman elder of the Black Root Clan and the grandfather to G'Nash. I know that he is a half-orc, his mother died in childbirth, the identity of his father is kept from him, and he is worried about his other five siblings that stayed behind to hold back the Black Sword Clan during the attack. He is afraid that the worst has befallen them."

"That's enough," Gh'Rys interrupted as he looked at the ground in shame. "How do you know all this?" He asked as he slowly looked up at her.

Isabella gave a shrug. "I needed to know your language so that we could speak. I asked the wolf spirit, Lucian, for guidance and he showed me what I needed to do, but the spell didn't just teach me your language. It gave me his memories too," she admitted, looking at G'Nash and then back to Gh'Rys. "Now, would you like to explain why no one wants to talk about his father?"

"It's because no one knows who he is," G'Nash answered, his voice weak and he turned his head to look at her. "They have suspicions on who it could be, but no one knows for sure."

Isabella flashed him a half smile. "Glad to see you are awake."

G'Nash squeezed the bridge of his nose. "What spell did you use on me?" He asked, sitting up with the help of his grandfather.

"I don't know the name of the spell," Isabella admitted with a shrug. "I'm sorry I used it on you without warning."

G'Nash waved his hand and shook his head. "You had to use it on someone to gain the ability to speak to my people."

Isabella rubbed her neck, the strain of staying awake was becoming harder with each passing second and she could feel her body wanting to succumb to slumber. "Are you well enough to move?"

"Are you?" G'Nash asked with an exasperated expression.

Isabella gritted her teeth as she slowly stood from the ground and got to her feet. She could feel her legs shaking, but she summoned all the strength in her body to keep them from failing her. "Your turn," she declared.

G'Nash gritted his teeth as he slowly made his way to his feet and with the aid of his grandfather, he was able to stand. "Shall we?" He asked with a half smile.

Isabella gave him a nod and turned to face her companions. "Are we ready to leave?" She asked, looking between her father and the wizard.

"Do they know where the city of Y'Melenor is?" Uthric asked.

Isabella shook her head. "The elvish cities are hidden with magic. We have to travel further west of here. The elves of Y'Melenor will find us and escort us into their city from there. Father, can you carry Irick?" She asked, looking over to Torgath.

"I don't need anyone to carry me," Irick announced, causing everyone to turn and look at him in shock. "I just need a wet linen square to clean myself up," he said, sitting up from the ground and running his hand the length of his face.

Isabella was surprised to see that her longtime friend looked to be healed. The lacerations that covered his face were nothing more than scars, his eyes were no longer swollen shut, and he flashed her a smile that slowly faded as he saw the orcs standing behind her. He leaped up to his feet, gritting his teeth in anger, but before he could move, an overly excited Uthric was on him. "This is beyond fascinating! How did the salve heal you so quickly?" He asked, examining the boy and stroking his long beard.

Irick knocked the hand of the wizard away from his face. "Are you alright, Isa? Have they hurt you?" He asked, stepping around the old man and up to her.

Isabella glanced back at the small band of orcs that were huddled together and then to her old friend. "They are friendly, Irick. They were prisoners of the Black Sword Clan just like you," she declared, placing a hand on his chest and trying to calm him down.

Irick glared at the orcs with such anger. "I don't trust them!" He declared through clenched teeth.

"Then trust me," Isabella begged. The fatigue that was growing in her body began showing through her voice.

Irick released a heavy breath through his nose and he looked into her eyes. "I'm keeping my eyes on them," he whispered softly.

Isabella gave him a nod. She could see that there was nothing that was going to change his mind and she didn't have time to try. "We are ready to move," she declared, pushing on the chest of Irick and causing him to take a step backwards toward the exit.

They slowly emerged from the tent. The camp showed the devastation of her attack against those that were guarding the prisoners and she could hear the hushed whispers of the orcs as they gazed at the carnage. Isabella led them out of the camp heading west with Irick at her side, the others close behind her, and they moved as swiftly as they could in search of the elven city, Y'Melenor.

Chapter 3
Y'Melenor

The flame of the campfire crackled. As it danced, its light drove away the darkness and its warmth pushed away the cold, but Isabella was more focused on the cooking meat that was stretched across the fire. The intoxicating aroma it was emitting made her mouth water. "How much longer?" She asked without breaking her gaze.

"Patience, *Wulgar*," G'Nash said from a half-smile as he turned the meat.

Wulgar, the name resounded in her head. It was a pet name he had given her two nights ago, it meant wolf girl and it was one of the many titles his mother carried before her passing. Gh'Rys snarled with disdain every time he heard the name mentioned, but other than a grumble the old orc never said anything to protest it.

"I'm going to starve to death," she cried out as her stomach rumbled and she sat heavily on the ground.

G'Nash chuckled as he sliced a thick chunk of meat free and made his way over to her. "Then allow me to save you," he announced, handing the ration over.

Isabella wasted no time in devouring the still sizzling meat. The juices washed down her throat, it felt as if she hadn't eaten in days, but in reality, this was the second time she enjoyed the succulent cooking of the half-orc. She flashed a smile to her savior as she gazed into his crimson eyes. She felt a connection to G'Nash, she didn't know if it was normal or if it was due to the spell she had used to learn his language, but she couldn't deny that she enjoyed the company of the half-orc.

"Is it good?" G'Nash asked from a smile.

Isabella gave him a nod. "It's delicious, but that's of no surprise," she mused with a scrunched nose.

The half-orc was a genius when it came to cooking and she could never get enough. She finished off the generous portion he brought her. "Think there will be any left?" She asked, looking over to still roasting meat that the others were carving into.

G'Nash chuckled as he shook his head. "I'll fetch you some more," he declared, making his way over to acquire her another helping.

Isabella turned her gaze to the beautiful lights that blanketed the night sky. She felt an ease come over her and she took in a deep breath. "Are you just going to sulk in the shadows, Irick?" She asked, turning to look behind her.

Irick stood with his arms crossed under his chest, his eyes fixed on the half-orc that was cutting meat free, and he shook his head. "I just don't understand how you can trust them," he confessed sourly. "They are brutes created for war."

Isabella released a disgruntled breath as she rolled her eyes. She was frustrated, she had been defending the Black Root Orcs for four days now and nothing she said seemed to get through to her friend. She understood that he had endured a great deal at the hands of the Black Sword Clan, but she needed him to see that not all orcs were the same. "Irick."

"Save your breath," Irick interrupted sourly. "I know what you are going to say and I'm not in the mood to hear it again," he said, turning his back, but looking back to her. "You weren't there to see what I saw. The bloodlust and rage that burned in their eyes when they beat me. It was a nightmare, Isa," he declared before releasing a defeated puff. "I'm afraid you are going to end up getting hurt," he admitted, closing his eyes tight.

Isabella felt a sting in her heart, but she wouldn't allow any weakness to show through. "I'll be fine, Irick. I can defend myself," she declared harshly.

Irick gave her a nod. "I know you can, Isa," he admitted before stepping into the forest and out of her sight.

Isabella was even more frustrated now. She knew of the bloodlust that the orcs could enter to give them an edge when it came to battle, but she also knew that those of the Black Root clan only used it when they had to in order to defend their home or their life. She had explained that to Irick, but it appeared to fall on deaf ears. She pulled her legs up and let her head rest on her knees.

"Are you still hungry?" G'Nash asked softly.

Isabella lifted her head from her knees to see the slight smile of the half-orc and she retrieved the large chunk of meat he was offering. She wasted no time in sinking her teeth into it while he sat down beside her. "Do you think we will make it to Y'Melenor tomorrow?" She asked, tearing another bite from the chunk and chewing it loudly.

G'Nash gave her a shrug. "I'm not sure. I have never been to the elven city," he admitted, ripping into his own portion of meat. "I do hope we find it soon. It would be nice to get some rest that wasn't filled with the worry of being discovered by the Black Sword Clan," he declared with a mouth full of food.

I wonder if Kirkland is awake, she thought as she finished off the meat that G'Nash had brought her. She released a heavy sigh as she thought of her brother. She pulled her legs up against her chest and let her head rest on them. She was tired, but every time she closed her eyes she was plagued with dreams of the rift. The endless void, the cold that chilled her bones, and the menacing voice that called out to her from within. She felt her body shiver from the mere thought of that lifeless place.

"Are you cold?" G'Nash asked, covering her shoulders with a wolf's pelt they had taken from the camp and wrapping his arm around her.

She wasn't cold, but she couldn't deny the warmth she felt having him close to her. She looked up into the crimson eyes of G'Nash. The half-orc was the same age as her and even without the spell she used to learn his language she could see that he had endured much growing up. His body was covered in scars, a large one stretched across his forehead, but she could still see a softness in his eyes. She had seen the heart he carried, the love for his people, for the land, and that he would give his life to protect them. She reached a hand up to let it rest on the side of his face. The two of them lost themselves in each other's gaze, but as they started to draw closer, a sound from within the forest drew her attention.

"I'm sorry," G'Nash exclaimed, shaking his head and separating from her.

Isabella put a hand over his mouth and quieted him so that she could listen. The sound of heavy footfalls echoed out, twigs snapping under the weight of those approaching, and they carried the smell of death. "Someone is coming!" She announced, standing up from the ground and rushing toward the others.

"Who comes?" Gh'Rys asked, lifting up a battle-axe they had taken from the camp and what remains of the Black Root Clan gathered around him.

Isabella shook her head. She didn't know who was coming or how many, but she knew from which direction they would be coming from. "They are coming from that way," she declared, pointing and Torgath stepped in front of her.

"Black Root, prepare to fight. For honor and glory!" Gh'Rys yelled and the others roared with a mighty cheer.

Isabella sniffed the air, the smell of death was growing stronger and the sound of heavy footfalls were loud enough that everyone could hear them. She lowered her body, her heart was racing, she didn't know who was coming, but if their intentions were to attack, she would make them regret it. G'Nash stood at her right side, battle-axe held tight in his hands and Irick stood at her left. She could see him shaking, the smell of fear emitting from him was palpable, but he continued to stand at her side.

"Grandfather, is that you?" A voice called out from the forest.

Gh'Rys trembled causing him to drop his axe and he lifted his arm up to his chest. "Lo'Nash!?" He cried out. "Can that really be him?" He asked, taking a step toward the voice, but being grabbed by the others standing close to him.

Lo'Nash was the eldest grandson to Gh'Rys and he was the one that rallied the others to stand with him against the Black Sword Clan to give the others time to escape. Isabella knew from the memories she borrowed from G'Nash that everyone had given up hope of ever seeing them again, but she had a bad feeling in the pit of her stomach. The smell of death lingered heavily in the air and it was getting stronger. "G'Nash," she whispered, reaching out to touch the forearm of the half-orc. "I have a bad feeling," she declared softly.

G'Nash released a heavy sigh. "I thought I would never see him again. I thought even Lo'Nash couldn't withstand the Black Sword Clan. I should have known better," he admitted from a wide grin.

Isabella squeezed the arm of the half-orc, but before she could voice her concern, those that were approaching the camp emerged from the shadows and into the light of the campfire. She looked out at a small group of ten orcs. Their bodies covered in poorly bandaged wounds, they were out of breath, and they all looked exhausted. Lo'Nash painfully brought his arm up to rest on his chest. "I'm glad we managed to find you," he said, bowing his head in respect.

Lo'Nash stood a hand taller than his grandfather. He had long black hair that was coated in sweat and it flowed down to rest upon his thick shoulders. He was covered in bloody bandages. One wrapped around his head covering his right eye, one of his fangs was broken, the brown woven trousers he wore were tattered, and he looked to be on the verge of collapse, but he fought to remain upright. Despite his injuries and his obvious fatigue, he gritted his teeth, clenched his fists, and puffed out his chest at the sight of the strangers that stood with his clan. "Who are these outsiders? Are they elves?" He asked.

Isabella squeezed the forearm of the half-orc causing him to look at her, but she never removed her gaze from those that just entered their camp. She didn't trust them, something felt off, and she sniffed quietly at the air, but the heavy smell of decay turned her stomach causing her to feel nauseous. She sunk her fingernails into the arm of the half-orc causing his face to twist in pain and the smell of his blood was just enough to drive away the awful aroma she was picking up, but G'Nash wasn't too pleased with her action.

"What is wrong with you Wulgar?" He asked loudly.

Lo'Nash clenched his teeth together, a flash of anger burned in his left eye, and he took a single step closer. "What did you call her?" He asked in rage.

G'Nash brought up the arm that she wasn't holding, she could smell his fear, and she released a low growl in the direction of Lo'Nash. She knew the half-orc's past, she lived through it thanks to the spell, and she knew all the torment that his oldest brother put him through. He was among those that disagreed with G'Nash receiving the name of his father. The half-orc wasn't born of Du'Nash and because of that he should not be given the name, but his words were lost in the wind. His mother wished for the half-orc to be given the proud name of Nash and so it was bestowed upon him.

Lo'Nash snarled, showing his broken fang even better in the weak campfire light and he took another stomp toward his half-brother. "You have no right to be giving anyone that name, small fang," he grumbled.

"The matter of the name can be dealt with once we are safe in Y'Melenor," Gh'Rys quickly interrupted as he rushed to his grandson and placed a hand on his chest.

Lo'Nash grumbled as he pointed a finger at the half-orc. "This isn't over," he declared through clenched teeth.

Isabella watched as the others stepped up to embrace their grandfather and she knew each one by name. She could see the twins Bu'Nash and Gu'Nash who were born a year after Lo'Nash. They were a hand shorter than him, they looked to be as strong as him, but their fangs were unbroken and decorated with silver rings. The next to approach was Lu'Nash, the youngest male child born to Du'Nash and he was the smallest of them. He embraced his grandfather, but he was only able to lift one arm to do it. The other was covered in blood covered bandages and his left eye was black and swollen shut, but he refused to let anyone help him.

The last to step into the light was that of Du'Nash's only daughter, Vivic. She was slightly taller than Lu'Nash, she had a slender body that was covered in muscle and she walked with a limp. A bloody bandage covered her thigh. She wore rough leather pants that matched the material of her brothers, but where they wore nothing, she had a thick leather strap that covered her chest. Her long black hair stretched to the small of her back and she smiled at her grandfather as she embraced him.

The other five orcs that traveled with them greeted the others heartily and Isabella was starting to feel as if the smell of decay was just due to the wounds that covered the bodies of the survivors. She released the forearm of the half-orc, but her ears quickly perked up as a familiar sound came to her. The twang of a bowstring being released resonated and she could hear an arrow cutting through the air. She quickly pushed the half-orc to the side, causing him to stumble over his feet, and come crashing to the ground. It felt like her body was moving of its own accord. She growled in the direction the sound came from and with haste she snatched the arrow just before it could find purchase in her shoulder.

She sniffed heavily at the arrow. She knew that had it hit her it wouldn't have killed her, but it would have kept her from using her arm until it healed. The aroma coming from the projectile was unfamiliar to her. It was earthly and sweet. The make of the arrow was unlike any she had ever seen. It was long, flimsy, but durable as she bent it to see where its breaking point might be. The head of the arrow wasn't metal like the ones her father would use back home. The wood of the arrow was just sharpened down to a fine point and the feathers at the end of it were solid white. It was beautifully crafted, but she didn't understand why it was fired at her.

She looked to G'Nash who managed to get back to his feet. "Who's there?!" He screamed, after he realized that she might have just saved his life.

A soft and slow clap came from within the treetops, but she couldn't pinpoint exactly where it was coming from. "I am impressed," a song-like voice called out from the shadows and she was surprised she could understand it.

She looked over at the half-orc and she could tell that he understood the language. *The spell didn't just give me his language, but all the languages that he knows*, she thought to herself. "We are not enemies of the elves. We have come in search of refuge from the Eye of Avgrunnen and those who have sworn fealty to it," she called out in the melodic language.

"What language was that?" Uthric asked softly, stepping up beside her and placing a hand on her shoulder.

A gentle breeze washed over her, cooling her sweaty brow, and easing her fleeting mind. She could faintly hear the soft footfalls of others quickly surrounding them, their sweet earthy scent mixing with that of the decayed, and the sound of them using the trees to gain higher ground on them. Her ears perked up as she could hear bow strings being pulled taut. She couldn't determine their actual number, but she believed they would stand no chance in a battle against them.

Uthric cleared his throat and squeezed her shoulder causing her to lose her concentration. "Are you going to tell me what language you used? I know it wasn't orcish, their tongue is so harsh and the other was more of a soft melody."

Isabella inhaled deeply of the fresh air that was blowing across her face, carrying the scent of the elves, and she gave the old wizard a nod. "It's the elven tongue."

"How did you come by their language?" Uthric asked in haste.

Isabella gave him a shrug. "I believe it was the spell I used on G'Nash. It didn't just give me his memories and the orcish tongue, but all the languages he knows," she admitted, her eyes searching the dark forest for any signs of those that were surrounding them.

She found that her sight was improving, just like her hearing and smell. She could see the shapes of those that were hidden within the darkness. She didn't know which one was talking to her, but she watched as they moved sure-footed through the tree branches with an uncanny quickness. It looked as if their feet barely touched the branch as they danced through them. She still didn't know their actual number, but those she could see were ready to attack should they have to. "Who are you?!" She asked loudly.

"I am *Revalor Simimar*, first son of *Dalyor*, son of Eridin, and blood of the silver archer," the voice called out from within the forest. "Are you the *Maiden of Lucian?*"

Isabella found him, she could see the shape of him as he stood perfectly balanced on a tree branch, his bow nocked with an arrow and pointed at her. She held her hands up to show that she was unarmed. "I have been given many gifts from the wolf spirit, but I'm not sure what you mean by being his maiden," she admitted, taking a single step closer to the forest.

"If the wolf spirit has bestowed gifts to you then that would make you his maiden," Revalor said, easing the tension on his bow string and placing the arrow back in the quiver on his back. "We have been searching for you," he declared, leaping from the branch.

Isabella was confused. "If you were searching for me, then why did you attack me?" She asked as she continued to watch him.

Revalor chuckled at her question as he continued to approach. He looked to be gliding across the ground. Each step was elegant and made little sound. "Lucian came to our elder three nights ago. He told her of his maiden, a girl of great power, but that you were lost and being hunted by orcs. He asked that we save you from them. I wasn't attacking you with my arrow," he admitted as he cleared the trees and stepped out into the weak light of the campfire.

She marveled at him. He had long silver hair that was tied in several places with twigs that still had leaves hanging on them. His skin was smooth with a light green hue, his chin was rounded, and he had high cheekbones. His violet eyes sparkled in the light, he had a charming smile, his slender body was covered in a robe made of hemp, and it was covered in bark to give him more durability. He cocked his head to the side slightly. "Until this moment I have never missed my mark, but you caused me to miss the orc and then caught my arrow. It was very impressive," he admitted with a shrug. "Are these orcs with you?"

Isabella gave him a nod and he released a heavy sigh. "We have never hosted orcs within our walls of Y'Melenor. Whenever we were dealing with the Black Swamp Orcs, we would always meet them within the *Evergreen Bog.* The wet and muddy ground would give us an advantage if they wished to lure us into a trap," he said with a smile. "I'm guessing that you won't go without them," he observed, placing his hands on his hips.

"If you intend to take me to your city, then they go with me," she declared, putting her arms down and looking around at the mixed company she stood with.

Revalor shrugged. "It can't be helped," he declared, giving a nod to the others that were still posted in the trees. "Let the others know that they will have to be blindfolded. We will escort them to *King Jaspen Theodred* and he can decide if they can stay within the city," he remarked, as he pulled free a sash made of hemp and approached her.

Isabella relayed the message of the archer to the others as the other elves moved closer. Torgath, Uthric, and Irick all agreed to the demands of the elf. Gh'Rys wasn't too keen on the idea of being blindfolded. That would put him at the mercy of the elves. He voiced his concern about giving up his sight, but her eldest grandson was able to convince him and everyone was made ready to travel. Isabella looked at Revalor who was ready to put his hemp cloth over her eyes and she recoiled from it. "This better not be a trick," she announced loudly.

Revalor flashed her a soothing smile. "I swear on my name and honor that I mean you no harm, maiden. I only wish to keep the secret of our city," he declared softly before fixing the blindfold over her eyes.

Isabella felt uneasy in total darkness. The absence of light drove her back to the void and that voice. *Useless mortal! Begone from my sight!* The words echoed in her head causing her body to tremble. She felt alone within the darkness. Powerless. But the touch of Irick entangling his fingers with hers on her left hand and the strong grip of G'Nash taking hold of her right, helped her dispel the nightmare that had taken hold again. She stood reassured and vigilant as the others were being huddled around her. She could hear the soft whisper of Revalor.

As the wood elf finished speaking his incantation, she felt a strong whirlwind engulf her. Fear gripped at her as her memories of the vortex came rushing back along with that voice that spoke to her from the darkness. It made her feel sick, her head was pounding, and her stomach twisted in knots, but she continued to remain steadfast against the cyclone that was threatening to knock her off balance. The whirlwind quickly dissipated, leaving her disoriented and weak. She fell to the ground, expecting to feel the soft embrace of the forest bed, but instead she scraped her knees on a hard surface.

"Are you alright?" Revalor asked softly.

Isabella quickly stood up from the ground. Her knees were stinging and she could feel the blood trickling down her legs, but she pushed the discomfort from her mind. "I'll be fine," she declared proudly. "Are we already in the city?"

"That we are," Revalor revealed as he removed her blindfold and allowed her to take in the beauty of the city.

Y'Melenor was constructed around the trees and the homes were built from those that had fallen on their own. A soft melody was being sung by small orbs of light that danced all around the city, the roads were made of large polished stones slightly covered by dried leaves. The trees were intertwined with each other, like two hands clasped together, making them strong at the base, but leaving a gaped opening usable for shelter. The small orbs danced around every structure within the city. They were the light source of the place as the sky was blocked by a mixture of orange and red leaves.

Y'Melenor was a breathtaking place of beauty, but Isabella found herself more concerned with the hundreds of wood elves that had encircled them. They were dressed in robes made of hemp and covered in bark to provide protection. Some of them carried long wooden spears and some had bows, but regardless of the weapon, they all had them pointed at those they deemed outsiders of their home.

Revalor tossed up his hands as he stepped in front of her. "Calm down everyone," he commanded softly.

"Have you lost your senses?!" A voice called out from the crowd. "Bringing orcs into our home. The king will banish you for sure this time!"

The voice was much different than the others she had heard. It still held a melody to it, but it was colder, darker than the others, and the elf that it belonged to was different. Most of the elves she could see were slender of body, but muscular. They had platinum hair of varying length, they all had violet eyes and their skin held a green hue, but looked smooth to the touch. Their facial structure was different for each one, but the one that burst forth with finger pointing was completely different from the others.

He was a hand shorter than the others, his hair was cut short, and it was slightly darker in color. The color of his eyes were also darker, but she could see a hint of violet in them. His face was covered in a short trimmed blond beard and he shouldered through the crowd and into the clearing where they were. Anger twisted his face. He was grinding his teeth as he pushed the point of his finger into the chest of Revalor and his eyes burned with rage as he looked around him at her. "Do you not even fathom the danger you have brought upon us by bringing them here?" He seethed.

"You need to take a step back, Veran, before I forget that you are from a noble house," Revalor threatened while knocking the finger away from his chest.

Veran looked taken aback at the response he received. "You forget yourself, archer. I am a Regynald, I have king's blood in my veins," he replied, pushing his finger into the chest of the archer once more.

Revalor grabbed the finger and twisted it causing the male elf to drop to a knee. "Your grandfather was once a king to our people, but his anger and rage brought us to the brink of extinction. It was his ill-gotten plan to raid the druhir city of *Drunidr* that cost my grandfather his life and it was after that he was exiled from our city. You are lucky that your father was respected by King Gorre or else your whole house would have been exiled," he said before releasing Veran's finger and allowing his prisoner to go free.

"I understand that you all were beguiled into thinking that an enemy had breached our city's defenses, but you have nothing to fear. The *Silver Battalion* will keep watch over those brought to see the king and elder," Revalor assured them with his soft voice. "Now, clear the street so that we can escort them to the throne," he requested with a bow.

The tension slowly eased as the elves dispersed back into the city, but Veran remained before the archer. "This is not over," he warned before turning and making his way back the way he had come.

"Just like his grandfather," Revalor observed with a shake of his head. "Let's get to the king and explain what's going on," he said, looking back to make sure all blindfolds were removed and he led them through the city.

"Isabella," Uthric called out. He was panting for breath as he tried to keep stride with her and the elf. "What spell did he use to bring us here so quickly?" he asked.

Isabella figured that magic had something to do with their arrival into the city. "How do you know he used a spell?" She asked the wizard.

Uthric cleared his throat as he sucked in a deep breath. "It felt like a teleportation spell, but there were some minor differences. The ones used back home never caused disorientation and I am curious if it was intentional or if the spell for teleportation is just that different."

Isabella rolled her eyes unintentionally. "The wizard wants to know what type of teleportation spell you used to bring us here," she softly whispered to the elf at her side.

"Our magic is sacred," Revalor said calmly.

Isabella relayed what the elf said to the wizard. He gave a disgruntled nod before slowing his pace to match that of the others and she released a heavy sigh. "Are you sure you can't make an exception for the old man? He was looking forward to learning all he could about magic from this place, but more importantly he is looking for a way to help my brother," she said, glancing at the elf.

Revalor shook his head as he held out a hand and let one of the orbs of light land on the tip of his fingers. "These are called *Ignis Fatuus* and they are the spirit of those we have lost. When an elf dies his magical energy will become one of these. In this form we take care of nature, that's why you see them mostly around the trees of the forest, but they are also known to guide those who have become lost," he said, moving his hand gently, causing the orb to float off his hand. "That is all I can tell you for now. Once the meeting with the king and elder has concluded, I will put your request for the old man before the elder."

Isabella gave him a nod as he brought them all to a halt. The building was different from the homes she had seen making her way to the royal hall. It was built to blend in with the trees that grew around it, it was the tallest structure within the city, it had windows that were covered by dried leaves, a tree went through the center of it, and it was turned into a tower with several guards standing at the top. The guards stood with long wooden spears at the doors. They were covered in the traditional armor made from bark and they carried oval wooden shields. They crossed their weapons as Revalor approached. "Why have you brought orcs to our city?" The guard on the left asked loudly.

"I fear you have overstepped this time," the one on the right remarked.

Revalor gave a shrug. "The wolf maiden refused to come without them. Go tell the king and elder that we have arrived," he commanded, and the guard on the right pushed open one of the doors and slipped inside.

Isabella exhaled as she squeezed the bridge of her nose. She still felt weak. Her stomach was twisting, but she fought against retching. "Everything alright?" Revalor asked without breaking his stare at the guard.

"Just feeling disoriented from the spell you used," she admitted, shaking her head and rubbing the back of her neck.

Revalor broke his gaze to look at her in bewilderment. "That's not possible," he remarked, turning to take hold of her shoulders and pulling her close.

She was taken aback by the sudden movement of the elf, but she lacked the strength to react to him. She gazed deep into his violet eyes and a spark ignited within them. She felt as if he was looking deep into her spirit and uncovering all her secrets. He placed a hand on her cheek. "When was the last time you slept, wolf maiden?" He asked, releasing her and crossing his arms under his chest.

Isabella shook her head, clearing it of the enchantment of looking into his eyes and rubbed the back of her neck. "I slept the night before," she lied.

She hadn't been able to close her eyes for no longer than a few moments since arriving in this world. Every time she tried, she was reminded of that place, the one made up of darkness, the one void of all life except for that voice and the thought of it made her body shiver involuntarily.

Revalor squeezed her shoulders causing her to look up at him. "I can see it in your eyes," he admitted, releasing her and shaking his head. "Perhaps the elder can help you, but you need to rest or it is going to kill you," he stated before turning to stand at her side.

She was trying to process what he had said, but before she could remark on it the guard returned from within the royal hall. "King Jaspen has given permission for the wolf maiden to enter, but she is to be escorted by Revalor. The others are to be taken to the holding cells," he said loudly, but he spoke only in the language of the elves.

G'Nash being one of the only others who understood what the elf had said, quickly stepped up beside her. His chest was swelled with pride, his muscles were tightened and bulging as he pointed his finger at the elves before him. "I will not let Wulgar out of my sight!" He declared loudly in the broken tongue of the elves.

Isabella quickly turned to place a hand upon the chest of the half-orc, she could feel the thick muscle flexing beneath her hand, she could see the fire that was burning in his crimson eyes, but she forced his focus on her. "This is why Revalor is getting so much hate for bringing us here. You need to calm down and respect the wishes of their king. Show them that they are wrong about the orcs, about you," she said in her common tongue.

Torgath released a heavy sigh. He had been silent since they left the Black Sword camp with those they saved. She had asked him if everything was alright and he assured her that he was fine, but she could tell that something was eating him up inside. She knows that he misses her mother. This is the longest he has ever been from her and he was full of worry over her brother, but despite everything he was going through, he knew what she needed. He placed a thick hand on the shoulder of G'Nash and pulled him back a few steps. "Calm yourself. She is capable of taking care of herself. She is after all my daughter," he said from a forced half-smile.

G'Nash turned to look at her father and she could see the rage subside in the eyes of the half-orc. "The elves are going to take us to a place where we can tend to our wounds and rest. Wulgar is going to speak to the king," he declared in the language of his people.

A hushed murmur echoed out from the other orcs, but Gh'Rys silenced them with the raise of a hand. "Some rest will be much appreciated," he declared, lowering his arm.

Isabella informed Revalor what was said between the orcs. "See that they are taken care of," he commanded and the archers saluted him before escorting the mixed company away from the royal hall.

She watched as her companions disappeared and she could hear the doors to the royal hall being pushed open. "Your friends will be taken care of. We shouldn't keep the king waiting," Revalor advised as he placed a hand on her shoulder and she slowly turned around.

The doors to the royal hall had been opened. She could see hundreds of Ignis Fatuus dancing within the long hallway, their soft glow reflecting off the polished marble floor and filling it with light. She could see paintings that decorated the walls on both sides. The somber eyes of the elves looked to follow her, but she felt compelled to approach one that depicted more than a single elf. An enormous tower loomed in the background, the silhouette of winged creatures looked to be perched at the top, elves with nocked bows stood ready to defend, but the image that called to her was the one of a young man that stood out from the others. He wore dark blue robes under ornate armor that covered his upper body. The chest plate was decorated with four gems, one placed just below the neck, another was on the far right of the chest with one on the far left and the last one down just above the belly button. He carried a twisted staff that held an amethyst secured at its head. In his other hand was a claymore of gold, but the silver edge of the blade could be seen. The pommel was that of a wolf, red gems adorned its eyes and the hilt guard was talons. On his brow was a crown of gold, it was also covered in a multitude of different gems in varying size and color.

"That was painted by *Bvorn Vorek*," Revalor said as he stepped up beside her. "He created the painting to immortalize those that stood with the wizard prime during the last battle with the blood god," he said, pointing to the tower. "Aster gathered all those willing to stand with him to face Bahaal. He knew that he would require a great deal of time to construct the alternate planes of existence and then he would have to banish the blood god. Many great warriors sacrificed their lives to defend the tower while the wizard worked and in the end he managed to banish the blood god, but Bahaal wasn't the only one that was banished that day."

"The Great Banishing," Isabella interrupted with a whisper.

Revalor gave a shrug. "Is that what they call it in your realm?" He asked, but didn't wait for her to answer as he released a heavy sigh. "That's a fitting name for it," he remarked, reaching out to touch the painting and then letting his hand drop to his side.

"That's what Uthric called it," she admitted, looking back at the portrait. "He told us that Aster sacrificed himself to banish Bahaal and his army, but before he could tell us anything else we were pulled through the vortex that brought us here."

Revalor placed his hands on his hips. "I wasn't there for the battle, but I've been told stories about what happened. My entire family stood with the wizard prime that day. The plan was to hold back the army of Bahaal while Aster siphoned enough magical energy to perform his spell. If done correctly it should have created a single mirrored plane to which he would cast the blood god and his horde into, but something went wrong," he explained, pausing a moment to collect his thoughts. "No one truly knows what happened that day or what spell was used by the wizard, but instead of one mirrored plane it created two. *Dorcha'Helvetti*, is what we call the one where the blood god was banished to and the rest of us made a home here in Tylwyth Teg'Villi," he said, looking at her with a forced half-smile.

"I don't understand," Isabella confessed. "If the plan was to only banish the blood god's army, then why did it also pull the other races through?"

Revalor shrugged. "The best theory I've heard is that the spell used was supposed to pull through any that had been touched by the blood god, but it was unable to differentiate between those that were created by him and those that fought against him and because of that it pulled all those that stood against him through also," he said, releasing a heavy sigh before turning away from the painting. "We've wasted enough time. Let's get moving," he declared before making his way down the hallway.

Isabella took one last look at the painting and she rushed to catch up with her escort. She continued to glance at the other paintings, but never stopped to truly take in their beauty as Revalor led her down the hallway in a slight haste. He brought her to a stop just outside a small wooden door, an image had been etched into it depicting several different animals, but she felt drawn to the howling wolf over the others. She reached out to touch it, but as her fingers graced the surface of the door, it opened slowly to reveal what it had been concealing. "Do as I do," Revalor said and upon her agreement he entered the room.

Isabella marveled at the elegantly decorated chamber, vines stretched from floor to ceiling and a mixture of different colored flowers appeared to bloom all along them. There were no windows in the room, but it was still being adequately lit by the Ignis Fatuus. A massive tree was at the center of the room that extended beyond the ceiling and a chair had been carved out of it. The king of Y'Melenor sat graciously upon it. He looked younger than her brother and his boyish face was smooth of hair, but his deep violet eyes told her that he had seen much in his time. His emerald green cloak was parted just enough to show the light brown robe he wore underneath, his leather pants were tucked into leather boots, and strands of platinum hair reached down to rest upon his slender chest. A woven crown of twigs sat upon his brow and in his hand he held tight to a small wooden scepter, but she could see the hilt of a sword sticking out of his cloak at his waist. With his eyes closed as they approached and while taking a knee, Revalor spoke. "I have brought the maiden as you requested, your highness," he said without bringing his gaze from the floor.

King Jaspen released a heavy sigh. "I don't recall asking for orcs, Revalor," he spoke in a displeasing tone as he stood up.

"I did what I had to, my king. The maiden refused to come without them, your highness," Revalor remarked, lifting his gaze up.

King Jaspen toyed with the scepter as he examined her from his dais. "What is wrong with her? She looks like she could collapse at any moment."

"Her mind has been touched by the bringer of calamity, the rider of darkness, the destroyer of worlds, and the god of blood," a soft, grandmotherly voice called out as a cloaked woman stepped around the throne and began descending down the dais with the aid of the king.

Isabella watched as she cautiously took each step. Her long green cloak flowed behind her and it was fastened with an emerald leaf broach at the neck. The woman's face was concealed by the hood, but long strands of silver hair could be seen resting on her chest. She walked with the help of a twisted staff and the forearm of the king. After they emerged from the last step, she released her grip on the king. She pushed back her hood to give sight to her face. Her eyes were full of life and she had a cheerful smile. "I am known as the elder, but you can call me Aleesia," she said while trying to catch her breath.

"Grandmother, you should sit and rest," King Jaspen advised, ushering her to sit on the bottom step of the dais.

Aleesia shook her head. "I will be fine," she said, looking back to Isabella. "It is her that I am worried about," she remarked, pointing a thin finger at her. "Bahaal's power still lingers on her, he is trying to break her will and I must stop it. Tell me, child, how do you feel?" She asked, ever so sweetly.

"Tired," Isabella answered without a second thought.

Aleesia hobbled over to caress the side of Isabella's head. "That is the source of his power. He plagues the mind of those that will not submit to him freely. You have a strong will, but even you have your limits. How long has it been since you came here?"

Isabella nervously moved her head from the carefree touch of the elder and rubbed the back of her neck. She didn't know how long it had been since she arrived in this plane. "I'm not sure, but I believe it has been eight days," she guessed, rubbing her tired eyes.

"Eight days," Aleesia repeated the number and looked to the others. "You have lasted longer than some of our greatest warriors. I can see why Lucian bestowed his power to you," she said from a grandmotherly smile. "Let us waste no more time on this and cleanse you of his shadow," she declared, ushering for her to follow.

Isabella was fatigued, her eyes were heavy, and it took every ounce of energy she could muster to command her legs to move. They made their way to the back of the throne room. An enormous pool had been carved out of the floor, the Ignis Fatuus danced upon the surface of the water, and she could see all the way to the bottom. There was an opening in the ceiling that allowed moonlight to pour down onto the pool. She could see a mixture of different colored flowers that bloomed all around and their sweet aroma filled the room. She felt a peace wash over her, one that she hadn't felt since the vortex stole her from her world.

"You must disrobe," Aleesia announced softly.

Isabella gasped as she scanned the room, but she couldn't see any sign of the others and the elder chuckled. "My great grandsons have already gone. They know what has to be done to cleanse your mind, my dear," she said from a soft smile.

Isabella was nervous, but she slowly removed the clothing that covered her body. "What should I do with these?" she asked, holding her clothing in each hand.

Aleesia clapped her hands and an elegantly dressed elf stepped through the door at the side of the pool. She was dressed in a white robe, her platinum hair bounced on her shoulder with each step, and she wasted no time in retrieving the clothes. Her nose twisted at the sight of them, but she made no comment as she retreated back through the door carrying the items. "Now that your body is ready, we shall begin the process of cleansing your mind. When you are ready, step into the water," she instructed as she sat on the side and lowered her feet down into the pool.

Isabella made her way over to the edge, looking down she could see her reflection, her dark brown hair was tangled, and dirt covered her face, but her almond shaped eyes showed just how tired she was. She eased herself down the steps leading into the water. The warm liquid relaxed the muscles as she walked and it made her feel at peace as she made her way toward the other side. She could hear the elder humming a soft tune, but she didn't know the song. Her eyes grew heavier, threatening to close as the water reached her neck and darkness took her.

Isabella opened her eyes to find that she was once again within the cold embrace of the void that brought her to this plane. *Useless mortal!* The words echoed in her mind and it made her body shiver. Her eyes burned, her head was pounding, she was fatigued, she wanted nothing more than to sleep, but even in the darkness of the void she couldn't force her eyes closed. *Useless mortal!* The words echoed in her mind once more. She was broken and she whimpered in defeat.

"Keep your courage, my dear," the voice of Aleesia called out through the darkness.

Isabella opened her eyes, she couldn't see the elder, but she could sense her. "How can I fight him? I'm just a useless mortal," she repeated the words that echoed in her head.

"You are not useless," Aleesia said, reaching out and taking hold of her shoulder. "You are the maiden of the wolf, the Wulgar of the orcs, the alpha of your pack, and you are stronger than him. Now stand up," she demanded, holding out her hand to help her up.

Isabella slowly got back to her feet with the help of the elder, but a laugh echoed out of the darkness. "Is that you, Aleesia? I always wondered if the elvish life span extended to that of a half-breed," the voice of Bahaal said, his voice calling from all around them. "Guess it does, in a manner of speaking. How much longer do you have?"

"You have no power here, Bahaal," Aleesia said, ignoring his question and speaking through clenched teeth.

Bahaal's laugh echoed out and it caused the darkness to quake. "You should look around, half-elf. You have entered into my world. Here I hold all the power," he announced as the darkness took form and he looked at them through crimson eyes.

"How is this possible?" Aleesia asked, bravely, but the quiver in her voice gave her away.

Bahaal moved a hand and the darkness formed into a massive throne for him to sit upon. "The veil between the planes is weakening and it is increasing my power. Soon, I will be free of this prison. Then I will hunt down those responsible for imprisoning me," he announced happily.

"I will not allow this to happen," Aleesia declared, holding out her hand and closing her eyes. "You will never leave Dorcha'Helvetti, but you will relinquish the hold you have on this girl!" She said, whispering an incantation under her breath.

Bahaal laughed hysterically. "You are trying to use magic, that's cute," he said, standing from the throne and pointing a finger at them. "The wolf maiden belongs to me or at least she will," he declared, waving his hands and creating a black orb.

Bahaal held the item out to examine it before shaking it and causing the smoke to clear. An image started to take form, but she couldn't see it from where she stood and the blood god held it out to give her a better look.

Isabella watched as the smog revealed her brother. His breathing appeared shallow, his bed sheets were soaked in sweat, and her mother was weeping uncontrollably at his side. She wanted to run for the item, but was stopped by Aleesia. "He is toying with your mind. Resist him," she whispered.

Bahaal laughed maniacally as he tossed the orb behind him and it disappeared in the shadow. "I will make my offer to you once more, mortal girl," he said, stepping closer toward them. "Join me. We will rule every realm side by side. I will grant you more power than you could ever dream of and I will give you what you desire more than anything. I will save your brother," he offered from an evil grin.

Isabella was torn. She didn't trust Bahaal, but she desperately wanted to rescue her brother from the pain she had caused him and she struggled with making a decision. *He is a deceiver. He is only trying to manipulate you. See through my eyes,* the voice of Lucian echoed in her head softly.

Isabella closed her eyes and the wolf revealed to her the deception of the blood god. She could see all the torment he caused before he was banished the first time. She saw the havoc he wrought the second time by using what he learned from his first fight with the wizard prime and he used his blood magic to create an army. One that would require a greater deal of magic to remove. She witnessed the countless souls slaughtered by his actions and how he cared not for it.

She opened her eyes, but she could feel that they had changed. The wolf was giving her a sight to see the true form of Bahaal and she could see that he was nothing more than a corrupted elf. She growled at the blood god causing him to stop his approach and his face twisted in anger.

Use the gifts I have bestowed to you, Lucian said as his voice faded to the back of her mind.

Isabella felt a surge of power flow through her, the fear that once paralyzed her was gone, and she looked at the shadow in anger. "I belong to no one," she growled as she stood to her feet. "I am Isabella Strongfellow, the daughter of a farmer, the wolf maiden, I am known as wulgar to the orcs and I will never be yours," she declared, pointing a finger at the blood god. "You will never escape your prison!"

A fire erupted from the chest of Isabella, taking the form of an enormous dire wolf and it stood proudly before her. Bahaal gritted his teeth in anger, but she could see the fear within the eyes of the blood god. The enchanted creature snarled at the enemy, snapping its massive jaws at him, but composing itself as it looked at the maiden and bowed its head. "Contain him!" She commanded, knowing that the blood god couldn't be destroyed or else they would have done so long ago.

The fiery wolf glared at its intended target, its flames growing even more intense as he took a single step closer toward the blood god and roared a fierce howl before bounding toward the shadow. "I will be free!" Declared Bahaal as the two of them collided.

A brilliant light caused Isabella to flinch, but as she slowly opened her eyes, she found that she was floating within the pool. The soft moonlight cascading down to bathe her in its glow. She released a soft sigh, the darkness that once plagued her mind was now gone and now having peace, she slowly closed her eyes to rest.

Chapter 4
NaShorn

Isabella slowly opened her eyes. She was disoriented and confused. The soft glow of the moon that she was basking in was gone. It was replaced by the sight of a wooden roof and she could feel that she was no longer floating in water, but resting on a soft bed instead. The Ignis Fatuus danced around her, their warm glow washing over her. She released a heavy sigh as she sat up to see that she was within a bedchamber, but one she didn't recognize. She was wearing soft garments of pale green that covered her completely and at her side was an unconscious G'Nash. She rubbed her eyes, helping them to adjust and she nudged the leg of the half-orc causing him to startle awake.

"Are you finally awake, Wulgar?" He asked, smacking his lips and rubbing his own eyes.

She felt different. She had forgotten the last time she ever felt like she had actually rested a full night. "Where are we?" She asked, rubbing at her forehead.

"We are inside the magically constructed house the elves built for us," G'Nash explained, rubbing his own eyes.

She shook her head as she tried to stand, but found her legs were too weak to hold her and the half-orc had to catch her before she collapsed to the ground. "Easy," G'Nash said, placing one of his hands on her hip and the other was tucked under her shoulder. "You have been sleeping for almost three full days."

The news came as a shock to her, but before she could give voice to what she was thinking he continued. "We have been taking turns watching over you, and your father has been making sure you stayed clean," he assured her as he helped her walk toward the door of the room and out into the hallway.

Three days, the words echoed in her head as he helped her down the hall to a privy. *I've lost so much time being in this world.* "Kirky," she softly whispered the name of her brother as she remembered the ritual with Aleesia.

She thought about what the blood god had shown her causing her stomach to twist and she lowered her face down to rest inside of her hands. "Please be alright, Kirky. I am trying to get back to you," she promised, drying her eyes and inhaling deeply through her nose. "But I have to do something about Bahaal," she whimpered as she stood from the wooden privy and washed her hands within a bowl of water. "How do you fight a god?" She asked, running a wet hand down her face.

You will need to gather more animal spirits, the voice of Lucian echoed in her head causing her to yelp in fright.

"Everything alright, Wulgar?" G'Nash asked through the closed door.

"I'm fine," she exclaimed quickly. "I'll be out soon."

She rubbed her temples as she closed her eyes. The vision of a forest was laid out before her. Curled on the ground was Lucian, his black fur bristled in the cool breeze, and he lay with his muzzle against his legs. "There are more of you?" She asked, taking an easy step closer.

Lucian lifted his head, his fiery gaze fixated on her. "There are many more animal spirits and some who have yet to select a champion. I will do what I can to guide you to them, but it will be up to you to gain their trust. I believe that with their power you will be able to stop Bahaal, but only if you can get them to join in your cause," he declared before yawning.

"Where can I start?" She asked, placing a hand on the head of the wolf and rubbing his soft fur.

Lucian showed his enjoyment at being touched. "I can sense the durable rhyno spirit, NaShorn, within the swamp of Bog'Alor. Go, plead with him to take a champion and stand beside you in stopping the blood god," he encouraged with a lick on her cheek.

She chuckled lightly at the touch of his tongue and it snapped her back to reality. She looked around the privy before opening the door to a startled G'Nash. He looked at her with wide eyes. "Bog'Alor," she yelled, stepping free of the privy and letting the door close behind her.

G'Nash scratched at the top of his head. "I'm afraid I don't understand, Wulgar," he declared.

"Lucian spoke to me," she exclaimed. "He told me how to stand against Bahaal and told me to seek out NaShorn in the swamp of Bog'Alor. Do you know where that is?"

G'Nash shook his head. "I'm afraid my knowledge of places is limited to the northern part of *Sapphire*, but Gh'Rys could be of assistance. He has traveled all over the island," he said, leading her down the hallway and to the stairs.

She walked behind the half-orc, examining the structure of the house, and it looked like the inside of the trees she would often hide in. They made their way down to the first floor and found the old orc shaman sitting at a table. He was drinking deeply from a horned cup, eating a slab of venison that was barely cooked, and he released a heavy sigh as they approached him. "I see you are finally awake," he exclaimed, tossing a chunk of the meat into his mouth and chewing it slowly.

"I need to get to Bog'Alor," she said quickly.

Gh'Rys shook his head. "And I need my freedom," he exclaimed loudly.

Isabella could feel her anger boiling. She didn't understand if it was just his words, his tone, or the look on his face that was prompting her rage, but she fought against the urge to attack him. "The elves aren't keeping you here. All you have to do is give up your weapons," G'Nash said, the sound of his voice calming her slightly.

"Give up our weapons? That's what a weakling would do," Gh'Rys announced, shaking his head and looking away from the half-orc.

Seeing the pain on her friend's face was more than she could withstand and she slammed a closed fist against the table. "That is enough. If the elves want you to give up your weapons and you refuse, but they continue to let you stay within their city that should mean something! If you can't see that then you are blind!" she yelled, but quickly covered her mouth in shock and she looked to G'Nash.

Gh'Rys chuckled darkly. "I admire your spirit," he said, sitting his empty cup down and pushing back away from the table. "Why are you trying to go to that dreadful swamp?"

Isabella let a slight growl escape, but shook her head. "I go there to search for NaShorn," she declared through clenched teeth.

"Why do you seek the rhyno spirit?" He asked, licking grease from his teeth.

Isabella could feel her anger burning within her as she looked upon the old orc shaman. "I have to gather the other spirit animals if I hope to contain Bahaal in his prison. I was told by Lucian that NaShorn resides within Bog'Alor. Now will you help me or not?"

Gh'Rys squeezed the bridge of his nose. "The swamp is a dangerous place. The creatures that call it home are amongst the deadliest in the land and then there is the curse that has been placed upon it. Bog'Alor was where a decisive battle for Sapphire took place. Thousands of lives were sacrificed. Their blood is said to fill the streams and their spirits call to those who come. Saddened by their quick demise they look to bring others into that sadness," he released a sigh as he stood from his chair and gripped his staff. "I will show you the way to the bog, but you will need to get an elvish escort to go with us. We will need their keen sight if we hope to ever find it," he declared while shuffling off through the home.

"Where are you going?"

Gh'Rys stopped at an entrance way and looked back to them. "I'm going to see which of our people is foolish enough to go with us. We will need more than sight to survive that hellish place. Now go see the king about our elvish escort," he demanded as he disappeared into the next room, but they could still hear his staff tapping against the floor.

Isabella released a heavy sigh, but she wasted no time in leaving the house and making her way through Y'Melenor. She arrived at the entrance to the royal hall, the two guards crossed their polearms as she stepped up to them, and they stood unmoving. "What purpose do you have here?" The one on the right asked.

"I have come to speak to King Jaspen," Isabella declared. "I need help finding NaShorn in Bog'Alor."

The two elves shared a deep concerning look, but she could hear someone approaching them from the east. "That is no place for the living, wolf maiden. How certain are you that the rhyno spirit is there?" Revalor asked, stepping up beside her and bowing his head in respect.

Isabella looked to the woodland elf in surprise. "Lucian told me that would be where I could find him," she declared.

Revalor scratched the back of his head. "I'm not wanting to doubt the word of the wolf spirit, but just recently we banished the blood god from your mind," he released a heavy sigh as he looked into her eyes. "Let's go see the elder. If she can make certain that the voice was that of Lucian, then I will escort you to Bog'Alor myself," he said from a smile.

"I will await your return, Wulgar," G'Nash announced as the two of them stepped past the guard and G'Nash walked over to sit at the edge of the dirt road.

Isabella gave him a nod as she walked beside Revalor. They entered the royal hall, walked down the familiar hallway of paintings and into the royal chamber. The throne of twisted wood was empty. King Jaspen was only in the throne room during official meetings and their arrival was unannounced. Isabella took a moment to look around the room, she could see the pool of water where she was freed from Bahaal's icy grip and the royal chamber was filled with Ignis Fatuus. They wasted little time crossing the room to the door at the side of the pool, Revalor knocked heavily upon it and it was opened to reveal the elvish lady that came to gather her clothes during the ritual.

"What brings the Silver Captain to the elders personal chamber?" She asked, elegantly and sweet.

Revalor bowed his head. "Vivienne, I have come to see grandmother. I need her to determine who provided the information to the wolf maiden."

She moved to speak and was interrupted by a voice from within the chamber. "Let them enter," Aleesia said weakly.

Vivienne pushed the door open further and stepped to the side so that the two of them could enter. The chamber was large, decorated in flowers of multiple colors that filled the room with a sweet smell, potions of varying color lined the walls, a small bed just big enough for the elder was pushed to the far wall, and Aleesia was getting out of it as they stepped into the room. She flashed them a soft smile. She tried to take a step away from the bed, but stumbled. Revalor rushed to help keep her from falling. "You will have to excuse me. I still haven't fully recovered from the ritual," she admitted from a soft smile, but with the aid of her grandson she made it over to a wooden table and drank the blue concoction that rested upon it. "What did Lucian tell you, child?" She asked, sitting the empty bottle down.

"He told me that the strength of NaShorn is within Bog'Alor. Gh'Rys is willing to show me the way, but said we will need the keen senses of the elves if we hope to survive the marshland," she said, stealing a glance at Vivienne.

She didn't notice it the first time they met, but the elf resembled her mother. Their eyes contained the same passion, the way she stood against the door with her arms folded, and the glare she was giving them. If she didn't know that they were in a different plane she would have mistaken Vivienne as her mother, but she released a heavy sigh. *I must be missing my mother more than I realized,* she thought as she looked back at the elder.

"Come here child and let me see you," Aleesia requested as she sat back down on the edge of the bed.

Aleesia reached out to place both her hands on the forehead of Isabella as the wolf maiden kneeled before her and the elder whispered a soft prayer to the elements. A swirling gust of wind danced around them. Isabella could see her home, Sparrow's Lake, the pristine lake, the lush filled crops, the forest where she used to play, and the sun peaking over the horizon. She felt peace come over her, but sadness gripped her as the image of her mother came to her mind. She was standing at the door of their small home, smiling, her eyes full of life, and Kirkland was leaning against the wall. She felt the warmth of her tears.

"Father?" Aleesia called out in a whisper as she released the forehead of the wolf maiden and fell onto the bed.

"Grandmother!" Revalor called out as he rushed over and took hold of her hand.

Aleesia smiled up to him. "I am fine, child. I now understand why she was able to hold back the icy grasp of Bahaal for so long and I believe I was wrong in my original assumption of her. She would have fought against him until her death," she said, pulling her hand free of Revalor and placing it on the side of Isabella's face. "She is of our blood. A daughter of Eridin. My first son," she declared.

"What do you mean?" Revalor asked, looking back to Vivienne as she quickly stepped up to look at the elder.

Aleesia released a soft sigh. "Eridin was always my most stubborn child. Father used to say he took it after my mother's side. He had a love before the Great Sacrifice, but after the wizard prime casted his spell they were separated. He missed her deeply and it would appear that she gave birth to a child after the banishing. The wolf maiden is a product of that love. Though I call her a daughter of Eridin, it would be more accurate to say she is a great descendant of our bloodline. She, like all other half-elves, is blessed with a long life, but nothing like that of an elf. That is why Lucian chose you, my dear. You are a descendant of a powerful bloodline. My father, Guthric Maximus, was renowned for his prowess on the field of battle, but he wasn't just a killer. He had a mind for diplomacy. With his words alone he managed to gain a settlement in Hyland, the first man to ever do so and he brokered peace amongst the elves and giants. He was respected by all the races. Bahaal tried to corrupt him, but his heart was too pure. I miss him every day," she admitted as her eyes filled and she struggled to fight against them.

Revalor pushed the gray hairs out of the face of his grandmother. "I have never heard you speak of your father before," he admitted.

Aleesia flashed a half-smile. "The pain of talking about him was too much for me, but when I saw her mother. Her eyes were like looking into his," she released a soft sigh. "The information she received was from that of the wolf spirit. Both of you should accompany her to the marshland of Bog'Alor. She is going to need your knowledge of the plants that grow there and you will need to make sure they stay safe. You might want to find some more of your archers to go with you," she declared from her smile.

Revalor gritted his teeth. Isabella could see that he was fighting the tears that begged to fall and he reached out to kiss his grandmother on the forehead. "Find peace, grandmother," he declared before making his way to the door.

Vivienne wasn't able to fight against her emotions. "I will make you proud, grandmother," she exclaimed, kissing the hand of the elder.

Isabella stood from the ground, but Aleesia reached out to take hold of her hand. "Will you stay with me for a short time, child?" She asked, sweetly.

Isabella looked back at the other two, but they exited the room and closed the door behind them. Aleesia released another weak sigh. "There is much that needs to be told to you, but I fear my time is almost done," she declared.

Isabella was confused. The fables that she was told growing up were that the elves were blessed with eternal life, but here she could see that it was a lie. Aleesia was fading, her breathing was irregular, and she looked weak. "I thought elves lived forever," she admitted, taking hold of the elder's hand.

Aleesia chuckled lightly. "True elves are blessed with a very long life, child, but I am like you. I am only half-elf," she said with a smile. "Don't fret about me shedding my mortal coil. Soon I will join with the other Ignis Fatuus of this land. Then I will be reunited with the loved ones I have lost over the many, many years I've had," she paused to take as much of a breath as she could. "Let's not waste any more time on that. I have to tell you about the spirit animals and the price that you will have to pay if you are to contain Bahaal in the void," she paused to choke back a cough and release a heavy sigh.

"I'm unsure of how many spirit animals were created by the wizard prime. What I do know is that the power given is different from those that worship and those that the spirit deems to be a champion. I know that you have felt what I am saying," she flashed a slight smile. "That burning rage, the fire of desire, and the heightened senses of a wolf. You still fight against letting Lucian have full control, but you will have to open yourself to him if you want to defeat Bahaal. That is the price you must pay, that is the price that any champion has to pay. You must become one with the spirit animal, you must give your life to save the world. Only then will you be given the power to contain the blood god."

"I believe in you, child," she said, her voice growing weaker, and her breathing becoming shallower. "Go, find the other spirit animals, but give those they choose as champions the warning that wasn't given to you. Let them know the price that will be paid," she placed a hand on the side of Isabella's face, but she didn't hold it there long before it fell limp on the bed and she exhaled her last breath.

Isabella's heart stung as she looked upon the gladsome expression of Aleesia. The body of the elder began to glow a brilliant white as an Ignis Fatuus emerged from her chest and it circled around Isabella as she wept over the lifeless body of Aleesia. "I am sorry this happened. I will find the other spirit animals and I will stop Bahaal for you!" She declared, standing from the bedside, and holding out her hand so that the Ignis Fatuus could land on it. "May you find true peace," she said before the glowing light flew off and she made her way out of the chamber.

Isabella made her way through the chamber, but as she rounded the throne, the doors burst open and King Jaspen rushed in. The once strong, regal king, came to an abrupt halt at the sight of his beloved grandmother and she could see his immense sorrow from the unfallen tears that swelled in his eyes.

"Grandmother?!" He managed to whimper before a flood of emotion washed down his face.

Isabella closed her eyes causing a lonely tear to run from them and King Jaspen collapsed to his knees. "I am too late!" He declared, smashing his fist against the floor.

Isabella knelt down beside the heartbroken king and placed a hand on his shoulder. "Your grandmother was beyond words. She was wise, strong, and proud of her grandchildren. She deserves to be grieved, but unfortunately our time is limited. Bahaal threatens to break free of his prison. He wants to rule the worlds and we have to stop him. I have to go to Bog'Alor. I have to gather the power needed to stop him, but I can't do it alone," she said, letting her thumb rub his shoulder.

King Jaspen ran his arm across his reddening eyes and looked up at her. "What do you need?" He asked, pushing himself up off the ground and dusting his knees clean.

"Your grandmother has commanded that Revalor and Vivienne go with me, but I'll need some more of your elvish archers to succeed. I will also need your permission to take the orc shaman and any orcs he managed to talk into going with us."

King Jaspen was fighting against his sadness, but he shook his head in agreement as he took in a deep breath. "I'll see that it is done. I can spare some archers. If Revalor is going I am certain that some of his troops will go regardless. I shall draw up the conscripts and send them over to the orcs house. Revalor can use his magic to escort you all from the city," he said as Isabella placed hand on the door that would take her out. "Bog'Alor is dangerous. Be sure you take care out there and please try to bring my cousins home. I have lost all I dare to stomach for now," he declared.

Isabella gave him a quick nod as she stepped through the door and into the hallway. She understood the pain he was going through. She feared that she would never see her mother or her brother ever again and the thought of losing them was unbearable, but she hardened her heart to that pain. She had to remain focused if she was going to stop Bahaal and save the world from the chaos he would unleash if he were freed from his prison. She emerged from within the royal hall. The guards standing post looked heartbroken, but remained steadfast. She bowed her head to them as she stepped past them and G'Nash stood from the ground and began to speak. "Revalor explained what was happening. He has gone with the other elf to acquire supplies for our journey to Bog'Alor. Though I never had the pleasure of meeting the elder, I can see that she must've been a remarkable woman. She managed to touch your heart in such a short time," he said, reaching out and brushing a tear from her cheek. "Do you want to rest before we leave?"

Isabella shook her head. "We need to see who else will go with us to Bog'Alor. Uthric and father should be within the library," she said as the two of them made their way through the streets of Y'Melenor.

She could hear the hushed talk of the elves as they passed. They were disgusted that G'Nash was able to walk the streets beside her. She could also hear the soft footfalls of the ranger tasked with keeping an eye on them as they moved through the woodland city. Veran Regynald had told any who would listen that the orcs being in Y'Melenor was a bad omen and that it would bring the downfall of the city. It was also rumored that the dethroned king had fled the city with a small group of followers, but she didn't have time to worry herself with that as they quickly approached the glamorous structure the elves used as a library.

She stepped up to the four-story building. Elvish scholars stood outside speaking of lore and the knowledge they were researching within the structure. She pushed open the door to see the enormous shelves full of tomes. At the center of the room were elves practicing their magic and at a long wooden table she could see those she was searching for. Her father wasn't much of a learner, but he hovered over the shoulder of Uthric as the old wizard turned pages within a tome. The two of them were searching for any knowledge of how they could open a portal home.

"If you are going to watch me read, can you, do it in a way where you aren't breathing on me?" Uthric asked, slamming the tome he was reading shut and turning to look at Torgath, but flashing a smile. "Isabella! I hope you haven't come here for good news. We still haven't found a way to open a portal," he confessed, standing from the table.

Isabella exhaled an exasperated sigh. "You haven't found anything?"

"I have found much," Uthric admitted. "I have discovered the many wars between the races, the creation of creatures to stand for each, the fall of kings, the rise of kings, the separation of the elf race, and much more rich history, but if your question is focused on a portal home," he paused to run his hand the length of his beard. "The answer is no, I haven't found anything on that," he admitted in a defeated manner.

Isabella squeezed the bridge of her nose. "Do you think the answer is within this library?"

"I don't know if the whole answer is within this building, but I believe that a clue will be uncovered here. If I could find a moment's peace to work," he whispered in a grumble while looking at her father, but she could hear him plainly.

"I have to go to Bog'Alor in search of NaShorn, father, would you like to join me?" She asked, placing a hand on the arm of the massive man. "I have been told that the marshlands were dangerous and I could use your help keeping the others safe."

Torgath rubbed the back of his neck as he looked back to the old wizard and to the tomes that were piled high on the table. "I will lend you my strength daughter," he exclaimed as he pulled her in and embraced her with a tight hug.

Isabella always felt safe and vulnerable in the arms of her father, but it wasn't the time for her to show weakness. She needed to gather the other spirit animals, she had to defeat the blood god and keep the world safe. She pushed away from her father. "Are you ready to head for the marshland or do you need to gather supplies?"

Torgath shrugged. "I just need to find my scythe and gather some food to last us. Where are you going from here?"

"We have to go back to the orcs house. Gh'Rys was gathering some orcs to go with us on this quest," she admitted as they made their way toward the door.

"Then I shall see you there," Torgath announced as he pushed through the door and out of the building.

"Thanks be to you Zephyr for sending me that girl," Uthric whispered, but Isabella could hear him plainly and it made her chuckle.

Isabella and G'Nash stepped free of the building, a gentle breeze blew across their faces and with it came the familiar scent of her friend. *Irick?* She thought to herself. She hadn't seen him since she was purged of the blood god's influence. "What's wrong?" G'Nash asked, his voice snapping her back to reality.

"Nothing," she remarked while shaking her head. "I have to check on something. Can you head back to the orcs and wait for me there?"

G'Nash gave her a gentle half-nod of his head. "I shall do as you ask, Wulgar," he declared as he stepped away and made his way toward the orc's home.

Isabella inhaled deeply through her nose, the scent of Irick was heavy around her, but she couldn't see him. *Listen to your instincts. Follow the direction where the scent is the strongest,* the voice of Lucian echoed in her head and she did as it instructed. The trail of her friend led her back to where they had entered the city, but that was where his scent faded. It was as if he had just disappeared upon arrival. She scratched at the back of her head. *What are you up to, Irick?* She asked herself, but looked around to see the attention she had drawn to herself.

Isabella shrugged before she made her way back through the street of Y'Melenor. She was lost in thought about Irick. She wondered what he could be up to. She hadn't seen him since they arrived in Y'Melenor and the last time they spoke was within the makeshift camp before the elves showed up.

"Are you ready to go?" Revalor asked, snapping her back to reality and she looked up to see him approaching her.

He was dressed in black leather, a bow was strapped to his chest, on his back was his enormous quiver full of arrows, on one hip was a smaller quiver, and a short sword and satchel hung to the opposite hip. His platinum hair was pinned to the back of his head by a small, but elegant twig and he flashed her a smile. Vivienne was dressed in the same manner at his side. Behind them were five more archers. She rubbed the back of her neck as Irick was pushed from her mind. "I am. I was just on my way to see how many orcs were going with us."

She led them through the streets of Y'Melenor. Those they passed were whispering about what they believed happened to the elder. They all believed that it was due to the ritual. They were saying that the fight with Bahaal in Dorcha'Helvetti was just too much of a strain on Aleesia and her body just couldn't recover from it. Though no one outright said it, Isabella knew that everyone blamed her. She blamed herself for bringing about the demise of the elder, but she couldn't allow her emotions to drive her. She hardened her heart to the pain that was dwelling within and continued to walk at a quick pace toward the house of the orcs.

She reached up to knock on the door, but it opened before her knuckles could find purchase. G'Nash stood in the doorway and she could see her father behind him. "Are we ready to go?" Gh'Rys could be heard, but not seen from behind the two massive bodies that blocked the exit of the home.

"How many orcs are going with us?" She asked, as the small group entered the house.

Gh'Rys stood with his staff held tight in his hand, his animal skin cloak pinned at his neck, and he shook his head. "There are three of us going, wolf maiden. Me, G'Nash and my eldest grandchild Lo'Nash. The others are still trying to recover from their most recent defeat."

Revalor shrugged. "Just try to not get in our way," he declared, pushing through to the center of them. "Are we ready to go? Once we are out of Y'Melenor, I'm not coming back until we have reached the marshlands. We will not be returning to the city just because you forgot something," he declared, looking at the orcs.

"We are ready, elf. Let's go," Gh'Rys scoffed as the elves whispered an incantation and a gust of wind swirled around them.

Isabella watched as the foyer of the house they stood in disappeared through the whirling vortex and was replaced with a forest. The orcs heaved at being transported in such a way. Her father was disoriented and placed a hand on his head as he steadied himself. The elves checked their belongings to make sure everything was where it needed to be. Isabella exhaled a soft sigh. Since the darkness of Bahaal was purged from her, she no longer felt the effects of magic being used on her. "We should get moving. I don't want to lose daylight," she said, looking up to see the early morning sun that peeked through the small gaps between the treetops.

Isabella walked ahead of the group, the dense forest was barely an obstacle for her as she leaped across an enormous root that was protruding from the ground and she sniffed heavily of the air. The trip felt familiar to her, she didn't recognize the forest, but there was something about the direction they were going. The elves were leaping from tree branch to tree branch and she could hear the heavy footfalls of those moving behind her.

The group rushed as quickly as they could, but the sun was starting to fade and the wildlife were beginning to encircle them. She didn't know how much further Bog'Alor was, but traveling at night in the forest was ill-advised. She came to a halt. Lowering her body she sniffed heavily, picking up the scent of the creatures that were watching them from within the shadows and she could hear her group inching closer to her, but it was her father that reached her first.

"Everything alright, daughter?" Torgath asked, inhaling deeply through his nose and slowly exhaling from his mouth.

Isabella nodded her agreement. "It's getting dark. We should make a camp and wait for daylight," she announced loudly for all to hear as she turned to the treetops.

She whistled, a call that Revalor had taught her. It was how the elvish rangers communicated without giving away their position and as her call echoed off the trees the elves descended down around them just as the orcs emerged from within the forest.

G'Nash was the first, followed by the others, and Gh'Rys was the last. Revalor examined each one, he could see how they were each panting for breath, but Torgath looked to be unfazed by it. The elvish ranger shook his head. "You are remarkable," he exclaimed, stepping closer to the farmer. "You are as big as them, but as swift as an elf," he observed, turning his gaze to Isabella. "I can see where you get your strength from," he remarked, smiling at Isabella.

"If you think I am impressive, you should see her mother," Torgath said with a light hearted chuckle.

The old shaman quickly found a log to sit upon, coughed violently as he tried to catch the breath that was stolen from him, and he sucked air through his mouth. "It's not much further now, but we shouldn't try it until dawn. We will need the light of the sun if we hope to stay out of the marshland's death traps," he advised, looking to his grandchildren. "Go fetch us some wood so that we can build a fire to keep us warm and keep the wild animals at bay."

Lo'Nash and G'Nash went separate ways to do as their grandfather commanded. Torgath sat down beside the orc shaman. "We will keep watch from above," Revalor said as the elvish rangers leaped back into the trees.

Isabella released a sigh as wood was brought back by the two orcs and a fire was quickly built. She watched as the orange flame danced around. She thought about the time before the vortex, the story that Uthric told her and how their campfire then changed to show them images of what he was describing. She then thought of her mother and how distraught she was over Kirkland before she left. As she thought of her brother, she remembered how he used to be before the witch of the woods used her spell. She knew that her brother always had a fixation with magic. His eyes would always light up to hear that a suspected wizard was in the village and how he would often obtain books from them to read. He was destined for great things, but because of her he was in a never-ending slumber.

"What's wrong?" G'Nash asked, taking a seat beside her.

Isabella shook her head without looking at him. "Just thinking," she admitted with a sigh.

"Thinking about home?" G'Nash asked, pulling free some elvish bread and breaking it.

Isabella gave a nervous nod. "I am worried about my family that was left behind. When the vortex took us," she paused to exhale. She had told the story more than once and she looked up to G'Nash, who had heard it on more than one occasion, but the half-orc looked at her while breaking the bread and handing half of it to her.

"I understand the reasoning for your worry, Wulgar," he admitted, taking a bite out of his portion. "We will find a way to stop the blood god and get you home. I swear it."

Isabella's heart raced causing her face to flush. She didn't know how to respond to the promise. She flashed an awkward smile and pushed her hair behind her ear as she looked down to the bread in her hands. "Do you think we will make it to Bog'Alor by morrow's end?" She asked in an attempt to change the subject.

G'Nash gave her a nod as he finished his portion of the bread. "I have never been to Bog'Alor, but from what my grandfather said it shouldn't be much further. The passage through the overgrown trees is what has slowed us. If we all could walk as swiftly as elves then we would have probably already made it, but some of us are heavy of foot," he said, looking around at those who were lying beside the campfire to sleep. "You should rest, Wulgar. We do not know what comes or how we are to gain the trust of NaShorn. You need to be prepared for anything," he said, looking back at her. "I will watch over the camp."

Isabella was reluctant, but there was something about the half-orc that just made her feel safe. She was comfortable around him and she knew that everything was going to be fine with him to protect her. She yawned, her fatigue catching up. She sniffed the air making sure that none of the creatures lurking in the shadows had moved any closer. She laid over on her side, pulled her knees up to her chest, and just listened to the sounds of the forest. She knew the predators stalking their camp were being held at bay by the elves, the campfire provided adequate light to assist G'Nash should any sneak past the keen sight of the archers, and with a soft sigh, she drifted off to slumber.

"Isabella?" The voice of Revalor woke her from her slumber and she slowly opened her eyes to see the elf standing over her. "There is something you need to see," he exclaimed, extending his hand to help her up.

She rubbed the sleep from her eyes as she yawned. "Where are the others?" She asked, sleepily while looking around.

Revalor gave her a nod. "They are waiting for you," he declared.

Isabella was dumbfounded at his remark. "What do you mean?" She asked in bewilderment.

"It's probably best if you see for yourself, wolf maiden," Revalor said, ducking under a low hanging branch and stepping free of the forest.

Isabella gasped as she looked out over the marshlands of Bog'Alor. Even though the houses were no longer there and the pristine waters were murky, she recognized the place. It was her home, it was Sparrow's Lake, but the countless dead that had fallen during the battles of long ago had turned it into a wasteland. A soft melody filled the air and she could see the others of her group tied up and laying on the ground. They struggled against their restraints to break free, but the elvish archers stood over them.

"What's the meaning of this?" Isabella asked, stepping back from Revalor, but keeping her eyes on the others.

Revalor shook his head. "Can't you hear it?" He asked from a smile. "They are calling to us," he said, closing his eyes and inhaling deeply.

"Have you lost your mind?" She asked harshly, but realized what he meant.

She could hear the soft melody. Once she focused on the words, she could tell it wasn't a song being sung, but a spell being cast. *I can shield you from the effects of the magic, champion, but you will have to deal with those enthralled by it yourself. The spell affects the emotions of those that hear it. It is easy for people to mask their true feelings, put on a fake smile, and pretend that they are not on the verge of breaking, but the spell shows their true self. Their anger will burn at them, their hatred will consume them, their love will suffocate them, their sadness will drown them and, in the end, it will take their lives. If you don't stop it,* Lucian's voice cautioned her within her head.

Isabella nodded her agreement to the wolf spirit as she widened her stance before the elf. "Revalor!" She yelled out. "You need to stop this," she declared, charging toward the archer, but she missed with her attack.

Revalor swiftly dodged her. He brought up his knee and smashed it into her stomach, knocking the wind from her. She fell to the ground, coughing violently as he stepped back away from her and nocked an arrow in his bow. "Why would you stand with orcs?" He asked, looking back at those he had tied up and back to her. "They eat our kind. They can't be trusted, even the half-orcs are still orcs."

Isabella pushed herself upright, she was fighting to regain her composure, but stood valiant against him. "I don't fully understand who the orcs used to be. I wasn't there during the Great Banishing. I wasn't there when they were created and I haven't seen any of the battles that transpired before the wizard prime sent them away. I'm not going to pretend that I have read books about them or that I cared enough to hear about their history when the races were brought to this plane, but what I do know is this."

"I was stranded here by a vortex that pulled me through Dorcha'Helvetti. I was cursed by the blood god that almost drove me mad, but through it all G'Nash has shown me nothing but respect and through that he has earned my trust. Out of respect to your grandmother, Aleesia, I will not let you die here, but I will also not let you kill those who have put their faith in me. The choice is yours to make, elf!" She declared.

Isabella could feel her body changing through the anger. She growled as her bones cracked and popped. They were reforming. Her fingernails fell off turning into claws, her nose grew into a snout, her teeth became sharp fangs, and the bones in her legs reformed to be more wolf-like. She didn't understand what was happening. Her anger was becoming fear as she became a monster and she could feel tears forming. *We are becoming one, my champion. Don't fight against me. Let me give you the power you will need to overcome this. Worry not, this transformation isn't permanent, but it is something that you will be able to call upon in the future. Just as long as you don't fight against me now,* Lucian declared within her head.

She didn't know if she should trust the wolf spirit, but she did know that she lacked the power to stop the elves alone. She gritted her teeth, a low growl emerged from her throat, and she gave into the power that was filling her body. Her transformation was complete. She unleashed a bone-chilling howl as she pointed a claw at Revalor. "Make your choice, now!" She declared through a voice she did not recognize.

"Allies to the orcs must be slain," Revalor declared, releasing the arrow from his bow and quickly nocking another.

Isabella snatched the arrow from the sky, snapping it in her fur-covered hand. She charged toward him, dodging the others as they fired on her, and she slashed at Revalor. The elf swiftly leaped back, but he wasn't prepared for her to be so quick with another attack. The black claws sliced through the bark of his leather armor and she sunk her teeth into the wooden gauntlet of his left arm. She could taste his blood. The upper arm was covered by the bark, but his under arm was only protected by leather. She shook him violently causing him to release his bow.

"Stop!" Vivienne cried out as Isabella slung Revalor several feet away with ease.

Vivienne rushed over to kneel beside her cousin. "I can break the enchantment," she said, coating her fingers in a green paste and applying it to the lower arm wound that Isabella just gave him. "I will explain soon, but for now we have to dispel the others. This concoction must be applied to a wound for it to work. Can you handle that?" She asked, tossing the small pouch toward the wolf maiden.

Isabella was deflecting the attacks from the other elves, but managed to catch the bag. She reached into the bag and gathered a healthy portion on her claws. She looked at the greenish mixture and gave a nod to Vivienne before she charged toward the others. They fired quickly at her, but with her new found speed and agility she found it easy to dodge their projectiles. She swiftly danced through the enchanted elves. Letting her claws rake across the vulnerable parts of their tree-bark armor and only using enough force to break the skin so that the concoction could mix into the bloodstream.

She made quick work of the elves, but as the last one wallowed on the ground, she felt a sudden sharp pain in several parts of her body. She thought she had dodged all of them, but in her haste she hadn't noticed that a few of them had found purchase. Despite the pain, she plucked them from her body as she walked over to Vivienne and kneeled beside her. "Is he alright?" She asked, tossing the last of the arrows away from her.

Vivienne held tight to her cousin. "He is resting, but what about you?" She asked, looking over to the wolf maiden.

Isabella looked down at her claws and fur-covered body. "Lucian said it wasn't permanent, but I had to do something to keep them safe," she declared, closing her eyes.

Isabella could feel her anger subsiding and her body was once again changing. Her bones cracked, popping back into position, her snout shrank, her fangs retracted, and though it sounded excruciating, she felt no pain as she took the form of a girl once more. Her clothes were torn to rags that barely covered her. "Let me help," Vivienne said, whispering an incantation, mending the clothes.

Isabella released a sigh of relief. "Thank you," she exclaimed, scratching the back of her head. "Why aren't you affected by the spell?"

"Who says it didn't?" Vivienne asked, looking up from her cousin to the wolf maiden. "I was drowning in sorrow over my grandmother, but I quickly realized that something wasn't right. I used the Eucilipsis Flower on myself. That's what I was doing while you were fighting my cousin," she admitted, pushing the hair out of his face.

Isabella released a sigh. "I'm sorry. I can't believe Revalor attacked the orcs," she declared, looking at those still tied up.

Vivienne shrugged. "Revalor will play nice with all the other races. He will act his part to keep the peace, but deep down he believes that the woodland elves are the superior race."

"You don't believe that?"

Vivienne shook her head. "I believe that each race has a part to play," she paused to look back at those tied up. "Even the orcs have their purposes."

"Can I ask you what a Eucilipsis Flower is?"

"It's a rare flower that is grown only in Y'Melenor. Its magical properties drive back that of enchantment," Vivienne declared, inhaling deeply. "You better use it on the others before they break free of the ropes."

Isabella agreed as she stood up and made her way over to those tied up. The elvish archers that she freed from the spell were rolling around in pain as the spell was being broken and she looked back at Vivienne. She knew that the elf maiden must've undergone the same outcome when she used the concoction on herself, but you couldn't tell it by looking at her. She released a sigh as she kneeled down beside her father. She could hear him whimpering with his face buried in the ground. Pushing him over to his side she could see that his face was already contorted in pain, a stream flooded down his cheeks mixing with the dirt and he gritted his teeth as he tried to break free of the rope. "Untie me, daughter!" He demanded through clenched teeth. "Your mother calls me. I must get to her!"

"I'm sorry, father," Isabella said, slicing a small wound on his shoulder and rubbing the paste upon it. "We will see mother again soon, but I need you now."

Isabella placed a soft kiss upon the side of her father's forehead and he looked at her with the saddest eyes she had ever seen. "Daughter. I miss her," he exclaimed before the agonizing pain took him.

She released a sigh as she moved to G'Nash next, but the half-orc just shook his head. "I do not require the remedy, Wulgar. The spell has no effect on me."

"How is that possible?"

"I have come to terms with what I am," he admitted nonchalantly. "I have spent my whole life hearing that I am an abomination, that I have no place amongst the orcs, but I have no hatred for my own kind or any other race for that matter. I seek to enlighten all that race should not be a factor on how someone should be treated. That's why I didn't fight against the elves when they attacked us. My brother on the other hand," he said, looking over to Lo'Nash who was tied up beside him. "He killed three of them before he was brought down."

Isabella moved to undo the bonds of the half-orc, but was stopped by the sound of battle. She looked out where it was coming from and she could finally see the marsh of Bog'Alor, but it felt familiar to her. She shook her head as she realized it was where her home was back in her plane, but the pristine lake was gone. Not much water remained, the stream that fed into it was blocked and she could see what looked like phantoms fighting before her.

Orcs rode on creatures with black wings as they clashed against elves who were riding on lions with honey gold wings, but the sky wasn't the only place of battle. Beasts of war were stomping across the field, carrying towers on their back, and the dead were piling up. Their blood soaked into the ground. The streams of crimson flowed in every direction and the sight of it was disturbing. She wanted to turn her gaze from it, but she lacked the strength to do so. She helplessly watched as elves, orcs, giants, beasts, and even some humans were cut down during the onslaught.

"Lucian, What is going on here?" She asked dumbfounded.

You are seeing an echo of the past, champion. This is the battle that tainted this land. It was the first to happen once the spell was cast by Aster, but it wasn't the last. Many heroes fell here that day. I will shield your mind from it so that you are not trapped within the past, Lucian said and with the blink of her eye the vision of the past faded from her sight.

G'Nash flexed his arms causing the ropes that bound him to snap and he leaped up to wrap his arms around her. "Are you alright, Wulgar?"

Isabella shook her head. She was far from alright, but she couldn't dwell on the things that were bothering her now. She had to free the others and find NaShorn before nightfall. She did not want to be in Bog'Alor during the night. She handed some of the paste to G'Nash. "You have to mix this with the blood of your grandfather. Make a small cut on his shoulder and rub it in. This will break the spell of this place. I will do the same to your brother."

G'Nash stuffed his fingers into the paste to coat them and moved to do as she asked. Gh'Rys wasn't just tied up, but he was gagged too. The two of them had been rendered unconscious by the elves before they were restricted by the ropes and Isabella found herself wondering why they hadn't already killed them before she arrived. She made a small cut across the shoulder of Lo'Nash, black blood oozed from the wound and she quickly rubbed the paste into the wound.

The ground trembled underneath her. She could hear the heavy stomp of something charging toward her and she looked out and saw another phantom coming at her. The beast was a rhyno and was quickly getting closer to her, but it looked different than the other phantoms she had seen before. *Move champion!* Lucian screamed and she instinctively leaped over Lo'Nash to get clear of the charging beast.

The rhyno came to a stop, but turned to look at her and G'Nash rushed to stand at her side. The beast snorted as it looked at them. "Who are you?" Its question came from a serene, but gruff voice.

"I am Isabella Strongfellow, the champion of Lucian and I have traveled far to see you NaShorn," she said, taking a knee in respect.

The rhyno snorted while shaking its head. "Why have you come, wolf champion?"

"The veil between the planes is weakening and the blood god grows stronger with each passing second. I need the help of the animal spirits to keep him contained," she admitted, slowly lifting her eyes to look at the rhyno. "I have come to ask that you lend your strength to me so that we can prevent his escape."

NaShorn snorted as it laughed. "If the veil breaks there is no containing the blood god. We were created to keep him in his prison, but the only way for us to do that is by keeping the veil from falling. His power is too great for us, but Dorcha'Helvetti siphons his power, keeps him weak enough that we can hold him back and keep him from bringing death upon the world."

"So, you won't help us?" She asked, through the pain she felt in her heart.

"I never said I wouldn't help you, wolf champion," NaShorn said, stomping the ground before her. "But your sights are set on the wrong target. We will need to prevent the veil from falling. If we can stop that then we can contain Bahaal in the prison designed for him."

"Then you will help us?"

NaShorn tossed his head back in agreement. "I will lend you my strength, but like Lucian I will need a champion. Have you been told the difference between those we lend our power to and our champion? We have granted mortals a small portion of our power so that they can do magic, the druids of the world, but a champion is a spiritual bond between us and the mortal. It's a bond that can never be broken. It's also a risk for us. Should the mortal succumb to death then our spirit will vanquish with them. That's why I can't champion someone without them showing me they are worthy. I do not wish to die any time soon," he declared, looking around at the people that followed her. "Have you brought me a worthy champion?"

G'Nash gritted his teeth and stepped in front of her. "I will be your champion, NaShorn!" He declared, standing with clenched fist.

NaShorn scrutinized the half-orc intensely. "What makes you think you are worthy to be my champion?"

"I have fought my whole life. I have stood shoulder to shoulder with those that despise my existence to protect my home, to defend those who hate me, and I did it not expecting to receive gratitude or acceptance from them. I did it because they were my family. They couldn't see beyond the fact my father was not orc, but I could see beyond their hate. My strength comes from my heart and I will show you just how strong I am if I have to. We need your power to save this world!" G'Nash declared, taking his stance to wait for the rhyno to charge him.

NaShorn lifted himself up on his back legs and crashed down on the ground. "If your words are true, then you would make a great champion, but taking a person at their word alone would be folly and I haven't survived this long by taking unnecessary risks," he said, tossing his head back and pacing ahead of them. "I will have the truth of your heart, I will see the darkest parts of your mind. I will test your body's endurance and if it is lacking, then you will perish. Do you accept your fate regardless of the outcome?" He asked with a snort.

G'Nash glanced at Isabella. Taking in a deep breath he flashed her a half-smile and turned his attention to the rhyno spirit. "If I prove to you that I am worthy, then will you join us?" He asked and the rhyno nodded. "Then do what you have to!" He declared loudly.

"Wait!" Isabella moved to protest, but her words fell on deaf ears as the rhyno stomped the ground.

The horn flashed a brilliant white as the spirit raised up on its back legs and a streak of lightning struck the tip of its horn as the rhyno slammed its front feet back down. The world shook, the ground cracked from the beast and it traveled toward a stalwart G'Nash. The proud half-orc stood, with legs shoulder length apart, his arms were tensed making his muscles bulge, and he waited for the test of the rhyno, but as the crack reached him, it stopped.

G'Nash never flinched, he looked like a statue as he waited for the test to begin, but Isabella had no way of knowing what to expect. She shook her head. *What's happening Lucian? Is he going to be alright?* She asked the wolf spirit.

NaShorn is testing the endurance of the half-orc. Right now, inside his mind G'Nash is reliving every single harsh moment of his life and then some. We have no true way of knowing that someone is worthy, but the rhyno believes this will help, Lucian answered patiently.

Isabella watched as a stream of tears poured down the face of the half-orc. She remembered seeing what all he had endured when she used the spell to learn his language and she didn't know how he had survived it then, but now to go through it all a second time. She turned her head, looking away from the pain and suffering he was enduring.

"All of this didn't break me when I was younger, it doesn't break me when I think back on it, and it will not break me now!" G'Nash yelled as his body shook, but he continued to stand in defiance to the spell.

NaShorn's horn flashed again and G'Nash stumbled slightly, but never dropped to a knee. The rhyno tossed its head around before speaking out loud. "You have shown to have the endurance to withstand the harshest of storms. You have a great compassion where others would have cursed the world and turned to darkness. Your loyalty has no boundaries, even for those who have shown that they despise you. I admire you, G'Nash of Black Root Clan and if you accept I will take you as my champion."

"I accept," G'Nash answered quickly.

NaShorn shook his head. "Do not accept without knowing all the details, would-be champion. If we try to join and something goes wrong it will kill the both of us. There is no way of knowing what could go wrong or why it would, but if you accept that you might die this day, then we can try."

"I would gladly give my life for….," G'Nash said, but paused only briefly to look at her and then to the rhyno. "….for this quest in saving the planes from the blood god. Do what you must!" He declared, puffing out his chest to ready himself.

NaShorn lowered his horn and charged toward the half-orc. "Trust in me. Put your faith in the knowledge that I am not wanting to harm you, but help you. We have to join as one. Our spirits must unite for you to become my champion," he declared as he collided with the half-orc and a brilliant light burst from them.

G'Nash groaned as the spirit of the rhyno slowly pushed into his body. Isabella couldn't imagine the pain he was going through, but she was also confused. When she joined with Lucian it was different. The wolf came to her in a dream, it spoke to her and then disappeared. She didn't even know that they came together to where she could use magic until she actually used it on the bandits and then Uthric explained the situation to her, but here she is watching the animal spirit unite with that of her friend.

Our union was done differently, champion. I did not want to break your soul and so you were given my power slowly. This is more dangerous, but if the two of them survive, then your friend will be given the full power of NaShorn, Lucian explained calmly.

An immense explosion knocked her from her feet as the rhyno spirit was completely engulfed into the body of G'Nash. She pushed herself up where she could see, but the half-orc had dropped to both knees. She rushed over to him, he looked lifeless and unmoving. She placed a hand on his broad shoulder. "G'Nash! You have to be alive!" She screamed as she shook him, but the body of the half-orc slumped to the ground. "He can't be dead," she cried as she collapsed on his chest.

She was overcome with emotions, but a gentle callused hand gripped hold of her shoulder and squeezed it. She could feel the chest of the half-orc heavy as he drew in a breath. "I am not ready to leave you, Wulgar. I made you a promise and I am not one to break those," he declared. His voice was weak, but he was alive.

Isabella was happy, but she couldn't stop the water that was flowing from her eyes. She smashed her hand against his thick chest. "If you ever scare me like that again. I'll kill you myself," she said through a sniffle.

The echoing sound of a horn drew their attention across the marshland. Over the soggy, murky ground they could see an enormous army standing and waiting. At the front of them were five riders, the one out front was dressed in black leather and a whip of black was curled up on his hip, but his porcelain face was uncovered for the world to see. His platinum hair swayed in the wind and his light violet eyes sparkled as he smiled at them. The horse he was riding was as black as a moonless night, but the eyes were crimson red.

At his side sat two warriors each. The one closest to his right was dressed in tattered robes of brown. He looked human with long, white hair that adorned his head and face. His eyes were cloudy in color, he held tight to a tome in his right hand, and a staff in his left. She moved her glance to the slender elf that was sitting beside him. The elf was garbed in tattered green clothing, a crown of thorns rested upon his head, he held tight to a bow, a large quiver of arrows were on his back, and his eyes were cloudy.

On the other side of the porcelain skinned elf sat a dwarf with skin unlike the ones she recognized from home. His dark black hair stretched down past his shoulders, in his hands was a small warhammer, and on his head was a throne of bronze. He had bronze rings in his beard and his eyes were also cloudy. At his side was an orc, his fangs pierced with thick golden rings, two emeralds embedded at the tip, and his body was covered in scars, but his eyes matched the others that were on horseback. She couldn't outright see the others that lined up in battle formations behind them, but she could imagine that their eyes were the same.

A soft wind blew through their ranks and it carried a familiar scent to Isabella. Her eyes went wide as she came to realize where she recalled it from. She rushed over to Lo'Nash. He had remained unresponsive to the Eucilipsis Flower remedy. Where the others had screamed out in pain, he was motionless and as she turned him over, she could see why. The orc was no longer breathing, his chest had stopped its function of rising and falling indicating that he was alive. She looked out to G'Nash who was kneeling at the side of his grandfather who had woken from the enchantment, but was now frantic.

Gh'Rys was muttering something and all she could make out from it was the name. Du'Nash. She looked out across the field to see the orc that sat upon the steed beside the dwarf. She didn't know what the legendary warrior looked like, but she knew from the memories of G'Nash that he had died a very long time ago. She looked down at Lo'Nash, then back to the orc warrior atop a horse, and then to G'Nash. "They all have the same scent," she whispered as she realized the scent was carried by all those that stumbled upon their camp that night, the night before they were brought to Y'Melenor and she was dumbfounded.

G'Nash lifted his grandfather to his feet. "You speak nonsense, grandfather. Du'Nash died. That can't be him," he declared, shaking the old orc.

"I'm telling you it is him!" Gh'Rys declared, loudly. "I don't know how, but that is him. He has come back."

"That's not the worst of it," Revalor announced, his voice still weak and his body wavering as he approached. "That is King Virion Regynald with them. We exiled him after he attacked a kingdom under control of the druhir. We lost many great warriors that day and I can see them all with him now. There is my grandfather, Yllaven Simimar."

Isabella looked out at the steadfast enemy and shook her head. "Why aren't they attacking?" She asked, looking at those around her.

"They are observing us," Vivienne declared. "They are watching for what we will do now that we have seen them."

Revalor struggled, but he managed to nock an arrow in his bow. "We have no choice. They know how to get in Y'Melenor. We have to stop them!" He declared loudly and the other elvish archers nocked arrows in their own bows.

Isabella looked around at her makeshift army. They were all still fatigued from being within the enthrall of the spell. They could barely pull their bowstrings back, Gh'Rys was barely standing, and her father was still weeping on the ground. She shook her head. "Our only hope is to take a warning to Y'Melenor. Take the others back to the city. Tell the king of what is coming and we will try to give you as much time as we can," she announced as she closed her eyes and prepared for her transformation.

Her skin stretched, tearing apart to reveal dark fur beneath it and her nose became a snout with razor sharp teeth lining both the top and bottom. The bones in her legs snapped causing the knees to turn backwards, her fingernails turned into black claws, her blue eyes became emerald green, and she unleashed a howl as her transformation was complete. She growled as she looked over to see G'Nash going through a change of his own.

The half-orc's skin turned a stone gray, his muscles doubled in size, his snout had a large horn at the very end, and a smaller one appeared just behind it. The clothes he was wearing shredded as he grew in size, his black eyes grew smaller as he snorted white smoke from his nose, and he flexed his arms, admiring his taut muscles. He unleashed a roar as his transformation came to an end.

The two of them stood in the way of the undead army that wished to cross the marshland on their way to the forest. She could hear Revalor gathering the others, helping her father and Gh'Rys from the ground. She looked back at him. Without words being said, he understood what she needed and he gave her a nod. He quickly made his way back into the forest with the others, leaving the two spirit animal champions to do what they were meant to do.

Isabella snarled at the undead, but then looked to her ally. "Are you with me, G'Nash?"

"Only death will remove me from your side, Wulgar and even then it won't be without a fight!" He declared loudly.

The commander of the army held up his hand, his smirk never fading, and as he brought his arm forward, the army at their back charged toward them. Isabella's growl turned to a howl as the two of them charged toward the army.

Chapter 5
Escaping Sapphire

The battle with the undead was intense for just two. Even with their magic it was taking a toll on them and Isabella knew that she didn't have much more to give. She slashed at them, sunk her teeth into their rotting flesh, tossed them into the others, and used them as meat shields to block the rain of arrows that came from the undead archers. She was unaware of just how many they had killed, but their numbers seemed to never dwindle. She stabbed her claws into the chest of one, held it up to let the arrows penetrate its back and then tossed it into the crowd that was closing in on her.

"I've had it!" Screamed G'Nash as he stomped his foot and the ground began to separate under his command.

She watched as a great divide between them and the undead army formed. Anything standing where the ground was separating was at the mercy of nature. Trees from the forest, huge chunks of dirt, and the undead that were bent on attacking them, all fell to the depths of the canyon. The undead army was lined up looking out at them and the sound of bows being fired filled the air. Isabella took cover behind G'Nash, the half-orc's new skin was tough to pierce. The arrows snapped as they hit him and he turned to look down at her. "We need to get back to Y'Melenor. We can't defend the city," he announced, turning his head to watch more arrows fly at him.

Isabella's heart sank. She still held hope that they could turn it around, but as she looked around her friend, she could see the leader of them. He looked so regal sitting on top of his steed. He was unnerved by those lost in the battle and he held out his hand. A small orb of pale green light filled it. She could see him smirk as he tossed the orb into the sky. The soft song that once filled the air ceased and it was replaced with that of those buried beneath the marshland coming to life.

They could see the ground heaving beneath their feet and G'Nash grabbed her shoulders. "We have to retreat!" He screamed over the sound of the arrows snapping against his back.

Isabella shook her head as she looked to the tree line that would take them back to Y'Melenor and she slowly agreed that their only option was to retreat. The two of them made their way from the divide. She walked in front of him so that the arrows couldn't reach her and the two of them entered the protection of the forest. They were away from the enemy and the arrows of the archers couldn't reach them here, so they transformed back into their normal forms to conserve their magic. Their clothes were tattered, they barely hid their nakedness, but they didn't expect to need clothes and they didn't have time to worry over trivial things.

Isabella adjusted what she had left of a shirt to make sure she was covered, pulled up her pants and held to one side with her hand, but G'Nash wasn't as lucky as she was. His animal form was thicker than the wolf and nothing of his previous clothing survived. He looked around. Lo'Nash was just outside the forest and still tied up, but his clothes were intact. He quickly rushed over, stripping his brother of his pants and putting them on. He could see the warriors of lore rising up from their watery graves. They were disoriented, but looked at him. He shook his head as he rushed back to her and without speaking, the two of them ran back the way they remembered coming from Y'Melenor.

Isabella ran ahead of G'Nash, her slender body making it easy for her to avoid the obstacles that slowed her friend, but she knew that they couldn't get into Y'Melenor without the aid of a woodland elf and she just hoped that she could catch up to Revalor before they entered the city. She ran, leaping over tree roots, slapping low hanging branches out of the way, she only paused to sniff the air, searching for the familiar scent of her father and running in the direction it was going.

She didn't know the distance between them and the undead army or how much longer it was going to take for her to reach Y'Melenor. She paused to lean against a tree, her lungs were burning, her legs ached, and the forest was blanketed in darkness, but she could see clearly thanks to the wolf spirit that was united with her and she waited for G'Nash.

"Is something wrong, Wulgar?" He asked while trying to catch his breath.

"Just need to catch my breath," she admitted, inhaling a deep breath and exhaling slowly. "Father's scent is getting stronger. They can't be much further ahead of us," she exclaimed, but paused as her ears perked up and she sniffed heavily. "King Jaspen?" She asked, turning to look in the direction the scent was coming from.

King Jaspen dropped to the ground from within the trees. He was dressed in a crown of twisted maple decorated with gorgeous gems, dark green garments that were covered in thick bark, a long sword hung to his hip, a bow crafted from white wood was wrapped around his body, and a large quiver of arrows hung from his back on the opposite side of his sword. He looked at the two of them. "I was told that you two were fighting an army. I was coming to help," he declared, looking around.

"We have to get back to Y'Melenor!" Isabella declared taking a step closer to the king, but being held back by an arrow that sunk into the ground at her feet. "I'm not going to hurt you. I am trying to warn you."

"Revalor said that the army they encountered at the marshland was one created from the undead. We couldn't be certain that you hadn't succumbed to them."

Isabella rolled her eyes. She understood his concern, but they didn't have time to fight amongst themselves and she shook her head. "How many warriors did you bring with you?"

King Jaspen's look showed his unwillingness to answer the question, but Isabella didn't have time to convince him. "The orcs that were with us are a part of the undead army. I didn't realize it before, but after fighting against them they all carry the same scent of death. Please tell me that you didn't bring every warrior from Y'Melenor," she begged through clenched teeth, but she could see by the wide eyes of the king that it was exactly what he did and she looked to G'Nash who pushed back his shoulders making them pop.

I'm ready for round two. Let's go and pray that we aren't too late," he declared, stepping closer to the king, but paused as he could hear bows being pulled taut.

King Jaspen held up his hand and whistled. They could hear the others within the trees using their magic to go back to the city. "We have to hurry," he declared, closing his eyes and whispering the incantation that would teleport them to the city.

The wind swirled around them and the forest melted, but as the city of Y'Melenor took shape they could see it burning. Cries of pain echoed out, the Ignis Fatuus was scurrying around as Isabella looked around at the carnage. She could see countless bodies of elves littering the ground, their lifeless bodies scarred with gruesome cuts. Some had teeth marks in their flesh, some had a face frozen in fear, and others were twisted in agony, but all of them were dead. She sniffed the air, hopeful of finding the scent of her father or even her friends that were left behind, but all she was greeted with was smoke, blood, and death.

"I have to go! I have to save as many of my people as I can," King Jaspen declared as he stumbled forward. "If you manage to escape this, head east. On the third rising of the sun, we will travel to the lands of *Tanzanite*. There we will seek refuge with the *High Elves*."

"Shouldn't we stick together?" Isabella called out to him.

King Jaspen gritted his teeth. "I'm going to the royal hall to save my family and I would suggest you do the same. Revalor took your father to the orc house," he said, disappearing into the smoke.

"Are you going to check on your grandfather?" Isabella asked, looking at the half-orc.

G'Nash shook his head. "I'm going with you. As Gh'Rys has told me many times, he can save himself and doesn't require my help."

Isabella knew the struggle he endured growing up as a half-orc within the tribe and she placed her hand softly on the side of his cheek, but without saying anything the two of them made their way through the carnage of Y'Melenor. She looked around at all the dead elves. The same ones that were whispering harsh things about her and her friends just a few days ago, but now they lay silent in pools of their own blood. Though they didn't make her feel welcomed within the city, her heart still ached for them, but she didn't have time to dwell on her feelings for the lives lost now.

She could smell the stench of flesh burning as her house came into sight. Her mind raced with the images of her father being slain in the carnage and it was more than she could bear. Weeping she continued to run, but outside she could see the mutilated bodies of the twin orc sons of Du'Nash. Gu'Nash was feathered, his right arm had been cut from his body, his head was cut from his shoulders, and he lay lifeless on the ground. Bu'Nash had fallen prey to the same fate as his brother, but his head was still attached, although only barely, and both of them were burning.

Around them lay dozens of elvish warriors. She could hear fighting coming from within the home and without thought she rushed toward the door. G'Nash was behind her, but she didn't wait for him as she put her shoulder into the smooth wooden obstacle that stood in her way. She burst into the house. She could see that her father was locked in battle with Lu'Nash and though the orc was the smallest of the brothers, he was holding his own against the massive Torgath. They weren't using weapons, instead, their hands were locked in a test of strength. Foam formed around the mouth of Lu'Nash, she could see the anger in her father's eyes, and he roared as he forced the orc to his knees.

"Do you think you will keep me from her? Do you think you can stop me from getting back to my beloved? You are mistaken and I'll kill all who try!" Torgath screamed as he drove his forehead down onto the nose of the orc and blood gushed forth.

Gritting his teeth, the enormous man tightened his grip on Lu'Nash's throat and the sound of bones crunching echoed out. The orc cried out in pain, but Torgath wasn't done as he twisted to the side, lifting his enemy off the ground and slamming him into the wall beside them. He had released his grip as the orc got airborne and he let him smash through the wall into the room next to them.

Isabella gasped at what she was seeing. She knew that her father possessed an unnatural strength, but she had never seen him so angry and so overcome with bloodlust. The fury that was pouring from him with each hit was unnerving and she looked over at G'Nash.

The half-orc was twitching, she could only imagine the torment that he was feeling and she placed a hand on the back of his shoulder. As she turned back, she saw her father saunter through the hole that was made, straddle the beaten orc that was scrambling to get up, and start slamming his fist down into the face of his enemy.

"Father, that is enough!" She screamed and snapped the behemoth back to reality. "What has gotten into you?" She asked, putting her shoulder in front of the half-orc.

"I'm so sorry, I don't know what came over me" Torgath uttered, looking down at the black blood that soaked his hands and then up to them.

G'Nash shook his head. "I wanted to intervene. Of all my siblings Lu'Nash was the only one who was ever kind to me and had it not been for NaShorn I would have tried to stop you. The rhyno held me in place. Told me that my brother was long gone from this world and the creature that Torgath was killing was nothing more than an empty shell. Still," he paused to choke down his emotions and closed his eyes. "The pain of seeing him beaten wasn't easy," he admitted with a heavy sigh.

Torgath slung his hands to clear as much of the blood as he could with the motion and he looked away from them in shame. "I'm sorry. I tried to talk reason into him as he attacked, but when he stabbed me with the knife, I lost control and all I could see was rage. The thought of never seeing my family again was more than I could bear and I gave in to my anger. I'm sorry for that," he apologized, turning his gaze slowly back to them and shaking his head.

Isabella released a heavy sigh. "It was frightening to see you that way and I hope to never witness it again," she said, looking away from her father shamefully.

Torgath released a heavy sigh. "I am truly sorry that you had to witness that, daughter and to you, G'Nash. I am sorry for the pain I've brought you," he declared, turning his gaze to the ground.

G'Nash gave an understanding nod, but held his tongue as Isabella looked around. "Where is Irick and Uthric?"

Torgath took a deep breath. "Uthric was still at the library, but I haven't seen Irick. I'll go see that the wizard is alright. Think you can track the boy?"

Isabella just gave him a nod as she stepped up to the side. "Uthric and I will wait for you at the library. Try to hurry, Bella. We have to escape this place," he declared before stepping past the half-orc and leaving the house.

G'Nash watched the mountain of a man as he disappeared into the smoke carrying his enormous scythe. The half-orc turned his attention to her. "Do you want me to go with him?"

Isabella shook her head. Once, she would have asked the half-orc to because she always thought her father too gentle to take care of himself, but now she could see just how strong he really is. She rubbed the moisture from her eyes and walked out of the house. "We have to hurry. This city couldn't have just fallen to the resurrected orcs that we brought. We have to figure out what we are up against and find Irick," she announced before rushing back into the burning city.

As they ran through Y'Melenor, she still couldn't pick up the scent of her friend, but she could hear the sound of combat echoing through the dark smoke. *This is ridiculous*, she thought, abandoning the search and heading toward the fighting. She quickly came upon the battle. Several undead made up of men, women, and children were slaughtering elvish warriors that were cornered against a burning wall. "For Y'Melenor!" One of the warriors screamed as the corpses piled on top of him, but holding out his hand toward the building. "Grund hear me," he managed to whisper before a small undead child ripped his throat out with its teeth and the building collapsed on them.

Screams drew her attention toward another group. The undead shambled toward the elvish survivors. They had arrows sticking out of their chest, but they weren't showing any signs of stopping and she unleashed a howl that cleared the smoke from around her. The undead turned to look at her, giving the elves the opportunity to deliver a killing blow to their would-be attackers and the lifeless bodies fell to the ground as their heads were cut from their shoulders.

"You need to escape the city. Go east. King Jaspen is gathering all those who escape there. Head for Tanzanite to seek refuge with the High Elves," she announced and they agreed before making their way to a safe place to escape.

G'Nash placed a hand on her shoulder. "We have to give up our search for Irick. If we don't escape soon then we are going to burn with the city," he declared.

Isabella felt a sting in her heart. She knew the half-orc was right, but she didn't want to abandon her friend. He wouldn't even be caught up in all this if it wasn't for her. She begged him to help her reach her father back before the vortex, back before everything got so hectic, and she knew he only agreed because he had a crush on her. Now he is lost in the burning city of Y'Melenor, probably scared and confused. She released another sorrowful howl to the sky.

"This is your fault, Isa," the voice of Irick could be heard, but she couldn't see him because of the smoke.

"Irick?" She called out.

The sound of boots hitting the ground grew louder. She didn't know if it was actually her friend, but whoever it happened to be was coming closer. She widened her stance. If it wasn't Irick she would be ready to fight. Her knees became weak as her friend emerged from within the smoke. He was wearing brown leather, his hair had been shaved completely, at the center of his forehead was painted to have a white eye on it, and he had a sword drawn with blood on it. He carried a look of anger as he sneered at them. "I didn't even want to leave the stable, but you begged me to and I could never tell you no. I love you Isabella Strongfellow. I love you with my entire being, but you could never love me that way could you? He said, pressing closer. Your heart has already been stolen by this half-breed, he accused, snarling at G'Nash. Bahaal promised that if I helped him, he would give me my heart's desire, but you will never be mine. You just won't accept it no matter who tries to will it. I have come to accept that and I have given my heart to another."

The sound of someone approaching echoed out over those dying and to their surprise Vivic emerged to stand at Irick's side. She was dressed in armor made from the bones of a creature that Isabella didn't recognize, she carried two small black blade daggers that curved to a point, and she smiled as she put her arm around the waist of Irick. The two of them shared a kiss before he looked back toward the champions. "Isn't she perfect?"

"She's dead, Irick!" Isabella declared loudly. "Her and her brothers were all resurrected from the dead by that commander we saw in Bog'Alor!"

Irick shook his head. "I know how the spell works, Isa. Doden explained everything. You see, Bahaal told me in the void that brought us here, that if I helped him escape, then he would make you mine, but after seeing you with the half-orc, it was more than I cared to stand and Doden came to me. The druhir showed me that the blood god's power was limited, but not his. He told me that I could have anyone I wanted and he gave me Vivic as proof. You see, he reanimates the body and rekindles the spark of life to bring them back, but the only difference is they are servient to him. They will do anything he asks of them. All because he freed them from the cold grasp of death. So, if I want you, then all I have to do is kill you," he explained with a mischievous smile.

"I will not allow that," G'Nash said as his body started to transform.

"You think I am not prepared for magic?" Irick asked, pulling free a gem and whispering into it.

The gem flashed a brilliant blue and a whirlwind blew through the city pushing away the smoke and putting out the fires that were burning bright. Isabella could finally see all the destruction that had befell the city. Vivic gasped as her lifeless body collapsed to the ground at Irick's feet. The city of Y'Melenor shimmered and the illusion of its majestic scenery faded, revealing that it was all built within the treetops. Large wooden planks made the streets, linking one tree to the other and at the center was a massive ancient tree that Isabella didn't recognize. She shook her head. She didn't understand what Irick had done, but the city looked different and she felt different. She felt like something was missing within her.

G'Nash was dumbfounded. He was in the process of transforming, but something had stopped it. He looked out at Irick and unleashed a throaty growl. "You think I need NaShorn to fight?!" He screamed, charging toward him.

The half-orc drove his shoulder into the stomach of the young man, lifting him off his feet, but as the two of them collided, G'Nash cried out in pain and Isabella watched Irick repeatedly stabbing the side of the half-orc with a small dagger. A stream of crimson poured from seven different wounds as G'Nash tossed Irick away from him and stumbled around trying to keep his feet. The dagger was sticking out of the last wound on his side, buried to the hilt and he groaned in agony as he pulled it free.

"Is that the best you got?" G'Nash asked, spitting blood on the ground and grinning back at him with blood-soaked teeth. "The *troggs* of *Nin'Shire* have hurt me more than this," he declared, but she could see that he was bluffing.

Irick stood from the ground, pulling free another dagger and his longsword. "That so? Want to charge me again? I can promise it will be the last time you ever do something so foolish," he declared, pointing the tip of his sword at the half-orc.

"Stop!" Isabella screamed, causing G'Nash to stop his charge and the two of them looked at her. "It is my fault that you are here, Irick. I used your feelings for me to convince you to come and that was wrong of me, I see that now, but G'Nash has done nothing to you. You want me, you desire me. Well. Come and get me!" She declared, holding her hands out as if she had claws, bending at the knees and taking a transformation stance.

Irick chuckled as he looked at G'Nash. The half-orc had stopped his pursuit, but he was still close by. "You are just trying to distract me so he can finish me."

Isabella shook her head. "G'Nash, go see to father," she demanded, but the half-orc started to oppose. "I can deal with him," she declared and he went to do as she commanded.

"It didn't have to come to this, Isa," Irick announced, tossing his weapons to the side. "All you had to do was give me a chance. Was that asking too much of you?"

Irick charged her, she swiped at him as if she had claws, but he dodged her attack and drove his fist into her face. She stumbled backwards. She had never been punched before so she didn't know what to expect. The attack split her lip causing it to bleed and she dropped to a seat on the ground. She licked the blood from her lip. "That make you feel good? That make you feel more manly?" She asked, standing back up from the ground. "That's the last one," she declared, charging toward him.

Irick threw another attack at her, but she dodged it by ducking and lifted her own fist upward in retaliation, catching him under the chin and causing him to stumble back. The sudden shock of being struck caused him to lose his grip on the gem he was holding and it clanged against the ground coming to a stop at her feet. "This has to end, Irick," she declared, driving her heel down on the gem and shattering it.

The rush of magic washed over her, Y'Melenor shimmered, and it was once again hidden. Irick tossed his hands up in defeat. "What happened to you, Isa? I remember when you didn't even like magic, but now you can't function without it," he said, getting up off the ground.

"You are so selfish!" She declared through clenched teeth. "You would sacrifice everything to appease your desires and not even consider the consequences of that action, Irick. You're right, I couldn't love you. I will do all I can to save this world, even if I have to kill you to do it," she announced as she began to transform again.

Irick shook his head, stung by the insult and charged toward her.

Isabella felt like time had stopped. She was able to see everything that had played out. She saw him lift up the blood covered dagger, conceal it, and now he came toward her with it. Without thought she moved instinctively to the side letting the small blade miss her, but without hesitation she pushed her fingers into his chest as they became claws once more. She could smell the blood pouring from his wounds and feel the warmth of it as it ran the length of her arm, but what got her was the look in her once friend's eyes. He was scared, it was like a veil was lifted from him and he couldn't believe what was happening.

Irick reached up pushing her claws deeper into his chest and held it there. "If I can't have you, Isa, then I choose death," he declared as he dropped to a knee.

Isabella gasped as she dropped down with him, her hand still plunged into his chest, she knew that if she removed it then he would be dead in moments and she wasn't ready to say goodbye. She choked on her mixed feelings, she liked Irick, it wasn't love, but she felt a kinship to him. She felt terrible that she begged him to help her, she wished she could go back and just leave the village without him. She looked down to see the wound she had inflicted on him, but he placed a hand on her cheek to bring her gaze back to his.

"I have always loved you, Isa," he said, weakly. "Do not take heed of what I said in anger. This was never your fault. I knew the risk of leaving the village and I chose to do it. It wasn't your fault that I listened to things that were beyond my understanding. Put my faith in those who told me what I wanted to hear. I am the one at fault here, Isa. You have to stop Doden and his Eye of Avgrunnen. They want to break the veil. Doden believes," he winced in pain.

"No one has the power to defeat the blood god," she said in his moment of silence.

Irick chuckled, blood streamed from the corners of his mouth and dripped on her arm that he was still holding against his chest. "He doesn't want to defeat him, Isa. He believes he can absorb his power and make it his own. You have to stop him," he choked out with a cough before lying back on the ground, but still holding her claw in place. "I'm sorry for what I did. I'm sorry for bringing death upon this city. Please, let those who survive know that I wish I could take it all back, if I could," he whispered as he breathed his last.

Isabella sobbed as she looked down at her friend. Overcome with emotion she bellowed a blood chilling howl into the sky and pushed her forehead gently against that of her dead friend. "I'm sorry, Irick. I wish that I could have loved you the way you loved me," she declared through the heart break.

"Wulgar?!" G'Nash screamed as he ran toward her.

She could see that behind him was a hundred woodland elves, Vivienne, her father carrying his blood-soaked scythe, and both the wizard and orc shaman. They were out of breath, but keeping at each other's pace at the back. G'Nash was the first to reach her. He kneeled down beside her, prying the dead hands of Irick from her arm and replacing them with his own strong hands. "Are you alright?" He asked as he gently raised her head from the chest of her dead friend and pulled her against his own.

She could hear the rapid thumping of the half-orc's heart. She could smell the salty sweat that covered his body and she cried harder into him. "I killed him," she declared softly.

"You did what you had to, Wulgar," G'Nash assured her as he wrapped his arms around her and squeezed her gently. "He was driven mad by the touch of Bahaal, just like you, but he lacked your strength to resist. If you hadn't killed him then he would have killed you and doomed the world to an unforgiving darkness."

She knew that the half-orc was right, but that didn't help heal her heart. She could feel the bloody wounds on his side from Irick's attack against him. They were starting to heal thanks to the magic of NaShorn. She looked up into his crimson eyes. "How do you feel? I can't stand to lose anyone else right now," she declared, placing a hand against his cheek.

"I am healing," G'Nash said, looking down at the wounds on his side. "NaShorn won't let me die so easily."

"We need to get out," Vivienne interrupted. "Can you walk?"

Isabella nodded as the two of them stood from the ground and prepared for the magic she would use to help them escape the city.

Vivienne, along with the other woodland elves, whispered an incantation causing the destroyed city of Y'Melenor to fade and they were brought into the forest, but they could hear the march of the undead army coming closer. They quickly checked to make sure everyone had been safely brought out of the city and they all moved east toward the shore with the woodland elves leading the way.

Isabella walked in a haze, her mind clouded with her memories of Irick and how they would play within the forest beside Sparrow's Lake. He would always try to protect her from the others and he was always there when she needed someone to talk to. But, that look….that look he had during his last moment. She breathed deep, trying to clear her head and she quickened her pace to catch up to Vivienne. "What happened to Revalor?"

"After we returned home, he took your father and Gh'Rys to the orc house and I made my way back to the royal chambers. Grandmother had just passed and preparations had to be made to lay her body to rest. I told King Jaspen what had transpired at Bog'Alor and he went to speak to Revalor, but I still had to take care of my grandmother's body. I cleaned her, dressed her in her favorite clothes, said a prayer over her, and that's when the attack happened," Vivienne breathed a heavy sigh as she recalled what transpired.

"I'm sorry," Isabella exclaimed sadly.

"Why?" Vivienne asked without stopping the march.

Isabella felt responsible for the fall of Y'Melenor. She insisted on the orcs being allowed into the city, she was the one that begged Irick to come with her. Had he not, then he wouldn't have been manipulated into being a puppet for Bahaal or Doden. She felt in her heart that everything bad that transpired to the woodland elves, was because of her.

Vivienne stopped walking, but commanded the others to continue and she grabbed the arm of Isabella. "You need to stop blaming yourself for everything!" She demanded, but looked over to G'Nash who had stopped following the others. "Do you need something?"

The half-orc hadn't let her out of his sight since they escaped, but he didn't have an answer to give to Vivienne and so he just shook his head. "I can take care of her should something happen. Follow the others and we will be along shortly," she demanded.

Isabella knew that he didn't take too kindly to being commanded, but she nodded in agreement and the half-orc did as she requested. Vivienne shook her head. "I know that it is easy for you to blame yourself and It will be easy for those who survive this endeavor to put the blame on you, but that blame isn't rightly placed. We had the orcs handled. If they tried to leave the house with their weapons, they would have been dealt with, but instead, the attack came from our own dead. The woodland elves lost in battles before you arrived in our world. They came and with them were countless others. Even that imbecile Irick isn't to blame. This attack was inevitable, but I'll tell you what can be blamed on you," she paused to get them moving again.

"You saved the lives of all those who survived the night. Had you not gone to Bog'Alor in search of NaShorn, then we would have been blinded to Doden's attack. Had you not stayed behind to hold his army off with the half-orc, then we wouldn't have been able to warn the king of his army and we wouldn't have been as prepared to escape when they attacked. We would have lost countless more lives than we did. You saved more lives than you know. You are a hero and you should never forget that," she declared.

Hero? The word echoed in her head. *Is this how it truly feels to be a hero?* She questioned herself as the two of them continued to walk through the forest in silence. *Being forced to kill a friend for the greater good? If this is what it takes to be a hero then I might not be the right choice.* She thought as a single tear trickled down her cheek.

A hero will always be plagued with making hard decisions, champion. We are bound together and I feel the pain you feel, Lucian's voice echoed in her head. *You are strong enough to endure this hardship, that's why I choose you as my champion. I believe in you. You will always miss your friend, but you need to understand that he could not be saved from the plague that had engulfed his mind.* The wolf spirit fell silent.

Isabella released a subtle sigh as they continued to travel through the forest. The sun had broken the horizon. It was the time of morning where the moon shared the sky but was slightly fading from sight. She thought once more of her friend, wondered if the memories she made with him would slowly fade like that of the moon, and she shook her head. She refused to believe that she could ever forget Irick or what he meant to her.

The forest had started to thin, the trees were further apart, and she could see further ahead than when they started. She could smell the salt of the sea getting stronger, but the smell of blood hung heavy on the air. The only comfort she had was that the scent of rot wasn't among the others and as they emerged from the tree line she could see more woodland elves resting along the shore.

King Jaspen was battered, his crown was missing, his armor had been broken, the leather underneath was tattered with cuts, and he had a fresh wound on his face. He was covered in blood, but he was examining the others to see who could still be saved and make comfortable those who could not. He dressed their wounds, applying a sweet-smelling salve to cuts, setting bones back in place, using his own clothes to splint the broken bone between two sticks, and then moving on to the next.

Isabella could see the fatigue on his face. He had fought to save all he could and escorted them to the shore. Where a lesser king would have worried more over his own wounds, this king sought to keep his people alive. She admired him as they approached the makeshift camp he had created and he breathed a sigh of relief. "Vivienne. I was worried about you. I'm glad to see you made it out and with others. I'm even glad to see the orc shaman right now," he admitted, rubbing his thumb across his forehead. "I have already treated most of these, but I could use the extra help," he said as the other elves that followed them moved to pick up where he left off and he finally sat down on the ground.

Vivienne rushed over to dress his wounds, but he tried to deflect her attempts. "Let me check you, Jaspen," she demanded hatefully.

"I am still your king," he declared.

"You were my cousin first," she said, slapping his hand away.

King Jaspen relented to her demand and let her check his wounds. "Thank you," he said, pleasantly to Isabella. "If you hadn't warned me when you did about the others, then I wouldn't have turned around and I shudder to think what would've happened then," he admitted as the salve was put on his cuts. "All those sitting here owe you so much, I more than anyone, and I vow to pay you back. On my honor as king of Y'Melenor, any request you ask that is within my power, shall be granted," he declared.

Isabella paused at the request made by the king. When she set out on her journey, it was to find a way to save her brother. Now she has the burden of protecting the world from a great evil. She released a heavy sigh as she shook her head. "I just want to get back home and help my brother, but I have to stop Bahaal if there is going to be any world worth him waking up to," she admitted, choking down the heartache that filled her.

King Jaspen gave a nod. "Then I will help," he announced loudly so that everyone present could hear his vow.

Vivienne blew on the salve to quicken its process of drying on the wound. "Where is Revalor?" She asked while examining the rest of him.

"I found him fighting against a small group. Those undead monsters had slain thirty of his warriors. He was wounded and barely standing, but still fighting. We managed to drive them back to their graves, he collapsed as the last of them fell to our blades, and with his last bit of strength he told me where my family was. He was protecting them, along with a hundred more survivors," he said, looking over at a large tree that grew alone on the shore. "I carried him from the city. He sleeps there, but he is weak," Vivienne gasped as she rushed over to him, behind her was Isabella and G'Nash.

Vivienne knelt down beside Revalor, rolling him over to see to his wounds. He groaned at being touched. He was covered in deep slashes across his chest, two that lined across his left eye and a long one that ran the length of his forehead. His forearm had been broken, he had a purple bruise on his right ribs, and three cuts on his legs. His wounds had been dressed and the broken bone was set with a stick tied to it, but they could hear a rattling when he breathed. Isabella knelt beside him and took hold of his hand.

Save him. I don't care how, I don't care what I have to do, but save him. I do not want to lose anyone else this day, she begged silently to the wolf spirit that was bound to her.

I will do what I can, champion, but the price we must pay will not be taken lightly. We will have to give him some of our life force to survive and even then, it might not work. It could just end up killing all three of us, Lucian warned, but Isabella just gritted her teeth. *As you wish, champion,* the wolf spirit echoed and a brilliant glow emerged from within her.

"What are you doing?" Vivienne asked while trying to pull her hand away.

"I'm saving him," Isabella declared as her body glowed brighter, her eyes turned light blue with very little white showing, and her teeth became fangs.

She felt the magic of Lucian flowing through her, coming together in her heart, with each beat it grew stronger, and with a quickness it shot through her arm into Revalor. The sudden rush of magic caused her to fall to the ground. She felt weak, but looked over at the elf archer as he took in a deep breath of air without restrictions and he coughed violently. She softly smiled at him as she reached out to move a blood-soaked strand of hair away from his face. "Welcome back," she declared before drifting off to sleep.

Chapter 6
Ursadelle, The Bear Spirit

Isabella slowly opened her eyes and yawned. She could hear the creaking of wood and the gentle rock of a ship, but she didn't remember ever getting on a boat. She placed a hand on her aching head as she tried to recall what happened before she succumbed to sleep. She remembered that Lucian had used a combination of magic and their life force to rescue Revalor from the brink of death as she carefully pushed herself up on the straw bed. She planted her bare feet on the wooden floor of the room and tried to figure out where she was.

The room was dark, but thanks to her bond with Lucian she could still see. A long table sat at the center of the room with chairs all around it and a round bronze tub was against the far wall, but it looked just barely big enough to lay in. A wardrobe sat in the corner of the same wall and a map covered the wall at the back. She believed it blocked a window as light could be seen peeking through small cuts all over it, but it wasn't enough to push away the total darkness of the cabin. An armchair had been pulled away from the table and was sitting at the side of her bed, but it was currently empty.

Isabella peeked under the linen sheet that covered her body and to her surprise she was completely naked. She groaned as her stomach rumbled. *What happened?* She thought as she made her way over to the wardrobe and pulled free some clothes she hoped would fit.

The linen shirt she put on could have been a dress as it hung to the top of her knees, but if she needed to fight, she couldn't do it in just that. She pulled up a pair of linen breeches to tuck the shirt into and using a small dagger from the table she cut a rope to tie around her waist. The boots inside were of no use to her as they would hinder her if she needed to defend herself, but she still had rope left. She cut two more pieces from it and tied the pants together at her ankles. She pulled back her wild, unkempt curly brown hair, tying a piece of rope around it to keep it away from her face and she breathed a sigh.

It will have to do. Now to find out where I am, she declared, looking at the only way out of the cabin and with caution she made her way toward it.

She eased the door open. Sunlight poured into the dark room from the crack causing her to squint her eyes shut and rub at them vigorously. She couldn't see, but she focused on her other senses. She could hear the heavy footfalls of others walking around on the wooden deck and the smell of sea salt and sweat hung in the air. *How did I end up on this boat? Where is father?* The questions burned in her mind as her eyes slowly adjusted to the light.

Her vision was still blurry, but she was able to make out a small group of workers on the deck. They were busy mopping, some were carrying large barrels of rations, she could only imagine it to be pickled or salted fish, and at the far end was a barrel that housed a wooden mug tied to its rim. She didn't know how many were on the ship, but she had to find out where her friends ended up. She feared that while she slept, they were attacked by pirates and taken captive. Her knowledge of a pirate's life was limited to what she learned from her brother, but she knew they could be ruthless in their pursuit of treasure. She thought about the story Kirkland loved to read to her. It was a tale regaling the life of a lady, born to a noble house within the Centurion Kingdom and she was supposedly beyond beautiful. The prince desired her hand, a nobleman from Slanderia sought her affection, and the king of Mador called on her, but she denied them all. They were asking for something that wasn't hers to give as her heart belonged firmly to another.

The man that won her affection was a commoner, a miner, but she saw beyond his humble birth. He stole her love with a gentle look and she knew from that moment he was the only person for her. When the others found out that they had been bested by a commoner, it drove them to declare war, but they had to be smart about it. The *Kingdom of Onyxium* was an island surrounded by mountains too steep to climb and the only way to gain access was through an enormous fortress built along the southern coast. It was these natural borders that gave them a sense of false safety. *King Olgar, first of the name to House Rose*, gave his blessing for his daughter to marry the commoner and those denied her hand, plotted just how they would take Onyxium as revenge.

Invitations were sent to all the kingdoms of Hyland. King Olgar was concerned about inviting the three who sought his daughter's hand, but feared refraining from sending them an invitation would only anger them more. He agreed to allow them access to the celebration, but they were only permitted a very small king's guard of twenty men to ensure their safety.

They complied with the rules set by King Olgar and suited twenty of their finest and fiercest warriors, but as their ships came to dock, they were greeted by a vessel of Onyxium. They were asked to give up their weapons before they could bring their ship to the port. It was a rule they hadn't prepared for.

In fear the Slanderian Nobleman gave the order to attack. His men were better trained, but of his twenty guards only five survived and he was grievously wounded. Sitting at the helm of his ship, he held an arm over his open gash, trying to keep his insides from spilling out, but a bloody smile slowly stretched across his face as he watched the others he conspired with take the fortress and with that he drifted off into eternal sleep.

With the fortress now under their control, they went to work on the signal they would use to let their reinforcements know. A giant pyre was built on top of the fortress and the flame from it could be seen all over Onyxium.

King Olgar was in a panic. He knew that they were signaling more ships, announcing their victory of taking the fortress and if he hoped to keep his kingdom, he would need to take back the port. He laid siege against *Fort Onyxia* for five nights, but the fortress was impenetrable. It was built to withstand armies and as the sun kissed the sky on the sixth day, he saw the ships of his enemies sailing into port.

His heart sank. He knew he stood no chance against their combined force. They would take his kingdom, but he wouldn't allow them the satisfaction of gaining his daughter. He escorted her north to a port he had constructed under a mountain in secret with the dwarves. They had built a simple wooden dock that was weathered and tied to it was a massive bireme that rocked patiently on the small waves that washed in from the sea.

Ruby Rose was etched on the side of the ship. The vessel was named after her and it was something her father hoped she would never see, but now it was their only way off the island. King Olgar watched as the forty knights he brought with him loaded the ship with their provisions, but his daughter refused to go. She knew that the king wasn't coming with her and she wasn't about to abandon him. Using force, her lover pulled her on board the ship and they escaped the fall of Onyxium.

They sailed south to the continent of *Gilavrath* and it was there she built her reputation as a pirate. Sailing the waters with her bireme, attacking the ships of the two that took everything from her, and selling everything that she gained from her raids. Those that sailed for her enemies were given options. They could join her and forsake their masters or be sold as slaves to the masters of DeGura. The cargo they carried was taken to be used to feed or arm her men and the ships that weren't sunk during her attack were fixed and sailed under her banner.

She was feared by all, but her tale ended in mystery. Some say that after the death of the last two that took her home, she just called it quits. Another tale is that she was killed in a mutiny and another is that she died of disease, but whatever the truth was, she was feared for her ruthlessness.

Isabella didn't know if those running the ship were pirates, but she didn't see any of her friends amongst them and she wouldn't risk everything on the small chance they weren't. She gritted her teeth as she watched one of them make his way over to drink from a barrel and decided he would be her first target. *I hope you are ready, Lucian*, she called out to the wolf spirit, but she didn't wait for him to answer as she shouldered through the door and rushed toward the man.

She waited for the transformation to take her. She was going to need the strength of the wolf if she hoped to defeat the crew of the ship, but she was growing weaker instead of stronger. She didn't understand why the wolf had abandoned her in her time of need. She tripped over her feet causing her to crash to the floor, but she continued to crawl toward the man. She would have answers to where her friends were.

"Wulgar?" The familiar voice of her friend echoed out and she looked over to see G'Nash carrying a plate of food. "Why are you out of bed?" He asked, dropping the plate of fruit and rushing toward her.

"Pirates," she managed to force out before falling to sleep.

Isabella laid on her back in the darkness, drained of energy, but she didn't understand why. "Lucian, are you there?!" She yelled as loud as she could.

"I am here, champion," the wolf spirit said with a yawn.

Isabella tried to move her head to look in the direction the voice came from, but she couldn't move. "Why can't I move?" She asked exhaustedly.

"I told you that saving the half-elf would be costly and that it could end up killing us. Though we didn't die, it did drain us of our energy."

The darkness was pushed away, giving sight to a pristine blue sky with white puffy clouds and a sun that was partially covered by them. "So, magic even has limitations in this world," she declared through her fatigue.

"Magic, even in this plane, is limited to the energy of the person using it," Lucian exclaimed through another yawn. "It doesn't take as long for those using it to regain the energy spent, but we parted with our lifeforce to save your friend. We will require another fortnight of rest to regain what we used and lost. You will be able to awaken soon, but try to not use any magic for a short time."

Isabella inhaled deeply. "What about the pirates?"

"What pirates?" Lucian asked bewildered.

"I woke up naked on a boat," she confessed. "My friends were gone and my father was missing. When I looked out of the cabin I saw a crew, but nothing of those I was with before we saved Revalor."

She could hear the wolf standing from the ground with a tired groan and his soft steps came closer to her. The wolf spirit licked her forehead. "Do you trust those that were around you when we saved the half-elf? Do you believe in the champion of NaShorn? Do you think he would allow anything to happen to you?"

Isabella released an exasperated sigh. "No. He would fight to the death to keep me safe, but what if that is what happened? He could have been killed by the pirates."

"NaShorn is not dead, champion," Lucian advised, lying beside her and nestling his nose against her shoulder.

Isabella was finally able to turn her head to look at the beautiful black wolf that lay beside her. "How can you be so sure?"

"The spirit animals are all connected. When one of us is extinguished, we feel it and I have not felt that emptiness of losing someone," he admitted, moving his snout to rest on her chest. "Wake now and seek them out, but don't over exert yourself, champion. Try talking to those you think are pirates," he suggested, turning his head to lick under her chin.

Isabella laid motionless on the hard bed made of straw. She figured that she was brought back to the cabin when she passed out on the deck, but she could sense that she wasn't alone like before. She didn't know who was there, watching her from the dark and her senses were of no help to her. The smell of salt lingered in the air, but from time to time she could pick up a small sniff of something that was sweet and sultry. Her stomach rumbled, she didn't know how long it had been since she ate, but she felt starved.

She exhaled a soft sigh. "If I open my eyes and you aren't someone I recognize," she exclaimed while turning her head to see who was watching over her.

"It is me, Wulgar," G'Nash said softly, pulling the chair closer and reaching out to touch her hand.

Isabella could see the plate of food resting on his lap, the steam of it lifted from the cooked meat that was waiting for her, but she forced her hungry gaze from the meal and put it on her friend. "Who is that with you?" She asked as the stranger used a tinderbox to light one of the tallow candles.

The man looked to be of average height for a human, his body looked bulky, but that could have been from the clothing he was wearing. He wore a red shirt tucked into brown breeches, a long sleeve red coat covered his body, and it hung down to the middle of his calves. His curly black hair flowed down, parting at his shoulders, his thick dark beard was decorated with gems in several spots, and he gave her a toothy grin. He dragged an empty chair across the cabin with his empty hand, positioned it so that he would be sitting at the side of the half-orc, and he adjusted himself on it.

"My name is *Captain Theodore LongShanks* and you are aboard my ship, *Faded Glory*," he said from a charming smile and a bow.

"Your ship?" Isabella asked before he had time to right himself.

"Aye, lass," Captain Theodore said, looking to the half-orc and then back to her.

"How did you find us?" She asked, dropping her hand down heavily on her leg and releasing a heavy sigh.

Captain Theodore chuckled as he sat back in the chair. "Good thing you were unconscious or we would still be on the shores of Sapphire," he said, scratching his chin. The stubble that had grown there made a raking sound and he gave a shrug. "We arrived at *Port EverGlade*, but all we found was death. Dead, headless bodies lay motionless in the dirt roads, buildings were burnt to the ground, and the smell of rot lingered heavily in the air. I had my reservations about docking at the port, but we were low on supplies. My chief officer led a search of the town. He was supposed to look for survivors and supplies that we could use to make the trip back to Tanzanite. I told him to be cautious, but nothing could have prepared them for what they encountered in that town," he said, his face turning pale as he cleared his throat. "They were attacked by decomposing men, their flesh sagged, wounds covered their bodies, their bodies shuffled slowly, and their numbers were too great."

Captain Theodore exhaled a heavy breath. "I watched my men deliver blows to these creatures that would kill a normal man, but they just kept coming. They killed everyone that went with my chief officer and then they carried their bodies off. I gave the command to turn back for Tanzanite. I was going to speak to the high elves about what I saw, but then the wood elves of Sapphire rushed for my dinghy. They danced around the monsters that were trying to kill them and paddled to my ship. They explained what was happening on the island and I brought my ship around the coast to pick you all up," he said from a forced smile.

Isabella understood what he had seen within the port town since she had already fought against the undead of Doden and his Eye of Avgrunnen cult. She released a sigh. "So, that's why you accepted our help as payment."

Captain Theodore nodded his head. "I was worried about sailing back to Tanzanite with the crew I had. It was a blessing from *Vatn* that brought your friends to me and brought me to the coast to rescue you."

Vatn, the name echoed in the head of Isabella as she recalled the story told to her by Uthric and she remembered that the name belonged to the elemental created from water. She inhaled a deep breath. "Where are we now?"

"We should be coming upon Tanzanite soon. We have been sailing across the *Shimmering Sea* for a fortnight."

"A fortnight?!" Isabella interrupted loudly. "I've been asleep for a fortnight?!" She asked, looking to G'Nash.

Captain Theodore chuckled. "At the very least," he declared, slapping his knee before standing up. "I must see my crew and check our bearings. You should eat. I'll come back to see you when I can."

"Is it possible to take a bath on this ship?" Isabella asked, stopping him at the door.

Captain Theodore gave a nod and pointed to the bronze tub beside the wardrobe. "I'll have some hot water brought up to fill it," he said, stepping through the door and closing it behind him.

Isabella pulled back the linen sheet that covered her and she was relieved to see that she was clothed. "Where is father?" She asked, pushing the blanket off her.

G'Nash handed her the tray that held her food. "Your father is resting in the crew quarters. He has been a tremendous help with seeing us across the Shimmering Sea. He had just left your side to go rest and I was on my way to replace him when you passed out again."

"What of Revalor?" She asked, eating from the tray.

"He is resting in the crew quarters," G'Nash said, making his way toward the table and pouring a glass of wine for her. "Vivienne said that he will live, but like you he has been asleep since you saved him and we have no way of knowing when he will wake," he said, bringing her the chalice.

"And the king?" She asked, taking the offering and drinking it to the last drop.

G'Nash took the empty chalice from her. "He is well. He works as part of the crew like the rest of us."

"King Jaspen is working on the ship?" She asked in disbelief.

G'Nash nodded as he refilled the chalice. "He was the one that made the deal with Captain Theodore, but only if he would allow you to rest within his cabin. The king would have stayed on that shore had he refused. You have become a champion to his people, Wulgar," he said, handing her the goblet and taking his seat beside her.

She exhaled a soft breath as the doors to the cabin were pushed open. Vivienne stepped through carrying a small bucket of water and behind her were six other female wood elves, the last one carrying elegant garments. The steam danced above the liquid as she floated across the hard wooden floors to the bronze tub, poured the water in, handed the empty bucket to the half-elf behind her and made her way over to the bed. She sat in the seat the captain had pulled up. "I'm glad to see that you are awake. I was afraid I wouldn't get to properly thank you for saving my cousin's life," she said, bowing her head and taking hold of Isabella's hand. "Your courage knows no bounds. I can see why the wolf spirit chose you."

One by one the other wood elves walked past the bed, bowed their heads, and thanked Isabella for what she had done for them. As the last of them exited the room, they closed the door, leaving the three of them alone and Vivienne smiled at her. "I am going to help you bathe, but you are going to help her over to the bath," she announced, standing from the chair.

G'Nash stood from his own seat, scooped his arms under the bends of her legs and at the small of her back. "Hold to me, Wulgar," he said, lifting her from the bed as if she was a newborn babe.

Isabella's heart raced as she held tight to the half-orc, resting her head on his thick rounded shoulder, and she felt at peace with him carrying her over to the bronze tub. He sat her down in a chair that Vivienne had pulled across the cabin. "Now, help me undress her," the wood elf announced, testing the waters with her fingers.

G'Nash's face flushed as he choked on the words that couldn't escape his throat and Vivienne shook her head. "Did you think she was going to bathe in those clothes? She needs to be undressed and I don't have the strength to do it. Now help me!" She declared angrily.

"Maybe this task is better suited for her father."

The half-orc turned to make his way toward the door, but Isabella quickly reached up to grasp his forearm. "It's fine, G'Nash," she assured him with a smile. "Will you please help Vivienne get me in the tub so I can relax?"

G'Nash was reluctant, but agreed to do as she asked. He used the small knife on the table to cut the rope she had used to tie the pants at her ankles and at the waist. He pulled down the top of the breeches so he could grab her hips, lifting her from the chair so that Vivienne could pull the pants off and he gently sat her back down as the half-elf removed the shirt that hung to her knees. His face flushed as he turned his gaze from her nakedness. "Was that the last thing? Is she ready to go into the water?" He asked, without looking at her.

"She is ready," Vivienne assured him.

He lifted her from the chair without looking at her. He positioned his body to where he could turn and lower her down into the water without seeing her naked body. Once she was seated firmly in the tub of hot water he made his way toward the door. "I will stand just outside here. Call on me when she is done," he declared without looking back and he made his way out of the cabin.

"That is a unique half-orc," Vivienne declared.

Isabella moaned as the water eased the ache in her muscles. "What do you mean?"

"I forget that you aren't from this world," Vivienne said in a surprised tone. "Most half-orcs take after their orc heritage and wouldn't have flinched at seeing you naked. There is more to him than I gave him credit for," she declared, lifting a linen square from the table.

"My brother would always tell me to never judge a book by its cover," Isabella said, letting the back of her head rest on the rim of the tub.

"Tell me more about your brother," Vivienne requested while dipping the linen square into the water.

Isabella leaned forward so that Vivienne could wash her back with the linen square and she exhaled a soft sigh. "I miss him so much. He got hurt because of me," she said, exhaling softly.

"I'm sure you aren't to blame," Vivienne retorted, moving the linen square down her arm and washing between each finger.

"I wish that was true," Isabella replied, sucking air through her nose. "Mother had sent him to fetch me for dinner, but I really enjoyed frightening him. So, I hid within the forest, forcing him to come find me, and that was when I scared him. He tripped over a root," she paused to let the memory flood her mind and ran her thumb under her eyes to wipe away the fallen tears.

"I thought he was hurt then, but when he woke up, a ball of fire emerged from his hand and burned the tree I had been hiding in. We didn't even have time to process what he had done before the witch of the woods came with her questions," she gritted her teeth at the mention of the old hag, but she released a sigh to calm back down. "She used vines to entangle us, blood magic on my brother to get the answers she wanted, and I was powerless to help him. I had to endure his agonizing cries as she did her crazy magic on him. I wanted to kill her, but by the time the vines released me she was gone," she said, resting her head back on the rim of the tub and closing her eyes.

It felt like a lifetime ago since the events with the witch happened, but she knew that in reality only a few months had passed. She released a sigh as Vivienne lifted her left leg out of the water and washed it. "The use of blood magic probably killed her," she said, lowering her appendage back down into the water.

Isabella turned her head to look at the wood elf. "You have blood magic here?"

Vivienne gave a nod. "It is a forbidden type of magic and my people stay away from it. The use of it is too unpredictable. We have tried to study it, as it is the power that is used by Bahaal, and we believed that if we had a better understanding of it then we would be able to stand against him, but found that it can't be controlled. That was before Aster approached our ancestors with another solution. He would banish the blood god to a realm where he could do no harm to others and we saw no other way to fight him."

"The Great Banishing," Isabella interrupted softly.

Vivienne nodded. "If that is what it is called. We call it *The Great Sacrifice*. It was a battle that changed the lives of so many, but that is a story for another time. Did the witch find out how your brother was able to conjure a ball of fire?"

Isabella gave a shrug. "I don't know. Kirkland fell into a never-ending slumber, the witch was gone, and father came to find us when he heard the screams."

"Fascinating," Vivienne exclaimed, moving to the other leg. "Humans in our world can use magic, but they require a focus of some sort to do it, they call upon the animal spirits to help guide their magic, or they use rituals for it. I'm curious to know how your brother was able to do it without any of that, myself," she declared, washing the rest of her body before lifting a goblet from the table and looking inside it.

"Uthric wondered the same before we were pulled into the rift. I just know that my power comes from Lucian," she announced as the wood elf poured water over her head, causing her to pause. "I wish I knew how Kirky was able to conjure magic without a focus. If he had a bond with an animal spirit," she stopped abruptly as the wood elf scrubbed her scalp to clean it from dirt and dumped another goblet of water over her head.

"Maybe the answer can be found in Tanzanite. That is if we can get the high elves to help us," Vivienne said, but her tone was full of doubt.

"You don't think the high elves will help us in this manner?" Isabella asked, using a new linen square to wipe her face.

Vivienne gave a shrug. "The difference in our people is so simple. The wood elves are mostly half-blooded and think we are only better than the races created by Bahaal, but the high elves are pure blooded. They believe that because of that they are better than all the races of this world and they aren't known for their hospitality towards outsiders. They even turned away one of their kings because he took a human wife after The Great Sacrifice. That's how King Virion Regynald came to our island and built his own kingdom, but lost it in a battle against the druhir's of Drunidr. He came to Y'Melenor with what remained of his warriors, enticed some of ours to join him in attacking the druhir's home, and then was exiled when he lost over half of those that traveled with him," she grimaced as she spoke of the past. "Our history is a dark place, but we have kept records of it to prevent us from repeating those mistakes. Unfortunately for the high elves, they believe the mistake that was made and should never be repeated is trusting a human to help us."

"That's awful," Isabella said, breaking the silence. "I have found good and bad in every race I have encountered on my journey. The orcs can be stubborn, but they value honor above all else," she exhaled as she shook her head. "I can understand the distrust that was built up over the long periods of warring against each other, but that was during the time they served Bahaal. They have changed since then," she declared, looking at the wood elf.

Vivienne gave a hesitant nod. "I have taken notice of that with Gh'Rys. He is skilled with magic and has helped me with tending to the wounded on this ship. We have given everyone on board some Eucilipsis Flower, mixing it in with the food to conceal it and it would appear that Doden's forces haven't escaped onto this ship," she said, furrowing her brow.

Isabella inhaled a deep breath. "That's good. Let's hope they aren't fond of water and never leave that island," she declared with a haphazard smile.

Vivienne gave her a nod as she sat back in the chair. "You are clean. Are you ready to get out or do you want to rest in the water for a while?"

Isabella released a sigh, resting her head on the rim of the tub and closing her eyes. She felt so much better now that she had relaxed within the warm water, but she knew that she couldn't just stay in the tub. "I'm ready to get out," she announced from a smile.

"I will get the half-orc."

"Let's not embarrass him any further," Isabella interrupted the wood elf as she started to stand. "I am capable of standing on my own," she declared, pushing herself up using the sides of the bronze tub.

Isabella shakes her body like a wolf and Vivienne laughs. "I took a bath this morning, Isabella," she remarked playfully. "You might be the champion of the wolf spirit, but that doesn't mean you dry like him. Here is a linen for you to use," she said, handing the towel to her.

Isabella chuckled as she realized what she had done. Using the side of the tub, she slowly stepped out, putting her feet firmly on the floor and taking the towel from the half-elf. She quickly dried herself as Vivienne prepared the elegant dress that was brought in. It was the first time that Isabella had really noticed it since it had been laid out for her and it was breathtaking.

The gown was a dark green in color, the neck of it was lined with wolf fur and it fit her perfectly. It flowed down to the tops of her ankle, but at the hips it fanned out giving her legs freedom to move. The upper half was snug against her body and there was no doubting she was a woman while wearing it. She rubbed her hands down the side, feeling the soft material it was made from and she looked to the half-elf that was speechless. "How do I look?"

"I don't believe the half-orc should ever see you like this. I don't believe his heart could handle it," Vivienne jested as she walked behind her to fix her hair and using a twig, she pulled it off her shoulders.

"Do I really have to wear this?"

Vivienne nodded. "We should be landing in Tanzanite before too long and King Jaspen wants you at his side while negotiating with the high elves. You can't show up looking like a ruffian," she said playfully as she examined just how well the dress fit. "You don't have to wear it now. I just needed to see how well my measurements were. You can take it off, but know that it is what you will be wearing once we dock," she declared while helping her remove the elegant gown and handing her linen clothes to put on.

Vivienne hung the dress inside the wardrobe and pulled free a fresh shirt. She tossed it over the head of Isabella. It hung down just above the knees, but it was the only thing that the wood elf gave her. "This is all you need to wear. It covers you completely and it will make you comfortable while you rest. I'll send others to empty the tub, but in the meantime, relax. I don't know the limits of your magic, but I do know that what you did to save Revalor should have killed you. It still surprises me to see you awake so quickly," she announced, making her way to the door and reaching out to open it.

"Would you send G'Nash back in, please?" Isabella asked, making her way over and climbing in the bed.

Vivienne laughed lightly. "I'll make sure your champion comes back in," she said playfully, but as she opened the door he was standing there like a stalwart statue. "She is ready for you," the half-elf said, stepping past him and making her way across the deck.

G'Nash stepped back, closing the door, but keeping his eyes away from the tub. "Are you dressed?" He asked, securing the doors.

"It is safe to look at me," Isabella said, snuggling down in the bed.

G'Nash turned to see that she was laying down and he made his way over to the seat. "Are you hungry? Are you thirsty? Should I leave you to rest?" He asked all his questions with haste without giving her time to answer.

Isabella placed a hand against his lips. "I just want you to sit for a while. I will rest better knowing that you are watching over me," she remarked from a smile.

G'Nash nodded his agreement as he shifted in the chair to get more comfortable and Isabella breathed a sigh of relief. "Good," she said, closing her eyes and letting sleep take her, but her sleep was short as the door creaked open.

"Did I wake you?" Torgath asked, stepping inside with a small candle and making his way over to stand by her bed.

Isabella shook her head as she yawned sleepily and smiled at her father. "I was just resting my eyes," she exclaimed.

"I'm sorry I woke you, Bella. I just wanted to check on you," Torgath said as soft as his gruff voice would allow. "When I heard you were awake, I wanted to come right then, but my duties on the ship required my attention. How do you feel?"

Isabella shrugged at the question and scratched the back of her head. "I'm getting stronger with every passing moment," she offered with a smile.

"I should be getting to my duties," G'Nash said, standing from the chair and offering it to Torgath.

"Have you slept?" Isabella called out after him.

G'Nash flashed her a smile as he pulled the door open. "I'm fine, Wulgar. I'll sleep soon enough," he promised, stepping out of the room and closing the door.

"I think he likes you," Torgath declared, sitting on the chair.

Isabella chuckled lightly. She could feel that the half-orc cared for her and she cared for him, but she didn't fully understand how deep that affection flowed or if it was due to the spell she had used to learn the languages he knew. She shook her head as she reached out to touch the hand of her father. "How are you, father?" She asked, trying to change the subject.

Torgath sat back in the chair, but kept hold of his daughter's hand. "I'm fine, Bella. Just wanting to find a way to get us back home."

She could hear it in her father's voice that he was tired, but she knew that he would never admit to needing a rest. She had watched him during the great harvest. When the others stopped due to exhaustion, her father would continue. He would start his work in the fields before the sun even kissed the sky and wouldn't stop until it became too dark to see. He would come home, tired from the day's work, but you couldn't tell it by looking at him. She squeezed his hand. For the first time she could see the fatigue eating away at her father and it broke her heart.

"You should rest," she announced from a forced half-smile.

Torgath shook his head, sitting up straight in the chair and composing himself. "I'm fine," he declared, placing the candle down on the other chair. "The captain said we should be seeing landfall soon."

Isabella's heart sank, she worried about her father, but she also knew just how stubborn he could be. "Vivienne said that we are going to seek help from the high elves."

"Land ho!" The unfamiliar voice interrupted and Torgath stood from the chair.

"The land of Tanzanite is in the distance," Vivienne said, opening the door and rushing in. "You need to get dressed before we dock. You should go help them bring the boat to shore," she said, ushering Torgath out.

"I'll do what I can. Take care of Bella," he managed to say in haste as he was pushed out the open door and it was closed behind him.

Vivienne turned to smile at her, but if it wasn't for her bond with Lucian, she wouldn't have been able to see it. "Aldmari," she whispered and all the candles within the cabin ignited. "Let's get that dress on you," she exclaimed, making her way toward the wardrobe.

Isabella groaned as she pushed the sheet off her and stood from the bed. "Do I have to wear that? What if there is a fight?" She asked in a discouraged tone.

Vivienne shook her head as she pulled the dress free. "Don't worry. I'll be close by with your champion. If a fight breaks out, we will save you," she announced playfully.

"My heroes," Isabella said, rolling her eyes as she stomped over and removed the clothes she was wearing.

The dress was pulled over her head with the help of Vivienne, a golden sash decorated with colorful leaves was tied around her waist, wooden shoes were placed on her feet, and her hair was twisted around and pinned at the back with a twig carved of jade. Isabella stood before a looking glass, the reflection she saw was unrecognizable, but she knew it was her because it mocked her movements as she ran her hands down the dress. The image of how elegant she looked reminded her of her mother and how she always wanted her to wear dresses.

"Perfect," Vivienne said from a smile. "You are ready to go."

Isabella released a moan. She didn't mind the dress from the waist down as it fanned out, giving her legs plenty of room, but the arms constrained her and made her feel like she was wearing chains. She pulled at the cuff of the sleeve. "Are we going to leave the ship at night?" She asked, turning her head to look at the half-elf.

Vivienne slapped at her hands to stop her from fidgeting with the sleeve. "I forgot that you haven't been out of this cabin since we boarded the ship," she said, from a soft smile. "It was almost morning before land was seen and the light of day should be on us before we make landfall. We just need to be ready when we do. Are you ready to step out on the deck?" She asked from her smile.

Isabella rubbed her eyes. She was ready to leave the cabin the moment she woke up, but the first attempt didn't end the way she had planned. She inhaled deeply and nodded her agreement as the two of them slowly stepped toward the exit. The door was pushed open, allowing the early morning light to flash into the dark room and it stung at her eyes, causing her to flinch, but she rubbed them gently to help them adjust before stepping out onto the deck. The crew of the ship was moving about making sure that everything was secured tightly. The salt filled breeze felt good across her sweaty brow and she could see in the distance the land they were sailing toward.

"You are looking better!" The captain screamed from behind her.

Isabella turned to see that the wheel of the ship was fixed above the chamber she was sleeping in, but it was so high that it prevented the noise from echoing down into the sleeping quarters of the captain. Thanks to her bond with Lucian, she could see him smiling at her and he waved his arm ushering for her to come up to where he was. She made her way up the twenty-two steps to reach the upper level with Vivienne behind her, but as she took the last step she was awestruck at the view.

"This is the reason why I sail the open seas," Captain Theodore said from his smile, but never taking his hand from the peg he was holding on the wheel. "Just a second. We have to change course slightly to make it to the land you see," he said, nodding to one of the sailors that stood beside him and the two of them worked together to turn the wheel.

Isabella could feel the ship turning in the water and once they were pointed directly at the landmass, the two of them gently let the wheel rest back to where it was. "It takes two of you to turn that wheel?"

Captain Theodore chuckled as he held it steady with one hand. "Not all of us are blessed with inhuman strength, lass. Holding the helm still isn't so bad, but when it comes to changing the rudders angle it can be a little more difficult. Would you like to hold it? I need to see what waits for us on the shore," he said, standing to the side and giving her room to step closer.

Isabella was nervous as she stepped up, she had always wondered what it would be like to sail on the seas when she was little, but she never dreamed she would ever get the chance. She reached out, taking hold of a peg and held tight to it. "A natural," Captain Theodore said with a nod while pulling out a looking glass.

He pulled to it causing it to extend and he looked through the smaller end. He scanned the direction they were heading, but made a discouraging sound. "I don't see anyone. I can see *Gulsbay Port*. I just don't see anyone there," he said, disheartened as he collapsed the looking glass and placed it back within his long coat. "Vatn watch over us," he prayed quietly.

"Do you worship all the elementals?" Isabella asked, without moving her eyes from the landmass they were sailing for.

Captain Theodore chuckled at her question. "Are you a believer of Zephyr?"

Zephyr was the only deity that Isabella knew about, but after meeting Uthric she found that she didn't even know much about the almighty they worshiped in her village. She shrugged her shoulders and the captain shook his head in awe. "Everyone should believe in something. We have worshipers of Zephyr here. I have heard the scriptures of this almighty and how he created everything. We have those that worship him on the ship. My chief officer worshiped him, may his deity give him rest, but we also have some that worship Deware as their almighty. Your religion doesn't matter to me, as long as you don't start trouble on the ship and I can rely on you in times of need," he declared from a smile.

Isabella rubbed the back of her neck as she looked back to see him. She didn't know what she believed in now, but she knew that she could trust Lucian. He had given her courage in times of need and he had given her strength and kept her going when she just wanted to give up. Maybe that was who she should be worshiping. She exhaled a soft sigh. "I don't know what I believe in anymore," she offered, turning her gaze back toward the landmass.

"Maybe you will find it on your journey, lass," Captain Theodore said, moving around to the other side and taking hold of the wheel with her. "I'll guide us close enough that the dinghy can be used. You should go see who is willing to row it to Gulsbay Port. Can't bring the whole ship in until we know it is safe, not after what happened at Port EverGlade," he declared with a sad tone, but he looked away from her and she knew that he was trying to harden his heart to the pain he felt over the ones he lost.

Isabella nodded to Vivienne and the two of them wasted little time going down the steps, but as they reached the bottom, they could see King Jaspen emerging from below deck. "It is good to see you up and walking around, and in elegant garments I see. You should present nicely to the High Elves." he declared with a smile.

They crossed the deck to meet in the middle and she bowed her head to him, as she had seen others do when they greeted the king, but he touched her shoulder gently. "You need not be so formal with me, Isabella. It should be me bowing to you," he declared, pulling her in and embracing her with a hug.

She hugged him back. "We need to discuss who is going to scout the port. Captain Theodore doesn't want to bring the whole ship in until we know it is safe from Doden's cult," she declared as they broke from the embrace and judged how much time they had.

Isabella looked at her dress and then to the king. "We should stay on the boat. If the cultists are there, we would be no good in a fight dressed like this," she declared, holding out her arm and tugging at the sleeves, but stopping after being slapped by Vivienne.

King Jaspen rubbed his smooth chin. "I agree that you should stay behind, but I am the king. I will stand with my people and not behind them," he declared.

"Make sure father and G'Nash go with you," she said.

She could see in his eyes that there was no swaying his decision, but she could at least make sure he was protected. He agreed to her terms as the sails were brought down and the clink of a heavy chain dropping an anchor into the depths of the water slowed their approach. When the ship came to a full stop, the deck was covered with those capable of walking and everyone was looking at the silent port-town that waited for them. Gentle waves smashed against the bow of the ship and seagulls flew overhead, but the town looked abandoned. The eerie sight and silence that was coming from it gave her a chill.

"Are you alright, Wulgar?" G'Nash asked as he walked up to her.

Isabella nodded and flashed him a forced smile. "I'm fine. It," she paused, biting her bottom lip. "The town. Something feels wrong. Be careful," she said, but her tone felt more demanding than cautionary.

G'Nash chuckled. "I know what you mean. NaShorn doesn't like the look of it either, but we are confident we can handle whatever lurks there. I promise that should something happen, I'll keep your father safe," he declared, slamming his fist against his chest and tilting his head slightly in respect.

"Just," she released a heavy sigh and shook her head. "Be careful over there. Scout it, make sure that Doden's Cult isn't lurking about, and then send us a signal."

"On my honor," he said with confidence.

"Worry not daughter," Torgath said, placing a massive hand on her shoulder. "I'll keep the little orc safe for you," he declared, chuckling and nudging G'Nash with his elbow.

King Jaspen stepped over into the dinghy along with four of his elvish warriors. They examined what was loaded within the small rowboat and got comfortable on the long benches, but kept room for the last two of their crew to board. "We should be going," he declared calmly.

G'Nash made his way over into the dinghy and stepped to the front. Torgath embraced his daughter tightly in his arms. "You have the strength of your mother," he whispered in her ear before stepping into the rowboat and moving to the back.

The two of them took hold of the rope and, using their immense strength, they slowly lowered the dinghy down into the waters and sat down taking hold of their oars. The king sat at the center of the rowboat while four oars were being used. Each one required the strength of two elves, but Torgath and G'Nash were able to move an oar by themselves.

Isabella watched as they soared across the calm waters. It took them only a few strokes to reach the dock, but for her it felt like a lifetime had passed. She watched as G'Nash was the first to step out of the rowboat, followed by her father, then two elves, the king and finally the last two elves. They slowly stepped into the town, swords drawn, bows nocked with arrows, her father's scythe at the ready, and they cautiously stepped toward the first home just off the dock. G'Nash peeked through a window, but crouched back down before moving deeper into the town and further away from the dock.

"We will know something soon," Captain Theodore announced, stepping up beside her and pulling free his looking glass. "My chief officer didn't make it much further than they are now before those creatures fell on them. Pray to all the deities worshiped that it's just empty," he finished as he scanned the whole town.

Isabella could feel her heart thumping against her chest, the dread of what could happen flooding her mind, and making her head swim. She should be over there with them, not standing idly by on the boat while others put their lives on the line, but she was without power. Lucian still needed time to regain his energy and without him, she would have put everyone in danger. She clasped her hands in front of her chest. *Almighty Zephyr, hear my prayer and keep them safe.*

Vivienne wrapped an arm around her. "They will be fine. They know how to deal with the undead monsters and the king knows to retreat at the first sign of danger or else he will have to deal with my wrath," she declared.

Isabella gave her a nod as she looked back to see that the group had made it to the center of town. King Jaspen spotted a water fountain centered within the town and held his hand straight up. A fireball shot up high into the sky and bursted with a thunderous boom. The sea became uneasy, the seagulls flying overhead retreated, and any enemies nearby would be alerted of their arrival. The group stood ready to defend or retreat. G'Nash was standing with his fist clenched down at his hips, the stance he took before transforming, but nothing came for them.

"Guess that answers that," Captain Theodore said, collapsing his looking glass and placing it back inside his coat. "Alright, lads. Let's bring this ship to dock!" He screamed. His crew roared with a cheer and he made his way back to the helm.

Isabella realized she had been holding her breath. She breathed a sigh of relief as she placed a hand up to her forehead and Vivienne chuckled. "I know what you mean," she remarked as the two of them stepped over to lean on the rim of the ship.

They stood in silence as the anchor was lifted by twenty men, others moved to fix the sail, and the wizard created a gentle breeze to fill the sail just enough to make it to shore. "Prepare to dock!" Captain Theodore yelled, causing the sails to be dropped, but the anchor remained unmoved.

Long oars were pushed through slits on the side of the ship and Isabella could hear those rowing below grunting with each movement that would propel the vessel closer to the dock. They moved at a gentle pace, the captain adjusting the helm to make sure that the ship stayed the course he wanted and as they pulled closer to the dock, the oars that would've hit it were pulled back into the ship. Several sailors leaped from the boat, landing on the wooden structure. Using the thick ropes in their hands, they tied the ship to iron buckles that were fixed to posts and it came to a halt. The captain made his way down from the helm and a long plank was pushed off the side and attached to the dock where others could leave the ship.

"Shall we see what the town has to offer?" Captain Theodore asked, ushering for the girls to go down the plank first.

Isabella pulled the bottom of her dress up just above the ankle and hurriedly rushed down the plank. "Be careful not to fall!" Captain Theodore screamed, but she was already clear of the boat before he could finish.

Isabella didn't wait for anyone as she ran into the town. At the center of it, she found her father and the half-orc searching around for any clues of what had happened to the townsfolk. "Wulgar," G'Nash managed to say before she embraced him with a tight hug.

"I was worried about the two of you," she admitted, releasing the half-orc and embracing her father in the same fashion.

"You shouldn't worry so much, Bella," Torgath said from a smile.

King Jaspen sheathed his sword, but was still accompanied by two of his elvish warriors. "We should remain on guard. We don't know what happened to the townsfolk, but we can see they left in a hurry. Half-eaten food had rotted within the plates they were served on. Where is Captain Theodore? I need to make sure it is alright our sick and injured remain on the ship until we have spoken with the high elves."

Isabella turned to see that in her haste to get to those she loved, she had left Vivienne and Captain Theodore far behind. She rubbed the back of her neck, trying to keep from knocking her hair down and she chuckled. "They are coming," she assured him.

"I'll go to them," he said, stepping to the side of Isabella. "Be ready to leave when I get back. I would like to speak to the high elves before nightfall."

Isabella agreed with him as he continued toward the dock. The two elvish warriors followed him and she turned her attention back to her father, but then to G'Nash. "Do you think the high elves will help us?"

G'Nash shook his head. "The high elves are pure of blood and hard to negotiate with. I have heard of them turning against their own kind just for being with another race. We are a combination of mixed blooded wood elves, orcs, humans, and me. I would be surprised if it doesn't come to a fight when we first encounter them," he declared, placing his hands on his hips.

"A fight between us would do no one any good."

"That's not how they will see it," Captain Theodore interrupted as he approached. Beside him walked Vivienne and the king. "The high elves believe they are untouchable."

King Jaspen shook his head as the group came to a stop just before her. "They are powerful due to their pure bloodlines, but they are far from untouchable. I have seen many of their strongest warriors and mages fall in battle," he said, rubbing his smooth chin. "It will take some convincing for them to even consider meeting with us. The magic I used to see if anyone was within the port should have gotten their attention. I would suspect they have already sent a scouting party to investigate us and that's why we have little time to just stand around."

"What is the plan?" Isabella asked.

Captain Theodore cleared his throat. "I have dealings with the high elves of this continent. They don't trust me, but they do trade with me. I will wait here for them and once they have entered the town, you will approach them with King Jaspen. Make sure that you announce who you are before you are seen, King Jaspen. Hopefully that will be enough to keep them from killing me," he said, half-heartedly.

"Then we should hide until they arrive," she said, making her way toward a house and pushing open the door.

The overbearing smell of rot caused her stomach to churn. She quickly covered her nose and mouth with her hand as she entered the abandoned house, making her way over to a small table that had two plates of decomposing food. She stacked them on top of each other. *Disgusting*, she thought as she lifted them and tossed them out the window. It didn't do much to help with the smell that lingered within the small home, but she was able to lower her hand from her face. She stood at the window making sure she could see the fountain as the others stepped in.

Captain Theodore gave her a subtle wave as he sat down on the rim of the fountain. He placed his left hand down into a pocket and with his right hand he let a golden coin run across his fingers. He was putting on a brave face, but she could see just how nervous he truly was. His crew carried cargo from the ship, placing it around him, and then going back to the ship to get more. He examined the crates, making sure that he hadn't lost anything while traveling. He broke the seal on one, pulled free an apple, looked it over, and took a bite. He nodded, but as he held the apple out an arrow knocked it from his hand.

Isabella quickly looked in the direction the arrow had come, she heard the snapping of the bowstring as soon as it was released, but she couldn't seem to locate the one who fired it. All she could smell was the rotting food left within the home, all she could see in the distance were abandoned houses, and all she could see beyond the town were the tops of trees. *Are the high elves capable of firing arrows that far?*

"What business do you have in Tanzanite?" A soft voice asked, breaking her concentration and drawing her attention to the edge of town, but she still couldn't see anyone.

"I am Captain Theodore LongShanks of the Faded Glory," he announced loudly, removing his hat and bowing his head slightly. "I have brought news of Sapphire," he said, placing his hat back on his head.

The creaking of a wooden door caused her to look in the direction it had come from and she could see a regal elf stepping from one of the abandoned homes. He was dressed in blue robes that flowed like silk and it looked like wind blowing behind him as he gracefully stepped toward the captain. He carried a longsword. The blade reflected the sunlight, he held it against his chest, ready to defend himself if need be, and he stopped just short of the fountain.

"I am Fortaine Del'VelRosa," he said, in a stern, but songlike voice. "and I know who you are, captain," he said in a voice of disgust. "How is it that you were able to use magic?"

Captain Theodore flashed him a coy smile and held out his hands. "Let me explain in full detail before you try to skewer me with that sword," he begged, but paused until the high elf rolled his eyes and agreed. "I've brought survivors from Sapphire, one of them being King Jaspen of Y'Melenor," he announced before taking a step back.

"You've brought outsiders to this land?" He said, taking a stance and holding the sword point at the captain.

"If you hurt him you will answer to my wrath!" Isabella screamed, throwing open the door and stepping forward.

Fortaine chuckled at the sight of her. "This human girl thinks she has wrath I should be concerned with," he mocked.

"It's not just her you have to worry about elf," G'Nash said as he emerged from the home with Torgath and the others behind him.

Fortaine's face twisted in disgust at the sight of them all. "Do you think I came alone?" He said, snapping his fingers and fifteen more high elves emerged with their longswords in hand.

"We did not come here to fight," King Jaspen declared softly.

Fortaine chuckled at him. "You came here to die," he said before making his attack.

The high elf's blade came toward her, the world slowed as he came closer and she knew that she didn't have the strength to stop it. She closed her eyes, preparing for the intense pain that would come from being stabbed, but the sound of metal breaking caused her to look. G'Nash had transformed and moved to defend her. His back was turned to the high elf, taking a chance that his hide was thick enough to deflect the tip of the sword, his dark eyes were fixed on her, his long ivory horn between them, and he reached out to rub her cheek. "Are you alright Wulgar?" He asked.

"What sort of monstrosity is this?" Fortaine asked, leaping away from them and letting his men encircle him.

"That will be enough, Fortaine," a female's voice called out from the direction the others had come and Isabella looked as she exited the same house.

The high elf female walked gracefully toward them, her light blue dress hung just above her ankles, she was decorated in jewelry that resembled the color of a full moon, she wore a crown of white diamonds that clung to her forehead, and her face was absent of emotions as she stopped at the side of the high elf. "He has been bound to NaShorn. The ancient Rhyno now protects him, to kill the foul half-orc would mean destroying that noble creature and that isn't something we can afford," she declared, looking out at them. "Why have you come to my kingdom?"

"Lady Yrula Har'VorNack. I, King Jaspen Theodred have come with grave news and wish to ask for the aid of the high elves," he announced, taking a knee before her.

Lady Yrula looked down her nose at him. "Save your words, wood elf. I already know of what has transpired in Sapphire. Our elders have seen the devastation and we have already taken measures to ensure the protection of our people," she said, holding out her arms. "That is why you find no one here."

King Jaspen nodded. "Then you will help us?"

"I will not," Lady Yrula interrupted harshly. "*La'Lilenor* has never been nor will it ever be besmudged by the likes of you, you, and most definitely not you or your kind," she said, pointing from the king to Isabella, but finishing with her finger at the half-orc.

"Are you not concerned about the monstrous army that could be coming for you?!" Isabella screamed in frustration.

Lady Yrula chuckled lightly. "Should the Eye of Avgrunnen land on our shores, we will then deal with it. They will find that we aren't as easily defeated as the half-breeds," she said with a smirk.

Isabella's anger grew, a light growl emerged from her throat and she moved to speak, but was stopped by King Jaspen. "I understand. May we get your permission to seek refuge at E'Amel, the wood elf city to the north of your territory?" He asked, bowing his head in respect.

Lady Yrula turned her back to them. "I shall have my mages teleport you to the border and you can seek out your kind from there. I can't just have you terrorizing my people," she exclaimed, nodding to Fortaine and he blew into a small wooden flute.

Six more elegantly dressed high elves emerged from a different house, rushed over to their queen, and bowed their heads. "Teleport these hoodlums to the border."

Lady Yrula stepped past her mages, but turned to look back at the group. "Careful with that temper of yours, girl. Not many would take being growled at with such kindness," she declared, turning and making her way back toward the house she had emerged from.

Isabella moved to speak, but in the blink of her eye she saw the abandoned houses replaced with tall trees, the smell of salt replaced with that of nature, and she could hear the wildlife rustling within the forest. She turned around in bewilderment. "What happened?" She asked, but she already knew the answer.

"They teleported us across their land," King Jaspen said as he looked at Vivienne. "Go see if they managed to send all our men or if it was just us that were sent," he commanded, but before she could move to do as requested, they watched as the others were teleported to them, and Captain Theodore was the last to appear.

"I said I didn't want to be teleported!" The captain screamed, tossing his hat to the ground and stomping his foot. "This has got to be a terrible jest. I told them I wasn't with you and not to teleport me and yet here I am!" He yelled, looking at the tree tops.

Isabella shook her head, but turned her attention back to the king. "Did you know that her elders held that kind of power?"

King Jaspen released a heavy sigh as those injured and sick on Faded Glory came through. "Vivienne, go tend to them. Make sure they are ready to move," he commanded and as she rushed toward the hurt warriors, he nodded his head at Isabella. "I figured they would have seen it in their visions. Just like those we travel to see now. Our elders have a unique gift that has been bestowed on them by Deware. The prophetic dream state and through that they can see what is to come. My grandmother had the gift, but it seems to skip generations. I don't have it, Revalor, as far as I know, doesn't have it, and Vivienne has never confessed to having it," he said, looking down to conceal his sadness at remembering his grandmother.

Isabella furrowed her brow. "Then why did we seek those pompous elves out? We should have just made our way to E'Amel," she declared through clenched teeth.

King Jaspen shook his head. "The dream state isn't always reliable. I had to make sure they were aware of Doden and his cult. Just because they hate us doesn't mean I want to see them hurt. Plus, I had hoped that they would see the vision of the undead army and be more willing to help," he declared in a huff. "Don't worry, Isabella. The city of E'Amel is much bigger than that of Y'Melenor and the knowledge there is vast. We will still be able to figure out where the other spirit animals are when we get there."

"How are we supposed to find the wood elves of E'Amel?"

"Don't worry. We have already found you," a female voice called out from a tree and they all looked to see that she was standing on a branch smiling at them.

Isabella could hear the string of bows being pulled taut and the wood elf gracefully made her way down the tree. "I hope you can forgive my distrust, but it's not every day we get visitors of such colorful variety," she said, taking a single step closer and looking at each person standing before her. "Our elders spoke of a creeping plague engulfing Sapphire, they even said we should prepare for survivors to come and to be of open mind when we saw them. I can now see why," she said, playfully.

King Jaspen took a knee before her. "Queen Lyranda Rosethorne, please forgive our intrusion in your land, but we have come carrying news of the black death that has swept through the land of Sapphire and we fear it could come for Tanzanite next."

"You need not kneel to me, King Jaspen," Queen Lyranda said, extending her hand for him to take. "I have prepared quarters for all of you and it looks like you have some that could benefit from our healers," she exclaimed, looking around at the injured within their party.

"You have my thanks," he said, bowing his head.

Queen Lyranda took hold of his hand and closed her eyes. A gentle breeze swept through them, the leaves rustled at their feet, the trees danced, and they were brought from the forest to the wood elf city of

E'Amel. Isabella was awestruck at the beauty of the city. It resembled Y'Melenor in many ways, but it was also very different. A peaceful river ran through the city in several places, coming together at the end to create a glorious waterfall, twisted branches made bridges that could be used to cross the streams, and wooden homes extended one story, but a few held a second story. The elves were all gathered at the center of the city. Hushed whispers filled the air as they manifested before them and little time was wasted.

The healers quickly examined the wounded and stretchers were used to carry them to a house where their wounds could be treated with the herbs and remedies grown within the city. Queen Lyranda bowed her head, but Isabella could see the spell she used took a lot of energy from her. The others moved to help their queen and she waved them off. "I'll be fine. Just need to catch my breath," she said with a forced smile.

Isabella thought of Aleesia, the grandmother to the king and the one that helped purge her from the darkness of Dorcha at the cost of her life. Queen Lyranda inhaled a deep breath. "If you will follow me I will show you to your house and we can discuss what has happened in Sapphire," she said, leading them through the city.

The house she led them to sat beside one of the rivers. The gentle sound of the water flowing was elegant and the home was the biggest within E'Amel. It was just two stories high, but was six rooms wide. Queen Lyranda stepped up to the door with a smile. "Welcome home," she declared, gently pushing the door open and allowing them to step inside.

They made their way to a dining area where a massive table sat that would accompany twelve all around it and she took a seat. She ushered for others to do the same, but the only ones that took a seat were that of King Jaspen, Uthric, Torgath, G'Nash, Gh'Rys, Vivienne, Captain Theodore and Isabella. The rest of them scattered through the house.

Queen Lyranda adjusted in her seat. "Now, tell me what happened to Sapphire?"

"We will need wine," King Jaspen declared, knowing the tale would be long and he would need something to insure his throat didn't fail him in the details.

Queen Lyranda nodded her head as she caught one of the elvish servants that was helping others in the house. "Bring us drinks," she requested elegantly and the servant bowed his head to do as she asked.

King Jaspen inhaled a deep breath as he began his tale with the arrival of Isabella and her quest of finding the spirit animals. He told her that it was his grandmother, Aleesia, that blessed the journey for the wolf champion and how she found the rhyno spirit, NaShorn within the swamp of Bog'Alor. He also explained what happened there and that he had heard rumors of a cult calling themselves the Eye of Avgrunnen and how its leader Doden was capable of miraculous things, but he never dreamed it was bringing back the dead. He told her of how they attacked his kingdom, of how Y'Melenor was lost and how he owed Isabella, not for saving the lives that were saved, but for also restoring the life of his cousin.

"I lack the knowledge of what spell was used, but had it not been for that magic, then Revalor would have died on the shores of Sapphire," King Jaspen admitted with a quiver in his voice and he looked down at the table top to compose himself. "We were rescued by Captain Theodore, brought to Tanzanite, and now we seek the aid of the elves of these lands."

Queen Lyranda gasped lightly with a shake of her head. "That's quite a tale, King Jaspen," she said, finishing her goblet and letting the servant refill it. "I'm not sure how much help I can be, but you have shelter here for as long as you need it," she offered from a smile. "Do you know where the next animal spirit is?" She asked, locking her eyes on the wolf champion.

Isabella shook her head and Queen Lyranda sat her goblet down. "How is it that you don't know where the animal spirits are? Aren't they connected?"

Isabella gave her a shrug. "Lucian said that they could sense each other, but he is still trying to recover after we saved the life of Revalor," she admitted shamefully.

Queen Lyranda reached out, taking hold of her hand. "There is nothing to be ashamed of, wolf champion," she said with a gentle squeeze. "You performed a miracle on the shores of Sapphire from what I hear and we all know the toll using magic has on a person. Let the wolf rest, but what about you?" She asked, pointing to the half-orc. "Can't NaShorn sense the other spirits like Lucian? What is the rhyno spirit saying to you?"

G'Nash shifted in his chair. "NaShorn isn't much of a talker. He is there to guide me in difficult times and give me strength when I need it, but other than that he is just quiet. I can try asking him though," he said, closing his eyes. "He says that he can sense two spirits close by. The closest being the bear spirit, Ursadelle. He suggests we gain her strength before seeking out the other," he remarked, opening his eyes slowly and exhaling a long breath. "The bear spirit can be found in a forest den within *White Lily Forest.*"

Queen Lyranda slapped the table top before standing from the chair. "I'll get you an escort. White Lily isn't far from here, we can actually teleport you there, but I'm not familiar where a den could be. Once you get there you will have to find that on your own."

"What about me?" Captain Theodore interrupted before she could get away. "I would like to get me and my crew back to our ship."

"I will have someone take you to your ship, but might I suggest you sail it to *Port Grum-Dale*. It's the closest port to E'Amel, it is run by dwarven cousins and they can be hard to deal with, but they are also in my debt. I'll send word you are coming," Queen Lyranda said with a smile. After the captain agreed she tapped her fingers on the hard wooden surface of the table. "Excellent. I'll get the escorts together. You find out who will be going," she declared, making her way out of the house.

Isabella heard the door close and she turned her attention to those still sitting at the table. "Who intends to go with me?"

"Are you sure it is wise for you to go, Wulgar?" G'Nash asked, placing a hand on her shoulder.

"I am the champion of Lucian," she declared, looking at the others. "This is my quest and I will see it to the end."

Torgath laid his hand on her other shoulder. "Then I shall accompany you, daughter. No harm shall befall you while I draw breath."

"I will walk at your side, Wulgar," G'Nash declared with a bow of his head.

Vivienne shook her head. "I should go, but I need to tend to our wounded."

"I must help Queen Lyranda plan our defense against the undead. Should they reach us here," King Jaspen said with a worried look etched on his noble brow.

"I used too much energy getting us across the sea. I will need ample rest to be of any use," Uthric said and Gh'Rys nodded his agreement.

Captain Theodore stood from his chair and lifted his hat from the table. "I would accompany you, but I have to get my ship," he said, bowing his head respectfully to them and making his way out of the house.

Isabella looked to her half-orc friend and then to her father. "Looks like it is just the three of us," she said, standing from the table.

"Sorry I'm late," the voice of Revalor echoed through the house.

Isabella gasped as he stepped up to the table. She rushed toward him and Vivienne did the same on the other side of the table. The two of them collided against him in a warm embrace, but he groaned from the affection. "What did I miss?" He asked, returning their embrace gently.

"We are getting ready to set out to find the bear spirit, Ursadelle," Isabella announced proudly.

"Sounds like fun," Revalor remarked from a smile. "When do we leave?"

"Are you sure you are up to going on this quest?" Isabella asked, looking him over.

Revalor rotated his shoulder causing it to pop. "I'm fine. Just a little stiff is all," he admitted, rubbing the back of his neck.

Isabella crossed her arms. "I'm glad to see you awake," she said as the door opened.

Four elvish archers stepped up to her. They were wearing leather armor covered in birch, their wooden helms outlined their faces, they carried long recurve bows, and a quiver that went from shoulder to shoulder full of arrows. The one at the front bowed his head. "I am General Norvian. I have been instructed to escort you through White Lily. Are you ready to go?" He asked, looking at the small group around the table.

Torgath stood from the table, lifting his massive scythe, the once innocent farming tool that had become stained with the blood it had spilled and G'Nash pushed himself up using the table. The two of them stepped closer to the wood elf general, but Revalor wasn't equipped for the journey. In his haste to make it to the house, he had forgotten to grab his bow and he released a heavy sigh at the realization of it.

King Jaspen stood from the table and unfastened his sword belt. "I will let you take *Wind Cleaver*, but I expect it back on your return," he declared, handing his cousin the sword.

It was the first time Isabella had taken notice of the sword. The hilt of it was twisted wood with hints of jade and the sheath was elegantly crafted with leaves of jade etched on it. Revalor bowed his head to his cousin as he took the sword and quickly fastened it around his waist. "Looks like I am ready," he declared from a smile.

General Norvian lowered his head, followed by his warriors, and they all whispered a magic incantation in unison. Isabella felt the familiar breeze of the teleportation spell blow across her brow and in a blink, she was transported from the city of E'Amel. She was standing within a forest, but it was different from the one where Queen Lyranda found them. The trees had vines that grew toward the ground, it looked like they were weeping, and white flowers bloomed all over them. The ground was softer under her feet, but the forest was denser than any other she had been in. She looked around in wonder.

"Queen Lyranda said that the bear spirit was within a den. The mountains just north of here would be an idle place to start our search," General Norvian announced and without hesitation he moved north with his men.

Isabella looked at the group that traveled with her. She knew that one of them would have to be the champion of Ursadelle, but she didn't know who. G'Nash was already the champion of NaShorn, she was champion of Lucian, and that only left a small number of those who could volunteer. *Maybe that's why Queen Lyranda sent two female warriors with us,* she thought, but pushed the thought to the side as they came to the base of the mountains. She marveled at the sight of the red rocks that made up the mountain, but there was no sign of any caves from where she was standing.

"Who dares enter my domain unannounced? You are either very brave or very stupid," the feminine voice said in a light growl.

"I am Isabella Strongfellow, champion of Lucian and seeker of the animal spirits," she announced loudly, stepping forward. "We need the strength of the guardians to prevent Bahaal from escaping Dorcha'Helvetti and we have come to speak to the great bear spirit, Ursadelle."

"You say that you are the champion of Lucian, but I can only sense the presence of NaShorn," the growly female voice said.

Isabella looked to Revalor and then back in the direction she believed the voice was coming from. "That's because Lucian is resting. Before we made our voyage here, we used a great deal of magic to save the life of someone and now he will need another fortnight before he is back to his full potential."

"You expect me to believe that Lucian would be so careless with his life?" The voice said, but it had moved to the other side of the forest.

Isabella took a small step back. "Lucian warned me of what could happen and I begged him to do it anyway. I had already lost my best friend, the city of Y'Melenor was destroyed, we were being pursued, and I wasn't about to lose anyone else. He granted me the power to save a life," she declared through clenched teeth.

"I can sense the burning rage within you," the voice said as the bear spirit stepped forward and shook its fur.

It had black fur with a yellow shape just below the neck, the long, thick claws tapped against the dirt as Ursadelle sauntered forward and stood up on her hind legs. Isabella could feel the power coming from the bear as it looked down at her. "What is your plan on defeating the blood god?"

"I will gather the animal spirits and contain him within Dorcha'Helvetti," Isabella said, looking into the eyes of the bear.

The bear chuckled at her. "Has Lucian told you the reason we were created?" Ursadelle asked, but didn't wait for her to answer. "We were created by Deware to bring forth the animals that fill the world and somehow we ended up becoming jailors to the blood god. We are able to bestow our power to those known as druids, but once we have taken a champion those blessed by us can no longer call upon our power. The world has already lost the wolf and rhyno spirit. You can't take all the animal spirits, girl. The druids would become powerless."

Isabella looked away, but kept the bear within sight. "I didn't know that. Lucian had never said that those blessed with his power would be without. Aleesia said you were created by the wizard prime during the Great Banishing," she admitted with a heavy heart.

"Fables are created to fit the teller of the story, child, but there is always a different version somewhere." The bear lowered back down to all fours and turned to walk away from her. "I can't turn my back on my followers. They need me."

"Joining our cause is the only way to protect your followers," Isabella begged.

Ursadelle turned her head slightly toward her. "I don't even sense a strong enough champion among you," She declared as she started back towards her cave.

"You are just scared!" Torgath screamed as he shouldered his way to stand beside his daughter and pointed his scythe at the bear. "You are terrified and that is the real reason you turn your back on this cause!”

Ursadelle roared in anger as she turned and stood back up on her hind legs. She was a hand taller than Torgath. “How dare you speak to me in this way!” She yelled, causing his hair to dance in her breath, but her father had no fear in looking down the gullet of the beast.

Torgath shook his head. “Unlike you I’m not afraid. You can maul me, tear me to shreds, but I will not go down without a fight. My daughter has endured so much in such a short time and yet she continues to fight for the world. She is only fifteen years of age, but she has shown more courage than people twice her age. She knows that if this blood god escapes, he will plunge the world into darkness, but instead of just giving up she continues to fight. If you walk away then you are a coward and if it is the last thing I ever do, I will make sure the world knows it,” he declared through clenched teeth.

Ursadelle lowered herself back to all fours and nuzzled her nose against Torgath. “Well spoken, my champion,” she announced happily.

“What?!” Torgath said in bewilderment.

“I needed to find a champion if I was going to give my power to the cause and you have shown me just how strong your bond is with her. Those who follow me are considered my children. I understand the devastating weight that can be put on your shoulders when trying to protect your young ones. You fear that you will falter and harm will come to those that you love, but it is in those moments that we find our true strength. I can sense that you are willing to stand against all odds and would never back down as long as it meant protecting your family,” Ursadelle said, standing back up. “Are you ready to accept me, champion?”

“Wait!” Isabella protested as she stepped between the bear and her father. “If you take the bear as the champion then you will be giving up your life.”

“If giving my life saves our family, then I will happily give it and stand at your side until the very end,” Torgath said, running his thumb down the cheek of his daughter.

Isabella gently rested her forehead on his, gave him a nod, stepped to the side, and the bear spirit collapsed onto the shoulders of Torgath. She watched as Ursadelle faded into the body of her father, his muscles flexed, his teeth clenched, and he fought against the pain he was enduring. A swirling wind blew all around them as he dropped to his knees, holding his arms against his chest. He started foaming at the mouth and he finally released a pain filled roar as the wind burst forth knocking everyone to the ground.

"Father!" She yelled as she crawled across the ground and rolled him over on his back. "Please be alright," she begged as she wept.

Torgath slowly lifted his hand to touch the side of her face. "I'm fine, daughter," he said, his voice carrying his fatigue, but he sat upright off the ground. "Ursadelle has told me where we can find Celeste, the wise owl spirit."

"Where might that be," G'Nash asked as he helped him back onto his feet.

Torgath rubbed the back of his neck. "She can be found in the snowy mountains further north, but she said we should proceed with caution through there."

"That's the home of the giants," General Norvian exclaimed, rubbing his smooth chin. "We should speak to Queen Lyranda before heading there. The giants aren't fond of outsiders within their territory. They see everything as an act of aggression and they fear everyone is out to take their land," he said, fixing his bow on his shoulder.

"Why would they think people are out to take their land?" Isabella asked, but before her question could be answered the elves used their magic to teleport them back to the city.

"The giants were promised a fertile island away from the other races if they helped during the Great Sacrifice, but instead they lost everything. We fought against them to lay claim to this forest and it wasn't an easy war. They are brutes that stand as tall as the oldest tree, they toss massive boulders with as much ease as we would pebbles. They have been known to eat my kind and they show no pain, but they are simple-minded. Their only battle tactic is relying on their immense strength. That is how we beat them," General Norvian explained as he led them through the city and up to a two-story home that was decorated by Ignis Fatuus. "If we are going to their lands, we will need permission from the queen. If we are caught by them, it could ignite another war between us," he said, opening the door and stepping through.

Isabella quickly followed with the others behind her. They walked down the long narrow hallway, the smell of trees lingered heavily in the air, and the Ignis Fatuus lighting their way and revealing the painted pictures that decorated the walls. She didn't stop to gaze upon them, but she was able to give them a quick glance. She could see how they immortalized a different elf, each looking more regal than the next, and the last one before they came to a door, was that of Queen Lyranda. She stood dressed in wooden armor that had gold inlay, making her look as if she was decorated in fall leaves and she held tight to a sword that was pointed to the sky.

The door was pushed open, the room reminded her of King Jaspen's royal chamber as the ceiling was so high it could barely be seen. The sunlight shone through cracks of the ceiling, a throne was positioned at the center with a long table, and she could see several elves sitting at it. Queen Lyranda sat at the head of the table with King Jaspen just off to her right, but the others Isabella didn't recognize. General Norvian stepped up and bowed to his queen. "We have succeeded in our mission, my queen. We have also gathered knowledge of another spirit animal. We have discovered that Celeste, the wise owl, is in the snowy mountains of the giants."

A loud commotion went up from those that Isabella didn't recognize at the table and interrupted General Norvian abruptly. They were all shouting of what could happen if someone was caught within the lands of the giants, how it would entice another war, and how the queen would be mad to allow it, but the queen appeared to pay them little heed as she closed her hands together. She slammed her hands down on the table causing silence to fill the room and she slowly stood from her chair.

"Isabella," Queen Lyranda started, her voice carrying a soft melodic tone as she forced a smile and sighed heavily. "With the threat that could be coming from Sapphire I just can't risk starting a war with the giants. They can't be reasoned with. They will see any transgression in their lands as an act of aggression and attack our home. I am truly sorry," she said, nodding to General Norvian and he bowed to her.

King Jaspen cleared his throat as he stood from the table. "We completely understand, Queen Lyranda and accept your decision. I will escort Lady Isabella back home where we may rest for a time," he said, bowing his head.

"Don't say anything," King Jaspen whispered as he came upon her and took her by the arm. "I will explain once we have arrived back at the house."

Isabella was upset, but she complied with the king's request. She bowed to the queen with respect, followed by the others who accompanied her, and the small group quickly made their way back toward the home that was conjured for them by the elves of E'Amel. King Jaspen opened the door, allowing her to step through first and ushered her to the table. "Can you be ready to leave by nightfall?" He asked, filling a goblet with wine.

"I don't understand," Isabella said, shaking her head and sitting down at the table.

King Jaspen slid a piece of parchment over to her. "The queen gave me that after she had hit the table."

General Norvian will escort a small party to the north, was written on it and she sat back in her chair. "I can be ready to leave, but we need to discuss who is going to be the champion of Celeste," she declared, handing the note back to the king.

King Jaspen declared, burning the note and tossing it down into an empty goblet. "I believe that I should take that responsibility."

"You are supposed to be a king, not a fool, cousin," Vivienne said, stepping from around the corner and leaning on the table. "You can't be a champion because our people still need you to rule them. Celeste is the animal spirit of a wise owl. I will be her champion," she declared with her chest swelling with pride.

King Jaspen groaned his disappointment, but Revalor shook his head. "How come I can't be the champion of the owl?"

"You have never sought knowledge, cousin," Vivienne revealed with a soft smile. "Your prowess came from your strength, but I was raised by our grandmother, taught the ways of our people, and where we came from. I am the right champion for the wise owl spirit," she declared with a nod of her head.

Isabella released a heavy sigh. "Then it is settled. We will be ready to travel by nightfall," she announced, standing from the table and stepping toward the exit of the room. "Everyone needs to rest up. We don't know what is waiting for us when we leave.

Isabella made her way through the house, finding a room that didn't have anyone occupying it, and she crawled on the soft bed of feathers. *Lucian, I hope you are almost recovered. I know you said it would be another fortnight, but I might need you when we find Celeste*, she prayed, closing her eyes.

I will be ready, champion, the voice of the wolf echoed in her mind as she drifted off.

Chapter 7
Celeste, The Owl Spirit

Isabella turned in circles, trying to find something that would give her an idea about where she was, but she didn't recognize anything around her. The mountains to the north were unlike any she had ever seen, the small town to her right was one she had never visited, and the old weathered sign that swayed in the wind was barely legible. "Merideth?" She questioned as she got closer and could finally make out what was etched into it. "Where am I?"

The town was empty, but the buildings looked properly maintained. She scratched at the top of her head. *Lucian,* she prayed, closing her eyes.

I am here, champion, he called out in her mind.

"What is this place? Why am I seeing it?"

This is a town back in Peili'Marfach Kone. I don't know why you are seeing it. I used to have some that lived here who worshiped me. Maybe that's the reason, but I am only guessing, he declared quietly.

The sound of metal clinking together drew her attention and she turned to see a man making his way toward the town on horseback. He was wearing a suit of black armor that made him look like he had dragon scales similar to the pictures she had seen. On his back was a massive sword that had an elegantly decorated hilt peeking over his right shoulder. He wore a wooden helm that ran the length of his cheeks and tied under his chin, but the only protection for his face was a nose guard that went between his eyes.

Isabella got an uneasy feeling as she watched the horse saunter toward her, bringing him closer and she clenched her fist together. "Who is that?"

I do not know, champion, but I sense a great power coming from him, Lucian offered as he manifested beside her and lowered his body toward the ground.

"I will not let you destroy this town like you did my village!" The stranger screamed, putting his heels into the side of the horse and making it charge toward her. "I will put an end to your tyranny here and now! If it's the last thing I do!" He declared, drawing the sword from the sheath, but as he was about to attack, she awoke.

"Are you alright, Wulgar?" G'Nash asked from the doorway.

Isabella groaned, her head pounded and she was confused. *Who was that and why did he think I was there to attack that town?* She questioned silently. She planted her feet on the floor and stood from the bed. "I'm fine, G'Nash. Has General Norvian arrived?" She asked, looking back to see that the sun hadn't fully set yet.

"Not as of yet, Wulgar. That's why I have come to see you," G'Nash said, taking a small step inside the room and closer to her. "No one would blame you if you stayed back to rest."

"Don't be foolish!" She interrupted harshly.

G'Nash lowered his head in shame at being scolded by her, but lifted his gaze to look at her. "I do not mean disrespect. I am just simply worried about you. We are about to go into a very hostile territory, one where we could be killed for just being there and you are without the wolf spirit."

Isabella interrupted him by holding out her hand, the palm facing toward the ceiling and a small ball of fire emerged from it. She held onto it like he would do a rock, twisting it around with the tips of her fingers and then smothering it out by clenching her hand into a fist. "I am never without Lucian, G'Nash, and he is getting stronger with each passing moment. I don't need anyone to worry about me. I'll be fine," she declared passionately.

G'Nash bowed his head to her slightly. "I am sorry, but worrying about you is something I cannot avoid. I will stand at your side and fight with all my strength to keep you safe," he exclaimed, saluting her with pride.

Isabella flashed a half-smile as she walked up and punched him lightly on the shoulder. "Together we will stop the blood god," she declared, sniffing the air. "Smells like someone is cooking. Let's eat before General Norvian shows up," she said, stepping past him and making her way toward the kitchen.

She stepped off the stairs and went through the dining hall. She paused to look at the long table that had twelve chairs, each filled with a person that came with her from Sapphire, but those sitting at the table weren't separated by race. They were together, laughing and telling tales of days gone. The elves spoke of orc warriors they admired from tales they had heard, the orcs sang elvish songs, but the light hearted melodies were changed by the dark and guttural voices of the orcs. Her heart felt lifted as she saw them getting along, she nodded to G'Nash as the half-orc touched her shoulder and the two of them continued into the kitchen.

A wood burning iron stove was being used by her father, an orc continued to stand patiently at his side watching him cook, and the sizzle of the meat intensified as it was turned over. "Are you hungry?" He asked, lifting it up, placing it on a wooden plate, and handing it to the young orc.

"Where did you get that?" Isabella asked, walking up to him.

"I killed it in the forest."

"Do the elves know that you have been hunting the beasts within their forest?"

She had spent enough time with the wood elves of Sapphire to know their diet. They consumed berries and fruits, but they were no strangers to the taste of meat. She also knew how they disliked those that hunted in their forest without their permission. She looked up at her father as she waited for him to answer.

"How do you think I got into the forest to hunt, daughter?" Torgath asked, placing another heavy chunk on the open flame. "The queen granted me permission and even sent me with a guide," he said, flipping the meat over to cook on the other side. "Now, are you hungry?" He asked again, presenting the cooked food to her on a wooden plate.

Isabella's mouth watered as she retrieved the plate from him, but as she accepted his offering, she inhaled deeply of the savory smell of her meal. "How are you feeling?"

Torgath gave her a shrug as he laid another chunk on the flame. "I feel stronger and my senses are heightened. Ursadelle is teaching me when she can. She is getting prepared for anything that might happen on our journey," he said with a heavy sigh. "I don't know how I am going to explain all this to your mother," he jested, turning the meat over so it could cook on the other side.

G'Nash held a wooden plate out for the food that was being cooked. "That'll do for me," he said, as the meat was placed on it.

"Good. You two go eat," Torgath demanded with a smile as he placed another chunk on the flame. "General Norvian shouldn't be much longer and we need to be ready to head north when he gets here," he announced, pointing the utensil he was using at them.

Isabella followed G'Nash out of the kitchen and the two of them found empty spots at the table that would allow them to sit next to each other. She ate from the cooked meat as Uthric shuffled into the room and took a seat across from her. He stretched, making his joints pop as he yawned. "How long did I sleep?" He asked, adjusting his eyepatch.

Isabella swallowed the bite she had been chewing and ran her arm across her mouth. "You've slept the whole day," she said, drinking from the goblet that was placed on the table by a wood elf servant.

Uthric let out another tired yawn as a goblet was placed before him. "Were you able to gain the power of Ursadelle?"

"We did," G'Nash answered as Isabella drained the contents of her goblet.

"Father is her champion," she announced as her empty chalice was filled back up.

Uthric nodded as he ran his hand down his beard. "Seems fitting, giving his immense strength. Have you determined the next one we are to seek?" He asked, sitting back in his chair and drinking from his cup.

Isabella gave him a nod as she toyed with the last bite of her steak. "We are going after Celeste, the wise owl spirit, but we have to wait until General Norvian shows up," she said, tossing the last piece of meat into her mouth and slowly chewing.

An eerie smile stretched across the face of Uthric as he gave a nod. "I supposed I should be the champion of this spirit," he said with confidence.

Isabella slowly shook her head. "Vivienne is going to be the champion."

"What?!" Uthric interrupted with a yell. "Why does she get that honor? I have spent my entire life in the pursuit of knowledge. I should be the champion of the owl!" He declared, leaping up from his chair.

Isabella shook her head. "Calm yourself, Uthric," she said, pushing the empty plate away from her and readjusting in her seat.

"What makes her more qualified than me?" Uthric asked, lowering himself back down in the seat and placing his arms on the table.

Isabella knew what Vivienne had told her cousin, but the old wizard that sat across from her had dedicated his entire life traveling the world, learning all it had to offer, and he seemed as knowledgeable as any. She shook her head. "I don't know what makes her more qualified, but I know that she has done as you have. She has spent her whole life learning all she could from her grandmother, Aleesia, and that has to be taken into consideration. If you would like to plead your case to the owl, then you are welcome to travel with us, but the choice of champion belongs to that of the animal spirit. They are giving up just as much as we are," she declared, looking to G'Nash who nodded his agreement.

Uthric sat back in the chair, crossing one arm over his chest and with the other he lifted up his hand to stroke his beard. "Fair enough. When do we leave?"

"As soon as General Norvian comes," Isabella answered, drinking from her chalice. "I would suggest you eat, drink, and prepare."

Uthric left the table without saying anything. "I will be ready to leave," he announced, making his way toward the kitchen.

Isabella sat back in her chair and sighed heavily, but G'Nash placed a hand on her shoulder. "Don't be discouraged, Wulgar. Letting the wizard come was the right choice to make. Let the owl spirit decide who should be the champion," he declared, pushing his plate across the table and drinking from his chalice. "I'm sure Celeste will make the wisest decision," He said as he nudged her arm slightly and flashed her a coy smile.

She giggled at the half-orc's attempt at humor. "We should gather supplies," she said with a flirty smile as she stood from the table and made her way toward the kitchen.

Isabella pushed open the door, but was greeted by Uthric. The old wizard was on his way back to the table, the sizzling steak resting on his plate, and he stepped to the side to let her enter the room. She nodded as she passed him. Her father was already working on packing dried meat into a small leather pouch and in another he had carefully packed loaves of elvish bread. He smiled as his daughter approached. "Has General Norvian arrived? I've packed rations that should see us through a week," he declared, stuffing more dried meat into the pouch.

Isabella shook her head. "We came to gather supplies for the journey, but you seem to already have that covered."

Torgath nodded as he handed her a pouch stuffed full of dried jerky. "I've got one for each of us. Just finished making one for Uthric," he announced, picking up the others from the counter and carrying them toward the exit of the kitchen.

They sat down at the table in chairs allowing them a clear view of the outside and they joined in the conversations that were already taking place. Torgath regaled them with his favorite tale from his childhood. The story was about a mercenary named *Aloric, the Emerald Dragon*, he was given the name due to the green dragon scales that his armor was made from, but the way he acquired the scales was a separate story than the one her father was recanting to those listening. The one Torgath spoke of was when Aloric was hired by the maer of *Torbeck*, a small village located in Mador Kingdom and his contract was to kill an evil hag that was abducting the children. She would lure them into the *Grimdale*, a swamp that was close to Torbeck, and once she had them, she would sacrifice them to gain power. Aloric hunted the old hag for a fortnight. He overcame many traps that were set by her, defeated every minion she summoned to protect her, and with each passing test he survived, she grew weaker before he finally killed her, but that was just one of his many achievements.

Isabella had heard every tale based on the fabled mercenary and that was one of the more reasonable ones that made her believe he actually existed, but there were some she just felt was made up to make the man more extraordinary. She chuckled at how lighthearted her father got when telling the tales of Aloric, but the front door opening caused her to sit up straight. She looked out the window to see that the sun had set during the fable and General Norvian stepped into the room with Vivienne behind him.

"Are you ready?" He asked, crossing his arms and standing firmly at the door.

Isabella looked around at the others and they stood from their chairs to get closer to the general. Vivienne shook her head as they approached. "Why is the old wizard coming?"

"I intend to make a plea to the owl spirit to be its champion," Uthric declared proudly.

Vivienne released a heavy sigh, but before she could speak General Norvian cleared his throat. "We don't have time to argue. We need to go," he said, closing his eyes and he cast his spell to teleport them quickly.

The room faded into darkness. The smell of those around the table was replaced with that of nature, a gentle breeze blew across her brow, and she noticed that she was now standing within the forest. She looked around, trying to get her bearings, but she didn't recognize anything. "Where are we?" She asked, focusing her gaze on the general.

"I brought us as close to the border as I could," General Norvian explained, taking a quick count of everyone. "A short league in that direction will bring us to the lands of the giants. Once we cross into their territory, it is important that you listen to what I say. They are primitive creatures and have poor eyesight. They won't be able to see us under the guise of night, but that doesn't mean they won't be able to hear us. So that means no squabbling about anything," he declared, looking between Vivienne and Uthric, but he didn't wait for them to agree before moving north.

The excitement was making Isabella's heart race. She had never seen a giant before, but she had heard tales of them from her brother. She had always imagined what they looked like, a race that towered over all others, and she looked at her father. She always thought he was a giant, but now she was going to see a real giant. She emerged from the forest into a small clearing, the barren land before her, and her heart sank. She expected to see behemoths moving around, their heads touching the sky, but instead all she could see was mountains, fields, and more forest off in the distance. "Where are the giants?" She asked, quietly.

General Norvian shook his head. "Did you expect to see them as soon as you stepped foot into their lands?"

Isabella gave him a nod and he released a sigh. "Have you never seen a giant before?"

She glanced at her father and the general chuckled. "Though your father is the biggest human I've ever seen, he is no giant. If the half-orc stood on your father's shoulders, then they would be the same height as a giant. They are massive creatures with immense strength, but they are slow and not very intelligent. That's why there is no reasoning with them. Now, stay quiet, keep close to me, and let's try to make it to that mountain before daybreak," he declared, pointing to a mountain not far from where they stood.

They crossed the grassy field to another small patch of forest, using the trees to conceal their presence, but there was still no sign of giants lurking about. They climbed the mountain, searching for a place to take shelter. The sun was breaking into the sky and she could see large fires burning brightly not far from where they started scaling the rocky surface, but she still couldn't see those she was hiding from.

"There," General Norvian called out quietly and she looked up to see the cave he was pointing to.

They pulled themselves up on the small ledge. The cave was enormous and dark. She peered inside it, but all she found was pictures that had been painted on the walls. The images depicted an enormous race hurling boulders, carrying spears the size of trees, and fighting against smaller images with bows.

"The *Gortek War*," General Norvian exclaimed, touching one of the images and looking back at the others. "After the Great Sacrifice we were disoriented. We had been ripped from our world and placed in this one. We did the best we could, but every race felt they were owed something. The giants thought this world was theirs, their prize for helping the wizard prime and they weren't too happy about having to share it with others. Their leader *Gortek Mountain Tooth* tried to take Tanzanite for himself. We tried to reason with them, but they wouldn't listen and after much death they finally relented," he paused to eat from the dried beef that was given to him by Torgath and he drank from the wineskin.

Isabella shook her head. "Gortek Mountain Tooth," she repeated the name as she walked through the cave and examined the other paints.

"Like I said," General Norvian started before taking another drink. "They are a primitive race and their names reflect that almost as much as their lifestyle."

Isabella furrowed her brow at what the general had said and went back to studying the cave drawings, but the sound of someone quickly approaching caused her to turn in defense. Through the darkness she could see the shape of someone just a hand shorter than her father rushing toward the general.

Isabella moved on instinct as she pulled General Norvian out of the way, but in doing so the attack struck her right in the center of her chest. She felt the air being knocked from her lungs, the world started spinning, and time stopped. She had never been struck with such force. She followed the arm that was attached to the massive fist that hit her. She expected to see a grown man, but instead she was greeted by an innocent face of a girl.

Her big brown eyes were filled with unfallen tears, her dirty brown hair was tied to the sides of her head, and she was frightened. Her clothes fit her loosely, hanging down to just above her ankles and she was screaming something, but Isabella couldn't make it out.

The attack had knocked her from her feet and all sound was muffled as she flew back away from her attacker. She thought that she would crash to the ground at any moment, but instead she felt as if she was floating. She turned her eyes up to see that she was within the arms of G'Nash and she could hear her father transforming as he rushed past her to collide with her attacker, but the woman cowered against the far wall and wept uncontrollably with her face buried against her knees.

"It's a giantess," General Norvian said, pulling free the longsword that was at his hip. "We have to kill her," he declared, taking a step closer.

"Stop!" Isabella commanded, getting to her feet from the arms of the half-orc and letting her senses come back to her. "This giantess is obviously scared," she pointed out as the woman cowered in the back of the cave.

"If she lives then she will inform the others and war will be brought on my people. I can't allow that," General Norvian declared, turning his attention back to the woman, but stopped as Torgath stepped in front of him.

"Move!" General Norvian demanded, but he was greeted by a low growl from Torgath.

Isabella shouldered past the half-elf and stepped up to the frightened giantess. "I'm not going to hurt you, but I need to be able to speak to you," she said as a bright light emerged from the palm of her hand and she lunged out, touching it to the forehead of the giant.

Isabella could see that she wasn't a woman, but just a small girl that was younger than she was. The cave was her sanctuary. A place she would come to play during the day and she was the one that painted the pictures on the wall. She had lost track of time the day before. She was asleep in the cave when they arrived and though she was frightened of them, she wouldn't just let them enslave her. Giants believe that elves use their magic to capture them, steal their lands, abuse them, and use them until their bodies give out. The girl was terrified of the magic Isabella showed, but hoped it would kill her when she placed it against her forehead.

"Rose not dead," the giantess said, looking at her hands.

Isabella shook her head and stumbled back a step. "Rose?"

"What spell did you use?" General Norvian interrupted, stepping closer to her.

Isabella shook her head and held up her hand to stop his approach. "I still don't know the name of the spell. It's just one that Lucian granted me to learn languages quickly, but it takes a toll on me and the one I use it on."

"Why Rose not dead?" The giant interrupted to ask.

Isabella forced a comforting smile and knelt down at the side of the giant. She searched for a way to say what needed to be said, but the language of the giants didn't allow for such words. "Not here to kill Rose. Isabella Strongfellow is name. Need to speak to animal spirit Celeste. Does Rose know where Celeste can be found?"

"If such a spell exists then why have we never heard of it?" General Norvian interrupted.

Isabella shook her head, but didn't move her gaze from the giant. "I don't know why the elves have no record of the spell," she admitted and put her focus back on the giant. "Can Rose help Isabella on quest for owl?"

Rose shook her head. "Rose knows the way, but why Isabella not kill Rose?"

"We should head back to E'Amel," General Norvian talked over the giant. "Queen Lyranda needs to know of this spell. If you could teach us how to do it then it could benefit us with negotiations with these giants and the other races of this world."

"Rose safe with Isabella," she said, ignoring the half-elf, but looking back to see he still held tight to his sword. "Put away your weapon! You are scaring her!" She commanded, but the half-elf chuckled at the request.

"Scaring her?" General Norvian mocked angrily.

Isabella let a low growl emerge from her throat. It had been a while since she felt the power of Lucian and she didn't know just how much she missed it until now. "I said to sheath the sword," she demanded and the half-elf did as she requested.

Isabella flashed a soft smile as she looked back at the girl. "Not come to fight or enslave giants, Rose. Only need to speak to Celeste about saving world. Can Rose help?" She asked, standing up and offering a hand to the giant.

Rose nodded as she accepted the help to stand from the ground. "Rose can help. Follow Rose," she said, stepping up, but getting stopped by the general.

"Where is she going? We can't just let her leave."

"She is going to show us the way to Celeste," Isabella interrupted, stepping up and placing a hand on the pommel of his sword to keep him from pulling it.

"They can't be trusted," General Norvian exclaimed through clenched teeth. "The only place she will lead us is to more of her kind and then they will kill us."

"The fear you feel is understandable, general, but she feared the same thing from you," Isabella said, making room so that the giant could step past them and toward the entrance of the cave. "Their people believe that your people only want to enslave them with magic."

"If she fears our magic so much then why did she let you use it on her?" General Norvian asked, watching the giant as she stopped at the cave entrance.

Isabella released a heavy sigh. "She hoped that it would kill her."

An eerie silence fell over them, but the giant looked out of the cave and then back to them. "Rose will wait until nightfall to take Isabella to the owl. Others not understand," she declared, sitting down at the entrance and looking out over the land.

"What did she say?" G'Nash asked.

"She is going to wait until nightfall to escort us to the owl spirit. She doesn't want the others to see us in the territory because they wouldn't understand," Isabella declared, looking at General Norvian and then making her way to sit beside the giantess. "Get some rest. We will leave as soon as the sun sets."

No one questioned her, but Isabella could see that the general had positioned himself where he could keep an eye on the giant and she knew that the half-elf wouldn't be getting any sleep. She released a heavy sigh, placing a hand over her eyes and Rose wrapped an arm around her. "Rose thanks Isabella for not making Rose a slave. Rose has heard many bad things about being a slave to pointy ears," she said, an uneasy smile creeping across her face.

Isabella shook her head. She knew what the giant was talking about, but she needed to fully understand what she meant. "Rose. Isabella not understand what Rose mean by being a slave to pointy ears."

Rose shook her head. "Giants stood with wizard in fight against evil. Giants promised peace, but instead got war with pointy ears. Big flash, plenty of land, and then stolen. Giants used to build big structures for pointy ears, giants used as shields during war so that pointy ears can cower in back and use magic. If giants resist, then giant is killed. Giants hide in the north. Hoping that pointy ears leave alone," she admitted from a broken voice.

Isabella was confused and she scratched her head. "Isabella sorry giants have endured so much. Fear of dying the reason Rose not resist magic Isabella used?"

Rose inhaled deep. "Rose intended to resist after, but then Rose saw the heart of Isabella and hope filled Rose," she admitted, looking away from her.

Isabella's heart broke at hearing the words of the giant. She feared being a slave so much that she was ready to sacrifice her life. "Rose not have to worry about being slave while Isabella lives. Rose safe with Isabella," she declared, moving her hand from the chest of the giant to her own chest and then back again. "Isabella need rest."

"Rose watch over Isabella. Rose keep Isabella safe while Isabella sleeps," she announced from a wide smile.

Isabella laid on the ground at the side of the giant and let sleep take her. She dreamed of Merideth, but it wasn't empty like before. The townsfolk moved around, criers tried to entice those traveling to stop at their store and she stood at the eastern entrance like before. She scratched at the back of her head. "Why am I dreaming of this town again?"

"I don't know, champion, but I can feel the coming of that man," Lucian said, stepping up beside her and lowering his body to the ground.

Isabella turned to see him charging toward her on horseback, the sun reflecting off the black armor, the wooden helm that covered his head and face. He was pointing a sword at her that she believed would give her father trouble at holding, but this man was wielding it with a single hand. "You will not take this town, Raven King!" he screamed as he got closer.

"Is he even talking to me?" She asked, looking around, but saw no one else beside her. "Who is the Raven King?!" She screamed back at him and he halted his pursuit.

"What sort of madness is this?!" He asked, but a white flame engulfed him causing him to disappear and she woke up to a gentle shake of the giant.

"Isabella have bad dream. Rose hates when Rose has bad dreams," she declared, helping the wolf champion up off the ground. "Night has come. Rose show Isabella the way to the owl now," she announced from a smile.

"Are we ready to leave?" Isabella asked, looking at her companions and after they all agreed, she nodded to Rose.

"I should've just stayed at the bottom of the mountain," Uthric groaned, leaning heavily on his staff.

Rose touched the shoulder of Isabella to get her attention. "What elder say?"

"Uthric complain about climb down," Isabella answered with a soft smile.

Rose lifted the old man off his feet and tossed him across her shoulder. The giant's strength was remarkable. She was merely a small child, but was as strong as Torgath. "Rose carry elder down mountain," she exclaimed and against his wishes she carried him.

The group made quick work reaching the bottom of the small mountain. Rose sat Uthric down and he glared at her. "Don't ever do that again," he declared, stamping the end of his staff down into the soft ground.

"What elder say?" Rose asked, looking to the only person that could speak to her.

Isabella nudged the old wizard. "Uthric thanks Rose for the help," she lied and the giant flashed him a smile.

"Follow close to Rose. Giants go to sleep soon, but have good ears," she announced before leading them toward the snowy mountain.

They traversed over open fields of tall grass and Rose brought them to a halt at the edge of one of the many small forests. She pushed a branch out of her view and gazed out at a settlement so big Isabella thought it a town. "*Snow Peak Village,*" Rose exclaimed, looking at Isabella and nudging her head. "Rose home. Isabella almost to owl."

The giant moved through the forest until the village was no longer in sight and then led the group across a small field into another forest. With the help of Rose, they managed to reach the base of the snow-covered mountain without alarming the other giants. "Owl up there," she said, pointing high to a cave that could barely be seen.

Isabella gave her a nod. "Rose has Isabella's thanks. Owe Rose much," she said, putting a hand against her chest and tilting her head.

"Isabella owe Rose nothing. Rose still free and Rose has new friend."

"Why have you come?" An unfamiliar voice interrupted to ask.

Isabella pushed Rose behind her and looked in the direction she believed the voice came from. A low growl emerged from her throat as she searched for the source. "Who said that?" She asked through clenched teeth.

"You must be the champion of Lucian," the voice said, but where it was coming from still couldn't be determined. "Only one beholden to him would have enough courage to travel through the giants' land with half-elves."

"Celeste?!" Isabella called out loudly.

"I know why you have come, but you are too late, champion of Lucian."

Isabella was astounded by the magnificent creature before her. She had seen a few owls when she was a small girl playing in the forest, but those could've perched on her arm and this owl was so large that the branch it was perched on was bending slightly. Its feathers were as white as the snow, its big, icy, cold, blue eyes glared at her and it flapped its massive wings causing a strong breeze to blow through them.

"What do you mean I'm too late?" Isabella asked through the gust.

Celeste calmed herself and let out a hoot. "You seek the animal spirits to contain Bahaal in Dorcha'Helvetti, but the blood god will not be contained there much longer. He has already found a host for his consciousness and once his ritual is complete, he will escape his prison. Not even the wizard prime could stop him now."

Isabella looked to the others, focusing on her father and the half-orc before looking back to the owl. "Then we will kill him."

The owl whistled, but it sounded more like a laugh. "You plan to kill the unkillable?" Celeste asked, turning her head upside down.

"Nothing is unkillable!" Isabella declared through clenched teeth. "You said he has found a host for his consciousness. What if we destroy the host? Can he then be put back in his prison?"

Celeste flapped her wings. "I suppose. Without a host the consciousness of the blood god would return back to its original host, but that is if you can destroy it before he breaks the spell that binds him in Dorcha'Helvetti. Once he has done that, there is no stopping him."

Isabella nodded to the owl. "Then that is what we will have to do. Is the host Doden?" She asked, thinking that it would explain how he could resurrect the dead.

"I'm afraid the host he has chosen is in Peili'Marfach Kone," Celeste responded with a coo. "That's where I have sensed his power the most and it will be there you will have to face his host to keep him contained."

Kirkland and mother! She thought, worrying about the danger they must be in. Isabella nodded her agreement. "Then we find a way back home, find this host, and kill it. Will you help us?" She asked, taking a knee before the owl.

Celeste shifted her wings causing a gentle gust to blow through them. "I'm sure you know the dangers of what you ask of me. If I join my spirit to that of someone unworthy, it would destroy both of us," she said with a hoot.

"Use your magic to find a suitable champion," Isabella declared, ushering toward Vivienne and Uthric who stood vigilantly within the group.

Celeste twisted her head at the request. "I'm afraid you don't understand how magic really works. What one perceives as magic is just a way of life to another. No one, not even the wizard prime, knows where the power comes from, but we know the consequences of misusing it. Everything is based on chance. Have your selection come forward, let them explain why they should be my champion, and I will choose between them."

Isabella didn't have to say anything as the two of them stepped forward, taking a knee at the tree and lowering their heads. Vivienne cleared her throat. "I have spent my entire life learning all that I could from my grandmother, Aleesia. She taught me the ways of our people before the Great Sacrifice and after, but my pursuit was not limited to just her teachings. I was an advisor to King Jaspen of Y'Melenor and I was expected to negotiate with the other races to keep peace within Sapphire. I have also educated myself on how to grow flowers and herbs that many thought were extinct, but despite it all I still have more to learn and always keep an open mind ready for new knowledge. That is why I believe I would be a suitable champion," she said, lifting her head.

Uthric shifted his shoulders and the gem at the head of his staff glowed. "The half-elf is remarkable, but I have also dedicated my life in the pursuit of knowledge. I have traversed all of Peili'Marfach Kone in pursuit of it and since arriving in Tylwyth Teg'Villi, I have done nothing but expand on that knowledge base. I have taught myself the many languages that we have encountered, I know how to communicate with the elves and the orcs, and given time, I will learn how to speak to the giants. I have an unquenchable thirst for knowledge and I seek it out however I can. This is why I believe I would be the best option for your champion, great Celeste," he declared, looking up at the owl.

Celeste flapped her wings. "Both of you are worthy to be a champion, but I sense the half-elf is more suitable to contain my knowledge," she said, taking to the skies.

Celeste flew so high that they couldn't see her, but Isabella could hear her as she soared around them and quickly rushed down to grasp the shoulders of Vivienne. She lifted the half-elf up and a whirlwind of snow engulfed them. A brilliant light burst forth giving sight to the bonding ritual.

The sudden burst of snow caused the group to stumble, but Uthric wasn't capable of staying upright. He collapsed to the ground and shook his head. "Why? Why am I not worthy enough?!" He screamed through clenched teeth.

"You are limited by your mind, Uthric, the wandering wizard of Peili'Marfach Kone, and if I took you as my champion, you would be driven to madness. I am taking a chance that the half-elf will be capable of handling all my knowledge, but even that is just a hope," the combination voice of Vivienne and Celeste echoed from the light. "Don't give up on your pursuit of knowledge. Continue to follow the champion of Lucian. She will show you the great wonders you have yet to see," the voice said as the light faded and Vivienne drifted down to the ground.

Isabella rushed over to check on the half-elf as Torgath lifted Uthric off the ground and the old wizard dried his eyes with his sleeve. Vivienne looked at them, one of her eyes a light green, but the other a cold blue. "I know how to get you back home, but we should get back to E'Amel first," she declared as she stood from the ground on weak legs.

Isabella placed a hand on the shoulder of a frightened Rose. "Isabella go save the world. Rose go home. Rose stay safe with other giants," she said with a smile.

Rose nodded her agreement before turning to make her way back toward the village they saw and Isabella turned to look at those that remained in her group. "Can we use magic to reach E'Amel from here or do we have to go back?"

"We can't use magic from here. The distance is too far," General Norvian scoffed.

"For you, maybe," Vivienne interrupted. "We can use the power of the animal spirits to teleport us back to the city," she exclaimed, taking hold of one of Isabella's hands and that of G'Nash.

The others quickly made a circle around the group, standing hand in hand, and Vivienne's eyes glowed brightly. "Hold tight," she said before whispering an incantation that engulfed the group in a brilliant light and in an instant the group was standing in the center of E'Amel, but Vivienne fell to her knees.

Isabella moved to comfort her and Vivienne chuckled. "Guess I need to rest, but at least we are back," she declared with a smile. "We should all rest. I know how to get us back to Peili'Marfach Kone, but it will require us at full strength to do it," she said as Torgath lifted her from the ground.

Isabella agreed as the group made their way toward the house that was conjured for them by the wood elves of E'Amel, but General Norvian took his leave of them. He had to report to the queen about what had transpired on their journey. She knew that she would eventually have to explain her actions with the giantess to the queen, but those questions would have to wait. Her mind danced with images of her mother and brother. She wondered if he was finally awake, she wondered if her mother would even recognize her now, and with those thoughts, she climbed into bed to let sleep take her.

Chapter 8
Defending Tanzanite

A cold and eerie breeze cut through her as she stood in an open field. Isabella was disoriented, she didn't know where she was or how she got there, but she could hear the heavy footfall of an army approaching. The smell of death lingered heavily in the air and she knew that it was the Eye of Avgrunnen that was coming for her. Lowering her body, she began to transform, her flesh tearing combined with that of her clothes, her nose becoming a snout full of razor-sharp teeth, her toes and fingers forming into claws. She unleashed a bone-chilling howl to the pale moon that hung above her head as she turned her gaze in the direction of the army and waited for them to emerge.

"You are rather impressive," a soft, but cold voice called out from the shadows. "Why don't you join me, wolf girl? I would much prefer to have you with me alive than dead."

"Why don't you come out and face me," she growled intensely.

"It's too soon for that, wolf girl, but I am coming. By the time you wake in your warm bed, I'll be there," Doden said with an eerie laugh.

Isabella growled, waking herself up, but she laid still on the bed. Letting her eyes scan the room until she was confident that she was alone and pushing herself up, she rubbed her forehead. "Just a dream, but it felt so real. Just like that town," she exclaimed, moving her hand to the back of her neck.

I believe there is more to your dreams, champion, Lucian offered, his voice echoing quietly in her head.

"What do you mean?" She asked, moving so that her feet could touch the floor and using a linen square, she dried the sweat from her brow.

I can sense magic coming from you while you sleep. It was what drew me to you. I believe you have innate magic long before you became my champion, Lucian admitted.

Isabella yawned fiercely and stretched. "Does that mean I should worry about the dream? Is Doden coming to Tanzanite? I've never seen that part of the forest before," she admitted, scratching the back of her head.

A gentle knock drew her attention. "Is everything alright, daughter?" Torgath whispered through the door.

"Just a bad dream, father," she replied, standing from the bed and slowly walking across the room.

"I'm heading down for something to eat, care to join me?"

Isabella opened the door to see the soft face of her giant father and she nodded her agreement before the two of them made their way down to the kitchen to scavenge for food. The two of them found leftover cured meat of the wild boar her father had killed before they went to the north in search of the owl spirit. Pulling several slabs from the barrel of salt and sesame oil and laying it on plates, the two of them made their way back to the dining room. Torgath grabbed a jug filled with sweet wine that the elves were known for making well and they sat beside each other to enjoy their morning meal.

Isabella sank her teeth into the meat and tore off a hearty chunk. "How is Ursadelle treating you, father?" She asked, swallowing the food.

Torgath gave her a shrug, drinking deep from the jug and wiping the liquid from his mouth. "I'm getting used to having her in my head. She has taught me things I never thought I could learn. I look forward to sharing some of her stories with Kirkland and your mother when we get home," he said from a wide grin at the mention of his son.

Isabella couldn't help but smile at the thought of her brother. She recalled how he looked up to their father and how he was always reading his books. She exhaled a soft sigh. "Soon we will return to our plane, but we can't forget the reason we are going. We have to find the host that Bahaal has chosen and kill it. We have to save the world," she just managed to finish before General Norvian rushed into the room.

"Lady Isabella," he said, bowing his head and saluting her. "The queen has requested you come to her chambers."

"I was just finishing up," she declared, lifting up the last bite and tossing it in her mouth.

Torgath growled lightly as he finished his meat. "Need me to go with you, daughter?" He asked, draining the jug dry and slamming it down on the table, but not taking his eyes off General Norvian.

Isabella giggled at the way her father was acting. "I'll be fine, daddy. I'm sure the queen just wants to talk about the spell I used on Rose," she said, making her way around the table and the general escorted her to the queen's chamber.

Isabella walked through the familiar halls, the royal elves standing guard, saluting her as she passed and she repaid their respect as they crossed into the queen's chamber. Queen Lyranda sat at the head of a long table, to her right was an elegantly dressed man in robes of faded green with a ring adorning each finger, but none had the same-colored gem and he tilted his head at her as she entered the room.

"We have been waiting for you," Queen Lyranda said, ushering to the empty seat to her left and smiling. "Won't you have a seat?" She asked, pushing the chair out with her foot.

Isabella looked around the room, making sure that it was just the four of them, but General Norvian had stepped back out and closed the doors behind him. She felt that this meeting was due to the magic she had used on the giantess, but on the chance it was something else, she sat down and smiled at the queen. "What can I do for you?"

Queen Lyranda chuckled slightly at the question, but readjusted in her chair. "Well, General Norvian told me that you encountered a giantess on your journey and that you used a spell that granted you their speech. Now, I have searched through every ancient tome in our library dealing with magic and spoken to our elders, but we have never encountered such a spell that could teach you the language of another. Care to explain the spell you used?"

Isabella released a heavy sigh and shook her head. "I don't know what it is called. Uthric told me that it was an ancient spell used by druids, but with caution. If something goes wrong with the spell it could destroy the mind of the person doing the spell, the mind of the person it is being used on, or both. I have only used it twice. Once on the half-orc and on the giantess. It hurt G'Nash more than it did Rose, but I believe that has something to do with their age."

Queen Lyranda looked to the elf on her right. "Can all the other champions do this?" She asked, turning her gaze back to her.

They can, champion. The spell is known as teanga and it should never be used. I shouldn't have allowed you to use it, but the circumstances required it, Lucian said softly.

Isabella gave a simple nod of her head. "It's not a spell that is used or recommended to be used by the animal spirits. The only reason I was provided access to it was because the circumstances required it and there was no other way. When I first arrived in Tylwyth I knew nothing and only spoke the common tongue of my village, but then we encountered the orcs. The first one we had encountered had beaten my friend badly. Once we defeated them, we stumbled upon Gh'Rys who was chained with others of his clan and we couldn't speak to them. The spell was granted to me by Lucian so that I could communicate with them and determine if their intentions were the same.

"Can you teach someone else how to use this spell? It would come in handy when negotiating with other races," Queen Lyranda declared, clapping her hands together.

Several servants came into the room carrying wooden platters of a variety of foods and behind them were more carrying drinks. They moved gracefully around the room, sitting the items down on the table, and then with silent footsteps made their way out. Isabella sat back in the chair releasing a sigh. "I don't know how the spell works. I pray to Lucian, my hand glows, I place it on their head, and I take in their knowledge and experiences. There are no secrets between those I used the spell on and I," she declared, drinking from her chalice of sweet wine.

Queen Lyranda looked at her inquisitively as she chewed a berry from the plate. "When you use this spell on someone, do they gain all the languages you speak or is it limited to only learning theirs?"

Careful, Champion, Lucian warned in a whisper and she gave a shrug. "I'm not sure. G'Nash gained my knowledge, along with the languages I speak, but with Rose it was different. I saw her brief past, I gained her speech, and she claimed to have seen the heart of me. That's how she knew she could trust me, but when Uthric or any of the others spoke she asked me what they had said. I wish I could give you more answers," she admitted, turning her fixed gaze from the chalice and putting it on the queen.

"That makes two of us," Queen Lyranda huffed, but before anything else could be said, the doors to the chamber burst open.

General Norvian rushed toward the table and took a knee by the left side of his queen. "My lady, our scouts have brought to the city refugees of Port Grum-Dale."

"What?!" Isabella interrupted, slamming her fist against the table and standing up abruptly. "Isn't that where Captain Theodore sailed his ship?!"

"Indeed it was, lass," the voice of the captain called through the chamber from the door and she turned to see him standing there leaning on the shoulder of the elf guard.

"What happened?" Isabella asked as she rushed over and guided him toward an empty chair at the table.

Captain Theodore was covered in cuts on his face, two covered his cheeks, he had one that went up from his jawline to his eyepatch, his forehead looked like a cat had scratched him, his chest showed signs of enduring slashes, and he had a stab wound in his left shoulder that was still bleeding. Isabella shook her head as she looked back at the queen. "We need some fresh water and bandages!" She yelled the command at the queen.

"How dare you speak to her majesty in such a crude manner," the man on her right said, standing from the table and drawing his slender sword from its sheath.

The queen tossed up her fingers elegantly to stop him. "Please sit back down, husband. I can handle myself," she said and he obliged without hesitation. "Go gather the items she has requested," she gave the order to the general, but called out to him at the door. "Bring some Eucilipsis Flower too," she said, standing from her chair and approaching the wounded captain.

"I hope that you can forgive King Whelhalm for his abrupt behavior," she requested, looking back at the wood elf and then back to the captain.

Isabella was more worried about her friend than the rude actions of a king, but she nodded her agreement to forgive him and Queen Lyranda smiled at her. "Are you well enough to talk, captain?" She asked, helping him remove his clothes.

Captain Theodore was panting through the pain as the dirt and blood mixed with the sweat that covered his face. He tried to force a smile, but the action made him groan. "I believe I got another tale in me," he jested and coughed violently.

"Don't push yourself too hard, captain," Queen Lyranda said, ushering for a servant to bring over a chalice and fill it with some wine. "Can you tell us what happened at the dwarven port?" She asked, handing him the cup.

"It's bad," he declared, drinking the wine and holding out the chalice to be filled again. "I sailed the Faded Glory to Port Grum-Dale, the dwarves were already on the dock waiting for me, and they saw to my every need. I decided to stay a few more nights there to rebuild my crew. I moved from tavern to tavern in search of able-bodied sailors, but I also took the time to tell the tale of Sapphire and the undead horde that now claimed it. I hoped to warn them of the dangers, but no one believed me. At least, not at that time," he said, sipping the wine.

Isabella got an empty feeling in the pit of her stomach, she had a feeling she knew what had happened to the port-town, but she needed to hear it. She had to know that what she feared was true. "Eye of Avgrunnen has arrived in Tanzanite," she exclaimed in a whisper as she sat back in the chair and gazed into nothing.

Captain Theodore pointed his finger at her and winked. "Got it in one, lass," he admitted before draining the chalice for a second time. He shook his head. "Do you have anything stronger than this? I'm trying to drive some images out of my mind," he admitted, holding the chalice out.

"We need to know every little detail of what happened, captain and then I will see that you are given a drink so strong not even dwarves can handle more than a sip," she promised, filling the cup with more of the sweet wine.

"I'll try," Captain Theodore exclaimed, readjusting in the chair. "There was a red sky this morning and any worthy sailor knows to take warning should that happen. I made my way to the *Drunken Donkey,* it was at the center of town, but it was my favorite establishment I had found. I was halfway through my tale when I noticed the townsfolk scampering away from the water and when I stepped out of the tavern, I could see why. Twelve hulks were rushing toward the port-town at an unnatural speed, but they weren't showing any signs of slowing. They tore through half the town. The sounds of the wooden splintering, the ground tearing, and the buildings being smashed was unnerving. Through the dust, I could hear the sound of people being slaughtered. I fought against the undead that emerged and I cut down a dozen of them, or maybe it was just one a dozen times. I don't know if they can even be killed," he admitted, steadying his hand, but there was nothing he could do about the fear in his eyes.

Isabella shook her head. She recalled her fight against the undead horde in Bog'Alor and within the city of Y'Melenor. She understood what the captain felt. She had torn the enemy to pieces, but if she didn't remove the head, then they would just reanimate and fight on. She released a heavy sigh. "You have to destroy their heads. Without it, their bodies slump to the ground useless," she announced, looking at the queen. "Have you come up with a plan?"

Queen Lyranda sat back in her chair. "King Whelhalm will take those unable to fight south, seek shelter with the high elves, and request that they send their army north to aid us in the coming war," she said, examining the captain more thoroughly. "If the captain doesn't react to the Eucilipsis Flower, then he will accompany my husband on the journey with the other refugees, but in the meantime," she flicked her wrist and a servant came in carrying a small flask.

Queen Lyranda took it from the wooden tray. "This is *Dwarven Delight,* it is fermented honey, wheat, and jasmine. It takes four moon cycles for it to be ready, but none have ever drunk more than a single sip," she warned, handing it over to the captain.

Captain Theodore saluted them with it before taking a drink, but the liquid barely touched his tongue and it was enough to cause him to pass out.

Isabella quickly snatched the flask before it could fall from the captain's hand and she sniffed it. The smell of it was overly sweet, but the aroma of it told her senses of its strength. She pushed the cork back down into the flask and handed it over to the queen. "That's some strong stuff," she admitted as the general rushed into the room.

His arms were stuffed with bandages, in his hand was a vial of the flower extract they would need, and behind him was an elvish servant carrying a pail of steaming water. He applied the Eucilipsis Flower extract to the open wound at the captain's shoulder. They waited for him to react to it, but only Isabella knew what to expect. She remembered when they smeared the remedy on the half-brother of G'Nash and how he just succumbed to death after. The captain groaned and the sound of burning flesh sizzled from the wound, but the Dwarven Delight that he had drank, prevented him from thrashing around in pain.

Isabella knew he was still alive because she could hear his heart beating and felt the breeze of his breath as he snored loudly. She felt a sense of ease wash over her. She had feared that the captain had died in the battle and he was just a puppet for Doden's farce, but he had somehow survived. She breathed a sigh of relief. "How long do you think it will take for the Eye of Avgrunnen to attack E'Amel?"

"I have sent out a scouting party to see if they are advancing. I will know more soon on their intentions," General Norvian offered, standing from the captain and letting the servants clean his dirty body.

"Good," Queen Lyranda said, standing from the chair and looking at her husband. "You should prepare to leave, husband. I will send messages to those unable to fight to meet at the center of town and you can escort them south. Let's hope the high elves are willing to help us," she said, half-heartedly.

"I wouldn't rely just on that," Isabella whispered while rubbing her face, but she quickly snapped her fingers as an idea struck her. "The giants," she said excitedly.

Queen Lyranda shook her head. "They won't help us, wolf champion, and even if they agreed to it, how would we be able to communicate with them? You are the only one that knows their language and you are going back to Peili to stop a greater evil than this cult."

"That is true," Isabella exclaimed quietly.

Champion, Lucian started, but then sighed. *Use the spell on the queen and I'll try to shield your mind as best I can. I worry that her long life of knowledge will be too much for you. The same reason that Celeste didn't choose Uthric to be her champion, but if you want to pass the language of the giants to her, I will stand by your decision.*

Isabella nodded her agreement. She knew that someone other than her had to be able to speak to the giants once she was gone and the queen would be the best person to do that. "Lucian is going to try to pass the language to you without any harm coming to me, but you have to understand something, Queen Lyranda. This spell could leave us both brain dead."

"You can't," King Whelhalm interrupted, rushing toward his wife. "Let it be me. Our people need you to lead them, wife, but they have no need of me," he declared, placing a hand on her shoulder.

Queen Lyranda looked at the glowing hand of Isabella and then to her husband. "I have an opportunity to do something that our people thought to be impossible. I can unite the races of this land like he did before the Great Sacrifice and it has to be me that accepts it. My father would want it to be me," she said with a smile.

Who is her father? Isabella asked in a prayer to the wolf spirit.

We are about to find out, champion, he replied as she placed her hand on the forehead of the queen and the two of them were engulfed in a mystical white flame.

Isabella could feel the wolf spirit fighting to keep the knowledge of Queen Lyranda at bay, but he could only do so much. Images played through her head. She could see that her father was Aster, she learned how to fight, and wield her magic at the temple. The queen was younger than her at the time of the Great Sacrifice, but she still stood proudly on the field of battle. She was terrified of the bloodthirsty horde that charged toward her, but she dared not show it. In a burst of light the spell was broken and both of them collapsed to the ground.

Isabella was encased in darkness, her body wouldn't move, and she feared that she had died, but the fiery direwolf appeared before her. He was bigger than before. It was as if he had grown stronger since the first day she saw him and he bowed his head to her. *Rise my champion. There is still much to do,* he commanded.

Isabella nodded as she slowly opened her eyes to see the queen sitting upright on the ground, one of her arms was over the leg of her husband and General Norvian was examining her, but she pushed him away. "Go, check on Isabella," she demanded.

"I'm fine," Isabella exclaimed before the general could move. "Did the spell work?" She asked, pushing herself up into a sitting position.

"Queen Lyranda speak giant speech now," she replied with a slight smile. "Thank you, Isabella. You have given me a gift. I could also see why you were sent on this path. I want you to know that you are not to blame for what happened to your brother. I hope you continue to fight for our world. In your hands, I am confident we have nothing to worry about," she declared, standing up with the help of her husband and dusting herself off. "I know your time is limited, but I hope that you will go with me to speak to the giants. I could use your help gaining the trust of Rose."

"Did you see everything I know about the giants?" Isabella asked, slowly standing and rubbing her forehead.

General Norvian was tending to Captain Theodore who was blasted from his chair when the spell was broken. The queen, being helped off the ground by her husband, gently lowered herself down into a chair of her own. "Some," she remarked, drinking from the chalice her husband gave her. "I gained the languages first and then short glimpses of the half-orc and giants' life. I never knew that the giants feared us. We have never used them in the way they believe," she announced, handing the chalice back to her husband and ushering for him to take it to Isabella.

Isabella nodded as she accepted the offering of wine from him. "I will go with you to speak to the giants about helping protect this land, but only if you promise to not take advantage of their limited intelligence. They will give up life and limb fighting to protect their homes, but that doesn't give any other race the right to abuse that virtue. If they agree to fight with you in this, then you should be willing to provide them with an offering of land suitable for farming and give them the right to prosper like the rest of us."

Queen Lyranda nodded her agreement. "You are right, my father saw their potential back during the Great Sacrifice, but somehow we lost sight of that. Now that I know how they feel and I can now speak to them, I will make it right. They will always have a friend in the wood elves."

"That's good," Isabella remarked happily. "Now I would like to talk about your father," she announced, draining the liquid from the chalice and handing it back to the king.

Queen Lyranda shrugged. "What would you like to know?"

"What happened to him after the Great Sacrifice?"

"I don't know," Queen Lyranda answered quickly. "I was on the battlefield protecting his tower, the Maximus bloodline was with him atop the temple while he was conjuring his spell. I think he was trying to keep me safe by having me so far away, but there was no escaping the banishing. Only those not touched by the darkness of Bahaal managed to remain in Peili and the rest of us did the best we could," she elaborated as she readjusted in her chair.

Isabella nodded as she listened to the tale and crossed her arms. "I have heard tales of how powerful he was, but nothing on where he came from. I have never heard anything of his parents or how he came to have his abilities. Do you know your grandparents?"

Queen Lyranda shook her head. "Father never talked openly about where he came from. He was a human, like you, but how he became so powerful is a mystery even to me. I guess he was afraid of someone following in his footsteps and using that power for ill means. He was probably right to think that," she exclaimed, looking away from them. "Anything else?" She asked, forcing a smile as she turned her gaze back.

"Just one more thing," Isabella said, standing from her chair. "When do you want to leave for the giants?"

"Now," Queen Lyranda interrupted, standing from her chair. "If you are able, that is."

Isabella nodded her head. "I am capable, but we better let the others know where we are going. I don't want them to worry."

"You are right. General Norvian, move Captain Theodore to a more comfortable place to rest," she commanded and the general nodded. "Let's go."

"Wife," King Whelhalm interrupted. "Will you at least take some rangers with you?"

Queen Lyranda shook her head. "I want the giants to trust me and showing up with a unit of rangers is no way to do it. I will take the animal spirit champions with me, if they will go," she said, looking at Isabella and after she agreed the queen smiled. "Good."

Queen Lyranda crossed the room, placing her hands on the chest of her husband and the two of them touched foreheads. "Take those not able to fight south, my love. Keep them safe for me," she said, turning so that they could kiss. "Protect our children."

"Until I breathe my last," he declared with a half-smile.

"Good," she said before turning and walking toward the door with Isabella beside her. "I shall return with a force big enough to make sure our home remains safe," she declared, opening the doors of the chamber and the two of them made their way out.

The city streets were filled with injured refugees from the port-town. Isabella cautiously proceeded through them, her heart breaking as those being treated wailed in pain, and those that couldn't be saved lay motionless on the ground. The smell of the Eucilipsis Flower lingered heavily in the air. The other animal spirits were doing what they could with magic, but it was taking a toll on them. Isabella shook her head. "This is his plan," she exclaimed, causing the queen to turn to her. "Doden let them escape, he wanted them to come to us because he knew we would exhaust ourselves helping them, and then he would be met with little resistance when he attacked."

"That's amazing," Queen Lyranda said with a half-smile. "If it wasn't for the spell, I would never believe you were only a girl of fifteen. You have a better mind for battle than most of my generals. Stop what you are doing!" She yelled bringing a halt to the work being done.

Isabella rubbed her chin as she thought of what needed to be done next. They couldn't just let the injured die, but they couldn't exhaust themselves either. "Champions of the animal spirits, head back to the house and rest up. The Eye of Avgrunnen has come to Tanzanite. We are going to need our strength to stand against them. Citizens of E'Amel, if you are unable to fight in battle then lend your hands to help the injured and others prepare for battle. I am going to gather reinforcements, but I do not know if I will make it back in time. Should the enemy attack, hold them off the best you can until I return," Isabella gave the command, but everyone waited for the queen to give a nod and those with an animal spirit approached her.

"Where are you going?" Torgath asked as he came up to her.

"The queen and I are going to the north to speak to the giants about helping us defend Tanzanite."

"When do we leave?" G'Nash asked, cleaning his brow of sweat.

Isabella shook her head. "All of you are going to the house to rest. We need to be ready to face Doden when he comes."

"What about you? You don't need to rest?" Vivienne asked, placing her hands on her hips and taking in a deep breath.

Isabella shook her head. "I have to go with the queen. She is going alone to show that the giants can trust her, but we are going to need Rose's help and the giantess will just flee from her if I don't go to make the introductions."

Vivienne shook her head. "I don't like it, but what you say is true. The giant wouldn't even look at us until you used your magic on her and even then I don't think she trusted the rest of us. Just be careful."

"Why can't I go with you?" Torgath asked, crossing his arms under his chest.

Isabella furrowed her brow. "When the attack comes, they will need the strength of Ursadelle and NaShorn the most in holding them off. I just need you to trust me on this," she said, placing a hand on his massive shoulder.

"I'll go with the girl," Uthric said, approaching them from the side, his staff clicking against the ground as he was stroking his beard with his other hand.

"That doesn't make me feel any better," Torgath said through clenched teeth. "It should be me going with her. I'm her father."

"I already told you why you can't go, father," Isabella interrupted, shaking her head, but before anything else could be said, she found herself standing in the forest and the snowy mountain in the distance.

Isabella looked around, the queen's hand was gripping tight to her shoulder and she offered a soft smile. "Sorry about teleporting you without warning, but you guys were wasting time and I couldn't get a word in at all."

"I understand. I just need a moment to regain my senses and I'll be ready to go," Isabella said with the wave of her hand.

Queen Lyranda gave her a nod and stepped forward to the edge of the forest. "I've never been this far north of my kingdom. Do you know where we might find the giantess?"

Isabella rubbed the back of her neck. "There is a cave not far from here. She likes to go there to play and paint."

"Then that is where we should go, but we shouldn't draw attention to ourselves until we've had time to speak to Rose," Queen Lyranda said and they got moving.

They moved through the forest with Isabella at the head of them. She was using her sense of smell to make sure that there were no giants in the direction they were heading and as the sun reached the midday sky, they stood before the cave entrance. Sniffing at the breeze that blew around her, Isabella knew that Rose was within, but they could all hear her singing a happy song to herself.

"Isabella come see Rose," she said without moving closer to the cave entrance.

A cheerful scream echoed out and they could hear the giantess rushing toward them. "Rose miss Isabella, but why Isabella come back?" She asked as she emerged from within the darkness and her eyes widened. "Isabella bring evil pointy-ear ruler. Why Isabella hate Rose now?" She asked from a broken heart.

Isabella shook her head. "Rose mistaken. Isabella bring Ruler Lyranda to speak to great chieftain. Bad people have come to take homes and make giants slaves. Lyranda plan to stop it, but need help," she said slowly and softly.

She could see the confusion on the young giantess's face. "Rose afraid great chieftain eat Isabella. Rose not strong enough to fight other giants," she admitted, hiding her face in shame.

Isabella pulled her hand away so that she could see her and she flashed her a simple smile. "Isabella protected by wolf spirit. Isabella strong, but pointy-ears need help to defend home or else home be taken by bad men."

Rose nodded her agreement. "Rose take Isabella home and she can speak to great chieftain. Rose do what Rose can to protect Isabella."

Rose lifted Uthric off his feet. "Rose remember elder doesn't like to climb," she exclaimed, throwing her over her shoulder and climbing down.

With the giantess leading them, they made short work of the terrain between the mountains and came to a stop just as the village came into view. Isabella looked around. She could see giants working in a field, tilling the dirt, but as one of them stretched, his gaze fell on them and fear struck him. "Pointy-ears have come to steal us! Rose already taken. Must inform great chieftain!" He screamed as he rushed into the village and the others followed.

"Rose no slave," she said in a confused tone.

Isabella touched her arm, but before she could say anything a roaring scream echoed from the village and the ground began to shake. Rose shook her head. "Great chieftain on his way. Rose try to explain."

Isabella didn't know what to expect of the great chieftain to the giants. The ones working the field were so tall that all three of them could stand on each other's shoulders and still be too short to look them in the eyes. She couldn't comprehend why they would flee from them in terror, but before she could ask, the giant chief rushed through the gate and stood before them.

He was a hand taller than the other, a long gray beard hung down to his chest, his head was clean shaved, he carried a huge oak tree as a club, and a gray garment wrapped around his waist and hung to his knees. "Thieving pointy-ears no take Rose. Come take Great Chieftain Tortek," he declared, resting his club on his shoulder, swelling his chest and smashing his forearm against it.

"Great chieftain," Rose started, stepping away from them as she spoke. "Rose in no danger. Isabella save Rose. Ruler Lyranda come to ask help from great chieftain. Bad people come to home and want to take home."

Chief Tortek lowered the head of his club down. "This some trick of pointy-ears. Tortek no let his people be slaves no more to pointy-ears!" He screamed through clenched teeth.

"Chief Tortek wrong!" Queen Lyranda screamed back in his own language and the shock of it caused him to lose his grip on his club. "Ruler Lyranda never take giants as slaves, but a wrong has been done to the giants. One that Lyranda will make right. Once home is safe," she promised, bowing her head.

Chief Tortek shook his enormous head and picked his club back up. "Giants have many tales of pointy-ear deception. Tortek need to protect his people, but Tortek afraid to trust pointy-ears like ancestors did," he said, looking to the sky.

"Ruler Lyranda understands what Tortek going through, but if giants do not help pointy-ears defend home, we cannot win," she said, looking away from him.

"Tortek will send group of giant warriors to help, but pointy-ears need to leave Isabella to see that giants return home after battle."

Queen Lyranda looked at Isabella and shook her head. "Isabella needed for fight against bad people."

"What are they saying," Uthric said, leaning on his staff and stroking his beard.

Isabella looked at the old wizard and shook her head. She had completely forgotten that he couldn't understand the giant speech, but she slowly stepped closer to him. "He is asking that we leave someone here as a token of good faith that we won't take those he sends as slaves."

"I'll do it," Uthric volunteered with haste, but held up a hand to keep those that would protest his decision quiet. "This is going to be a decisive battle and I'd just get in the way. My magic isn't what it used to be," he admitted through a heavy sigh.

"Uthric," Isabella started, but she was hushed by him.

"When we passed through Dorcha'Helvetti to get here, I encountered the blood god in that darkness and he told me that my body was failing, but he could give me back my youth," he confessed, looking away from them in shame. "All I had to do was find out all I could about the animal spirits and their champions. I just had to find a weakness he could use and he would grant me immortality."

"What did you discover?" Isabella's question came out as a growl.

Uthric chuckled lightly. "I found friendship," he said, walking over to sit on a boulder and releasing a heavy sigh. "The thought of never dying was enticing, but what's the point of living forever if it is under the thumb of a tyrant?" He asked, but didn't wait for an answer. "The end of my life cycle is coming. I can feel it with each spell I cast and I've come to accept that."

Isabella ran her thumb under her eyes. "Thank you," she said, embracing him with a hug.

"The world doesn't owe me anything. Just make sure that you defeat Doden so we can go home and I can find someone worthy to take my journal," he said from a smile that smoothed out his wrinkles.

"Rose stay with elder and keep him safe," she said, placing a hand on his shoulder.

"She speaks our tongue?" Uthric asked in bewilderment.

"Rose?" Isabella started with a shake of her head. "Rose speak Isabella speech?"

The giantess shrugged slightly. "When Isabella touch Rose's head something happened to Rose. Me. Understand. Your. Words. Elder. But. Still. Hard. for. Me," she said with a smile full of pride.

Isabella chuckled as she placed a hand on her shoulder. "Uthric help Rose better understand. Take care of Uthric, please."

"Rose take care," she promised, taking the old wizard by the hand and leading him across the terrain toward the great chieftain.

Chieftain Tortek whistled loudly causing a horde of giants to crowd around him and he turned to look at them all. "Pointy-ears need giants help. Bad men come. Wanting to take home. Giants stand with pointy-ears in war and pointy-ears will make right the past. Tortek has token of faith no giant will become slave to pointy-ears. Who want to fight for home?"

A loud cheering roar went up as the great chieftain began to point to those he thought suitable to go and they all stomped over to stand by Isabella. They were granted fifteen giants of varying size and they stood before them. They carried large trees like they were clubs and Isabella looked to the queen. "Can you teleport all of us to the city?" She asked, scratching her head.

"I will teleport us as close to E'Amel as I can," Queen Lyranda said, lowering her head. "*Vindr*," she whispered the name of the element of wind.

Isabella could hear her speaking the name and around them swirled a strong wind. The spell never really bothered her, but she was curious how the giants were going to handle it. She looked around the leg of the one in front of her, catching a glimpse of Rose walking with Uthric and in a blink, they were replaced with a lush forest. The giants stumbled, some grumbled their distaste for the spell, but only one had to take a knee to recover. She shook her head as she looked around and realized she didn't recognize anything she was looking at.

"How far are we from E'Amel?"

Queen Lyranda chuckled, but fainted as she tried to speak and Isabella rushed to catch her before she could collide with the ground. "Are you alright?" She asked, cradling the queen.

Lyranda forced a soft smile to her. "Just took more energy than I thought to bring all of us here, but we are still leagues away from E'Amel. We need to go that way," she said, pointing weakly to the southeast.

"My queen," General Norvian said as he dropped from a tree, followed by a hundred elvish archers and the animal spirits.

General Norvian aimed his nocked arrow at one of the giants. "What did you do to her?" He asked, through clenched teeth.

"Put your bows down!" Isabella screamed. "The giants aren't to be blamed for this. She used up a lot of magic to teleport us here and she just needs to recover."

General Norvian was hesitant, but released the tension of his bowstring. He tossed up his hand giving the command for the others to do the same and he released a sigh. "I will have some archers take her home to rest, but we need to go west. We need to join those I've sent to encounter the enemy and keep them from marching any further into the forest."

Isabella nodded her agreement as she handed the queen over to one of the four archers and in a blink, they were gone. "Army moves to encounter bad people. Giants ready?" She asked, turning to look over her shoulder at the massive behemoths.

A ground shattering roar went up from them as they turned to head in the direction of battle and with them marched the elvish warriors being led by General Norvian. Isabella quickly found her companions and joined them as they marched through the forest, but as they moved, she took notice that the giants were just shy of being taller than the trees. The top of the tallest head was right at the peak and their bodies were massive. If one laid on its side across the ground then all the citizens of E'Amel could hide behind it. She was lost in thought as the smell of decay hit her and she could hear the shambling feet of the enemy ahead.

She could sense that they were close, making her heart beat faster. She felt the cold sweat bead on her brow and her nerves made her hands twitch. She was courageous and strong, but fighting still made her uneasy. She exhaled a deep breath as they emerged from the forest and looked upon the enemy across a field of grass.

The undead force was brought to a halt in ranks. They wobbled as they stood shoulder to shoulder in rows of forty across and looked to be eighty deep. Their numbers were too many to really count, but she worried about if they had what it took to stand against them. They were all dressed in tattered clothing, carrying a variety of weapons, some still had pieces of their armor matted to what remained of their flesh, and they roared a bone chilling scream as the army of living took form before them.

A rider on an undead destrier galloped forward. The horse had only one crimson eye, one of its ears had been chewed in half, and its ribs showed on the right side, but he walked as if it still drew breath. The monster sitting on its back was clad in rusted silver armor, the only pauldron left was in the shape of an eagle's head, and it covered the right shoulder. He lowered a maul that he was holding in his right hand. The stone weapon was stained brown from all the dried blood it had drank over the years and he pointed the head of it at the living.

"Doden has requested that you surrender. He has no problems with adding you to his undead, but he would prefer having you alive. All you have to do is kneel before him and accept him as your savior," the cold and dark voice of the rider said from behind his visor.

"Archers!" General Norvian yelled, causing a sound of arrows being nocked to echo out. "Aim!" He commanded and they lifted their bows. "Let's give him our answer warriors of E'Amel!" He screamed as the arrows flew from the strings.

Isabella watched as the volley dropped down into the ranks of the undead, but from the hundreds of arrows only three monsters fell permanently to the ground. "Champions, what say we give an answer of our own!" She declared as her body began to transform and the others did the same.

The cracking of bones, the ripping of flesh echoed loudly over the battlefield and from it, the four champions stood ready to face the undead horde. Isabella growled before howling, G'Nash stomped his foot as he snorted air through his nostrils, Torgath roared, and Vivienne took to the sky. She flashed a toothy grin at the rider. "We would rather die!" She barked before looking at the giants. "Bad man wants giants to surrender. Show bad man strength of giants!" She growled as they obliged by uprooting nearby trees and throwing them with ease.

Isabella watched as the logs crushed the undead, taking out hundreds before coming to a stop, and they remained without movement. There was no reanimating those killed by the giants. "Enough!" Doden screamed, a voice she recalled from her dream and he galloped his palfrey to the frontline. "Why do you resist me, wolf girl?" He asked, bringing his horse to a halt at the side of his general, but not giving her time to answer. "Join me and I'll make you my bride. We can rule this world together," he offered, readjusting himself on the back of his horse.

Doden was slender in body, but tall. He had long platinum hair that hung down past his chest, purple eyes looked from behind a helm made from a rhyno's skull, and bone shards from an animal lined his wrist, ankles and neck. He carried in his right hand a scepter, a clawed hand held to a large round orb that was pulsating a purple color, a short sword hung at his hip, and he patiently waited for her to give him an answer.

"I will never join you," she growled in response.

Doden's face flashed with anger as he turned his attention to his own army. "Kill them all!" He commanded, pointing his scepter toward her.

The general at his side put a horn to his lips and blew. The sound it produced caused her to freeze in fear, but as she looked around she could tell she wasn't the only one it was affecting. *Lucian, I can't move,* she prayed to the wolf spirit in terror.

It's the horn, champion. It will pass for those of you with an animal spirit, but it will take a moment. You have to stop that general to help the others before it is too late.

"We need to stop that general, but we have to protect our allies too. G'Nash and father will attack the horde. Vivienne, keep an eye out from the sky. If any should break through their defense take care of them and I'll kill the general," she commanded.

They rushed toward the undead army, Isabella ran behind G'Nash. Lowering his head he stampeded through the enemy, making a path for her to get through and at the end, he doubled back to do it again, but she wasn't able to watch his second passthrough as she had to reach the general that was still blowing the horn. She was running on all fours, covering the distance as quickly as she could, and as she pounced toward the general, he tossed the horn away, but an unseen force blasted her side, knocking her to the ground. She slowly pushed herself up to see Doden was pointing his scepter at her. "You should've joined me, wolf girl," he declared, looking to his general. "I can handle her. Go kill those giants," he commanded before sliding from the back of his horse and taking a step around to where he could see her.

The general bowed his head. Putting his heels into the side of the beast, he charged toward the giants and behind him came twenty more on horseback to help him.

Isabella held to her side, the blast from the scepter had knocked the air from her, but she pushed herself back up and gave a quick glance around the battlefield.

The elves were firing their arrows as quickly as they could, but the undead forces of Doden just continued to march toward them. Arrows were sticking out of their rotted flesh and many of the elves had either forsaken the fight or drawn their swords to stand against the undead that became too close for ranged attack.

A giant cried out causing her to look in his direction and she watched as one of them collapsed to the ground. Several spears were protruding from his chest and a few were sticking out of his head.

She could see G'Nash being overrun by the undead soldiers. They were slashing at his thick hide and their crude weapons were cutting through, wounding him more than most could survive, but he continued to fight against them.

Vivienne was soaring overhead, but as she dived down to attack, a net was flung over her and a dozen undead soldiers pulled her to the ground. She struggled against the trap, trying desperately to fly back up, but realizing her efforts were futile, she drew two small daggers and began to fight those that entrapped her.

A roar drew her attention and she could see her father. He was swiping at the undead, his massive paws slashing across their rotted flesh, and knocking them down, but they didn't stay down. He was quickly overrun by the enemy and though she could no longer see him, she could hear him fighting with every ounce of his strength.

Isabella felt a sudden dread of lost hope come over her. The thought of never seeing her brother and mother again caused tears to swell in her eyes. Her mind filled with the story-telling moments she had shared with her father and she felt a heavy guilt for taking them for granted. Suddenly, her eyes went wide with an epiphanic look.

Lucian, can we defend against his magic? I have a plan, she declared in a prayer to the wolf spirit.

I will do what I can, champion, but don't overdo it, Lucian cautioned back.

Isabella pushed herself back up to her feet and shook her body. "Is that all you got?" She asked with a chuckle.

"Insolent whelp!" He screamed, pushing the head of his staff out and blasting her again.

She widened her stance, digging her heels into the ground, but the force of the spell still caused her to slide backwards. "Figured that one would've had more power behind it. Guess you aren't as strong as you think," she said, attacking his ego and causing him to yell in anger.

She could see Doden gripping the scepter tighter in his hand, pushing it forward, causing the orb to glow brighter and brighter with each attack. She brought up her arms to protect her face as each blast hit her directly, but she refused to go down. She growled as she looked around at the battlefield and she could see that they had endured casualties. The general was using magic to make duplicates of himself and using the clones, he was able to kill two giants. Twenty elves were injured or dead, but they did manage to kill five of the general's men that were riding with him. Her heart pained at the fact they had lost lives, but another blast hit her and she could see that some of the undead dropped to the ground.

Her legs were getting weaker with each blast, but she fought to remain upright as the onslaught of Doden's attack continued to come. Blast after blast she felt her body getting weaker and enduring all she could, she dropped to her knees, but kept her arms up. She could hear Doden screaming in frustration as he unleashed yet another powerful attack and it was more than she could handle. Her arms fell to the ground, she was doubled over, and she could see that she was starting to shift back to normal.

She was having trouble catching her breath, she scanned the battlefield to see that over half the undead were dormant on the ground and she looked out at a sweaty Doden. She forced a chuckle as she moved her gaze back to the ground. "I can see why you wanted me to join you. You aren't strong enough to rule a world alone and need my strength to do it."

"I'll show you what real strength feels like!" He screamed, focusing every ounce of energy into one, final blast.

Isabella watched as the crystal at the end of his scepter pulsated rapidly and pushing the scepter out toward her, he blasted her with a paralyzing blow, forcing her on the ground. She lay motionless, the world around her growing dark, but she could hear the necromancer fighting to catch his breath while dragging his feet to inch closer to her. She couldn't move and dread filled her. *Lucian,* she cried out in desperation.

I'm here, champion, the wolf said and she could feel a small amount of energy filling her body.

"Now to finish this," Doden said and she could hear him lifting the scepter up weakly.

Using the small amount of reserved energy given to her by Lucian, she pushed herself up from the ground and charged toward Doden. She was still in the process of shifting back to normal, but her fingernails were still claws, and she hoped it was enough to end his tyranny. She plunged her right hand into his chest, causing the druhir to cry out in pain, and forced him to drop the scepter to the ground. The crystal's glow faded, the undead returned to their eternal slumber, and she stood over her enemy.

Doden looked around at what remained of his army. Those of his men who were still alive were fleeing and all of the undead had returned to their eternal slumber. "I don't understand," He said, turning his frightened gaze back to her. "Avgrunnen promised that I would usher in a new world and rule it at his side. How did this happen? Mercy, please," he begged, bowing his head and weeping.

Isabella was fighting against her body's urge to slumber. She lifted his head and moved closer to his ear. "Mercy," she whispered, her voice cold. "I will show you the same mercy you showed all the others. You brought terror and pain to the innocent. You burned their homes, killed their loved ones, forced them to fight against their heroes, tried to kill me, and worst of all," she paused, choking back the tears that wanted to fall. "You made me kill my best friend. Here is your mercy," she declared, using the claws on her left hand to slice his throat.

She watched as the blood poured from his wound, but her strength was fading and she dropped to the ground. She laid beside him, unable to move her gaze to see him suffer, but she could hear him gasping for air. He wiggled beside her, struggling to hold onto life and all at once he fell silent. She released a heavy sigh. *Finally,* she thought, but lacked the strength to utter the word and darkness took her.

Chapter 9
Returning Home

Isabella stood in the familiar town of Merideth, the sun rising over the horizon and giving light to the land. The townsfolk were preparing their shops, setting out a few simple wares to entice people to come in and shop their more expensive offerings. She slowly walked through the streets, but was alone. She hadn't felt the presence of Lucian since they fought against Doden and that worried her.

Reaching the northern exit of the town, she sat down, letting her back lean against the wall and she looked across the grassy field. "Lucian, are you still with me? Did I push us too hard?" She prayed silently to the wolf spirit, but no answer came to her.

She lowered her head in sadness. *I am here, champion. I'm just recovering from our encounter with the necromancer.* Lucian said and a sense of peace washed over her.

Isabella could hear the sound of a galloping horse far off to the north. She stood up from the ground, more confident now that she knew the wolf spirit was still with her, and she watched for the strange man on horseback. She was tired of dreaming of this town. She had questions that she felt only the man could answer, but she would need to keep him from escaping like before. As the horse emerged from the forest, she could see him clearly. His black armor reflecting the weak light of the morning sun, his wooden helm with the visor pulled over his face, and the massive sword pointing at her.

Even though this is only a dream I caution you to be careful, champion. I know not if this gift was given to you by Droyma or Nightmyre, Lucian advised and with a nod of her head she charged across the field.

The stranger halted his horse as he came closer to her and he raised his visor. "Who are you?" he asked, tightening his grip on his sword hilt.

"I am Isabella Strongfellow. Who are you?"

"Sir Samuel of House Maximus. I am a knight of Manidai. Are you working for the Raven King?"

"I've never heard of such a king? Who is he?"

Samuel pointed his sword in the direction of the town and as she turned around, she could see a massive raven hovering over Merideth. The townsfolk were fleeing in terror, taking shelter in their homes, and some were escaping the town altogether. The beast screeched causing the ground to quake, fire rained from its eyes down onto Merideth causing massive destruction, and as the smoke settled, nothing remained but rubble. She could hear the screaming of those dying within the town, the smell of burning flesh caused her stomach to churn, and anger took her.

"We are dreaming," Samuel announced, slowly riding up to stand beside her. "I have had these dreams before, but this is the first time I've ever encountered another like you within them."

Isabella shook her head. "I don't understand," she admitted, looking up at him.

"I can't pretend to know myself," Samuel said, steadying his horse. "I witnessed the destruction of my home and much more, but still the reasoning for it eludes me. At first I thought it was because of these artifacts I've been hunting," he admitted, looking down at the armor that covered his body and then to the sword. "But that doesn't explain why you are having the same dream as me or why we are aware of each other in it."

"If you would like an explanation to it all then join me," the raven screeched as it approached and shifted into a cloaked figure before them.

She could clearly see that it was a man, but his appearance looked off. It was as if he was using a spell to make himself look different and she could almost see through it. He was wearing a cap of raven's feathers, the cowl gave him the appearance of a raven's head, and he carried no weapon she could see. She didn't know who he was, but what she could sense was the power he wielded.

"Even you, young lady. I can open your mind to all sorts of fascinating things. I can tell you why you are having prophetic dreams and why the three of us are able to communicate within them. I can even grant you a greater power than you already have. All you have to do is join me," the raven spoke as he turned his attention to the knight. "Stand at my side and give me the artifacts you possess, Sir Samuel of

House Maximus," he said, holding out his hand as if to accept the items, but the knight shook his head.

"You seek to release the blood god and I can't let you put this world in danger," Samuel declared, pointing the tip of the sword at the cloaked figure.

The Raven King chuckled as he shook his head. "I'm going to kill Bahaal."

"You intend to kill the unkillable?" Isabella interrupted to ask the same question that Celeste had asked of her.

The Raven King's chuckle turned into a laugh as he placed his hands on his hips and winked at her. "He is only unkillable to those too weak to do it. I can kill him and restore the world to how it is supposed to be. Join me, make this easy," he requested from a half-smile.

"Easy?" Isabella repeated with a chuckle. "What makes you think defeating a blood god will be easy? I was torn from my home during a time that my family needed me. I endured the bonding ritual to become the wolf spirit champion. I have fought orcs, druhirs, undead, and a necromancer. I crossed great leagues to gather the strength needed just to contain the blood god, but you intend to free him from his prison and kill him so easily? What makes you think you are strong enough?"

The cowled man flashed a coy smile. "I am the Raven King. I have never known defeat," he declared, puffing out his chest.

Isabella growled. "The blood god is too dangerous and needs to remain locked away. If you continue to seek his release, then I will introduce you to defeat," she declared as her body started to shift.

The Raven King chuckled lightly. "Such a pity," he said, flicking a finger at Samuel and consuming him in a white flame.

Isabella pounced toward him, but as they were about to collide, she woke in her bed. She was sitting upright panting for breath, sweat poured from her brow, and her head pained her. She groaned as she looked down at all the bandages covering her body. *What happened,* she thought as she scanned the dark room. She was alone, but she recognized that she was back at the house the wood elves of E'Amel had magically constructed for them.

She tried to stand out of bed, but her legs were too weak to support her and she fell back down on the wooden frame. *Guess the fight with*

Doden took more out of me than I realized, she thought, squeezing the back of her neck and moving her head around.

Isabella's legs tingled as life returned to them, but the rest of her body was just as stiff. She exercised her shoulders, rotating them in a circular motion, lifting them to her ears, holding them there for a moment, and then letting them rest back down. It was a technique her father used every morning after a hard day's work of harvesting. She then stretched her arms and back causing the bones to crack. Stretching made her feel a little better, but her legs still tingled. She massaged the muscles of her thigh, trying to get the blood to flow faster and she focused on getting her toes to wiggle while they rested on the hard floor.

She felt better, but she was still sore. She pushed herself up off the bed, her knees cracked, her legs were wobbly, and her ankles ached, but she was standing. *Now to make it to the door,* she declared, looking across the room and slowly making her way toward the exit.

She couldn't recall the last time she hurt so bad. She thought about the time when she was much younger and had fallen out of an enormous tree. She was playing with Irick and he was wanting to steal a kiss from her so she climbed to the top to escape him, but as she reached for a branch, it broke. She recalled how it felt to fall, like she was floating until she collided with the ground and it knocked the breath from her. She remembered the next day being back out in that forest with the gang, playing knights and bandits without an ache at all. She missed those days, the ones where the only thing she had to worry about was boys trying to kiss her and what games they were going to play.

She released a heavy sigh as she reached the door. "Made it," she exclaimed with excitement as she opened it to see G'Nash stepping past. "Did we win?" She asked, causing him to yelp and jump in fright.

"You're up already?" He asked, shaking his head and stepping closer. "We figured you would sleep at least a month to recover."

Isabella leaned against the doorframe. "Guess I'm stronger than I look," she exclaimed playfully. "How long have I been asleep?"

G'Nash scratched the top of his head and she could clearly see he was trying to add up just how long she had slumbered. "Twenty and two days have passed since you fell asleep on the field of battle," he said, reaching out to examine her.

Isabella pushed his hands away from her. "Did we win?"

"We did," G'Nash said, crossing his arms over his chest. "Thanks to you, but your father is cross with you over it. We have been trying to convince him you knew what you were doing the whole time, but he doesn't believe it."

"Where is he?"

"Should be in the kitchen or at the table eating. I was just about to head down. Care to join me?" He asked, stepping back a bit, giving her room to exit.

Isabella gave him a nod as she placed a hand on his chest. She could feel his heart racing and hers began to flutter as she gazed into his eyes. She was aware of his feelings and she would be lying if she said she didn't feel something for the half-orc, but she still couldn't act on it. If they were going to stop Bahaal, then it meant someone may have to make a sacrifice and she couldn't take the chance of their feelings getting in the way. "I could eat," she declared, with a heavy heart and he quickly lifted her off her feet.

"We would move much faster if I carried you," he announced as he walked before she could interject his offer. *He couldn't make this any harder could he?* She thought as she tried not to focus on his bulging muscles against her body.

She could hear her father talking about his favorite person in the world, the mythical monster hunter, Aloric, and it caused her to smile. She would never again take for granted the fables he wanted to tell her and G'Nash gently nudged the door open. The tale he was telling was the time the hunter was summoned to the kingdom of Mador. A creature had taken up residence in one of the mines. They had sent wizards and knights to deal with it, but none had returned. They offered to give him the title of lord, a title that would come with a keep, land, servants, and a modest chest full of gold. Satisfied with the offering, he ventured to the mines of Bal'A'Dur.

The iron mine was a glamorous dwarven kingdom. Many went there just to marvel at it, but the Bal'A'Dur dwarves disappeared shortly after the Great Sacrifice. No one seemed to take notice until rumors came from those that ventured there and survived. None that entered the mine ever came back, but those who had yet to enter spoke of the terrifying screams of those dying inside and the intense heat they felt from outside. The king of Mador sent a small envoy to investigate, but when they never returned, he sent a moderate sized force to do what the others couldn't. A mix match of knights, knight-errants, squires, and wizards. They ventured into the mine, but only a handful returned, mostly the squires that were too afraid to enter and they told the same tale. Any that stepped inside didn't return.

That's when Aloric came. He was just finishing up slaying a wyvern in one of the southern villages of Mador and the maer had informed him of the beast of Bal'A'Dur. The hunter of monsters came, he heard what was promised, he listened to the stories told, made his preparations, and left for the mine. He pulled a wagon that had seven barrels within it. Two contained salted venison for him to eat, two had mead for him to drink, and the others were filled with water, but no one knew why he was taking water with him.

He unloaded the barrels with water, placing them at the entrance of the mine and the last one he laid on its side. He drew his mythical claymore of silver and with a kick he forced the barrel to roll into the darkness of the cave. Like he was told, an intense heat filled the air, the wood splintered under it and the water boiled, but as it splashed out of the barrel, an agonizing screech echoed out. He poured the contents of the second barrel over him and he charged into the cave with his sword held high.

He confronted a bird of fire, but its flames had been put out by the barrel and he knew that it wouldn't be long before they returned. He had to kill it now while it was weak, but the monster fought against him. Using beak and claws, it attacked him as it tried to reignite that which was stolen, but the creature was no match against his skill with a sword. He cut the head of the monster off, causing it to turn into a pile of ashes at his feet and he quickly carried the remaining barrel of water down.

The ashes sparked as he pulled the cork from the barrel, a small flame was given birth, and he kicked it over causing it to wash the ashes away into the mine. He made his way to the throne of the mine, taking the crown of the Bal'A'Dur dwarves, and heading back to the castle. He presented it as proof he had slain the monster. That was when he became Lord Aloric of House Syr, the words of his house 'from the ashes, we will rise,' and his sigil was that of a bird on fire he called the phoenix. It was one of the more unbelievable tales her father would tell of Aloric, but his story was cut short as they entered the room.

"Bella!" He yelled, standing from his chair and rushing toward her. "How do you feel?"

"Hungry, but strong," she exclaimed, but her father wasn't amused.

"I told you to stop doing careless things. My heart can't take it," Torgath declared, holding his hand over his chest and shaking his head. "You should've let me take care of that filth," he said, pushing her hair out of her face.

"We didn't really have time to strategize on what needed to be done," she explained as G'Nash sat her down in a chair and food was brought to her. "I had a plan, but it needed to be done with finesse. We all know you can't do anything delicately," she said playfully, looking at him before she started eating.

"Still," Torgath said, sitting beside her. "How did you know that would work?"

"From your stories, father," she admitted with a smile. "It was what Aloric did to beat that hag. He forced her to use up all her power until she was too weak to fight back against him and then he killed her. Looks like it isn't just a useful tool against hags," she chuckled, drinking from her chalice to wash down the meat she had been chewing.

"Knew those stories were good for something. Told your mother that, but she didn't believe me," Torgath said with a chuckle.

"Oh, good. You're up," Vivienne said, stepping into the room and taking a seat at the nearly filled table. "I have found a spell that will open a rift to take us home and Queen Lyranda said that she can teleport us to the island where we have to go."

"What island?" Isabella asked, finishing off the meat on the plate and drinking the last drop of wine.

"The mirrored island of where Aster banished the blood god and we made the great sacrifice to stop him. When you are ready, we can leave," she announced as food was placed before her and a chalice filled with wine.

Isabella rubbed her eyes and released a sleepy yawn. *HOME.* The word resonated in her mind, reminding her of why she began her journey. *I'm coming to help you Kirky,* she thought, making her heart race at the thought of seeing not just her brother, but her mother as well. She released a silent sigh as she thought of her adventure and came to realize she couldn't just leave Tylwyth until she knew it was safe. She needed to know what happened to the giants. The last thing she remembered was seeing two of them dead during the battle. She was also worried about Uthric. The old wizard was stubborn, but she came to love him as she would a grandfather. Then there was Captain Theodore. He was badly beaten and barely alive when she set out to face Doden. She also wondered if King Whelhalm had returned from the high elves or if they even helped at all. She inhaled deep, the food had helped soothe her hunger, but it did nothing to cure her curious mind.

She flashed a happy grin to Vivienne and looked around. "Do we have any news of Uthric or how the giants handled losing two of their own?"

"The great chieftain was saddened by the loss of his people, but he understood their sacrifice was for the betterment of the world. As for Uthric, he has decided to stay with them," Vivienne announced, swallowing the berry she was eating. "He intends to teach Rose all he knows. Apparently, the spell you used opened her mind and she is the first giant to ever be able to use magic."

Isabella thought of the giantess and the great things she believed Rose would do. "Speaking of the giants. What is going on there?"

"The great chieftain wasn't happy about losing any of his people, but he understood they died fighting. Queen Lyranda has given a great portion of her northern kingdom to them for harvesting and the giants have agreed to continue protecting the wood elves from enemies. Seems things have been mended between them. The queen has also started investigating why the giants believe the elves are taking them as slaves. I blame the high elves, but she believes it is just a fable that got out of control. I guess only time will tell."

"Did the high elves help at all?"

Vivienne shook her head. "There was no real need for their help, but when King Whelhalm arrived, they turned him away. They told him that they could only worry about true elves and that if all the woodland elves were slain, it would be a great service done by the necromancer. They are truly vile," she declared with a distasteful look.

Isabella couldn't believe how evil the high elves were. They were real monsters, but she continued to hold hope that some had good within. She released a sigh as she shook her head. "What about Captain Theodore?"

"He has gone to help rebuild Port Grum-Dale and then he is going to rebuild his crew. The dwarves are going to build him a new galley for his help. He is going to call it Isabella's Glory. He is rather excited about it."

Isabella's face flushed at hearing the name of the vessel, but quickly regained her composure. "Then I guess the only thing left is for us to go home," she said, reaching out to touch her father's hand and smiling.

Vivienne pushed what remained of her food away from her. "Then let's go."

"Right now?" Isabella interrupted, looking around at everyone.

The others at the table stood and saluted her. "We will defend Tylwyth until you return," an elf said. "We will fight together to banish the hatred and rebuild," remarked an orc. "For honor!" They all screamed in unison and she bowed to them.

The champions made their way from the house, but as Isabella exited the home, a small gathering was waiting for her outside and a cheer went up. She looked around, she could see Rose, but the other giants were too big to enter the city. General Norvian stepped up to her as she cleared the door. "You are a true warrior. I would gladly fight by your side any day," he declared, saluting her, but moving so the next could approach her.

"Thought you could escape without saying goodbye?" Captain Theodore asked, stepping up with open arms and pulling her in for a hug. "Sorry I wasn't there in the final battle."

"Don't be sorry. Had you not brought us news of his arrival, then we wouldn't have been prepared to stand against him and those you saved in Port Grum-Dale wouldn't be here without you. You have nothing to be sorry for," she exclaimed from a smile.

"Be safe, lass. I'll pray to every elemental that you are kept protected," he said, stepping away to make room for the next.

Uthric shuffled toward her. "Following you has been one of the greatest adventures I have ever had the honor of being a part of. You have shown me a world full of magic and wonder. I've decided that I will be staying with the giants to insure that no one will ever again misuse them, but I want you to have these," he said, conjuring three tomes to appear. "These are my writings, the knowledge I have gained over the centuries while walking the world. You should be the one to continue filling the pages with knowledge learned."

Isabella reached out to accept the offering as a tear streaked down her cheek and Uthric flashed a simple smile. "I do have one favor to ask. If you ever run into Lillith Stoneheart, tell her that Uthric the wandering wizard has finally found a home and that he misses her," he said, kissing her forehead gently.

Rose rushed forward knocking him to the side and almost making him fall to the ground. She embraced Isabella like a sister. "You have helped open mind. Elder teaching much, but still got much to learn," she said in a broken common tongue that most would understand.

"You are going to do great things, Rose. I believe in you," she said, pushing the hair out of the face of the giantess.

Rose bowed her head and moved so that King Jaspen could step forward. "You are a wonder to behold. Through your undaunting courage, you stopped Doden and his army of undead. You have shown us that not one race is better than the other. Each of us has a strength that can help us rebuild our world. You have given us hope of a brighter future," he announced happily.

"What are you going to do?" She asked, wiping the tears from her eyes.

"I'm going to go rebuild Y'Melenor. It won't be an easy task without Vivienne, but she has something more important that requires her attention," he said, looking to his cousin and then back to Isabella. "Though Doden has been defeated, there is a greater threat that awaits you. May the elements bless you on your journey to contain the blood god," he said, bowing his head to her and stepping to the side.

Gh'Rys came forward carrying a small dagger. The sheath it was concealed in had the image of a dire wolf's head etched into it at the hilt and the maw was open as if you pulled the blade from the wolf itself. The blade was elegant, with orcish writing going from hilt to tip that read, 'Wulgar the protector,' and the hilt of it was black with a red gem at the end of the pommel. He handed the dagger to her. "This was my daughter's most prized possession. To earn it means that you have earned the title of Wulgar and to my people, that means you are more revered than any chieftain. My grandson saw greatness in you when I was blinded by hatred. You continued to protect me, my people, and now I see how ignorant I was. You are Wulgar, protector of all!" He declared, holding his staff high.

Isabella held tight to the gift, but embraced the old orc shaman as if he was her grandfather. "Lead your people the right way. There are still going to be tribes that don't understand the new way and they will need your guidance to show them a better path," she said, releasing her hold on him.

Gh'Rys nodded his agreement as he stepped back and Revalor came forth. She could sense that something was wrong with him. A darkness seemed to surround him that made her feel strange and he took a knee before her. She reached out, taking hold of his shoulders. "What is wrong with you?"

"Dorcha," he exclaimed, looking up at her. "When you brought me back from death, I was in Dorcha. I didn't become an Ignis Fatuus, but instead I was sent to that dark place. It still haunts me. The things I saw, the torture I endured. Be careful. You have to pass through that darkness to get home and there are things dwelling there that can't be overcome," he admitted as tears streaked from his eyes.

"How can I help you? Can you be purged like I was?"

"Queen Lyranda has been trying," he said, wiping the tears from his eyes. "She believes that because I was dead at the time, it has plagued me more than it did you, but she is hopeful that soon I'll be cleansed of it. Just promise you will be careful."

He stood back up after she agreed to his request and he stepped back to allow Queen Lyranda to approach. "We owe you so much. We would have never been able to stop him without you. I don't know how we could ever repay you," she admitted, bowing her head.

Isabella chuckled. "Saving people is what I do these days," she exclaimed playfully. "You don't owe me anything. Teleporting us to the island where we can get home is plenty, but if I might ask a favor. Do right by the giants, help those hurt in Sapphire recover, and try to get through to the high elves. I believe there is good in them somewhere," she said from a smile.

"It was a great pleasure to meet you, Isabella Strongfellow, Wulgar, Champion of Lucian, and I pray that you are kept safe on your journey to come," Queen Lyranda said, lowering her head, followed by the others in attendance and they began to chant in unison.

"I'm going to miss all of you so much," Isabella managed to say before she was teleported from E'Amel and brought before a dilapidated tower.

She recognized the tower from the painting she had seen, but trees had grown into the structure, vines climbed the length of the sides, and it appeared that the forest had nearly taken the land back. She felt an increase in power flow through her and she looked around at the others. Vivienne inhaled deep as she drew images in the dirt. "Aster built his tower on this island because it is either where the magic force of all the worlds meet or its the starting point for it. That fact is unsure, but it is a place where magic is strongest and he knew he would need a great deal of power to complete the spell that would banish Bahaal. We are going to tap into that power to open the rift. Everyone needs to hold hands," she said, taking hold of Torgath and G'Nash.

Isabella released a heavy sigh. She was a touch away from going home. She had given up hope of ever seeing her mother and brother again, but now the way was before her. She looked at the three faces standing with her. They were patiently waiting for her to seal the circle so they could complete the ritual and open the rift, but she was hesitant. She thought of all the friends she had made, the memories she made while in Tylwyth, the adventures that could still be had, and the work that was going to be needed to rebuild what Doden ruined. She shook her head as she stepped up and took hold of the hands needed to complete the circle. Though she wished she could stay in Tylwyth, venture the open seas with Captain Theodore, rebuild Y'Melenor, and continue to live her life of adventure, she needed to ensure her brother's safety. She worried about him and her desire to see him and her mother were greater than anything else.

"Are we ready?" Vivienne asked, looking at everyone. As they all agreed, she closed her eyes.

Isabella watched as the half-elf started to chant while lowering her head and they did the same. She could see them inside her mind, G'Nash, Vivienne, her father, but between them were their spirit animals. They were all joined together, their power coursing through them and she could feel the vortex starting to open. She slowly opened her eyes to see the rift spiraling around overhead and she felt her body being lifted from the ground. She remembered the first time she was pulled through the vortex, the fear that had gripped her and how young she felt then, but now she smiled. *I'm coming Kirky, stay strong,* she thought as she was pulled from the ground and into the rift.

"Whatever happens we can't let go. We have to keep our bond until we have passed through to Peili," Vivienne warned as they were pulled into the rift.

Isabella could feel the grip tighten from those she was holding hands with and she realized that their placement was on purpose. Lightning passed through the whirlwind, giving sight to things outside and she could see hordes of monsters in the darkness. They were gathered around a black temple, they looked to be attacking the door of it, and creatures flying overhead were diving down at a man who was swinging a staff at them. In the vast darkness, she could see that he wore faded blue robes, tattered from wear, his cowl was chewed on, his staff was weathered, and his gem glowed as they passed over him. He blasted a winged creature, jumping on its back while it was stunned. He quickly grabbed hold of its wings and forced it to carry him into the rift.

Isabella was dazed at what happened, but before she could put thought into it, the whirlwind subsided and she was standing in the same place where they had left Tylwyth. She looked around, the temple was derelict, but nature had yet to cover it over like before. The ground was soggy as if it had recently been flooded and she looked to those that traveled with her. She was finally home.

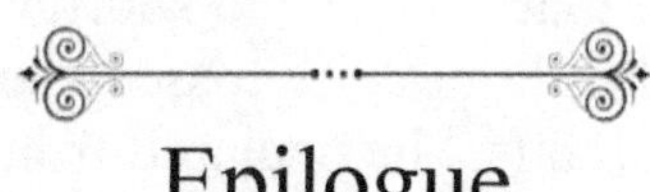

Epilogue

A man stands on top of a dilapidated tower. He wears armor of black dragon scales, on his head is a wooden helm, he carries a claymore of silver, and a shield that had an image of all the elements spiraling down to a point at the center. A shadow looms over him, his eyes are wild, and he laughed maniacally as lightning leaps from dark cloud to dark cloud.

The mysterious man stood with sword held high, his mouth was moving, but his words went unheard as a bolt fell down on the tip and the blade glowed brightly. He pointed it toward the beasts that stood across from him. "I will break the chains that bind and you are powerless to stop me!" He declared over the rumble of thunder.

The beasts stood on their hind legs. The first to attack was that of a rhyno. It stood two hands taller than the man, its body was thick with muscle, it had a long snout with a long horn at the end, and it charged toward him. The roof of the tower shook with each stomp, but as he got closer, the man deflected it with the shield. The sound of bones snapping echoed out as the head of the creature was forced to the side and the rhyno-beast dropped to the ground.

A terrifying roar went up as the others attacked. The owl creature flapped its wings to take to the sky and the bear rushed forward. It was just as tall as the rhyno creature, but its body was covered in fur. It had a shorter snout, but the teeth looked sharp and the saliva that covered them glistened as the rain started to fall. It swiped a massive claw at the man, but he quickly ducked under the attack and before the bear could process what had happened, the tip of the lightning sword pierced through its heart.

Before the bear could drop to the ground, the man lifted a hand, his lips moved, but his words continued to go unheard as the white feathered owl over head became entangled with something and the man quickly dropped his arm toward the ground. The owl creature screeched as it was violently brought down out of the sky and collided with the stones of the tower.

The man flashed a smile at the only remaining beast across from him. A bipedal wolf that was a hand shorter than the rhyno and slender of body. It growled at him as he tossed the shield he was carrying to the side. "Let's finish this," he declared from his smile.

The wolf howled as it pounced toward the man, but he made no effort to move as the claws scratched across the armor. The black scales glowed brightly as it absorbed the attack and he quickly clasped his hands around the throat of the beast. It fought against his grip, but each attack was absorbed by the armor and the life started to fade from the creature.

The wolf monster started to shift from beast to that of a young girl with shoulder length auburn hair as she was still trying to break free of the man's grip, but was no match for the stranger's strength.

"Kirky, help me!" She squeaked.

"No!" Kirkland cried out as he leapt up in his bed.

His head was spinning, he was disoriented as he looked around the room and he came to realize that he was in his room. "What happened?" He said, but reached up to rub his throat.

He tried to move, but his lower body refused to budge, and his door burst open to reveal his mother rushing in with Vepters. "He's awake! Thanks be to Zephyr," she screamed, rushing in to comfort her son.

Kirkland tried to clear his throat, but it was too raw. "Where's."

"Told them that remedy would wake even the dead," the oldest vepter interrupted.

Kirkland exhaled in discomfort. "Where's."

"This needs to be documented," another interrupted.

Kirkland was becoming frustrated. His throat hurt too bad for him to have to keep repeating the same word, but his dream had him worried. "Where's."

"We still need to evaluate him. He endured blood magic and survived," the third vepter interrupted while pulling out parchment.

"Enough!" Kirkland screamed as loud as his throat would allow and he took the hands of his mother. "Where's Isabella?"

Magdalene looked to the vepters in shame and then back to her son while shaking her head. "She snuck out to find your father. He was going to the Library of Zephyr to research how to help you and they haven't been seen since."

"How long was that?" He interrupted to ask.

"Six months ago," she said, kissing his hands.

"I have to go," Kirkland announced, tossing back the sheets and trying to make his body move, but found it still unresponsive.

"You can't walk. You have been bedfast for six months now," the oldest vepter said, stepping closer.

Kirkland shook his head. "My sister needs me!" He screamed in anger as a rush of power flowed through his body.

His throat no longer hurt, he could see that his body was glowing, and he was able to move his legs. He stood from the bed as he slowly turned back to normal. "What do you know of dilapidated towers that might hold some importance," he asked the vepters.

He didn't know where the tower was in his dream, but he knew that his sister needed him and he was going to save her, no matter the cost.

About the Author

I grew up in the hills of Kentucky and doing so taught me how to seek adventures through my imagination. I have always adored fantasy. Some of my greatest memories involve the many hours I would spend just playing with my friends outside, in the hills or valleys and roleplaying the video games we often played. We were LARPing long before we understood what it actually was.

My love for fantasy grew when I was introduced to the wonderful works of J. R. R. Tolkien. Reading the words he had weaved on his pages, helped me to escape to a world of remarkable adventure and I wanted to give that to others, if I could.

I also drew inspiration from Dungeons & Dragons. At first, I was a player, creating a character who would live a life of adventure. From there developed a spark that enticed me to create my first campaign. I developed a world of mystery, filled it with characters for my friends to interact with, created lore, and watched as they traveled through the land unlocking all the secrets it held.

I wanted to share with the world the imagination I was engaging my friends in. So I began putting it down on paper. I just want to do for others what the great J. R. R. Tolkien did for me, so many years ago. Bring joy.